Books by Diane Haeger

Angel Bride
Courtesan
The Return

Published by POCKET BOOKS

ANGEL BRIDE

DIANE HAEGER

POCKET BOOKS

New York London Toronto Sydney Tokyo Singapore

This book is a work of fiction. Names, characters, places and incidents are products of the author's imagination or are used fictitiously. Any resemblance to actual events or locales or persons, living or dead, is entirely coincidental.

An *Original* Publication of POCKET BOOKS

POCKET BOOKS, a division of Simon & Schuster Inc.
1230 Avenue of the Americas, New York, NY 10020

ISBN: 0-671-86481-5

First Pocket Books printing September 1994

10 9 8 7 6 5 4 3 2 1

POCKET and colophon are registered trademarks of
Simon & Schuster Inc.

Cover art by Mitzura Salgian
Cameo inset by Yuan Lee

Printed in the U.S.A.

To my brother, Stephen Seltzner,
the first really important man in my life,
with great respect and admiration for the
person you've become . . .

All families have their secrets

FARQUHAR

Prologue

Hangchow, China
1862

"So it is tomorrow that you return to America," the old man said simply as he gazed out across his own delicate garden, past a pond strewn with water lilies. Past a small red bridge.

"My father is furious with me for having stayed so long as it is, Li. This was not what he had in mind when he sent me to negotiate for silk with your son."

They sat together on a veranda open to the pond that shimmered like liquid silver in the setting sun. Beyond lay the hills, some capped with pagodas, rising gently through a ring of opalescent mist. One of the men sat in a red silk robe, his sagging skin the color of almonds. His voice was as gentle and persuasive as a familiar melody. He belonged to this place: to the hills, to the water, to the peace. The other man—young, tall, and blond—did not. He was *yang jen,* a foreigner. A man who had come for one reason and stayed for another, here in the the City of Heaven.

"And you are unhappy about the journey that lies ahead?"

"Not so much the journey as what I will find at the end of it."

"It is said that there is perfection in simplicity, my young lion. Think of nothing beyond today. There is perfection in that."

Li Kao Chen turned his head slowly. He looked at Chandler Tate only briefly before he turned his gaze toward the other red-pillared pavilions, the blue tiled roofs, and the misty hills beyond.

"I am not certain I know what you mean, Li."

"Perhaps not now. But one day it shall be as clear to you as the sky above us."

Chandler was too distracted to comprehend the sage message in the old man's softly spoken words. He was too taken up with his return to America. To a place and time too complex, too unforgiving, for the man he had become here. He had come to Hangchow to buy Chinese silk. "It is good business to deal with a man face to face," his father had said. But Benjamin Tate's son had found more here than fabric, and he had stayed for the lessons this place had to teach.

"How can you be so certain it will ever be clear to me?"

"Because, young lion, it is written."

Chandler took an uneven breath. "I don't want to go back. I have found peace here."

"But happiness waits for you there."

"Oh, I'm not so certain of that," Chandler countered, his mind struggling to conjure a steadily fading image of Cynthia Fortham. She was the girl he had stubbornly sworn to his father that he would marry, for little other reason than that she was unacceptable. A girl who now was as foreign to him as a stranger.

"One day you will be certain," the old man assured him. "Peace is not in a place. It is not in these hills before us, nor in this garden."

"Peace is inside of me."

Li Kao Chen smiled slowly. "So you have learned."

"I have learned only how much there is yet to learn."

"Then you have learned well."

The old man, his beard and mustache long and snowy, his body as gnarled by time as the trunk of an oak tree, came slowly to his feet with the encouragement of an ivory-handled cane.

"Come inside with me. I have something to give you."

Chandler followed him silently through the open, painted screens past the elegant lacquered furniture. "What is this?"

"You have been here long enough to know what it is, my young lion."

"But why would you give me a bolt of your son's finest silk? It takes so long to make that precise shade of blue."

"I give it to you because you have come to see its value, not only its cost."

"I see so many things I did not see before I came here."

The old man leveled his dark, watchful eyes on Chandler. "Give it to *her* in the form of a beautiful gown."

Chandler thought of Cynthia again, waiting for him back in Boston. Waiting to marry a Tate. To capture him like a prize. She would never understand. She was not capable of comprehending this place or these people. The exquisite simplicity of their lives.

"But to whom would I give something so precious, Li?"

"Only to the *one*," Li Kao Chen replied precisely.

"I really cannot imagine that there is one in all of Boston deserving of something so rare."

"Perhaps not in this place you call Boston. But you shall find her," he said in a tone of complete assurance. "You have only to look for her with your whole heart for it to be so."

The circumstances that had propelled Chandler toward Cynthia Fortham had nothing whatsoever to do with his heart. He had been an angry young man back in America. So full of the need to rebel against the structured, aristocratic life to which his father had so rigidly consigned him. He had asked her to marry him to spite Benjamin Tate. Chandler knew now, as he prepared to return to her, that it had been the biggest mistake of his life.

"I wish I could be so certain of the future as you are."

"When you find her, you shall be."

"I am not the same man I would have been if I hadn't come here," Chandler said, his voice ringing with emotion.

"What you have found you will not leave behind. It will go with you, a part of you now."

"You make me believe it. But if she really is out there, the one you describe, exactly how long will I have to wait to find her?"

"You are young, and impatience tempts the young lion to spring before its time, much as impatience shall tempt you." The old man smiled through teeth that were brown and slightly rotten. "You will not wait. And yet you will find her just the same."

"It is an awfully big world out there."

"It is the head of a pin," said Li Kao Chen.

Chapter

1

New York City
1871

"FANTASY WILL GET YOU NOWHERE, FOOLISH GIRL!"

Tessa closed her eyes and sagged against the red brick wall of the alley. It was not the first time she had chided herself for daring to dream, and she was quite certain it would not be the last. But even now, glancing back at her father's milk wagon and the waiting swaybacked mare, she could not help but surrender her mind to the fantasy one more time.

She had drawn near to watch a parade of New York's finest ladies and gentlemen emerge from their cabriolets and shiny broughams, and then move up the crimson-carpeted steps into the elegant Hoffman House Hotel. Men in their top hats and crisp silk cravats assisted ladies in smart button shoes and ribbon-tied bonnets. Diamonds flashed. Glorious silk skirts whispered like clouds, spilling onto the stone steps as the ladies made their way inside. The last man twisted the tip of his thick, glossy, black mustache as he swung an ivory-topped cane.

Their carefree laughter echoed back down the alley where Tessa waited for her father. She wore a modest gray skirt

5

and high-necked white blouse, her copper hair tucked neatly beneath a simple straw hat. The people who frequented the Hoffman House were from a world she had read about, dreamed about, a world entirely apart from her own.

"A bit like peering through a keyhole, isn't it?"

An unexpected voice—a man's thick, clotted baritone—plunged through the faraway laughter. "There is always the possibility of encountering something terribly naughty. And the prospect of that is *so* delicious!"

She hadn't heard him coming. Tessa's head snapped back to see a man standing beside her; watching what she had seen. His elbow was balanced casually against the brick wall as his paunch strained his belt. He must have come from the service entrance behind her.

The blood drained from her face. Then it shot back like Vesuvius, and her face grew hot and red with embarrassment. She glowered at the black-bearded face of a man in top hat and dark cutaway coat. He grinned raffishly as he held a half-smoked cigar in the corner of his mouth. His expression said clearly that he had caught her in something compromising.

"I'm afraid I haven't the slightest idea what you mean."

To her denial, the stranger only laughed: a deep, provocative and intimidating sound. "Oh, don't you?" he asked, glancing back to the hotel entrance and pulling the cigar out with thumb and forefinger.

"Believe me, you are not the first young woman of modest means I have encountered standing outside here, waiting, hoping to be asked inside. So you needn't bother with the pretense."

"I assure you, you have made some sort of mistake, sir," she replied, stiffly.

He laughed again, an ugly, grating sound. "Just the same, I am prepared to show you a good deal more inside than you would ever see standing alone out here."

"I beg your pardon?"

He leaned closer. His warm breath smelled of stale cigar

smoke and brandy. "You really are surprisingly lovely for someone so . . . unfortunate."

Tessa flinched at the suggestive tone in his voice.

"Allow me to buy you a cup of tea."

"No, thank you."

Now it was he who stiffened. "Apparently you haven't any idea who I am, my dear. I am Alfred Dunne."

"I'm afraid I am far too common to be impressed with your name, sir," she shot back with a hint of sarcasm.

"An invitation from someone like me is one you are not likely ever to receive again."

"I shall take my chances."

Nonplussed by her rejection, he continued a moment later. "So tell me. Why else would a girl of your less-than-fortunate means remain here in a dim back alley if not hoping for some sort of invitation inside?"

"My father delivers milk to the hotel," she replied in a tone sparked with anger, glancing back at the empty wagon behind them. "What is your excuse?"

"Clever, for a milkman's daughter," he grinned with raised black brows and a short condescending nod. She had matched him word for word, slight for slight, and she had held her head proudly. "I find that the back door is often the safest way out if one is intent on retaining one's anonymity."

"Clever, perhaps, but not very dignified . . . for an aristocrat."

A smile lengthened his lips and his coal-black eyes glistened. "You've a spark of fire. I like that. Are you certain you wouldn't care to reconsider?"

"Very certain."

"I truly could make it worth your while."

"A shame we will never know for sure."

He ran a thick finger across her shoulder coaxingly. Tessa bristled at the sickening sensation. "I would strongly advise you, sir, to remove your hand."

"Now I *know* you have no idea who I am."

"And why is that?"

"Because if you did you would know that Alfred Dunne has seldom, if ever, taken anyone's advice."

"That could prove most unfortunate if you were to encounter my father."

In the silence, his eyes followed hers back to the service entrance and the sight of a stocky, well built Irishman approaching them with short, powerful strides.

Alfred Dunne retracted his hand quickly. "Then again, I always say the mark of a wise man is knowing those rare occasions when he would be well served by taking advice."

Tessa's grin was slight. "I thought you might see it that way."

The stranger quickly tipped his hat, glancing back at her. "And to think, for at least an afternoon you might actually have seen for yourself how the other half lives."

"A cross I shall be forced to bear," she dryly replied as he moved around the corner and out of sight.

Tessa pulled off her straw bonnet once he was gone, and ran her fingers through the copper tresses that tumbled down around her shoulders. She tried to catch her breath. She was trying not to cry. It was not the first time she had come to the Hoffman House Hotel with her father to deliver milk. Nor was it the first time she had longingly watched the fashionable parade of ladies and gentlemen enter and leave the hotel. It was, however, the first time in her life she had been made to feel like a strumpet.

Breathless and flushed, she climbed back into the milk wagon and waited for her father to settle into the seat beside her. Tessa wiped the tears she could not quell from her eyes before he could see them. Foul, pompous leacher! she seethed silently. If he was an example of a real aristocrat, I would rather be dead than married to one!

She had made the right decision for her future, Tessa decided angrily. After that tasteless and disappointing first encounter with a man of means, she was certain of it.

The leather seat creaked beneath Charlie Murphy's weight as he settled in beside her, wiping the perspiration from his brow with a single sweep of his hand. The old, maple-colored mare jerked and snorted beneath the already blazing late-morning sun.

"Only two more stops," her father said in a weary, graveled voice tinged heavily with an Irish brogue. He gripped the reins with short, powerful hands and clucked at the overburdened horse.

Tessa glanced down at her own plain beige skirt and thin brown shawl. Her mind jerked again. For the briefest moment, before the stranger had torn a jagged hole in her elegant fantasy, it was she who was going in to luncheon at a linen-covered table, like a real lady. She would eat with real silver on china dishes and sip wine from fine crystal and speak of inconsequential things.

She closed her eyes tightly as the images clashed together in her mind. Fantasy and reality. The two would never meet. Not for her. In one brief encounter, the strange man had made it something ugly, dark. Something from which to run. Yes, she had made the right decision. After this morning, she was certain of it. Now, if only she could find a way to confess it convincingly enough to make her father believe it also.

She slumped back against the wooden bench and closed her eyes. Other carriages and horses clopped by on Twenty-fourth Street churning up dust and dung, their harness chains jingling. The Murphys rode in a plodding rhythm to the mare's gentle clop into the heavy, rumbling traffic on the busy city street amid a tangle of maroon and green phaetons, barouches, victorias, and reckless hansom cabs. Flat-bedded drays carrying barrels and sacks, and enamel-sided delivery wagons all passed them easily.

The tin cans rattled against one another as the one-horse milk wagon steadily made its way across New York City. Every day, Charlie Murphy delivered his heavy cans full of milk to various establishments along Broadway. But it was only on Wednesdays, when he delivered to the fashionable Hoffman House, that Tessa offered her company. It was an opportunity to catch a glimpse of another life, a snatch of fantasy. One that, at least for today, had been entirely ruined by a boorish stranger named Alfred Dunne.

"You're awfully quiet today, lass," Charlie remarked, glancing over at his daughter. "Ye used to love it when I delivered there."

Her expression was distant. "I'm just tired, Da, that's all."

He smiled, believing her, and flicked the reins again. A warm summer breeze tossed her hair back off her shoulders.

"It won't be long now," he said with a weary smile.

Tessa nodded absently and opened a small volume that she kept in her brown knit shawl, trying to chase the morning's darker images from her mind. This volume had been her mother's favorite. Reading it kept Claire Murphy alive for her daughter.

The cloth cover enclosed the ragged-edged pages of poems by William Blake. "Fine ladies read poetry," her father always said, urging her to better herself. "You are your mother's daughter," he would tell her every night before she fell asleep. "You deserve the life o' privilege I took her from in Ireland. Not the life we found here."

Charlie and Claire Murphy had dreamed of America, the land of opportunity for them and for their daughter. It was to have been a place to begin again, away from Claire's angry family, who said she had married beneath her.

But Claire, pregnant with their second child, had not survived the sea voyage, and Charlie had always blamed himself. Now he was determined that his wife's hopes for Tessa, and his own, be realized. The daughter would find the dreams that the mother never had. To that he was absolutely committed.

By late morning, the deliveries had all been made.

Charlie Murphy walked, heavy-footed, a pace ahead of Tessa, down Tenth Street to the neat brownstone boarding-house where they rented two rooms. Brian Sullivan, a firm, broad-shouldered young man with tawny brown eyes and a ruggedly handsome face, stepped down the front steps as they neared.

"Miss Murphy," he intoned in a deep, masculine voice, bearing the same Irish brogue as her father's.

"Mr. Sullivan," Tessa returned sweetly, lowering her eyes to the young Irish policeman, who was another of Mrs. Gallagher's boarders.

Charlie Murphy glowered at his daughter, then at the young man, whose muscles filled his shirt and bulged beneath rolled-up sleeves; a man he knew very well had set his sights on winning her.

"Warm day, it is," Brian remarked.

"One of the warmest," Tessa agreed, lifting a hand to push the hair from her eyes.

As she moved up the first step Brian brought a small book from behind his back and thrust it toward her. The book was bound in sable-colored leather and was worn and slightly ragged at the edges of the binding. "I've brought you another book."

Tessa's eyes lit with pleasure and surprise, and her lips parted slightly as she reached out for it.

"It is by some fellow named Thackeray. Mrs. Broadhurst thought you would enjoy it since you liked the others she recommended."

She slowly fingered the pages, which smelled old and rich and deliciously musty. "I still cannot quite believe that a wealthy old woman is willing to loan such precious books to me."

"She loans them to me, Tessa." Brian corrected her with a spark of pride raising the timbre of his voice. "You'll remember that I was the only one brave enough to go up on her roof that night to rescue her old tomcat."

"Or fool enough," Charlie Murphy grunted. "They say she's got at least twenty of the dirty little buggers."

"Twenty-eight, to be exact."

The two men's eyes met. Charlie Murphy was the first to turn away.

"Mrs. Gallagher has a fresh pitcher of lemonade in the kitchen."

"Thank you, Mr. Sullivan, but my daughter does not wish to spoil her appetite for supper," Charlie replied, taking Tessa's arm and leading her firmly up the next two front steps.

It was the same sort of coolly polite encounter in which the two men had engaged every Wednesday afternoon for the past year: one trying to win her, the other fighting valiantly to keep that from happening. Both for the same reason: for love of Tessa.

"Thank you for the book, Brian," Tessa said sweetly. "It really was thoughtful of you."

"I'll have to give ye that," Charlie Murphy agreed. "'Tis the only way my Tessa could ever read those kind o' books." Clearly uncomfortable with the emotion of gratitude, he ran his other hand across his nearly bald head, where only a skein of copper-gray hair remained. "Now, Mr. Sullivan, if ye will excuse us."

But, as the last word left his lips, the stout Irishman faltered and clutched the iron railing.

"Da!" Tessa cried out.

Brian grabbed hold of Charlie's arm to keep him from falling.

"'Tis nothin'," Charlie gasped.

But he did not protest as his daughter and Brian each took an arm and led him up into the shadowy parlor to an overstuffed green chair. Around them was heavy maple furniture. Macramé lace lay on the backs of chairs and cultivated ferns dotted the room. In the heat of summer it was oppressively still, with no sound but the droning tick of the mantle clock.

"'Tis just a bit too warm," Charlie added, drawing a handkerchief from his moist white shirt pocket and dabbing his forehead.

"It's not *that* warm, Da," Tessa disagreed, her thin copper brows narrowing into a frown of concern. "But it has been a difficult week, I will agree to that. Up before dawn every morning, and lugging those heavy cans. How much longer do you think you can go at this pace?"

"As long as I'm breathin'," he stubbornly replied.

Brian loomed beside Tessa over the cranky Irishman. "Can I get ye anything, Mr. Murphy?"

"What ye can get for me, Sullivan, is a few moments' peace."

"Saints preserve us!" Mary Gallagher huffed as she pushed commandingly in through the double kitchen doors, hands on wide, apron-covered hips. "Now what have ye done to yourself?"

"What I've done is my job. Nothin' beyond that to concern yourself with."

She regarded him with deep-set eyes. "A bit o' pride, is it now, man?"

"The mark of any good Irishman!" he puffed.

"And the downfall. Here, let me have a closer look at ye." She took his chin in her hand and turned it firmly from left to right, studying him for a moment. "A wee bit o' coriander is all you'll be needin'. I'll brew it up in a tea for ye."

"You're a midwife, Mary Gallagher. Not a witch!"

"Da!" Tessa gasped. "She's only trying to help!"

"Another of her foul-tasting potions is help I'll not be needin'!"

"Oh, you will drink it, Da, and you'll thank her for it afterward," Tessa said stubbornly, before she followed Mrs. Gallagher back into the kitchen.

As Mary Gallagher poured boiling water over dried herbs a blue china cup, Tessa sank behind her onto the edge of the kitchen table.

"How is he?"

"Faith, I'm only a midwife, Tessa," she averred, still turned away. "I cannot say for sure."

"You're far more than that, Mrs. Gallagher," Tessa pushed until the old woman with red-gray hair and dim blue eyes exhaled another breath and reluctantly turned around.

"What I see, lass, is not good. His color is pale and the

shortness o' breath seem to be with him more and more. 'Tis his heart, I think. The coriander tea helped it at first, but now . . ."

"Can you do nothing else?"

"I'm not a doctor. I learned a bit about herbs back in Ireland is all."

"He needs to stop working," Tessa declared painfully. "You see enough to know that."

"You're both like family to me and I have offered him your rooms here at no charge, but your da's a stubborn man, lass."

"That he is, but I am every bit Charlie Murphy's daughter. I'll not let this get out of hand."

"You told him, then, what you plan to do?"

Tessa averted her eyes. "No. But I will."

"Is there no other way than marryin' a man ye don't love?"

Tessa could not help it. She stiffened defensively. It was a move partially against the question and partially against her own conscience. "I do love Brian."

"We have known one another far too long for a lie like that to fester between us."

Mary Gallagher's eyes leveled on Tessa in the silence following her declaration, holding them there until she recanted.

"Well, I care for him, that much is true, and I cannot simply let my da slip further and further away from us. Brian has a good job and he can provide for both of us with it. He has promised."

"Charlie still won't let ye take work o' your own?"

"He doesn't even like the fact that I help you with the babies as much as I do. He says it isn't dignified for ladies to work. And no matter how many times I tell him I'm not my ma, he stays determined to make me over in her image. Marrying Brian is the only path he has left me."

"'Tis a noble enough notion, lass," Mary Gallagher observed, "but a lifetime without love is quite a price to pay for it."

14

"It would be worth any price," Tessa replied without the slightest hesitation. "If only it saves my da."

Even after his second cup of coriander tea, Charlie Murphy still needed to be helped into his bed. And tonight was not the first night. These past few weeks, especially beneath the pall of stifling summer heat, he had really begun to frighten his daughter with his rapidly failing health.

Wishing to take no more chances tonight, Tessa pulled back the quilted bed covers and held his arm as he lay back against the downy, white pillows she had propped up behind his head. Then she opened the single window to let in the fresh evening breeze. The parchment-colored curtains flapped as they let in the sounds of the city—the clopping of horses, the jangle of harnesses—and the sweet, fragile fragrance of the flowers growing down below.

Tessa turned back around and ran a hand across the back of her own moist neck. She sat on the edge of her father's bed. To her dismay, even though the room was cooled by a hint of dampness and the feel of an oncoming summer rain, he looked worse than he had in the parlor. His skin was pasty and moist. Most frightening was the labored sound of his breathing.

"What is happening, Da?" she asked softly, squeezing his moist fingers.

Charlie looked up at his daughter, trying to smile but managing only a cough instead. "'Tis nothin' more than the long day, lass. I'll be fine by mornin'."

"How can you tell me that? Look at you! You're white as a sheet! And you're burning up!"

"Nothing a little splash of good Irish whiskey wouldn't help along."

When Tessa frowned at him, he said, "Well, it'll take something strong as that to wash away the taste of that tea!"

She reluctantly went to the top of a large bureau and poured her father a liberal tumbler of the amber liquid, her heart pounding in her chest. If anything should happen to him . . . But that was unthinkable. He was all that she had in the world. She could not lose him. And she would not, no matter what the cost. If he would not let her work, then she would marry Brian Sullivan. On that point she would remain firm, even after she had found the courage to confess it to her father.

"Let me take a job to help, Da. Please," she urged him one last time, knowing even as the words left her lips what the answer would be. "I'm a grown woman now. I should be earning my own way."

"No!" His hazel eyes darkened as he raised the glass to his lips with a shaky hand. "I'll not have it!"

"It is the way things are for people like us. Everyone else helps their families out. Why are you being so stubborn about it?"

"We've been all over this, lass," he frowned up at her, his bushy gray brows merging. "You're not like other girls."

"But I want to help, Da."

He lapsed into a moment of recollection. Taking her hand and bringing it to his lips, Charlie softly kissed it. "I know, and I love ye for it. Truly I do. But, Tessa, me lass, ye were not meant to do for others, mending their clothes, nor seeing to their laundry. You are your sainted mother's daughter, and ye were meant for somethin' greater. I've believed that about ye since the day ye were born. And so, rest her soul, did she."

"Wishing cannot make it so," she softly countered. "You know that."

"I know nothin' o' the sort," Charlie Murphy declared with a firmly set chin that doubled just above his collar. "It will happen. *That* I know," he said with such utter confidence that, for a single, glimmering moment, Tessa nearly believed it, too.

"'Tis that young woman yesterday who lost her child that has upset you. Being down there amid all o' that despair has made ye lose sight of your dreams," he suggested, drawing forth a battered pipe from his shirt pocket as he set down the now empty glass.

Tessa lifted her chin a fraction.

"You needn't deny ye've been accompanyin' Mary again, lass. She told me about it herself."

Tessa rose up from the corner of her father's bed, went back to the bureau across the room and began rearranging things so that he could not so easily see her face. He was right, as always. It had affected her more than she cared to admit. The hopelessness. The despair. The death of a child whose life had never really begun. She had hoped today that a trip to the Hoffman House, the fantasy there, might clear her mind of that.

"It was such a beautiful child, Da," she said in a whisper. "It is a ghastly thing to see when there is no life in them, you know?"

"I know," he replied almost as softly, having lost a wife and newborn son on the ship bound for America.

Charlie Murphy had first forbade his daughter to help the midwife in whose house they had lived for nearly two decades. He was convinced that any work, even that, was beneath what he hoped for her. But he also knew that his strong-willed daughter needed something to occupy her time. She needed a purpose of her own. And since he was not about to let that purpose be the sort of employment left to immigrants, he had at last given her a tacit agreement to her insistence that she help Mary Gallagher.

"Then you're not angry with me?"

"Ye know I don't approve of ye workin'," he said sternly. "But I also know Mary Gallagher, and that woman could have changed the mind o' Judas himself!"

"She doesn't force me, Da. Honestly. And I only help her when there is too much for her to do alone. There's more call than time for a midwife who'll not always require money."

"I'd like to say I understand it, but I don't. Not when ye have yer readin', yer books. Ye love them as much as yer dear mother did."

"But alone they're not enough."

He puffed out a breath of smoke and looked across the room, studying her. "There'll be somethin' more to come for ye in this life, Tessa lass," he said with complete assurance. "Ye'll see."

She came back and sat down on the edge of the bed beside him. "I know what you wish, Da. And I love you for it," she said quietly. "But isn't it just possible that you're wrong?"

"It'll happen," Charlie repeated with a confident smile, hearing the frustration that hung in the air between them.

"But I will be twenty in the autumn. When exactly do you expect this wondrous thing will occur?"

"When ye least expect it," he weakly chuckled, but it was not the sound she remembered. "'Tis how true love is."

The laughter she had grown up hearing was rich and full of life. When Charlie Murphy chuckled, his plump face went the color of ripe berries. There was comfort for her in the visage of that proud and sturdy Irishman as there was in no other. Tessa looked away, wondering what he would say when she finally found the right words to confess the truth.

Her decision to marry Brian Sullivan was not so full of passion as of determination. Brian had a good job and a steady future. And he was such a kind, sweet man. She didn't love him, not in the way a woman should love a man, that was true enough. But she cared for him deeply, and he could provide not only for her, but for the three of them.

Life was full of difficult choices, she silently reminded herself, and this was one choice she was determined never to regret.

But the day had been too long and too difficult for confessions. Even in the face of Brian's kindness toward her and toward her father, Tessa could not wrench the truth from her lips. Not quite yet.

"Sometimes I think you have more faith in me than I have in myself," she said instead.

Charlie puffed on his pipe, filling the room with its sweet, heady fragrance. "'Tis true enough, I expect. At least when it comes to miracles."

She lit a chipped glass lamp on the small table near the window and the dim, beige room quickly deepened to rich gold and shadows. When she returned to him this time, it was not to the edge of the bed. Instead, she lay down beside him, her head on his shoulder, as if for a moment she could be his little girl again; as if his proximity could actually make her believe what he believed.

"Be patient, lass," Charlie softly bid her as he stroked her copper hair, still unbound and loose and long down her back, the pipe smoke whirling around them. "He will come one day. I know it."

His endearingly gruff tone was always so full of faith, Tessa thought. A father's blind love made him believe in miracles. Tessa closed her eyes. Yes, she wanted more. She wanted what those women going in and out of the Hoffman House had been given. And she wanted love. God help her, she probably always would. But no amount of wishing alone would save Charlie Murphy's life. It was up to her. Tessa meant to do it, no matter what.

Chapter

2

TESSA CLUTCHED HER SKIRT AND STEPPED UP THE NARROW FLIGHT of attic stairs as soon as her father had finally fallen asleep. The opening and closing of the little rounded door was soundless and she stood alone in a ring of light and shadows cast through the windows by the streetlamp outside.

"Brian?" she called softly into the shadows. "Are you here yet?"

At the same moment she smelled the musky scent of his skin, Tessa spun around and fell into his husky, solid arms. In a single, fluid movement, he tipped up her chin and pressed his lips onto hers. One hand moved down the length of her body, the other played at the nape of her long, elegant neck.

Tessa felt his heart widly beating against her chest as he pressed his tongue into her mouth and crushed the rest of her to him boldly. He moved against her thigh so that she could feel his aching hardness. It pleased her to know he still wanted her that desperately. She may have outgrown these ardent kisses of his, and even his passionate caresses, but never the reassurance they brought.

Tessa's hands shifted restlessly from Brian's chest across his broad shoulders and down his firm, square hips. They were so close that she could feel the waves of tension shooting through him; the little involuntary pulsing movement. No longer the child she had been at the beginning of their friendship, Tessa was now keenly aware of the power she had over this man who wanted to make her his wife. Her only wish was that she still felt even a shred of the passion he felt for her.

Brian groaned and at the same time, drew back. His breath was ragged and heavy. "Did ye tell him about us then?" he asked hoarsely, fighting to hold her at arm's length as he swallowed with difficulty. "What did he say?"

Tessa leaned against the attic wall. "I couldn't do it."

Having heard the catch in her voice, Brian reached up and gently turned her face back to his. "Ye haven't changed yer mind then, have ye?"

"Oh, no. Nothing like that. He just looked so dreadful, Brian, even after he had eaten, and I didn't want him going off to bed having something like that to keep him from the rest he needs."

"He'll never accept me for a son-in-law, ye know."

"Well, he will just have to sooner or later, won't he? I mean to marry you, Brian Sullivan, and to make you a good wife."

"I know that ye . . ." His voice caught on the words. "Well, that yer feelings for me are not as strong as those I bear for ye."

"I have never lied to you about that," her eyes darkened. "But you were the world to me from the time I was a little girl. I have never even known another man. And I do believe with all my heart that we have enough between us to build a fine life."

"And ye're certain there was no other reason ye couldn't manage to tell him?"

"I'm certain."

"Good," he said, breathing a kiss and a little sigh of relief into her thick, loose hair. "Because I couldn't bear to have ye change yer mind now, when I've come so close to havin' ye. And as for love, I've enough in my heart for both of us."

Not waiting for her to say anything more, he pulled her against his rigid body once again, this time even more forcefully, as once again his lips descended onto hers. "Lord above, I want ye, Tessa Murphy," he murmured achingly. "I'm not a'tall certain how much longer I can wait to have all o' ye!"

His scorching fingers trailed a hot path from her chin down along her neck to the crevice between her breasts. Tessa stood quiescent as he unfastened the top buttons of her white cotton blouse. She let him rub the tip of his finger gently over the surface of her breast then bend down to take one taut nipple into his mouth. Her back arched as he pressed her against the wall, both his fingers and lips playing across her breast. Tessa swallowed hard, pushing down the idea of this forbidden coupling. In her mind, it was not sinful since she had agreed to become his wife.

"Ye've just got to tell him, lass," Brian murmured again as he dragged his lips up the bare flesh of her chest, tracing a path across her throat and back to her lips. His tongue plunged into her mouth seductively until he finally found the strength to pull away again. Carefully, he refastened her blouse, knowing he could go no further until they were man and wife.

"I want to tell him. You know that I do. But now just really isn't a good time."

She saw a discordant glint of amusement in his soft spaniel eyes as Brian brushed back his own unruly russet hair from his forehead. "Well, ye could keep it from him altogether. But I fear he wouldn't take kindly a'tall to the fair surprise o' findin' us sharing a bed one fine mornin'."

"I've been meaning to ask you about that," Tessa began carefully, turning away from the light. "We will still be able to help him once we're married and have a home of our own, won't we? What I mean is, do you still agree to let him live with us?"

"Charlie Murphy livin' beneath a roof o' mine is not an easy thing to conjure," he barked out with a sudden gruff laugh. "Are ye so certain that the ol' bear will consent to it himself?"

"You leave the ol' bear to me. I just need to know for certain you'll not change your mind."

Firmly, Brian took her shoulders and turned her back to him, as the soft golden glow from the moon passed through the small latched window and across both their faces.

"I shall do the best that I can by ye both, lass," he said with deep-voiced conviction. "I may never be a rich man, but ye'll not find a need to work for anyone once I've made ye my wife. Nor will yer da."

Tessa softened and her eyes glistened with a sudden mist of tears. "I'm just so awfully worried about him. He can't die, Brian. He's the only family I have left in the world."

"I'll be family to ye one day."

"I know, and I love you for it. But it's not the same thing as the prospect of losing the last of your flesh and blood."

Brian ran a hand along the line of her jaw with infinite tenderness, seeing her stricken expression. "Ye know I'd give ye anythin' I had to give."

Tessa flung her arms around Brian's thick neck, seeking comfort against his firm, muscular body. "I do know that."

"But, my sweet lass," he sighed, wanting more than anything in the world to possess this bright spirit, to have her all to himself forever. "I am a simple man with little more than myself to give ye."

She kissed him again. "That'll be enough."

"I can only hope that's true," he sighed.

"It will be, Brian. It will be."

Chapter

3

CHANDLER TATE BREATHED A HEAVY, BOREDOM-FILLED SIGH.

It was a deep, long-winded sound, almost painful. He was trying valiantly to listen to the frivolous banter passing back and forth before him in the gilded, exclusive Beacon Hill ballroom lit by heavy, hissing gas chandeliers. His enthusiasm for this event was equal to what he might have felt for a ladies' tea. And at this particular moment, Chandler thought ruefully, he would even have preferred something so tedious.

Felicity Pettigrew, gowned in white satin, and as carefully coiffed and jeweled as a china doll, clung fast to his arm. Unlike her escort, she was clearly fascinated by the pompous droning of Phineas Weld. Foolish girl. She was far too ambitious for her own good, and it was making her desperate. They had never had a thing in common, Chandler thought irritably. No matter what the rest of Boston, and his sister in particular, preferred to believe.

"Well, Tate, my good man, then do you agree with me?" Everyone's eyes shifted from the paunchy, balding

Phineas Weld to the tall statue of a man with thick waves of golden hair and a dazzling white smile. Chandler Tate elegantly stood in a dark cutaway coat with a sleek silver-gray waistcoat beneath, and slim, dark trousers.

Chandler was among the wealthiest, the most handsome, and certainly the most eligible men in Boston. The story of his family's rise to great wealth a generation before was one of the most inspiring on the eastern seaboard. Before his parents' untimely death, Chandler's father had been considered a genius among the nation's self-made men. A millionaire by the age of twenty, Benjamin Tate had left his legacy of ambition and drive, as well as the majority of his considerable fortune, to his only son, and it seemed that everyone in Boston now wanted to hear what old Tate's heir had to say.

"So then, Tate my good man," Phineas Weld pressed, "what do you think?"

"What I think is that I make it a point never to disagree with my host, especially just before supper. It really is not at all good for the digestion," Chandler replied with a sly grin that made his blue eyes sparkle. It also concealed the fact that he had not heard the question or the discussion that had preceded it.

Still, adept as any politician, and every bit as charming, Chandler had managed to say the most clever thing. The group of well dressed men around him, with muttonchop sideburns and round potbellies, began to chuckle out loud.

Felicity laughed too, but just enough. It was the perfectly controlled, mirthful sound that ended as abruptly as it began. Her smile faded along with her laugh.

"Take me out for some air, Chandler, would you?" Felicity asked coquettishly, and yet it was more of a command, as she squeezed his arm tighter.

"Watch out for that one in the dark of night, Tate ol' boy," Phineas warned beneath his breath. "They say she has every intention of capturing your heart as well as your name."

In that mission, she had a good deal of assistance, Chandler thought ruefully. He glanced across the room at his ever-resourceful sister, Daphne, who had not torn her blue, watchful eyes from the two of them the entire evening. She could watch whatever she pleased, Chandler huffed with a defiant scowl, but for Felicity Pettigrew, his sister's dearest friend, there wasn't a chance in hell of her ever becoming his wife.

He even despised the notion of being alone with her. But the stale air and the predictability of evenings like this were choking the life from him. A breath of fresh air would be welcome just now, and since Felicity had absolutely no intention of releasing his arm to let him go off and find Lydia Bailey, Chandler was about to be forced into taking her along.

They maneuvered past the crowds of dancers and little cliques of well-heeled guests in their silk, feathers, and grandiose bustles, all sipping champagne and gossiping. They walked steadily, purposefully, past everyone until Chandler could feel the cool night air coming in from the terrace through an open glass door. He could breathe again.

"This way," he directed the young woman whom he had reluctantly agreed to escort that evening, pulling her small hand with such exasperated force that he could feel her begin to lose her balance.

Outside, amid the sweet fragrance of rose and jasmine, Chandler began to regain his composure. He leaned, stiff-armed, against the stone railing that faced down into the Weld's perfectly manicured garden. He inhaled deeply and, when he could bear it, he finally looked back at Felicity.

She was not an unattractive woman. She was actually lovely. Her hair was a rich, glowing mahogany, which she wore pulled tightly away from her flawless ivory face. She had a slender white neck, a perfect waist, and an iron core, one which he knew only too well was bent on capturing him. And she might have managed it once, a very long time ago. Before Cynthia. Before the nightmare and the sham of a marriage he had tried so hard to maintain. Before he had turned to the recklessness of married women; willing and,

26

safe mistresses like Lydia Bailey, who could not threaten his heart.

Chandler would have liked to feel something more than indifference for Felicity. It certainly would have relieved some of the old crones in their diamonds and pearls. Then there would be no reason at all for their raised eyebrows and clucks of disapproval for the life he had chosen to lead.

It certainly would have made things simpler. Felicity wanted to marry him. His sister wanted him to marry her. Of that, he was well aware. Felicity and Daphne had been scheming about that since they were children. But Felicity was far too much like Cynthia to be a viable contender in his heart or in his bed. She would never be his wife. Besides, Chandler had actually found a certain perverse pleasure, these past couple of years, in defying what the frivolous, narrow-minded Beacon Hill ladies thought he should make of his life.

Felicity grasped the railing, closed her eyes, and inhaled a breath. "Isn't it divine?" she purred.

"What's that?" Chandler asked, regretting his question even as he spoke it.

She opened her dark, gold-flecked eyes, expertly fluttering her long lashes. She gazed at him with her most seductive expression: lips slightly parted, eyes leveled upon him.

"Can you not feel it?"

He was already beginning to get irritated. "Feel what?"

"The air is charged, as it is just before a summer storm. I believe it's the two of us making it that way."

Chandler glanced up. There wasn't a cloud in the sky. But he knew what she was doing. He knew what she had meant for him to say in reply as she suggestively moved toward him, close enough for him to kiss her or to touch her any way he pleased. For the briefest moment, he even considered it.

But giving in to Felicity's artful attempt at seduction would be far too costly. The Pettigrew family was one of Boston's oldest and most venerable. No matter what temptation she now waved before him, a dalliance with Miss Pettigrew would be unacceptable unless marriage were to follow it.

He took a difficult breath. "Felicity, I have something I would like to speak to you about."

Her seductive smile broadened to one of eager anticipation. "I was hoping you would say that if we could only manage to find a moment alone."

"You are a lovely young woman, Felicity. And, in all of the years we have known one another, I have grown quite fond of you." He took her hand, knowing how quickly her expression—and her plans for the evening—were about to change. "Be that as it may, however, I simply cannot give you what you and my sister desire. Not now nor ever. And I thought it best I be honest about it."

She arched a single sculpted mahogany brow. "And what is it you think I want from you?"

"I think you—you and Daphne, that is—would like me to request your hand in marriage."

"My, we are full of ourselves this evening, aren't we?" she laughed more gaily and tossed her head.

"Am I wrong then?"

Felicity turned her back so that they stood beside one another, both leaning against the railing. She crossed her arms over her chest reflectively. He could see her waiting, calculating the precise moment to speak.

"I am fond of you, Chandler," she began carefully. "My father is fond of you, which you know quite well is nothing short of a miracle, since he favors so few people. He has promised to give us an interest in Branford Shipping as a wedding gift, as well as that house on Beacon Street you have been eyeing the entire time I have known you."

"I can buy my own house, thank you very much," he snapped, suddenly irritated at her flagrant attempt at purchasing something far more life altering than a place to live.

"Perhaps," she countered smoothly, her dark eyes shimmering in the moonlight. "But you cannot buy that house."

"And why is that, precisely?"

"The old woman who lives there has no desire to sell."

"Then what makes you think she would sell it to your father?"

Felicity laughed at that. "Chandler dear, my father is Charles Pettigrew," she said as though somehow he could have forgotten the name of one of the most powerful men in Boston. "Father simply made her an offer too attractive to turn down."

"He has already purchased a house for you and me?" Chandler gasped incredulously.

"Daphne and Lincoln are in complete accord with the move. My father acted with her approval."

The mention of his sister and brother-in-law sent such a wave of anger slashing through his veins that Chandler spun furiously away from this all-too-perfect young woman who was being systematically thrust upon him.

"Would it be so dreadful to marry me?" she asked more softly. An instant later he felt a feminine hand on his shoulder. "It really would be a splendid match, you know. A Pettigrew with a Tate. You and I would absolutely reign in Boston society."

Chandler spun back around with the fury of a whip, his body rigid with indignation. "I do not desire a match, successful or otherwise. If I do ever marry again, and at this point the prospect of that seems doubtful, I will choose the time and the woman myself!"

"Because of Cynthia."

"In part, yes," he answered carefully, pausing a moment more to carefully select words that would not betray secrets long buried. He must be more careful. Chandler could not afford to let his anger get the best of him.

"She and I married for all of the wrong reasons, and I have no intention of seeing history repeat itself. It is that simple."

Felicity tipped her head to one side. There was a long silence as she studied Chandler's angry expression. "That is a curious way indeed to speak of your poor dead wife. I was under the impression that you and Cynthia had been blissfully happy before the poor dear's untimely demise."

Chandler collected himself quickly, aware of the dangerous slip which his frustration had allowed him to make. "Of course you are right. She was my wife, the mother of my children," he said more carefully, more in control. "I only meant that, in the beginning, I pursued Cynthia precisely because my family disapproved. Rebellion, as they say, is the folly of the young."

Chandler gauged her response from the corner of his eye, prepared to continue on down a fabricated path as well worn as his defenses could make it. "Now, with both of our parents gone, I know Daphne believes it is her responsibility to find me a suitable wife. But age has given me many things, not the least of which is a powerful determination to live my own life and make my own choices."

"Can you not choose me, then, because you want me?" she asked more demurely and yet sidling up to him as brazenly as any back-street whore.

Chandler stiffened again. "That is just it. It wouldn't be my choice. It would be yours and Daphne's. She would believe she had finally won control of my life."

Felicity's sparkling chocolate eyes darkened to ebony. "So, you are rejecting me because of some nasty little sibling rivalry between you?"

"No. I am turning you down because I don't love you," he said bluntly. "I'm sorry if that hurts you. But you have pushed me to say it, and I do despise being pushed."

"I am asking you to marry me," she shot back incredulously, "not to love me, Chandler."

"What you are asking for is a merger, not a marriage."

"My father has always said a successful union has nothing to do with sentiment. If anything, that is the sort of thing that gets in the way of any real compatibility."

Chandler raked a hand through his full blond hair and looked at her. He could hear by her tone that she was serious, even desperate.

"That may be true in the boardroom," he said thoughtfully, "but it could not be further from the truth in the bedroom."

Felicity looked over at him now, too. "I could make you happy in either room, Chandler," she said, taking his warm hand. "I know that I could."

"My children, not my desires, must be my first concern. Surely you can understand that."

They were interrupted by the swishing of a taffeta ball gown. A figure came from the shadows and crossed the tiled terrace in the cool night air.

"Is it all settled then?"

Daphne Tate Forrester stood before them in an elegant and formidably stiff black ballgown. In spite of her straight, bronze-gold hair, sapphire eyes, and soft ivory skin, she had a panther-like quality, sleek but deadly.

Five years younger than her brother, Lincoln Forrester's wife was reed slender, almost gaunt. She was a presence with which to be reckoned in a crowded ballroom or on a moonlit terrace. She knew it. She had spent the majority of her life learning how to get her way. She had worked first on her father, becoming an unbearably spoiled child. She had honed her skills next on a bevy of well connected suitors. And finally, when those skills of manipulation were wrought to perfection, she had used them to land Lincoln Forrester.

Since the death of their parents, Chandler had treated his younger sister like a petulant child, whose babble must be listened to for the noise it makes, but then is easily disregarded. For her part, Daphne pushed him to his absolute limit at every available opportunity.

But there was more to their relationship than simple sibling rivalry. Anyone who had witnessed the icy public encounters between them in the past two years could see that. Daphne Forrester knew something deep and damning about her brother, something she held over his head and then taunted him with at her slightest whim.

Chandler pivoted to face her now, knowing even before he heard her voice that it was she who had followed them outside. He also knew by her brittle tone that it was she who goaded Felicity into her distastefully flagrant proposal of marriage.

"Is what settled, sister dear?" he asked cooly, intent upon making her confess her part in it.

"Why, your discussion of course."

"Whatever might you imagine we were discussing?"

"You tell me."

They played the game well. They were more like opponents than sister and brother, the way they cruelly toyed with one another, blanketing their animosity in a thick cloak civility.

"I'm afraid, Daphne," Chandler scowled at his sister, "this time I cannot tell you what you wish to hear." He nodded politely to Felicity and disappeared back into the crowded ballroom.

"What on earth happened out here?" Daphne demanded impatiently, her arched brows narrowing at the apparent failure of their plan.

"You told me it would work!" Felicity moaned.

"And so it shall. But you must tell me what was said between you."

Felicity's dark eyes widened as though she were about to cry. But no tears came. The wounded expression was done for effect.

"Your brother informed me that he did not love me, that he would never love me, and that if he married me in spite of that, you and Lincoln would believe you had won control of his life."

"Blast!" Daphne snarled. "You are absolutely the perfect wife for Chandler. The Tates are perfect for the Pettigrews. Why in heaven's name is he choosing now to be so obstinate?"

"Perhaps this was not such a good idea after all."

Felicity dabbed an imaginary tear from her eye as she thought of the gossip about Chandler and Lydia Bailey. "I'll not force myself upon any man, even one to whom my father has agreed to give a portion of his empire."

Daphne flinched, almost in pain. It was the first time she had heard confirmation that what she had hoped and planned for had actually been in the process of coming true. Thanks to the fortune that their father had made, son and daughter were left impressively wealthy, accepted into all of the right social circles. But their wealth and sphere of influence did not surpass the Pettigrew empire.

A marriage between her brother and her dearest friend was the only guaranteed means of gaining the respect and power Daphne had not quite yet attained.

"Perhaps we have made a mistake in this," Felicity suggested with a tone of resignation. "Your brother has made his feeling on the matter very clear. It is over between us."

"Oh, no it's not!" Daphne countered, grabbing the girl's silky-soft arms between her own long, bony fingers. "It is not over by a long shot!"

"But he said—"

"I haven't a care in the world what he said," Daphne cut her off. "Trust me, Felicity. This is far from over!"

He had taken four short strides back into the crowded ballroom, when he felt a feminine hand close firmly on his elbow from behind. Chandler knew by her perfume that it was Lydia Bailey.

Eyes all around shifted to them. Their liaison had been gossiped about for months and Chandler knew very well that even a lingering glance would be confirmation of what everyone already believed. Recklessly, he lifted the hand of the lovely, much older, Mrs. Bailey, and kissed it.

"I waited for you in the usual place last night," she said quietly as she smiled gaily beneath the curious stares and whispers.

Chandler nodded and smiled back at his elegantly aging lover with the fashionably knotted silver-blond hair, as though she had just complimented him. "I'm sorry about that. But I could not get away," he smoothly lied.

"Is there somewhere we can go? I really must speak to you."

"I seriously doubt it on this particular occasion," he countered, freeing her hand noticeably and stepping back to establish a more formal distance between them.

"Well, I simply must see you privately," she said more frantically.

Chandler saw, as he looked into her large and vivid blue eyes, that she was dangerously near to revealing the true nature of their relationship to everyone present. As little as it mattered to him these days, he knew what it would mean to her. And though he no longer felt the same tumultuous passion for her he once had, Chandler had no wish to see her ruin her life over a man she would never completely have.

"In the carriage house. Ten minutes," he relented as she turned away, her perfume lingering.

Ten minutes later, clothed safely in shadows, Lydia Bailey pressed her ample form seductively against Chandler and muttered in an aching whisper, "Oh, this week away from you has been such torture."

Her arms moved skillfully around his neck and she pressed her full lips against him, thrusting her tongue into his mouth. Chandler felt a familiar flame of passion flicker inside him at the erotic touch he knew only too well. His own hands played automatically at the cleft of her huge, ripe breasts as his need grew rigid, his body urging him to surrender.

"I can't, Lydia," he groaned, pulling away. "Not here like this."

"That never stopped you before," she said with a wicked little grin that once had charmed him.

"Well, I suppose there is a first time for everything."

"Is it that Pettigrew girl?" she asked when, for the first time, he turned away from her. "I know that she's younger, richer, and far more beautiful but, experience still counts for something, does it not?"

Chandler spun back on his heel and crushed her against him, taking her parted lips in a bruisingly sensual kiss filled more with nostalgia than with true desire.

Lydia clung to him once again. "I wouldn't blame you, you know," she said softly when they parted. "A Pettigrew really does have a great deal more to offer than I."

"Dear woman, believe me when I tell you it is not Felicity Pettigrew who has my attention this evening," he said firmly, still pressed against her.

"Good," she smiled. "Then shall we meet later? Martin's nurse will see that he is long asleep, and if you come through the service entrance even our housekeeper won't know you're there."

Once again, Chandler surrendered to the sensuous curves of a body he knew well and the taste of her open mouth. Lydia had certainly always been a willing lover, knowing exactly how to please him. How to make him forget. It would be so easy now again just to . . .

He pulled away from her and ran a finger over her smooth, full cheek. "I can't, Lydia," Chandler said again, though this time more firmly.

"Oh, I do so hate to hear you say *can't*. It is such an uninspired little word."

"I'm sorry, but—"

"Equally distasteful," she said with a winsome smile, then turned her full lower lip out in a pout.

"Splendid as the offer is, I do have to get home to my children. They have been quite a handful lately. They need to see more of me."

"You still haven't found a governess then?" she asked, fingering his lapels.

"If you have any candidates, I would love to know about them. I'm afraid I am fresh out of ideas at this point."

"I wish I could help you, darling, but you know perfectly well that my own children have been grown for years, now."

Ah, yes, he thought, his ardor cooling by degrees with the recollection of her six children, all nearly as old as he.

35

"Indeed they are at that."

"Well then, if not tonight, at least tell me you'll not disappoint me at the usual time next Thursday."

Their usual time had been just after he played cards with, among others, her youngest son. Tonight, for the first time in a very long time, Chandler found a bitterly sour taste in his mouth at that notion. What he had once found splendidly dangerous now made him feel a woeful burst of remorse for ever having allowed things to get this far with such a fine woman as Lydia.

Could it be that I am actually starting to feel something again other than this reckless indifference? he considered with surprise. *Good Lord, perhaps there is hope for me yet!*

Chandler took a horse cab home and instructed his own driver to wait for Felicity. Daphne, on the other hand, would have to employ whatever clandestine means she had used to come, uninvited, to the Weld's soiree, to take her home again.

He laid his weary head back against the soft leather seat and closed his eyes as the carriage swayed. The wheels clicked, over the cobblestones, past the golden glow of gas lamps. In spite of his confrontation with Lydia, his mind was still full of business. It was B.W. Tate & Company that held his mind now. A shipment of Norwich crepe was late in coming from abroad and he was at his wits' end.

This was the real reason he had chosen not to avail himself of his very willing mistress this evening. He had been straining to end things with her for some time now. Doubtless, like Lydia Bailey, his dear sister had plans for the evening. They would be riding back down Mount Vernon Street to some sort of tasteful little celebration in the Tate family parlor. No doubt, Daphne had even seen that chilled champagne was waiting.

"Damn her," he murmured, as the horses clopped a steady beat forward.

As a child, Daphne had been a force with which to be reckoned, chiefly because of the subtle feminine way she had been able to manipulate their father. But after Cynthia, and the absence of a proper hostess and mother figure for his children, she had quite slowly and methodically increased her influence in the Tate home.

Part of this complex meshing of their two lives, Chandler acknowledged as his own fault. After all, it had been at his request that she supervise the care of Alice and James when yet another governess departed. "Temporarily," he had said, for the sake of the children.

Losing Cynthia had taken a great toll on both of his children. Alice had cried herself to sleep every night that first year. James, three years younger, refused to cry. Instead, he covered his pain with a series of pranks, forcing four governesses to leave before they could decide to do so on their own. Just as he believed their mother had done.

Regrettably, Daphne, of all people, was now their greatest single influence. Childless herself, his sister pushed them, fussed over them, disciplined them, until even he could see them gradually becoming the regimented, elitist, Brahmin children he had come to loathe.

The horse cab did not proceed directly to Mount Vernon Street. The driver followed his instructions, leading Chandler down to the more modest dwellings on the tree-lined lower slope of Chestnut Street.

Chandler disembarked and stood before the three-story brick house for a long time, looking in. Golden light streamed through the lace undercurtains of the parlor window. Inside, people were moving about. There was laughter and music from a piano.

He leaned against a lamppost in a ring of shimmering light and exhaled a breath. It was the first time all evening Chandler had felt able to breathe anything but frustration and regret. Suddenly the heavy, black-lacquered door clicked open and a man drew near, down the four front steps.

"Is that you, Tate?" a man's voice asked through the shadows.

"It is."

"I was sure you'd be with Bailey's wife tonight," the man said casually.

"I've been trying to end that for weeks," Chandler scowled.

"Well then, why the devil didn't you come in? We're just having a nightcap."

"It's late." Chandler hesitated, stepping back. "I didn't want to intrude."

"Would a good, strong glass of brandy change your mind about that? It's French. Sylvie's father sent it from Paris last week. Smooth as silk."

Chandler pushed the reference to that particular city from his mind, as if he were pushing away evil itself. He despised Paris and all of the secrets that it stood for in his life. But the Winthrops could not have known that. No one but Daphne could.

He smiled reluctantly. "Well, then, perhaps just one."

Nelson Winthrop, a man of Chandler's height and age, but with warm hazel eyes and wavy brown hair, which framed a handsome boyish face, clapped his arm around Chandler's back. Then he drew him up the stairs.

"Didn't want to intrude," he parroted with a carefree little laugh. "You know as well as I that my beautiful wife adores you. I suspect she would just as soon have married you as me if you'd had the good sense to ask her first," he joked as they came into the warm, gas-lit foyer. "You both thought I didn't know, didn't you?"

Sylvie Winthrop came out of the parlor a moment later and stood beneath the arch between the two rooms, her smile warm and welcoming. She was a pretty woman, with maple-colored hair piled in a loose bun on top of her head and little wisps near her face and at the nape of her neck.

"Chandler," she said in her thick French accent, her friendly, liquid-brown eyes sparkling in the light. "Nelson didn't tell me you were coming by."

"That, my dear, is because I don't believe that until he arrived here, he knew it himself," Nelson replied, kissing his wife's cheek with a wide, humorous mouth curled as if always just on the edge of laughter.

"Well, it is always wonderful to see you," she said in that gentle, serenely wise way that was hers alone. "You're just in time for a glass of sherry."

"Have Mrs. Yates see to the good brandy instead, would you, dearest?"

Sylvie glanced across at each of their faces and quickly saw that Chandler's bore a restless, preoccupied expression. "Of course," she nodded.

"Where are those gorgeous children tonight?" Chandler asked distractedly as they went into the parlor and sat facing one another in two high-backed chairs covered in straw-colored silk.

"Good Lord, Tate, you really are in a stew, aren't you? It's after midnight. Those little hellions of mine are put to bed by their mother precisely at ten."

Chandler glanced up at the face of the tall clock in the corner behind Nelson, having had no idea until that moment what time it was. "Of course you're right. I just lost track."

"The Welds' party was that good, hmm?" Nelson asked, crossing his legs.

"That bad," Chandler replied, and only then did a weak smile touch the corners of his mouth.

"Ah, yes. It hasn't been so many years since I received an invitation that I cannot recall how dreary old Phineas's affairs can be," Nelson said, laughing easily.

"Do you ever miss it?" Chandler asked into the little silence that followed.

"Miss what?"

"The balls, the parties . . . society."

"You mean everything I gave up for Sylvie?"

Chandler nodded, as Sylvie returned and sat on the arm of her husband's chair. A stout, gray-haired housekeeper shuffled in and handed each of the men a full glass of French brandy.

Nelson took a long swallow of the amber liquid, then he leaned back in his chair as a contented smile turned up the corners of his thick, rosy lips.

"Occasionally, yes," he said, truthfully. "It's a way of life that is hard to let go of." Then he began to laugh heartily as he drew his pretty young French wife into his lap and wrapped his arms affectionately around her. "But I would do it all again in a heartbeat for this heavenly creature!"

His tone was lighthearted, but the truth was that Nelson Winthrop had lost his inheritance, his social standing, even most of his friends, by marrying the lady's maid who had served his mother. Five years before, it had been Beacon Hill's greatest scandal. Of all the lifelong ties he had made at Harvard, only Chandler Tate's had remained unbroken.

Chandler watched them together, still as playful as newlyweds. Their surroundings were no longer posh. The townhouse they occupied was far more modest than the one in which his Harvard friend had grown up. And the final humiliation was that Nelson had been forced to take a job at the New England Bank as a means of supporting his family. Even so, theirs was a marriage bathed in love, commitment, and an infectious amount of happiness. It was a marriage Chandler envied desperately.

"Speaking of children," Nelson began as he sipped his drink, "how are Alice and James getting on these days? Any luck finding another governess?"

"None, and I am afraid Daphne shall remain my albatross until I do."

"Then by God, man, you've got to find help. Or, at the very least, a wife!" Nelson's eyes twinkled.

"Not you, too?" Chandler groaned.

"Well. Certainly not the wife half of Boston has in mind for you."

Chandler's blond brows arched incredulously. "What? You don't believe Felicity Pettigrew is perfect for me?"

"Oh no, old friend!" Nelson chuckled. "Far from it. I think your dear sister's very socially appropriate friend would be the worst possible influence on Alice and James after all they have endured these past two years. If you don't mind my saying, what you need is someone entirely different, someone completely untouched by society, who will love you just because you're you."

The ease in this house was a contagious thing, and Chandler smiled more comfortably now, with the brandy and the laughter to warm him. He loved to come here, to share a meal with Nelson and Sylvie, and, if only for a little while, to remind himself that there were indeed such things as happy endings.

"I'll not be marrying again," he resolved with a sigh. "There's too much heartache in it."

"But there are equal parts of joy," Nelson countered.

"Not for me."

"Oh, I wouldn't be so certain of that," Sylvie smiled. "I'll just bet there is a sweet, kind young woman out there yet."

"Unfortunately, my dear," Chandler kissed her hand playfully, "you have already been claimed."

When he left the Winthrop house after two, Chandler was happy and content. The bitter aftertaste of his encounter with Felicity and Daphne was finally gone and he felt at last that he might actually be able to sleep.

As he wearily climbed the stone steps to his front door, Chandler was finally glad to be returning home to his children. Alice and James were the light of his life and he really had no interest in taking on another wife. Marriage had drained him entirely. For two years, the handsome and eligible Chandler Tate had been intentionally alone. There had been brief affairs, mistresses certainly, principally Lydia Bailey, but no one to really grow close to. Since Cynthia, he had shielded his heart with an iron will. No one would ever make him feel that kind of pain again.

Tiptoeing into the nursery, Chandler let out a heavy, satisfied sigh. In elegant canopied beds, one beside the other—with a chest full of toys between—his young son and daughter slept. Angels, he thought, as their shiny faces peaked out from beneath thick, downy covers. The grand room they shared was filled with dolls, toys, and all of the luxuries of a privileged life.

The children had given him the will to go on two years ago. Their innocence reminded him of the goodness still left inside him. For what they had given back to him these past two years, he had given them everything they desired.

Everything except a mother.

Gazing down at them now, so innocent, so full of need, he actually let the horrifying thought pass through his mind: Felicity Pettigrew as wife and mother. He could not contain the moan of utter disgust that moved from the pit of his stomach and across his lips following the thought. Society's pawn. Her father's puppet. "The perfect wife." The worst possible mother to his children. She was the mirror image of Daphne: controlling, calculating, entirely self-absorbed. Chandler would never marry a woman like her, no matter how badly his children needed the influence of a mother. They did not need a second female influence in their lives like that.

The creak the floorboards made as he crossed the room woke his son. The huge, scruffy sheep dog the children called Mayflower, who slept at the foot of James's bed, only lifted his head, however. He let out an impotent growl and then went back to sleep, drooling on the priceless needle-point coverlet.

James sat up, squinting in the light from the corridor. "Did you have a nice time, Papa?"

"Very nice," Chandler lied, sitting down on the edge of his son's bed. "Shouldn't you be asleep?"

"I tried, but . . ." James paused and looked down at the covers, holding the rest of his sentence.

"But what, son?"

"I promised Alice I would stay awake to find out if you asked Miss Pettigrew to be our new mother."

Chandler's eyes widened. "Where would you get an idea like that?" he asked, already knowing the answer.

"Aunt Daphne told us."

"Well, Aunt Daphne was wrong," he said firmly, suddenly

feeling an even sharper spasm of contempt for his sister's meddling than he had earlier in the evening. She had given them false hope of the worst possible kind. "I am not going to marry Miss Pettigrew and she is definitely not going to be your new mother."

James Tate, a towheaded, blue-eyed boy of eight, breathed an audible sigh of relief, then covered his lips with a small curled hand. "Alice wants you to marry her," he announced, trying to sound conciliatory.

"She does?"

"Yes. But I don't like her, Papa. When she comes here, she's always gazing at herself in our mirrors and telling us that children are to be seen and not heard when she knows you aren't listening." He lowered his voice a fraction. "I don't think she likes children very much."

"Then why does Alice want me to marry her?" Chandler asked, whispering the question and then glancing over to make certain she was still asleep.

"She wants a mother," he said simply and honestly. The pain of his son's confession stung Chandler's heart.

"And do you want a new mother, too?"

James considered the important question for a moment before he replied. When he spoke, he looked directly up at his father, his wide blue eyes glittering in the lamplight.

"Yes, but not Miss Pettigrew. I would like you to marry someone who is not always telling us to be quiet. Someone who will play games with us and take us to the park."

"I would like that, too," Chandler said truthfully, "but I am afraid it is not that simple."

"Are there no nice ladies anywhere who could love us?"

Chandler's heart contracted. He brought the small boy to his chest, desperately wanting to be all that his children needed, knowing that he never could be. "Of course there are, my boy. You and Alice are the easiest children in the entire world to love."

"Mama didn't think so," James said, hanging his head.

Chandler grew suddenly stern. "You must never say that, James. It is not true. In her way, your mother loved you

43

both. You must believe that. It is very important that both you and Alice believe that."

"Then why did she go away? She was always going away with those men, even before she left us for good."

Chandler took a breath and felt as though he were inhaling poison. It was the poison of deceit. Still, it was better that they should believe the lie than live with the shame of the dark truth of what had happened between their parents that awful night.

"People die, son. One day we all must. But you must never think your mother did not love you. Never. Do you understand?"

The child nodded his head that he did, but Chandler could see in the silvery-blue midnight shadows that he was not convinced. How to explain what had really happened to a boy of eight, he wondered. How to explain, indeed, when he still did not understand it himself. Life had been so simple when he was a boy, so full of privilege and innocence. Then there was Cynthia Fortham, and nothing in his life, or in theirs, would ever be the same.

"Will you look for a new mother for us?" the boy asked, lying back against the spray of fluffy white pillows. "Maybe the right mother for us is not here in Boston at all. Maybe that's why you haven't found her yet."

Chandler's expression warmed again. "And where precisely would you have me look for this exceptionally charming young woman who loves children and large dogs?"

"Maybe in a forest in a faraway land, like the one in the story you read last night?" he suggested, meaning Robin Hood.

"Perhaps that is as good as any place to start. Now, off to sleep with you," Chandler said, pulling the covers up over the boy's shoulders and gently kissing his smooth forehead.

"Angels watching over you, my boy."

"Angels watching over you, too, Papa," James whispered back with a weary smile.

Contented that his father had every intention of finding them a new mother, James closed his eyes and in no more than a few moments was fast asleep. Chandler shook his head. Damn Daphne! He had been forced to tell the child what he wanted to hear, knowing that it was never going to happen.

He hated his sister for making him lie to them.

He hated himself, knowing it was not the first time.

Chandler sat cross-legged and motionless on the floor of his bedroom. He faced an open window, undercurtains blowing toward him, as the early-morning sun streaked across his face and neck in a slash of opalescent pink light.

Dressed now in a loose-fitting pair of gold silk pants and a jacket in the Chinese design, Chandler finally opened his eyes from the meditation to which he had surrendered himself. He ran a hand through his thick hair.

He had not slept, only used the technique for calming the mind and body that he had learned in Hangchow. Last night it had seemed more important than sleep.

Finally, he stood and stretched, then walked over to the edge of his bed. The sheets and coverlet onto which he sank, like those in the rest of the house, imported by his father from Italy, had been neatly turned down. His blue-and-white-striped nightshirt had been laid neatly at the edge of the bed, and there was an untouched glass of sherry still waiting on the nightstand.

Everything had been prepared precisely as he liked it. But Chandler had noticed none of it last night. His mind had been too full of the events of the evening, of distasteful encounters and far too much talk about marriage.

It was often the habit of aristocratic Bostonians to select their spouses dispassionately, as Felicity Pettigrew had sought to do. As Cynthia Fortham had done. Love was a secondary consideration at best. Unless of course one meant to surrender everything, as Nelson Winthrop had done. The lucky bastard!

As Chandler sat on the edge of the bed, pushing away the thoughts he had spent an entire sleepless night trying to erase, his eyes drifted to the bedside table. Among the many things he had not noticed late last night was a letter propped against the lamp. When it caught his eye now, he took it up in his hand and drew it near. Chandler knew the handwriting at once. He would never forget it. The sight of that alone—the careless sloping letters—filled him with such instant rage that he felt as if he might explode.

"Jennings!" he shouted hoarsely. "Jennings!"

A moment later, a stout, courtly gentleman in butler's black and white pushed open the bedroom door and came inside.

"You called, sir?"

"When did this arrive?"

"The letter from Paris, sir? Yesterday afternoon after you had already left for the Welds' party."

"Burn it!"

"But, sir, you haven't even—"

"Burn it, I said! There is no one in Paris, or all of France for that matter, whom I care a thing about! Now burn it! Burn it to ashes!"

"Very well, Mr. Tate," the butler replied and withdrew once again.

It was several minutes before he could collect himself, the storm of hostility only just beginning to recede. Yet another promise broken, he thought angrily, glancing back to the place where the missive had awaited his waking. After the deal had been struck, there were to be no letters, he remembered. No visits. Nothing. It had cost him a small fortune to see that agreed to. Two years ago it had been worth the price. Apparently now, however, he was the only one still willing to live up to his word.

Chandler bolted from his bed and glanced into the mirror above his writing table. A strong, sleekly handsome face with compelling blue eyes stared back at him. For the first time in two long years, he could see his own stubborn streak in the set of his chin. It was an image that surprised him.

This morning, for the first time in a very long time, he saw the man he had been on his way to becoming. Before the deceit and the heartbreak. Before Cynthia. He could actually feel himself returning. The resourceful determination. The complete self-assurance. No one was ever going to force his hand in anything again, by God! No matter what dark truths they held over his head. Not Daphne, nor anyone else. The sudden sparkle of life in his eyes as he gazed into the mirror assured him of that.

Chapter

4

TESSA LIFTED THE SHAWL OVER HER HEAD AND WALKED ALONE down Hester Street toward Bayard Street to join Mary Gallagher in the tenements there. She pulled the shawl around her face so that she might blend with the other nameless, faceless immigrant women who had made this shabby neighborhood their home.

Some of them held bundles of vegetables wound in their dirty aprons. Some wore babies slung in faded shawls from their breasts. Others hung from windows amid flapping laundry, shouting into the street at the boys playing stickball below.

Around them, others haggled over wilted lettuce, yellow tomatoes, and bruised oranges sold from rickety carts along the streets. An ash barrel served as a counter for one toothless, wrinkle-faced old woman selling crusty wreaths of bread in the crowded makeshift street market.

This morning, another baby was in the process of being born amid the densely packed squalor and Mary Gallagher was the only midwife who would come without pay. Her father was right, Tessa thought as she moved through the masses. It was not easy to witness poor women strain and wail, suffering the agony of a process that would bring far more pain than pleasure to their lives. But by aiding Mrs. Gallagher, Tessa had begun to discover a strength inside of herself that she had not known as a young girl. It was that part of herself that made her absolutely determined to marry Brian Sullivan and save her father's life.

She hurried now, thinking of the woman Mrs. Gallagher had been tending since before dawn. She had gone there alone but the woman was ill and weak, and the child was not coming with the ease of the three before it.

"I fear it'll not be a pretty sight today, lass," Mrs. Gallagher's message had read. "So if you haven't the stomach for it after yesterday, I'll understand if you choose not to come."

Tessa took a deep breath and passed quickly by a butcher's doorway hung with a faded green awning, with big, dark sausages swinging beneath. A baby born dead was the most awful thing she had ever seen. But she could not disappoint the woman who had taken her on as an apprentice and who twice had trusted her enough to let her go alone to deliver babies.

She climbed a dozen crooked, rickety stairs and a dozen more after that to the grimy garret room with a sloping ceiling and one small, dirty window. It was dark and damp and the air was filled with the sour aroma of unwashed flesh and spoiled food.

Tessa had not been here before, but she had seen a dozen other squalid places exactly like it. There was scarcely enough room to turn around amid what passed as furnishings. A table of rough boards propped on boxes. A broken black iron stove. There were piles of rubbish in the corner and three hollow-eyed, dirty-faced children sat quietly near the door.

In a dark corner of the stifling apartment lay a gaunt-faced woman, her nightdress soaked with sweat. Olive-colored skin was stretched like parchment over her bones. Her ebony hair was matted and wet. She moaned softly, lying motionless beneath a rough, dun-colored blanket.

Mrs. Gallagher worked silently, checking the position of the baby, as Tessa laid a cool cloth across the woman's forehead. She did not protest above a whimper nor did her children cry. Their expressions were glazed.

A neighbor who had once met Mrs. Gallagher had sent for her, knowing the family would never be able to pay. She came anyway, believing that it was her duty to God for the better life she had found in this huge, bewildering land.

They worked silently over the woman, Tessa anticipating precisely Mrs. Gallagher's needs. Hot water. Clean linen. A pair of scissors and a piece of string to tie off the cord. All of it lay neat and ready, as she had been taught to make it. After the first few minutes, Tessa was as bathed in perspiration as the midwife. By the end of the first hour, her copper hair had begun to fall free from her neat, loose bun while she knelt beside the stained cot.

"It isn't good, is it?" Tessa asked, in a low voice, as she replaced the burning cloth on the woman's forehead with a fresh, cool one.

"She needs a doctor," Mary whispered back with an exasperated sigh. "Pray for them, lass. 'Tis likely the best we can do for either of them now."

By the end of the third hour, her own blouse was soaked through, and Mrs. Gallagher's expression had compressed into a scowl. The baby was still not properly turned, and it appeared to be battling the notion of joining his mother in so cruel a world. But Mrs. Gallagher was relentless. Through sheer determination and gritty Irish pluck, she had the woman out of her cot and squatting on the dirty floor beside it. And finally another boy was born, this one stillborn.

The dark-haired, gaunt woman, whose name Tessa had not been told, lay back in her cot and wept, never having even looked at the child. Tessa looked. Even wet and bloodied, she thought how this one, too, looked as if it were sleeping.

Mrs. Gallagher wrapped the still, bloody infant's body in

a blanket and handed it to Tessa. She shrank back, unable to bear the sight of another dead child so close to the last.

"Tessa, please," she said in a whisper of authority. "There is still much to be done."

"But what do I—"

"Take the child next door. The woman there will see it washed and readied for a decent burial."

As Mrs. Gallagher repacked her satchel, Tessa advanced slowly to the corner where the three other children waited. All of them now gazed up at her with a mixture of fright and curiosity. She knelt beside them and, without uttering a word, took three small pieces of molasses candy from a pocket in her skirt.

At first they resisted, unaccustomed to the kindness of strangers. But when the ragged, unkempt little girl finally reached out, her two brothers followed. Their faces lit almost in unison at the surprisingly sweet taste and Tessa was certain, looking at them, that it was the first bit of confection any of them had ever tasted. It wasn't much. Tessa knew that. In fact it was precious little. But it was the only bit of pleasure she could give, and she wanted— needed—to give it.

The little girl would have been pretty, she thought sadly, had it not been for the sooty smudges on her cheeks and the ratty brown hair, which had not seen a comb or a pail of soap and water for what she guessed was several weeks. Tessa's heart ached for the dim light in the child's wide eyes. The odds she faced in this life were insurmountable. Whenever she began to pity her own simple life, Tessa Murphy had only to come to Hester Street to look into the pale faces of these people, these children.

Crouching beside them, she reached down and slowly ran her hand along the child's cheek. She did not pull away, strangely trusting. Tessa had needed to touch a living child to try and somehow wash away what she had seen and felt.

In spite of the dirt, the little girl's skin was smooth like her own. What might her own life have been, Tessa wondered, kneeling close to the child, had it not been for her father?

For his relentless determination once they had come here to America.

God, Tessa thought, she owed him everything.

Out in the street a few minutes later, Tessa sagged against the soot-stained tenement and sobbed. The image of the little girl's face, another dead baby, the sour smell of the garret: They pummeled her now with an unyielding cruelty.

"I'm sorry, lass," Mrs. Gallagher kindly offered in her raspy Irish brogue.

She led Tessa to an old overturned crate and made her sit. After a moment, she sank down beside her with a little huff, then held out her hand. "Here."

"What's this?" Tessa asked of the coins pressed into the palm of her hand.

"'Tis your share."

"That woman can't afford to pay you."

"She didn't. But that doesn't mean I cannot pay you." Mary Gallagher curled Tessa's fingers around the money and smiled. "Take it, lass. You've earned it today."

Tessa wiped her tears with the back of her hand. "It's really because of my da, isn't it? Because he won't take anything directly from you."

"Does the reason really matter so much?"

"I suppose not." She waited another moment before she said, "I never knew it would feel so dreadful. That poor family has so much misery. And now they must face this."

Mary patted her shoulder. "Sometimes 'tis for the best. They have so little and there are already three young mouths to feed."

"But the woman wept for her child just the same."

"Oh, Tessa lass, these women cry for so many things," she sighed, wiping the back of her neck with a handkerchief. "For the life they left back home. For the disappointments they have found here. For the children who will suffer far longer than they."

"It is all just so sad."

"It is at that."

"I really don't understand," Tessa shook her head, and a loose copper strand brushed her forehead.

"What's that?"

"How do women do it?"

"Have babies ye mean?"

Tessa looked up, still shaken. "Oh, I know how babies come to be. That's not it. I just can't imagine how all of the horrid pain, the torture, even the chance of dying, could be worth it to any of them."

"'Tis love that does it. Makes a woman perfectly willing to give herself up, body and soul, with not a thought to the future," Mary explained simply, stuffing the handkerchief back in her skirt pocket. Then her kind smile fell to a lopsided grin. "Of course, you're not likely to discover the bliss of that if you're still determined to marry Brian Sullivan."

"Good!" Tessa said stubbornly. "The act of begetting a child sounds almost as gruesome as bearing it."

When Mary Gallagher did not argue or plead a case for love any further, Tessa looked back at her. "Thank you for this," she said, holding up the money. "It will go toward helping my da."

"Like you, I do at least wish he would slow down."

"After Brian and I are married it will all work out. I will see to it."

Again Mary Gallagher smiled. "You're right about one thing, lass. Ye're every bit yer father's daughter, stubborn as the day is long."

"And younger! Charlie Murphy doesn't stand a chance against me!"

"That, I do believe," Mary said with a little chuckle.

Tessa paused a moment more and glanced around the dark, grimy alley as she inhaled a breath of the warm, stifling air. "Tell me something, Mary. Does the loss get any easier to bear with time?"

"Never," the old Irish woman answered truthfully. "Not for someone with a heart as big as yours."

Chapter

5

TESSA HURRIED ALONE DOWN TENTH STREET.

She was still shaken by what she had seen yet again in the tenements. But tonight she would try to wash her mind free of it. She was going to the theater with Brian.

It was already ten minutes past five, and her father would be home soon, expecting his supper. She had also agreed to be ready for Brian at half past six, but she had lost track of time sitting alone on a bench in Tompkins Square, trying to collect herself enough to face them both with a smile.

As a surprise for her twentieth birthday the week before, Brian had purchased tickets to see the famous Lydia Thompson perform, and Tessa could not disappoint him. Secretly, she liked the notion of an evening out far more than she liked the sort of bawdy events Brian preferred. But one, unfortunately, did not come without the other.

She came out of her small, dark bedroom and stepped down the creaking stairs in her best black button shoes, the ones with the worn-down heels and scuffed tips. Tessa had been revived by a basin of cold water and a fresh cotton blouse. It wasn't at all like what they wore at the Hoffman House, but after the poverty she had seen again today, Tessa Murphy could scarcely pity her own modest wardrobe.

In the dining room, her father sat hunched over at the head of the oak table between the two spinster boarders, the Misses Baldwin. Mary Gallagher sat at the other end, and none of them was speaking. The only sound was the clinking of silverware against steadily emptying dinner plates. In one hand her father held a fork. His head was propped up by his other hand. The aroma of boiled cabbage and potatoes swirled around them all like a pungent cloud.

Tessa lingered in the doorway, her copper hair piled into a loose bun, watching her father for a moment. His eyes opened and closed and he looked as if his head was about to fall into his plate. She despised seeing him so weary. His round face was flaccid, as it had been the evening before. His breathing was still strained, and he had patently refused any more of Mary Gallagher's coriander tea.

"And where might ye be goin', lass?" he asked, when he finally looked up and saw her standing there in her best blouse with her mother's cameo at her throat.

Tessa took a breath and tipped up her chin as the two Misses Baldwin and Mary Gallagher looked up at her, too.

"I am going to the theater with Brian."

"Sullivan, is it?" he asked, his faded gray eyes narrowing circumspectly.

"Let's not start again, Da, all right? Brian very kindly bought two tickets to see Miss Lydia Thompson perform in her burlesque company as a present for my birthday."

"The man is in love with ye, lass. There was a great deal more to it than kindness."

"So what if he is?" she asked defensively, clearing away his plate and fork. Then she reached back to the sideboard behind him and put a clean glass and the whiskey bottle in their place. "Would that really be so dreadful?"

"Ye know how I feel about the lad, Tessa," her father said more softly, his concern for this child of his heart bleeding through the bitter tone of disapproval. The others at the table politely averted their eyes. "Ye deserve so much better."

She sank into the empty chair beside him with every bit of grace her mother had once possessed, but there was an angry determination in her eyes that pressed her to speak before she had thought clearly.

"Da, Brian works hard. You know that. He has a solid job. A good future. He can afford store-bought dresses for me and a place big enough for us all."

"So that is it, hmm? Finally we come to the truth." He took a long, contemplative swallow of whiskey and then set the glass back on the table. "Ye're entertainin' Sullivan so that ye can have some place to keep yer poor, sick ol' da."

"You don't understand, I—"

"Tessa, ye don't want to marry the man any more than I want ye to."

She averted her eyes, unable to look at her father for the truth suddenly out between them. At this very direct turn in the conversation, Mrs. Gallagher motioned to the Misses Baldwin, and all of them silently adjourned to the parlor, giving father and daughter a bit of privacy.

"You're the most important thing in the world to me," she said in a faint whisper, squeezing his hand. "You've cared for me all of my life and now I see a chance for you to stop working so hard. It is my chance to take care of you for a change. What precisely is so very wrong with that?"

"Tessa, lass," he said with sudden tears in his eyes and a flicker of a smile. "What a blessin' ye would have been to yer mother if she had lived to see the sort of woman ye've become."

He brought her hand to his lips and kissed it tenderly. "But listen well. Even if he had a home of his own to offer, I'd not live under Sullivan's roof, nor would I take his charity, we all knowin' how I feel. That would make me an even bigger hypocrite than you, my darlin' girl, and I'm full o' far too much pride for that."

"But I really want to do this," she said pleadingly.

"And I want to stop ye! I tell ye, lass, I'll not stand by and watch ye give yer life away for an old Irishman like me. Not without a fight!"

"I'd be doing it for both of us, Da. I cannot lose you, too."

He betrayed the slightest hint of a smile at that. "Now, lass, do ye truly believe I have any intention of dyin' before I see ye find that prince of yours?"

"I loved Brian that way once," she softly replied, trying to convince herself as much as her father. As she leaned back in the creaky oak chair, her copper hair sparkled like fire in the glow of the single lamp between them. "It was really not so long ago."

At that, Charlie Murphy laughed aloud. "Ye were a child then. 'Twas a fancy, not really love."

"I believed that it was."

"A lifetime ago ye did. The woman ye've become could never be happy with Brian Sullivan."

"And why not?"

"There's too much fire in yer heart to settle for a man like him."

When they both heard the sound of heavy footsteps coming down the stairs outside in the corridor, Tessa saw now that it was her father who stiffened. No matter what, the subject is closed, she thought, stubbornly. I know this is what is best for all concerned, and I mean to stick to my course!

"Now, Da. Please at least try to be civil to him tonight, won't you? For me?"

Charlie Murphy tapped his fingers on the table as his daughter looked back from the door. He wanted to approve of this man. He had tried so many times to think of Brian Sullivan as a suitable husband for his only child. But, heaven help him, he simply couldn't.

He watched silently, frustratedly, the firm, broad-shouldered young man with the strong, square face as he rounded the corner and lumbered into the dining room.

"Good evening, Brian," Tessa smiled sweetly, betraying nothing of the argument that had gone on before his arrival.

Brian Sullivan stood in the doorway, unwieldily formal in

his best suit of clothes, a green-and-white-striped shirt and suspenders beneath. His unruly russet hair and mustache were tamed and oiled. Try as he might to look sophisticated for Tessa, out of his dashing police uniform he looked awkward, at best.

Charlie managed only a glowering nod and a gruff, unintelligible growl in the man's direction before he lowered his head back into the glass of whiskey.

"You will have to excuse him. My da, it seems, is feeling poorly again."

"Well, ye must take it easy, Charlie. We were all so worried about ye," Brian said. But his kind observation fell into the chasm of strained silence that dominated the tiny, lamplit dining room.

When Brian could see that there was to be no more of an exchange between them, he drew a small gold watch from his coat pocket, glanced down at it, then pushed it back. "We best be goin'. Curtain is at eight and we've a fair walk ahead."

Tessa glanced back at her father one last time, hoping he would say something, anything, civilized. When it was clear that he was not about to relent, Tessa pulled the shawl up over her shoulders and turned toward the door. "Yes. We had better be going," she agreed, and moved out into the corridor. "Good night, Da," she said hopefully.

In response, Charlie Murphy only grumbled again into his now half-full tumbler of Irish whiskey, then turned away.

Part of what Tessa had looked forward to about going to the theater with Brian was the walk they would take along a portion of the Ladies' Mile afterwards. She had insisted that they walk past the elegant storefront windows, so that she could see all of the beautiful things on display.

Tessa was mesmerized by the splendid array of clothes, gloves, hats, and shoes. The golden things, her father called them. Things that were possible, with ingenuity and a bit of luck, for anyone to obtain in America.

Despite the lateness of the hour, the evening was still warm and full of activity when they left the theater. Together, they strolled beneath streetlamps amid dozens of other New Yorkers, all dressed impeccably, all going home to their aristocratic mansions, many on Madison Square. A dark blue barouche, accented in gold, slowed and then stopped at the curb beside them and Tessa tried to catch a glimpse beyond the carriage lamps of the elegant people inside.

Now, in the shadow of the bright gaslit bars and restaurants just off Broadway, Tessa had entirely forgotten about her morning in the tenements. At the moment, she actually felt carefree, thanks to Brian's thoughtful gift. As they began to walk again, Tessa linked her arm with Brian's muscled one.

"The show was great fun, don't you think?"

"Oh, yes," she agreed, meaning it.

They paused again, this time in front of a millinery shop. The window was low to the ground and fronted with a waist-high brass bar against which Tessa leaned. Silently, she studied three of the most elegant hats she had ever seen. Two were ornamented with brightly colored feathers. The third was black with gold braid and four yellow roses. All of them were framed in a window with thick, blue velvet draperies tied with gold cord.

"Which one do you like best?" she asked playfully.

In response, Brian stood stiff legged and perplexed, hands shoved into his pants pockets. "Oh, come now," she prodded, smiling sweetly. "Of course they're all divine, but you must prefer one above the others."

Brian lifted a hand and squeezed his chin between his thumb and forefinger trying, for her sake, to study them. "Truthfully, Tessa, I don't much care for any o' them. But then, ye know, I don't especially favor grand bonnets for ladies."

"Can you not imagine me in at least one of them, propped on my head, my long hair hanging down around it?" she asked, tipping her own modest bonnet to the side of her

head in the fashionable way the more costly ones were worn.
"Well, I am especially fond of the green one," she declared
when he said nothing.

"With all o' those feathers?" Brian croaked, wrinkling his
wide nose as his chin jutted out toward the glass. "Why, that
hat costs five dollars! 'Tis a fortune for such a useless thing!"

Tessa's heart sank. She could not help it. When Brian
looked over at her, his face, like the rest of his body, was
rigid with disbelief. He was so clearly uncomfortable with
opulence, even the fantasy of it.

"I am simply not accustomed to thinkin' of ye as the
grand sort o' girl who would have a place to wear somethin'
like that," Brian tried awkwardly to explain, when faced
with the disappointment in her eyes.

Tessa looked back out at the other people passing them
by. "When I was young, I used to dream of being a grand
lady, swept away by a handsome prince."

"I thought ye used to dream of marryin' me."

She doggedly pressed her reservations even further beneath her good-natured smile. "Young girls have lots of
dreams, Brian."

He leaned against the window beside her and took in a
heavy breath. For a few moments more, they silently
watched the people parade before them in the cool night air.

"What happened to them? Yer dreams, I mean," Brian
finally asked, glancing over at her as they stood in the
flickering yellow glow of a gas streetlamp.

"I don't know," Tessa answered a little sadly. "I suppose I
just grew up."

They stood on the dark porch of Mrs. Gallagher's boardinghouse, safe from the prying eyes of the passersby. A
cooling breeze rustled the flaming tips of Tessa's hair, which
she wore free from her bun, and as he paused, Brian reached
out to carefully brush them from her eyes.

"I want to say something to ye," Brian began in a halting
whisper. Then he stopped.

"What I mean to say," he began again, "is that I love ye

quite desperately. But, if there is some other reason ye have not told yer father about our plans to marry, I'd like to know it."

A slow smile kindled behind her shimmering green eyes and then spread fully across her face. What a day it had been. From Hester Street to Broadway. From a child's despair to an evening's entertainment. From stubbornly defending Brian, to her own dogged feeling of doubt. Life was full of such contradictions.

Tessa moved a step nearer, suddenly craving the musky scent of his skin and more intimacy between them to wash that doubt away. She loved the raw desire she always saw in his eyes when they were close like this. It would be enough, knowing that he felt it. Even if she could never feel the same thing.

Gently, Tessa pressed a slow, thoughtful kiss onto his lips. "Does that answer your question?"

"Because ye know well that I only want ye to be happy."

Again she kissed him, sweet and soft. Seductively. This time, as she felt his body stir against her, she wantonly ran a hand along the line of his neck and across his broad shoulder.

"You can be the silliest man sometimes, Brian Sullivan."

"Don't make light of this, lass," he warned. "I know only too well that yer da believes I am not the right man for ye."

"I love you. In my way, I have always loved you," she declared. "He will come around once we are married. I am certain of it."

Chapter
6

CHANDLER SAT ALONE IN A RED LEATHER WING CHAIR IN THE sun-filled library of his family home on Mount Vernon Street. It was early morning, just before he was to leave for his office down on Summer Street. His long, elegant legs were crossed at the ankles as he held up the morning paper. But he had read the same line three times. His mind was too full of the past, and of what the future held for his children if Daphne continued to be the dominant female influence in their lives. Other men's wives were not the answer to his pain. Nor, any longer, were they the answer to his passion. He knew that now.

Chandler absently lifted a cup filled with strong, dark tea from the side table, which was cluttered with part of his collection of Chinese porcelain. He took a slow sip of the special blend of tea Li Kao Chen had sent him, and then lay his head back against the cool red leather, hoping that it would be enough to relax him. He had not found time to do his meditation this morning and already he had begun to regret it.

"Good morning, brother dear."

The pungent fragrance of lilac water had preceded her entrance. Chandler opened his eyes to see his sister standing over him dressed in beige silk with a stiff lace collar; a tasteful rope of pearls was knotted at her breast. Her hair was neatly parted in the center and pulled back into the same severe bun she always wore. The style was less flattering now than it had been when she was eighteen, as it accentuated the fine network of wrinkles that had begun to develop around her eyes and small, pursed mouth.

"You're here early," he nodded absently, detesting the smell of lilac water almost as much as he disliked seeing her this early in the day. "No one left at your own home this morning for you to torment?"

Daphne ignored him. "Grand evening, last night. Felicity looked lovelier than I have ever seen her, I think."

"Mmm," he mouthed and looked back at the newspaper, not at all inclined to take the bait.

She perched formally on the edge of a hard mahogany chair at a right angle to his own, then folded her hands neatly in her lap.

"Now then, suppose you tell me what went wrong last evening. I had such high hopes for the two of you."

"Why, Daphne, whatever do you mean?"

Her expression quickly soured. She had been pretty once, he thought. But a lifetime of scheming had already aged her well beyond her twenty-nine years.

"Don't let's play games. You know perfectly well what I mean."

He put the newspaper down again as the expression on his own classically handsome face became a smirk, but his voice was openly hostile. "Oh, you must mean your intention to control every facet of my life from the boardroom to the bedroom."

"Sarcasm never did become you, Chandler."

"Curious," he shot back glibly. "I was just going to say the same thing about you."

Daphne appeared to soften. It was a calculated tactic.

"Oh, Chandler," she said, leaning slightly forward, her hard eyes widening. "I do so hate it when we quarrel like this. You are my brother, and I love you. You must know that I have only your best interests at heart."

As her icy blue eyes widened, suggesting sincerity, his own narrowed. "Of course you do. What other possible reason would you have for badgering me to marry a girl I detest?"

Her cool laughter was unexpected. "Oh, really, Chandler. What reason could you possibly have to detest Felicity? You've known her for years. She is beautiful, well educated, and she comes from one of the finest families in Boston."

"You mean one of the richest, don't you?"

"Do stop that," Daphne stiffened again. "You know how I abhor it when you make me sound so mercenary."

"That's right," he said, smiling, suddenly as impish and as pleased with himself as a delinquent schoolboy for having gotten to her. Just as she had gotten to him. "It can be so difficult at times to hear the truth."

They sat in glacial silence, as Jennings, the Tate family butler, attired in starched black with crisp white gloves and collar, served Daphne a cup of her favorite scorchingly hot Mandarin tea. He added just the right amount of milk and sugar. She dismissed him with a wave, then once again leveled her eyes upon her only brother.

"Very well. Let's stop the sparring, shall we?"

"Gladly."

"Lincoln and I want you to stop carrying on with Martin Bailey's wife and marry Felicity."

"I am aware of that."

"And?" she arched a slim blond brow expectantly.

"And there isn't a chance in hell of that happening."

"But you have been living this solitary existence of yours for more than two years," she reminded him. "So have your children. Haven't you made them suffer quite long enough for your hatred of Cynthia?"

Chandler's eyes shadowed and his lips became a single rigid line. As only she could, Daphne had successfully stirred the embers of a memory he wished desperately to extinguish, and they both knew it.

"You agreed never to speak her name before me."

"Oh, good heavens, Chandler! Has your heart hardened so much that you cannot look back fondly on at least some of what the two of you shared? After all of this time?"

"Not another word or I swear I shall—"

"Or you shall what? You listen to me, Chandler Tate. I suffered through that whole nasty business with you so that father, and the rest of the world for that matter, would never discover the awful truth. Or have you forgotten to whom you came in your darkest hour? Have you forgotten who came here and cared for your children when you were too devastated by what had occurred even to get out in the morning?"

"I am telling you, Daphne, you cannot force this! I will marry whom I like when I like and enjoy myself in the meantime! And there isn't a wretched thing you can do about it!"

In the silence, Daphne reached into a pocket in her skirt and drew forth an official looking document. "I haven't wanted to do this," she said with a calculated little sigh, "but it would appear I no longer have any choice."

"What is that?" he scoffed out the question.

"Certainly you recognize a codicil when you see one," Daphne countered, her voice once again as cold as slate.

Chandler took it from her with a quick, snapping movement and glanced down. His lips began to part slowly. "A codicil to father's will?"

"I had hoped there would never be a need to show it to you. But your arrogance toward me lately, and your persistence in going against the good of this family, has forced my hand."

Chandler scanned the paper and then lowered it into his lap, thunderstruck. "It says that father left you with the final say in B.W. Tate and Company. You?"

"If you do not remarry within three years, yes."

"You are trying to blackmail me?"

"Father would have called it firm persuasion."

"Damn!" He pressed a hand against his forehead with an incredulous moan and turned away from her. "I saw the will he left. He showed it to me himself years ago. What did you get him to do? Sign this on his deathbed?"

"All that matters, Chandler," she said without inflection, "is that father did sign it. After Cynthia was gone, he saw the way you were carrying on, and he began to doubt that leaving you with absolutely no one to keep you in check was in the best interests of the company or the family."

She gauged his anger before she continued. "Before his death, father came to believe that if you did not get this recklessness out of your system, the only choice left was to force you to marry. It was either that or he felt certain you would proceed in dragging the reputation of this family down into the depths along with you."

"So that is why you have been pushing me so relentlessly toward Felicity!"

"You need not contest the codicil, either. Horace witnessed father's signature himself."

Chandler stood now, clenching and unclenching his fists, trying to stem the tide of fury that threatened to overtake him.

"How much did you pay that old barracuda to help you? Father would never have agreed to this without Horace Merriweather's clever prodding!"

Daphne came to her feet and met him, both of them rigid and angry. "Lincoln and I didn't want to do this, but you really have left us no choice."

"Why not use your real ace, instead of just the company, if you mean to force my hand?" he raged, beginning to back and forth across the room.

"Even I have my limits, Chandler."

He stopped suddenly and spun back around. "Oh come now, Daphne. Don't tell me after this that you actually have a shred of human decency left!"

"You have misjudged my motives, I assure you."

"I think not! Why, of course!" He laughed viciously. "How silly of me. Revealing that particular skeleton in the Tate family closet would damage you every bit as much as it would me. And we couldn't have that, now could we?"

"How can you speak to me that way, Chandler? I am your sister!"

"You have made a drastic error in betraying me," he snarled. "I'll not be forced into marrying Felicity, no matter what you try to do."

"It doesn't appear that you have much of an option," she replied with a victorious little grin. "Apparently your beloved father trusted your judgment far less than he led you to believe. And your rebuff of a woman like Felicity Pettigrew, unfortunately, only confirms that he was right. Chandler, she really is so perfectly suited to you if you would only open your eyes."

"My God, you are a hateful woman."

"Not hateful. Just practical," she countered calmly. "I know what is best for this family. Father loved that about me."

"And I despise it!" he barked, turning abruptly away from her, his fists clenched in explosive rage.

In the silence, Daphne watched her headstrong brother for signs of capitulation. But all she saw was the fury. Responding expertly, she softened again. Daphne came up behind her magnificent, stately brother and pressed a hand gently between his shoulders.

"This piece of paper really means so little," she said, strangely docile now that she had delivered such a swift and unexpected blow. "We have worked so well together since father's death, agreed on almost everything for the good of the company and for the good of the family. There really is no reason for things to change now." She took the paper from his clenched fist and folded it, then pressed it back into her pocket. "See there? Now we can just forget all about it, all right? We shall simply say we have an understanding."

Chandler turned back around, his handsome, chiseled face now a crimson mask of fury. "Daphne, take the company and the legacy and go straight to hell with them both, for all I care!"

"Well I can see by a comment like that, that you have been spending far too much time with that tasteless Nelson Winthrop friend of yours, and that he has quite seriously warped your mind to your duty."

"I would sooner leave myself and my children penniless, as he had the courage to do, than condemn Alice and James to the sort of contrived existence you envision for them."

"Now, Chandler," she remained calm. "You don't mean that."

"The devil I don't!"

"Father was only trying to protect you and this family from the costly error you made the last time around."

"If I had listened to my instincts the last time around, instead of being so determined to stand against him, Cynthia would never have become anything more than my mistress. Certainly she would never have become my wife. For that error in judgment I have only my youth to blame. But from here on out I shall live my life as I see fit. Even if the cost is my company. Is that clear?"

Daphne sank back into the wooden chair amid the silence. Her arms on the rests, she propped her chin with a single finger as she watched him stalk to the door in four heavy-footed strides. As he clutched the brass handle, Chandler turned back around.

"You wouldn't abandon your duty to father's company. B.W. Tate and Company is your life."

"Just watch me!" Chandler seethed. "And you and that inept husband of yours can do with it as your conscience wills you. Quite frankly, I say to hell with you both!"

The heavy door crashed against the frame as he stormed from the parlor.

Through an adjoining door in his bedroom, Chandler looked into the pale blue room that once had been Cynthia's. It had been a very long time since he had allowed himself to come here to confront the past. Cynthia, he thought. No matter how she denied it, that was his sister's real blackmail.

Everything in the room was precisely as she had left it two years before. Bathed now in bright sunlight, which came in past the lace-edged curtains, the room was awash in feminine luxury. It was a style and design that made him physically ill now, when he thought how frequently his lust had once led him here.

Chandler glanced at the watercolor above the bed, a gift for their first wedding anniversary. Her silver-handled hairbrush, comb, and mirror were still neatly arranged atop the rosewood dressing table. So these things remained, along with the wardrobe of costly gowns that he had never quite been able to force himself to discard. His children would have wondered. So would the rest of the world. He was, after all, the grieving widower, and leaving any other impression than that was a chance still too dangerous to take.

As he leaned against the doorjamb, surveying the room, Chandler shivered. For a moment, he closed his eyes. It seemed like a dream to him now, their beginning and certainly their end. It would haunt him, he knew, for the rest of his life. He sat on the edge of her bed. Their bed. He heard only the quickened beating of his own heart as he remembered what else lay within these four walls.

"You rang, sir?" Jennings formally intoned as he stood in the doorway to Cynthia's bedroom that led into the corridor.

"Has she gone?" Chandler asked flatly. He was holding back the heavy red velvet drapery and gazing out the window to Mount Vernon Street, where a horse stood waiting, tethered to a hitching post.

"Your sister? Yes, sir. Miss Daphne left shortly after your meeting in the parlor."

"Splendid."

His lips were pressed tightly together as if to hold in the anger as he turned back around. "Jennings, I want you to ready a valise for me. I'll be leaving for New York this afternoon. You have strict instructions to give Daphne or that husband of hers not the slightest idea where I've gone or when I shall return. That is, until you feel that she is sufficiently frantic. I will trust you to know when the time is right."

"New York, sir?"

"I have got to get away from Boston for a while. I feel as if I am suffocating here," he confessed, raking a hand through his hair. "Naturally, for anything concerning the children, I can be reached at the Hoffman House."

"Of course, sir," the stately old butler nodded compliantly. "But if you don't mind my saying so, a trip now, when you have just received such an important shipment—"

"Will teach my sister a lesson. If Daphne and that useless husband of hers think that they can manage the entire company without me, then as of right now, they shall have a golden opportunity to try."

"But Miss Daphne knows no more about the import business than which of your costly fabrics she wishes to see made into her newest ball gown."

"True," Chandler agreed with an angry smile. "And Lincoln Forrester knows even less. But it seems that they have a terribly misguided impression of their own worth in the matter, thanks to my father and his wretched codicil."

"Rather a cruel way to teach the ol' girl a lesson, sir," Jennings wryly observed.

"Perhaps," Chandler considered thoughtfully. Then he looked back at his butler with conviction lighting his stormy blue eyes. "But I'll have no one—and I do mean no one—undermining and seeking to control me as she has sought to do. If Daphne feels so able to take over my life, let her try it. A week or two ought to bring her to her senses."

Jennings gasped. "Why sir, your sister will have things in a complete state! That will seem an eternity to her."

"As it will seem to me. That company and my children are my life," Chandler said.

"You are a man full of surprises, Mr. Tate."

"Jennings, ol' friend, you cannot imagine."

Chapter

7

AN HOUR BEFORE HIS TRAIN WAS SCHEDULED TO LEAVE, Chandler stood alone in his office on Summer Street, fingering a bolt of indigo blue satin. It was the one he had brought back from China a lifetime ago.

That purchase had been his finest coup. Negotiated for months, twice he had nearly lost the deal. But in the end, Chandler had won his price and his father's respect. Again, he glanced proudly down at the cool, smooth fabric sparkling like blue jewels. It would sell for a small fortune here. But this particular bolt was not for sale at any price. This costly silk symbolized his own coming of age, his dreams for the future, only a tiny glimmer of which had been rekindled last night.

As a romantic young man of eighteen, Chandler had vowed to turn this elegant silk into a gown for the woman he would one day marry. But he had never even shown it to Cynthia. She had not seemed quite worthy of so dear a part of himself, even when times were at their best between them. He had saved it for just the right woman at just the right time. And now, quite likely, he would save it forever.

Chandler moved a few steps further into the office that had been the focus of his life these past two years. It had helped him keep his sanity. A carved mahogany desk served as the room's focal point, with golden sunlight from the tall windows slashed across it. On Saturday morning, the octagonal building of hammered granite, and the rest of the business district, were like a graveyard. It was far more conducive to reflection than he liked.

B.W. Tate & Company was more profitable by a forty percent margin than it had been at the time of his father's death. He was proud of what he had achieved. And now he was risking it all by putting it into his sister's inexperienced hands.

Daphne had left him no choice. She had committed the most egregiously contemptible act of betrayal against her own brother, and she must be taught a lesson. Of course she would fail. That was not what concerned him. Rather, it was the cost of that failure that filled him with doubt.

For the last two years, this company had come to dominate his life, almost like a third child to him. He had cared for it, nurtured it, watched it grow and prosper beneath his tender care. Now he must cast it all into the hands of someone who could only bring it harm through her inexperience.

He let go of the silk and heaved a sigh that was full of misgivings. He did not want to go to New York. But blackmail? Bullying him into a marriage? Never!

He did not even particularly like New York, but it would be difficult for Daphne to locate him there. When she grew desperate, when she pleaded sufficiently with Jennings to tell her where he'd gone, only then would her brother consider it punishment enough.

Only then would he come home to Boston.

"You sent for me, sir?"

Chandler glanced up, having almost forgotten the primary reason he had come here before leaving. In the doorway, facing him, stood a white-haired old gentleman with deep-set eyes, muddy, lined skin, and a stooping gait. He held his gray felt hat in gnarled hands.

"Come in, Harlen," Chandler said, managing a smile for the worker who had been with B.W. Tate & Company the longest.

His father had hired Harlen Murray before Chandler was born, back when the company operated out of one room down at the end of the block. His eyesight was now poor, his usefulness insignificant. But Chandler retained him on the payroll out of sentiment and loyalty.

"I'm sorry to have bothered you on your day off, Harlen."

"It's never a bother, sir. I owe you more than I can ever say."

"But that is still to remain our secret, isn't it?" Chandler said, his slight smile broadening. "After all, it wouldn't do to have the rest of the workers know I have a favorite around here."

Chandler came out from behind his grand mahogany desk and motioned for Harlen to sit in the red leather guest chair opposite him.

"Of course, sir. I've not told a soul."

"So how is Martha?"

Harlen Murray winced as he lowered himself tentatively into the chair, a hand gripping each of the arms. "They tell me she won't improve much, Mr. Tate, but my wife is at least comfortable now, thanks to you."

"It is a good hospital, the Channing Home."

"The most expensive in Boston," Harlen gratefully reminded the young man that was both employer and benefactor. He added, with slightly lowered eyes, "You know, sir, that I can never repay all of the kindness you've shown to us both."

"And I can never repay the many years of loyalty you've shown this company."

"It wasn't really so much."

"Honor is vastly underrated these days I'm afraid, Harlen. But to the Chinese, and now to me, it is everything."

The old man leaned forward slightly in the red leather chair. "If you don't mind my saying so, sir, that strange place changed you. You've got a side to yourself now that your father never had."

"Some might say it made me too introspective."

"All I know for sure is that I remember the young man you were before Mr. Tate senior sent you over there. I didn't have much hope for you being any different from the rest of them back then."

"Quite frankly, Harlen, neither did I."

Chandler reached behind himself and took a large envelope that lay among the scattered papers. "I've got to go away for a little while, and I want you to have this to see you and Martha through until I return."

Harlen Murray knew that it was yet more money to help him pay the expenses in caring for his terminally ill wife. But before he could object, Chandler pressed the envelope into his hand. "Take it, my friend, and if you would, as a favor to me and to my father's memory, keep an eye on things around here while I'm away."

"You know I would do anything for you and this company, Mr. Tate, sir."

"Good," Chandler smiled. "I've a feeling the company, at least, is going to need you."

Chapter
8

DOWN IN THE STREET BELOW, THE SWEET IRISH MUSIC HAD ALready begun. There was a birthday celebration beginning. Tessa pulled aside the beige cambric curtains on her bedroom window and glanced outside. The night sky was bright, almost like daylight. Neighbors had lit their oil lamps and placed them on open windowsills. There was such a glow and sparkle that one could scarcely tell the lamps from the stars in the sky. Even her father would dance tonight. He would be happy, carefree. And, she hoped, healthy for a little while longer.

"Come on! We don't want to be late!" Charlie Murphy called anxiously to her through the closed bedroom door.

Tessa glanced out the window again. The neighbors had begun to gather. Already there were laughter and conversation, all of it laced with the remembered strains of a homeland Tessa had never known. Tonight, for a little while, the people who toiled long hours in the factories and on the railroads and in other people's houses could laugh and dance. They could forget.

It was precisely what she meant to do.

When Tessa opened the door, her father stood before her smiling, his chest bowed out and his hands pulling his best pair of green suspenders away from his good clean white shirt. His few threads of silver-red hair were wet and tamed away from his rough and ruddy face.

"You look handsome as ever, Da."

"And you, you look splendid as ever, Tessa me love." He extended his hand proudly to her like a suitor. "Shall we go then?"

Outside Mrs. Gallagher's boardinghouse, they strolled together into the crowd. Children in knee pants and pinafores laughed and rushed around them as Tessa looked up at the night sky lit brightly with the glow of oil lamps, candles, and stars.

The music was sweet and lively as the crowd enthusiastically clapped along. Women, their skirts lifted to their ankles, were dancing a spirited jig with the men. Everyone was laughing. Around the whirling dancers, in a ring that now included Tessa and her father, the people cheered and clapped.

"Come on!" her father beckoned with a wide grin as he tugged her toward the dancers.

"Oh, Da," she demurred. "You know I'm no good at it. Ma was the dancer."

"'Twas so," he winked, "but ye're the beauty. And besides, all lovely young lasses should know how to dance!"

Chapter

9

CHANDLER PULLED THE GOLD WATCH FROM HIS POCKET, FLICKED it open, and checked the time again. It was twenty minutes since the last time he had looked and not yet even ten o'clock in the morning. Around him in the wood-paneled Hoffman House lobby, pockets of actors and Wall Street magnates and bankers collected in their derbies and their tall black hats ready to begin the day. But Chandler, who sat nearly obscured by the fronds of two tall green palms in one of the overstuffed crimson velvet chairs, had begun his hours before. Another day in New York City ahead of him and once again, he was already bored to tears.

The vast lobby was grand. More than a dozen huge oil paintings graced its ornate molded plaster walls, along with Correggio's *Narcissus* and a collection of luscious nudes by Bouguereau. There were huge ormolu vases brimming with fresh flowers. Marble busts filled arched niches. Near the entrance, on lush crimson carpeting, stood two ebony statues of Nubian slaves, each one bearing a basket of fruit. But Chandler was too distracted to care about any of it.

He had been in New York for a week. He had gone to the theater and to dinner. He had seen the friends he wanted to see in an empty whirl of tedious social events. He missed James and Alice. He missed his work. He could not summon the courage to imagine what Daphne might be doing to the company he had so lovingly nurtured. But he had made a stand, so all he could do now was hope that his absence was accomplishing what it must.

Chandler shifted in his chair and propped up his chin with his hand. He needed a breath of air. A brisk morning walk. And regrettably, he needed to start formulating a plan for how he meant to handle his sister once he returned to Boston. Hopefully by then, even without an admission of defeat, he would find that she had learned her lesson.

Charlie Murphy's health had not improved.

The perspiration ever-present on his waxy forehead and the shallow breaths he took were enough to concern even Brian Sullivan now. In spite of their differences, Brian had offered to take on the old Irishman's deliveries until he felt better, and Tessa's father was just weary enough to acquiesce. The policeman generously took on the job in addition to his regular shift with the force.

She had ridden beside him in the milk wagon since before dawn, directing Brian toward each stop. Now, just past ten, they rode down Broadway to the clatter of horse's hooves and the crush of carts and carriages, rushing shoppers, and business people calling for horsecarts across the busy street. A poor young woman with unruly black hair and a dirt-smudged face sold posies on the street corner. A boy of no more than eight or nine held up three copies and shouted out the headline from the day's newspaper.

Brian guided the horse with a snap of the reins through a tangle of sleek carriages waiting near the Hoffman House's grand entrance. The late-morning air was already hot and oppressive again, and the back of Tessa's neck was wet. She brushed a hand beneath the back of her hair and directed him toward the smart hotel for one of their last deliveries.

As they waited for a string of traffic to pass so they could maneuver down the alley behind the hotel, Tessa linked her arm through his and snuggled against his powerful shoulder.

"I know that you and my da are not the best of friends, and yet you've agreed to help me do his job until he is up to it again," she said quietly, placing her other hand gently on his knee and inadvertently feeling the firmness of his thigh. "I don't know how I can ever thank you for that."

"Marry me," he shot her a contented smile. "I do believe that'll be payment enough."

After that, it all happened so swiftly that Tessa only saw a trace of the tall, elegant man who stepped out in front of their wagon where the street fronted the alley. He did so in the single moment that she reached over to press a kiss onto the thick, moist column of Brian's neck. But a moment was all it took. Tessa had no time even to shout a warning before he was knocked from his feet by a swift jutting clip of the horse's hoof and hurled into the street.

"Great God above!" Brian shouted as he tugged violently at the reins jerking the horse to a halt before she could trample the stranger.

"He's hurt, Brian!" Tessa gasped, jumping down and rushing in front of the wagon to the man lying prostrate and motionless before them. "Oh, Mother Mary! He's bleeding!"

As Brian stood gazing down helplessly at the bloody gash in the man's forehead, he felt a sharp stab of panic. The injury was very bad. But not so bad as their situation. The man lying before them was dressed in an expensive gray suit and gray silk waistcoat and there was a diamond stickpin shimmering from his lapel. This was not just any man. This man was a guest at the Hoffman House.

From that alone, Brian knew he would be the sort who could ruin him entirely for his carelessness. He had been in this unforgiving America long enough to understand the general feeling toward immigrants. An aristocrat would need no other excuse.

"We've got to get him to a doctor." Tessa cried, cradling the man's head in her hands.

"No! No doctor."

"But the poor man will surely bleed to death if we don't get him some help."

Brian tore a sleeve from his shirt and bent down beside her. "Here," he thrust it forward. "Use this to stop the bleeding."

"Are you going inside at least, for help?"

"I cannot do that! 'Tis too dangerous for people like us!"

"Well, we certainly cannot just leave him here! Saints above! We are the ones who ran him over."

"And the ones who'll wind up in jail for doin' it."

Brian glanced around again in sharp, nervous movements. He considered it a small miracle that the milk wagon and the shadowy alley obscured them. The handsome stranger with the shiny golden hair and square jaw began to moan as Tessa gently dabbed the blood from his forehead.

"Here now," Brian instructed, taking one of the man's limp arms. "Help me get him into the wagon."

"Our wagon?" she gulped.

"We'll take him home with us. You can tend to him there at least until we can convince him we meant no harm."

Slumped against her, the slim, elegant man was heavier than Tessa had expected. She tried her best to help Brian lift his crumpled, semiconscious body out of the street. He moaned again as Tessa pressed the torn cotton sleeve against his forehead in an attempt to stop the bleeding.

"What about his family? Shouldn't someone know we've taken him?"

"We'll worry about that if he lives!" Brian grunted.

Brian pulled to the curb in front of the boardinghouse in Charlie Murphy's milk wagon with the empty cans rattling behind.

"Will ye be needin' a hand, Sullivan?" a neighbor, whose voice was thickly laced with the familiar Irish brogue, called out from his sooty second-floor window.

"No. But thank ye kindly," Brian called back as the aristocratic stranger stumbled and slumped against him.

The children playing in the street stopped to look, and then gathered around the trio as they slowly took the first two steps up to the oak and glass front door of Mrs. Gallagher's.

"Scat now!" Brian dashed at them with a thick hand as Tessa opened the door.

She and Brian were struggling with the man as they stumbled through the entry and into the modest parlor whose bow front window faced the street. Hearing the commotion, Mrs. Gallagher flung open the kitchen door as Brian and Tessa heaved and sputtered from the weight of the man they were trying to lay down on the red velvet sofa.

"What on earth—"

"He's been hurt," Tessa huffed, pulling the man's arm from around her neck.

"I'll fetch some water and clean towels."

Brian lifted the stranger's legs up onto the sofa as Tessa pressed two throw pillows beneath his head.

"What in blazes happened to him?" Charlie asked, reaching the bottom of the stairs at the same moment that Mrs. Gallagher was dashing into the kitchen.

"It was an accident, Da. The man just walked out in front of the wagon. We didn't even have a chance to stop."

"'Tis stiflin' in here." Brian sputtered, out of breath. "Open a window, lass. The man needs air."

It was only another moment before Mary Gallagher padded back through the kitchen door carrying a steaming brass kettle full of water, an empty basin, and a towel. Tessa took up the collection of things and knelt down beside the sofa.

"He's dead."

"He's not dead, Charlie," Mary Gallagher scoffed.

"All of this blood has made his wound appear far worse than it is," Tessa whispered, running a fresh cloth through the hot water.

Brian was trying to think clearly enough to decide if they

had committed any real crime. He had not been a policeman long enough to know for certain. He hovered nervously behind Tessa as she gently cleaned away the ribbon of dried blood from beneath the makeshift bandage.

"Ah, but he's a handsome devil," Mary declared, standing beside Brian and stroking her chin. "Rich, too, by the look o' those clothes."

Still afraid of what they might face when the stranger woke, Brian turned to her with an expression of censure. "Thank ye for the water, Mary. Ye've been a great help. But I expect we can best deal with it from here."

When she placed her hands stubbornly on wide hips, not about to be expelled from her own parlor, Brian rolled his eyes and returned to Tessa's side.

"Why the devil doesn't he open his eyes?" he asked, shoving helpless hands into his pants pockets and then pulling them out again.

"I don't know exactly," Tessa answered, dipping the cloth back through the warm water, which now was pink from his blood. "But most of the bleeding has stopped."

"Thank heaven for that."

As they all hovered over him, waiting for him to wake, Tessa folded the man's hands across his chest and marveled at how long his fingers were. The nails were clean and perfectly shaped. She glanced up at his pale, golden face. The lips were firm and sensual. The nose was aquiline. All of his features were classically handsome but there was an unmistakable sensuality coiled behind his well groomed appearance.

"Perhaps he would be more comfortable if we got him out of this jacket," she suggested to her father and Brian who obliged her immediately by rolling the man onto his side so that she could pull his arms through the sleeves.

When Tessa touched his firm shoulder, an odd sensation shot through her. She drew in a steadying breath and sank back onto her heels. She studied his face, the contours of his jaw, the closed eyes with long dark lashes, and the perfectly sculpted pale mouth, struggling to put the sensation into some sort of context that made sense. When he moaned and reached for his head, she took his hand away and pressed it back against his chest.

"Shh," she tenderly implored him. "You must lie still or you're sure to start bleeding again."

"W-where am I?"

"I'm afraid you've had an accident. You stepped out in front of our wagon and there was no time to stop," Tessa carefully explained. "We weren't sure what else to do, so we brought you back home with us. You're at Mrs. Gallagher's boardinghouse on Tenth Street."

He reached for his bandaged head again and grimaced at the pain that his own touch brought. He remembered leaving the hotel. The frustration that had overwhelmed him. Circumstances in his life that he could no longer control. The need to walk. To breathe fresh air. To feel anything besides the anger. After that, everything was a blank.

"Who are you?"

"My name is Tessa Murphy." She smiled tentatively. "But now, sir, you have me at a disadvantage."

He swallowed dryly, gazing into eyes that were green, but unlike emeralds. They were the green of the sea. Deep. Unending. Their expression was full of kindness and concern for him.

"I am Chandler Tate, and I would like to offer you something for all of your trouble," he rasped, reaching for an adequate reward.

Tessa frowned and her color began to rise. "We could not possibly accept anything, Mr. Tate."

"Under the circumstances, it's the least that I can do."

"It wouldn't be right."

He could feel his throat constrict when he moved to push the issue. It was difficult to focus and he still was not altogether certain where he was. But even now, Chandler could see that this girl was the most extraordinary combination of determination and vulnerability. Her green eyes were wide and doe-like with trust, but her chin was set firmly proud against the notion of taking anything at all for an act of kindness.

"Now, lass," her father intervened. "If Mr. Tate would feel better . . ."

"But Da, Brian and I did so little."

Mindful of the disagreement between father and daughter, and with a headache too painful to enter into the debate, Chandler let the issue go, then moved to stand.

"I do thank you both for your hospitality but I really must be—" Before he could finish his sentence, Chandler grimaced again at the shooting pain, then stumbled. Tessa and Brian both shot to their feet and braced him on either side.

"Ye'll pardon me for sayin' so, I hope, Mr. Tate," Charlie Murphy intervened again, "but ye don't look as if ye're fit to go much of anywhere at the moment."

Feeling the room whirling beneath his shaky legs, Chandler wisely chose not to disagree. "Perhaps you're right at that," he said with a weak, half smile, and then let them help him back down onto the sofa. From there, he lay down willingly and allowed Tessa to cover him over lightly with a quilt.

"Rest now," she said in a sweet, fragile whisper.

It was only a moment more before he was asleep.

Chapter
10

TESSA KNELT BESIDE CHANDLER, WASHING HIS WARM FACE WITH A cool cloth and waiting patiently for him to wake again. The modest parlor was lit with the golden glow of oil lamps and candles, and the sun had begun to descend as he slept fitfully.

Charlie Murphy sat alone across the room in the lamplit dining recess. He was picking at the supper his daughter had hastily laid before him before she returned to nurse the stranger. Brian had chosen to busy himself upstairs for the remainder of the evening, not wishing any further connection with risk than was absolutely necessary.

Tessa was fascinated by this aristocratic and mysterious stranger with the smooth voice and kind eyes. He had been a patron of the Hoffman House and yet he was nothing at all like that vile Alfred Dunne. A quiver of excitement ran through her as her eyes played over his body while he slept. He was not an exceptionally large man, she thought, but he had a trim, athletic build that bespoke a man of physical discipline. She would not have expected that from one of his class.

Feeling more courageous with him asleep, Tessa reached out and ran her fingers across his broad shoulders and then along the length of his arm, as if he were some species altogether different from her own. His was certainly a different body than Brian's taut, muscular one.

Her childhood love was certainly powerfully built. A ruddy Irish bear. Chandler, on the other hand, was slim and lithe, and as elegant as a Roman sculpture. As she touched him, the same sensation quivered inside of her.

It was nothing she had ever felt for anyone else. It drew her. But it was at the precise moment when she reached out again that Chandler Tate opened his eyes. Tessa was caught gazing down at him, her fingers hovering over his chest as if she were fighting an inner battle not to touch him again. She sank back on her heels, her smooth cheeks flushing crimson as he looked up at her.

"Now it is you who have *me* at a disadvantage," he said with only a hint of devilish mischief lighting his inscrutable blue eyes.

Tessa knelt before him, suddenly feeling more embarrassed than she had ever felt before in her life. "How do you mean?" she managed to ask.

"It would appear that you know far more about me than I do about you."

She leapt to her feet, straightening the folds in her skirt. It was a nervous gesture. "I thought you might be hungry so I took the liberty of putting together a plate of bread and cheese for you," she said coolly.

Chandler watched her turn away and move to the small oak dining table in the lamplit recess across the room. Her costume was plain. A tailored beige skirt hung in folds beneath a simple ivory-colored shirtwaist. A cameo and lace collar accented her slim neck. Modest, yes. But she was surprisingly graceful for someone of her class. She had a natural elegance that some women of far better breeding never managed to attain, and her eyes were full of enough caring to take his breath away.

Tessa did not look directly at him again as she returned with the tray of cheese, Irish soda bread, and a glass of her father's precious Irish whiskey. "You must eat something," she said in a voice far more formal than the one that had greeted his waking.

"Thank you," he replied, taking a bite of the cheese, and hoping to say with his expression alone that something about her made him care what she thought.

When she stood back up, leaving him with his tray, Chandler found he could not stop himself. He reached out and took her slim wrist. "Stay and talk with me."

Tessa was still reluctant. She had embarrassed herself beyond measure by touching a strange man in the familiar, searching way that she had. And she had been caught. To make matters even worse, he had pointed it out.

"Please," Chandler said again, his eyes shimmering now in the steadily darkening room like two magic sapphire lights beckoning her almost as strongly as his words.

"Go on, lass," Charlie called out across the small room, to his daughter's great surprise. "Ye musn't be rude to our guest."

With a resolute sigh, Tessa finally sank onto the little empty place at the end of the sofa. "You're not from New York, are you?" she asked carefully as he began to eat.

"From Boston. I'm only here on business."

Tessa had never been out of New York, and with her marriage to Brian now only a matter of time, she was not likely ever to do so.

"Is it a nice city?" she asked, more as a way of keeping an awkward silence from falling between them than from true interest.

"Quite lovely. Boston is very old, steeped in the history of this country. You've never been there?" he asked, taking a slow swallow of the whiskey and feeling the throbbing in his head begin to recede with its warmth.

"I've never been much of anywhere. Except Ireland, if you can count that. I was born there, but my parents brought me to America when I was just a baby."

The Irish potato famine had chased thousands of desperate families from their homeland. Chandler had read about it at Harvard with a detached sort of empathy that came from never having done without. He had never actually spent time with anyone who had struggled for every single thing they had attained. Now the notion humbled him.

"My ancestors were Irish," Chandler offered, trying to kindle something common between them that would set her at ease.

"And have you been to Ireland?"

"Afraid not. London was as close as I got."

The faraway expression in her eyes quickly changed. Suddenly Chandler saw a glint of wonder there. "You have been to London, England?"

"I went to school there for a year when I was a boy."

"I've read all about it in Dickens."

"You enjoy reading then?" Chandler asked, trying unsuccessfully to keep the astonishment from his smooth, studied voice.

"Being an immigrant, Mr. Tate, is a disadvantage, not necessarily a lifetime devastation."

"Touché," he grinned delightedly.

"I see by your expression that I have surprised you." She smiled sweetly in return.

Surprised him? She had indeed. Tessa had countered with every bit of tact and savvy that Daphne might have used against him. Chandler was also surprised to see that the rigid, defensive expression on her face had suddenly softened into one of easy confidence.

He was not entirely certain what he would have expected of people like this before coming here. A firm social order throughout his life had kept him well insulated from the many servants who had always populated his house. Housemaids and the cook were up in the fifth-floor garrets. The butler in a basement apartment.

"What sort of books do you enjoy?" Chandler asked, feeling curiously at ease.

"All sorts. But I quite favor Dickens," she said and once again there was that gentle softness in her voice.

"Oh, yes," he smiled genuinely. "I have always enjoyed him too. *David Copperfield*."

"*Nicholas Nickleby*," she countered.

"*Pickwick Papers*."

"It was one of my favorites."

"Truly?"

"Believe it or not," she quirked a little smile.

"Oh, yes. The lass is readin' all o' the time, Mr. Tate. Takes after her sainted ma, she does," Charlie volunteered proudly, hoping to extoll the virtues of a lovely young woman with more intellect than education and more drive than opportunity.

"Then you are not employed?" Chandler asked, looking back at Tessa.

"She'll toil for no man, Mr. Tate," Charlie Murphy answered authoritatively for his daughter. "Not so long as I have breath left in my body to support us both."

"That is very commendable of you," Chandler said sincerely. But suddenly the familiarity and the surprising attraction he felt for this girl was making him uneasy. A complication like this was the last thing he needed in his life just now. Once again, he moved to stand.

"Are you certain you feel up to it?" Tessa asked, a gentle note of true concern highlighting her voice.

"It is getting late. Have you any idea where I might get a cab from here?"

"Down on the corner. They pass by quite often."

"Thank you," he nodded, touching the makeshift bandage still around his head, and feeling a flood of attraction for her. That he could feel such an all-encompassing sensation for anyone anymore had completely overwhelmed him.

Charlie walked slowly over to where the gentleman stood beside his daughter. "That may well begin to bleed again.

Perhaps you should allow us to accompany you back to your hotel."

"Oh, that won't be necessary. But thank you."

Chandler considered for a moment what people would think when he paraded through the lobby of the very elegant Hoffman House with a bloody shirt sleeve wound around his forehead. But it didn't matter. Suddenly nothing else but this lovely Irish girl mattered in the slightest.

Tessa accompanied him to the door and Charlie moved busily toward the kitchen with the tray of empty dishes. "It was a real pleasure to meet you, Mr. Tate," he called out with a friendly wave, holding open the kitchen door.

Chandler smiled, looking back at Tessa, her sparkling green eyes, and then replied sincerely, "The pleasure, I assure you, Mr. Murphy, was all mine."

"And thank you, Miss Murphy, for your exquisite care."

"We are just so relieved that you are feeling better."

She opened the door for him but Chandler lingered beneath it. "If you enjoy reading Dickens, might I recommend *Vanity Fair* by William Thackeray."

"I've recently read it, as a matter of fact," she replied, without missing a beat, and then quirking her own sly smile, added, "And I'm sorry to say that I found the prose a bit overblown."

Chandler could not help himself. At that, he laughed out loud. Oh, what a refreshing change a girl like that would be in Boston! Bright and pretty, with none of the pretense that Cynthia and Felicity possessed to excess.

To survive, Chandler had mastered conversation and repartee at an early age. It was bred into one from Boston society as were the knowledge of dancing and of which wine to select. A response from the mind, not from the heart. But not so, he thought, with Charlie Murphy's daughter. There was no need to work that hard with her. The way they had spoken with one another was easy, natural, almost like what he saw between Nelson and Sylvie Winthrop.

"Miss Murphy," he said, turning back around and bracing himself against the frame of the door. "I was thinking.

I've a few more days here in New York and there is a play I have been wanting to see. I wonder if you would do me the honor of joining me tomorrow evening."

Her reaction was not the one he had expected.

Tessa's confident sparkle began to fade by degrees and her bright smile vanished behind a frown. "I am afraid that would be impossible, Mr. Tate."

"Would you mind if I asked why?"

"To begin with, I haven't anything fitting to wear to sit in a theater beside someone like you," she divulged with only a hint of regret bleeding through her enormous dignity.

Now it was Chandler whose smile fell. It had been insensitive of him. Of course she was right. What could he have possibly been thinking? These were working-class people. Immigrants. They ate bread and cheese and rationed their Irish whiskey as if it were liquid gold.

"Are there other reasons?" he asked cautiously.

"I think that one is quite good enough."

Chandler moved a step back into the foyer and into the light. "Well, Miss Tessa Murphy, if that is your only objection to joining me tomorrow evening, you must promise to leave it to me and agree to let me escort you. I shall call for you at seven."

"But—" she tried to object until he began to raise his hand.

"It really is the least that I can do, since you and your father would not take my money," he said, having secretly tucked the bill beneath his empty dinner plate anyway. "And it is you who would be doing me a favor, since I truly do hate to sit through an evening of one of Shakespeare's tragedies alone. As to your attire, I shall have something suitable sent around for you first thing tomorrow morning."

"I cannot take your charity."

Chandler leveled his eyes upon her with a bit more gravity. "And precisely where would I be if I had said the same thing to you and your father earlier today?"

He had made his point. After all, he was offering an evening of theater. The sort of theater of which she had long dreamed of attending. This man was taking her to see a performance of the great William Shakespeare's work, not a bawdy burlesque show. It would be one evening of her life. Then, in a few days, he would return to his own aristocratic existence, and she would marry Brian Sullivan. But for at least one splendid evening, Tessa Murphy would have lived a fantasy.

Hopefully, she thought, gazing up into a face so full of power and possibilities, that one night would be enough.

Chapter

11

"As I live and breathe," gasped Charlie Murphy.

"I've never seen anything like it," Tessa uttered in an echo of disbelief, with a finger pressed lightly over her lips.

She and her father gazed down at the beaded, chestnut-colored evening dress that had just been delivered, along with shoes, bonnet, and matching gloves. Neither of them had ever seen anything more exquisite, not even on the women who went in and out of the Hoffman House. That even for a few hours she might possess something so lovely was beyond Tessa's wildest dreams. Her eyes played slowly over the thick folds of luxurious fabric. The beaded trim caught the light and glittered like ancient jewels.

Charlie's lips curved into a soft smile. "I knew it would happen for ye one day," he said in a voice peaked with confidence. "Ye had only to believe that it could."

Tessa's smooth jaw quickly hardened as she shot her father a remonstrating glance. "I shall thank you to stop that sort of foolish talk this instant, Da," she said severely. "Mr.

Tate is no more interested in me than he could ever be in one of his own hirelings, so don't be getting any of your foolish ideas to the contrary!"

"And do ye really believe ye are the only eligible young lady in all of New York he could find to escort if that were truly the case?"

"He was just being gracious about what we did for him yesterday."

"What ye did, Tessa me lass, was nearly cost the man his life, whether ye brought him here to mend his wounds or not. Why should he be grateful for that?"

"Oh, all right, so he doesn't see it entirely as charity."

"Not when faced with a daughter o' mine, he doesn't," Charlie countered proudly, pushing out his chest and snapping his suspenders.

Tessa pressed her hands onto her hips with a little huff. "You really must stop that or I won't go at all."

"Oh, very well. Call it what ye like, lass. But I shall never give up hope that my beautiful daughter is meant for somethin' great. And no matter what ye say, ye surely won't be changin' my mind about that."

"I wasn't going to tell you this until tomorrow, but I see now that you leave me no choice." She inhaled a deep breath, preparing finally to speak the words her heart had been fighting to keep her from saying.

"Brian has proposed to me . . . and I have accepted him."

"Marriage?" Charlie asked, the word sputtering forth. In the moment following, Tessa watched her father's expression go from true shock to irritation. "I'll not allow it!"

"What's done is done. I have already accepted him."

"And neither one o' ye bothered to come to me?" he asked incredulously, slumping down onto the couch.

"We knew what you would say."

"And ye sought to go against me wishes just the same?"

"It is for the best, Da. Brian really is a good man."

Charlie's lips twitched sourly. "Brian Sullivan is too common for ye!"

"I won't have you speak of him like that! He was my first

94

love. The man I wanted to marry when I was a girl. Now, finally he has asked me, and I mean to marry him, and that is all there is to it!"

She stood over her father, whose face, in spite of the anger, had gone deathly pale. She remembered the night before last when he had returned home so weak and full of fatigue that she thought he might actually die. A wave of tenderness swelled past her resolve, and Tessa sank onto the couch beside him.

She cared more for this man than for any other in the world. The one man she could not bear to lose. It was why she was marrying Brian: to save her father. And yet she had never seen him look closer to dying in her life. For a moment, neither of them spoke another word. They had reached an impasse.

"Ye know, child," he said finally. "I don't speak much about yer sainted mother, because even now the pain is sometimes too great a thing to bear."

"I know that," Tessa said softly, telling him he need not try now. She covered his rough hand with her own slim, smooth one.

"Yer mother was a great beauty in her day. Almost as beautiful as ye. I was always too proud to tell ye this, but in me, she married beneath herself," Charlie softly confessed, his eyes suddenly misting. "Her family was against me from the start because *I* was common."

"Da, you musn't say such a thing."

"'Tis true, lass. I had nothin' to offer her."

"You had your heart."

"Worthless!" he countered harshly. "When ye see where it got her. Not even a proper burial. But I was so certain o' myself back then, so certain that I could make her happy, that I would listen to no one. Her father pleaded with me to let her go. Even offered me money, he did. But it only hardened my resolve to have her. Like ye, I was stubborn. Because I had made the commitment and I meant to see it through, at any cost. I will always believe that cost was the love o' me life."

"I had no idea."

"No, 'tis not the sort o' thing a man confesses easily, nor proudly, once 'tis done. Tessa, lass," he said, suddenly looking up at her. "It is I who am to blame for yer dear mother's death on that ship. My prideful, arrogant heart took her life on the way to America, and I shall pay for the knowledge o' that for the rest o' me own days."

"She died in childbirth," Tessa tried weakly to counter.

"On a sea voyage that I forced her to take. Tessa, me dear, dear heart," he said, trembling as he took both of her hands. "I am tellin' ye all o' this now for one reason, and one reason alone. Ye deserve the chance yer sainted ma lost. The chance I took from her. Don't harden your heart to that. Brian Sullivan is nice enough, but he is too much like me. He is an ordinary lad who can never give ye the sort o' life ye will always crave. The sort o' life that is possible here, in America."

Tessa shot back to her feet. "Da, please! Look around you! This is not a fairy tale we're living in. The streets here are not paved with gold. This is our life, and Brian has offered us something safe and secure."

"There it is, then," he sighed. Tessa watched her father's gray eyes darken with comprehension as the words she had spoken pleadingly and without thinking hung like a sudden dark cloud between them. "Ye do mean to marry Sullivan for me."

"For both of us, Da."

"No!"

"I know my own mind," she stubbornly countered.

"Ye put on that dress," he challenged between labored breaths. "And then tell me that same thing, Tessa Murphy, if ye dare. If ye can tell me in truth that Brian Sullivan and the life he has offered ye is all that ye want, after that, then I'll challenge ye no more."

Tessa stood alone in her small, sun-dappled bedroom in Mrs. Gallagher's boardinghouse late that afternoon, trying in vain to catch her breath. She could not quite believe that the reflection in the mirror before her was her own. For the first time in her life, she thought her own image was breathtaking.

Chestnut-colored satin hung from her body like soft, shimmering waves and rippled in the afternoon breeze through the small, open window. The delicate cap sleeves and the bodice were all dotted with fringe and brown beads. Using a picture from *Harper's* magazine to guide her, Tessa had swept her full mane of copper hair up into a classic twist, crowning it with the elegant little bonnet accented by satin ribbons and brown satin roses. The beige satin evening slippers, beaded in ivory, molded to her feet as though they had been made exclusively for her.

She looked back up at her own reflection, startled again to see the elegant beauty who now faced her. As if this all were not enough, beneath her gown she wore a fine cotton chemise ornamented with delicate embroidery, with a whalebone corset and petticoat she almost had not known how to wear. Mr. Tate had spent a small fortune, she mused, on underclothes no one else would ever see. How could anyone possibly afford to be so utterly decadent?

Then she reminded herself.

He came from another world.

Beyond the oak door, she could hear her father pacing as he had done for the better part of an hour, huffing and muttering to himself in anticipation. Tessa knew what he would say, what he would think. Once he saw her like this, there would be no convincing him at all that Brian Sullivan was the right man for her. She was certain that the dress alone had cost more than poor Brian earned in an entire year. Even if he had been inclined to buy her something so impractical, he could never afford to.

This is only one night, and Brian has offered my da and me a lifetime, she fought now to remind herself. She looked around at the chipped iron bedstead, the simple wooden dresser with marble knobs and a pitcher and bowl on top. *I will learn to feel for him what a wife should. I will!*

Charlie wept when he saw her, and Tessa already regretted

her decision to go through with the evening. It gave her poor dear father hope that Chandler Tate was some sort of dashing and handsome knight who had come here to this side of town by divine providence and meant to sweep her off into the sunset. It made him believe in the notion that America could make his dreams, and her own, come true after all.

"Please, Da, you musn't cry," Tessa bid him, "or I shall only start myself, and that would be a fine state for Mr. Tate to find us both in."

"'Tis only that, standin' there, in that light, ye look more like yer dear ma than I have ever seen ye. How proud she would have been," he said brokenly, wiping the free-flowing tears from his eyes with the back of his hand as he inhaled a deep, soulful breath. "Ye're so very lovely."

"Thank you," Tessa smiled serenely, feeling for this brief moment in time every bit as privileged and lovely as any aristocratic girl might have.

"Here. I want to give ye somethin'," her father said, drawing forth a small gold pendant she had never seen before. Suspended from a delicate gold chain and set in fine gold filigree, was a glittering amethyst chip that sparkled in the afternoon light.

"It belonged to yer ma," he explained, with a teary smile, sensing her question. "She called it one of her special golden things. 'Twas the sort o' thing we always said ye were goin' to have here in America. All o' the golden things this country had to offer."

"I remember," she smiled, but it was a sad smile. She recalled all of the times in her childhood when he had told her that, and yet never had he shown her this precious pendant before now.

"She wanted these sorts o' things for ye, lass, because after we had been married for a time, she came to realize what it was to live without them."

Tessa fingered the delicate locket. "It's beautiful."

"Not so beautiful as me only daughter. Let me help ye with it."

He dragged his huge, rough hands over her bare shoulders and clasped the pendant behind her neck. Then he bent down and pressed his lips softly against her shoulder. For a moment, there were no words between them as she turned back around and ran a hand through his thinning hair. As he did, Charlie Murphy expelled a long breath.

It was at that moment a firm knock sounded downstairs at the front door. The commanding sound of it filled the house and Tessa's heart lurched. No matter how calm she had wanted to be or believed she could be, this really was the most exciting thing that had ever happened to her. Try as she might to the contrary, Tessa Murphy felt just like a princess.

She moved slowly down the staircase and toward the door, with her father behind her. She was trying to steady her hand enough so that she might reach out and turn the handle.

"Ye'll be fine," Charlie lovingly assured her. "Finally, lass, 'tis your time to shine."

Chandler Tate swallowed hard upon seeing the young woman who greeted him. He had known she would be lovely in the rich shades of satin and velvet he had personally selected, but he had not known how lovely. Nestled between her full, ripe breasts was the pendent her father had just given her. Tessa saw his eyes widen and then linger there momentarily before he looked away.

"Top o' the evenin' to ye, Mr. Tate," Charlie announced in his jolly Irish brogue.

"Mr. Murphy," Chandler nodded with a smile, but he was still unable to tear his eyes from the exquisite young woman before him.

"'Tis a lovely gown, don't ye think?" Charlie asked, puffing his chest out proudly.

"I do indeed," Chandler replied, silently marveling at the way in which the elegant fabric molded perfectly to her seductive young shape.

Fashion became her, Chandler thought as his eyes played

over her full breasts. Her slender waist. Her skin, above the low-cut bodice, was lovely, all milky apricot, and like her face, it bore a sprinkling of freckles.

"And I've brought this for you," Chandler said, dragging his eyes from the beauty before him as he drew forth a bottle of fine Irish whiskey that was tied with a red velvet bow. "For your hospitality and concern last evening."

Charlie's eyes lit with pure delight. "Jameson! Best there is!"

"I hope you enjoy it."

"Would ye be sharin' a drink with me then, sir?"

"I would be pleased to join you for a small one." Chandler smiled, then nodded obligingly.

Chandler took three even paces across the floor in his dark, elegant evening wear. Tessa stood with her hand on the still open door trying vainly to catch her breath. She was doing her best to keep her inexperience from showing. He must be accustomed to such incredibly sophisticated companions back in Boston. The sort of woman with whom she could never even hope to compete. The knowledge of that was most unnerving.

The only thing that helped at all was how he had looked at her in that first moment as they had faced one another at the door. The memory lingered now in her mind like a soft perfume. No man had ever had such respect for her and yet such pure fascination in his eyes at the same moment. Not even Brian Sullivan. And it was then, standing in the middle of Mrs. Gallagher's parlor between her father and this very handsome stranger, that a rush of confused emotion shook her again. This is only one evening, she fought to remind herself as Chandler and her father sank down in two stuffed blue chairs beside the fireplace.

"Your daughter tells me you are from Ireland," Chandler remarked, fingering the glass and looking more dashing than she thought anyone on earth had a right to look. She moved behind her father with her hands on the back of his chair.

"From Galway," Charlie replied, but in a tone of reluctance, preferring to think of his adopted country as his only home now.

"I've heard that Ireland is lovely, but I've never had an opportunity to see so for myself."

"Lovely and poor," Charlie replied a little sadly for the memories the declaration brought.

"But Mr. Tate has been to London," Tessa interjected, as her father took a stiff swallow of the whiskey. Her voice trembled slightly.

"London is it?" Charlie asked, as his daughter ran a nervous finger along the back of the chair.

"A large, crowded city much like any other, I'm afraid. I would much rather hear about Galway."

"'Tis very green, like all o' Ireland. And the skies there go on forever. They're crystal blue and full o' clouds as thick and rich as pillows."

As Chandler listened to her father, Tessa felt safe enough to lift her eyes. Now, for the first time, she saw the rich details of his suit, from the pale-blue waistcoat to the shimmering diamond stickpin in his cravat, to the impeccable shine of his black shoes.

The makeshift bandage on his forehead was gone. In its place, beneath carefully combed hair, was nothing more than a small burgundy scab. It was the only memento of the unconventional manner in which they had met. She thought that even with the imperfection, Chandler Tate exuded more power and confidence than she had ever seen before. And here he was, a man like that, standing in their parlor, calling on her!

Was it actually possible that through her father's faith alone, he was here? That Charlie Murphy had willed this for his daughter? Tessa's mind spun with a myriad of questions, while Chandler asked her father why he had left a place that sounded so lovely as Galway.

"Many reasons, actually, beyond the obvious. Me wife and I wanted a place to begin again. Our marriage was not approved of by her family," Charlie said truthfully. "There was little I could do there to provide her with the sort o' life she deserved, or the one they expected for her."

"So you came to America."

"She did not survive the sea voyage."

"I'm sorry," Chandler said sincerely, glancing up at Tessa. "But I am certain your lovely daughter is a great comfort to you."

Tessa suddenly felt the warmth of his smile like fire upon her. She burned beneath it. But still she said nothing. Charlie finished his whiskey. His eyes were on Chandler, watching him, studying him.

"She is my greatest comfort," he replied, "and my greatest achievement. I guard my daughter and her happiness with my own life."

"As well you should."

A short silence followed the understanding wrought between the two men. Then Chandler stood, still beaming an easy smile as he extended a gallant crooked arm to Tessa.

"Well, Mr. Murphy, I thank you once again for your hospitality."

"Must ye be leavin' so soon?"

"You shall forgive us I hope, sir, but the curtain is at eight, and I wouldn't want Tessa to miss a moment of *Romeo and Juliet*. I am told it is a very good production."

"Yes, o' course," Charlie replied with an easy smile to match their guest's.

What he had wanted to do was make an impression. He wanted this aristocratic young man to know that his Tessa was so much more than an immigrant's daughter. She was as lovely and desirable a young woman as he was likely to find. And Charlie Murphy meant to make her one opportunity count. Even if Tessa herself chose not to believe in miracles.

"Your father really is a splendid man," Chandler said as they descended the stone stairs into the cool night air.

"I certainly think so."

"And he has raised you entirely by himself?"

"Since I was three."

"What a tribute you are to him," he said glancing over at

her, no longer able to keep the pure admiration from his eyes as they stepped out onto the street. Before them sat a bright, shiny, green brougham with shimmering carriage lamps. Two sleek, beautifully muscled gray stallions harnessed in shiny silver waited with a coachman in a black cutaway coat and black hat who stood formally as he held the door open.

"Is this for us?" Tessa managed to ask brokenly as the neighborhood children buzzed around them like bees around a hive.

"How else would a lady expect to arrive at the theater?" he asked with a confident smile.

But this was no ordinary carriage and it was certainly not a cab. Tessa knew it the moment she sank against the rich, brown-velvet-covered seat. The doors and roof were upholstered in rich, polished leather. She had seen these private carriages riding around New York stuffed with well-heeled gentry, but never had she so much as dared to guess what one might be like inside.

Tessa watched Chandler slip into the velvet seat across from her; felt his weight, just as she heard the crack of the whip and felt the carriage lurch forward. Trying valiantly not to look astounded, she glanced outside at the neighborhood children giggling and calling after them, running beneath the windows as the carriage pulled away down the tree-lined street.

"Your father is right, you know," Chandler finally said above the loping canter of the horses and the din of street noise. "That gown really is becoming on you."

"The loan of the dress was more than gracious, Mr. Tate," she could not help but beam as she fingered the silken folds across her lap. "I shall do my best not to get it dirty."

"Oh, it is not a loan. The dress was a gift. And you really must call me Chandler," he said deeply. "Just as you know I must call you Tessa."

"Yes," she softly concurred, feeling a shiver of attraction, and turning away once again.

As they rode along in silence, Chandler found himself

wondering what it would be like to show someone like Tessa the sights of Boston. The Common. The Old State House. To see it all through such refreshingly innocent eyes. It really was the most magnificent city. He had allowed himself to forget that, as he had so many things. But she had such wonder. Different from a child's, but equally pure.

When the carriage came to a halt behind a line of others, it was before an enormous facade of white stone. Two great carved pillars at each side marked the entrance. Tessa stepped out, holding on to the firm, gloved hand extended by the coachman, into a collection of grand ladies in sweeping gowns and gentlemen in coats and top hats.

Chandler came out behind her, seeing what she saw, and then tucked her gloved hand into the crook of his arm. "I should have warned you that this evening would be a production in itself. But I can assure you, Tessa, that you look more splendid tonight than any other lady here."

"Enough to keep them from suspecting how deceiving those looks can be?"

A faint smile tugged at his lips. "Oh, yes. More than enough."

Tessa was trying to quell the violent beating of her heart as they strolled over the plush red carpet beneath the light of two huge glittering chandeliers. She was also trying not to gape at all of the diamonds and fur as she drank in the opulence, but Tessa had never been anywhere so elegant. This place was a world apart from the theater where she had gone with Brian to see Miss Lydia Thompson's burlesque show.

"I am told this is a wonderful production of *Romeo and Juliet*. The company is world famous," Chandler remarked as they settled into the red-velvet-covered seats of the box he had rented for the evening.

But Tessa had not heard him. She was looking over the gilded balustrade at the women in their silks and satins, their diamonds and pearls, unable to stop herself from comparing their costumes to her own.

Chandler watched her, trying to imagine what she saw. Yet he knew such a thing would be impossible. Their worlds were too different. His heart warmed. She was sitting so proudly beside him, not betraying even a hint of what great anxiety she undoubtedly felt. Only her rigid arm, as he had led her to their seats, had given her away. Knowing that, he marveled all the more at her poise and grace.

"Tate, my good man! Is that you?" A masculine voice suddenly boomed at them from the next box. "I had no idea you were in town."

"Alfred," Chandler returned with an easy smile, standing to extend his hand across the chasm between the two side balustrades. "And Eudora. How nice to see you both. I am here on business."

"And you haven't called on us? How terribly wretched of you."

"The trip was on rather short notice."

"Well, in any event, you simply must join us for supper," said the woman with the dark judgmental eyes as she fluttered her painted silk fan before a face that drooped into flabby folds.

"There is nothing I would like better," Chandler politely lied to the man's prying wife. "But I'm afraid we shall have to make it the next time. This trip I am simply swamped with work."

"Not tonight, I see," the woman returned, suspiciously craning her jeweled, wagging neck to see just who it was who was sitting beside the very eligible and equally elusive Chandler Tate. "Are you not going to introduce us?"

Chandler turned back around and glanced at Tessa, then he held out his hand and drew her into the light. "Mr. and Mrs. Alfred Dunne, may I present Tessa Murphy."

"Business indeed," the woman barked a short, soprano laugh. "Murphy," she then repeated, rolling the name around on her tongue and grimacing as if she were tasting sour fruit. "Irish, isn't it?"

"Every bit as Irish as Dunne, in fact," Tessa replied.

"My good woman," she stiffened. "Dunne is an old and venerable name in New York. It certainly does not connote a collection of immigrants."

"Perhaps not now. But we were all immigrants to this land once, Mrs. Dunne. Some of us just came over a little earlier than others."

Tessa's flawlessly timed jab, delivered in her sweet-toned voice, surprised even Chandler. No one ever got the better of Eudora Dunne, he thought. Especially not someone the old crone believed to be subordinate (which included most people in New York). He bit his cheeks to keep from laughing. When he glanced over at Tessa, however, her confident expression had faded. Her lovely face was white as stone. Chandler's eyes followed hers across the balustrade to Alfred Dunne.

The focus of the portly gentleman's attention, quite clearly, was Tessa. There was something unmistakably familiar and yet uneasy in both their expressions as they regarded one another.

"What a small world," Dunne smirked.

"Isn't it, though," Tessa replied past impossibly dry lips.

"Do the two of you know one another?"

Dunne answered him cautiously. "Our paths crossed briefly a few days ago."

"Oh?" Chandler stiffened slightly. "Where was that?"

"At the Hoffman House."

"Are you a guest there, young woman?" Dunne's wife asked coldly, her voice flooded with suspicion.

"My father delivers their milk," Tessa replied, tipping up her chin and not bothering to lie.

To that, Alfred Dunne laughed heartily. It was the same mocking sound she had tried to forget from their single humiliating encounter, when he had taken her for a trollop. She had been foolish to consider that, even for one evening, she might be able entirely to live her fantasy.

"She is lovely enough, I suppose," Alfred mused, index finger to his chin, "but isn't she just a bit beneath you?"

"Go to hell, Alfred!"

"Chandler Tate!" Eudora Dunne gasped. "The three of us have been friends for years!"

"No friend of mine would insult a lady."

"Who says *she* is a lady?" Alfred asked cruelly.

"I do."

A glacial silence followed as Chandler let the declaration cover the air already filled with the murmuring of people still filing into their seats down below.

"Miss Murphy is with me," he added angrily, his body now as tight as the string of a bow, "and if you plan to address either one of us further, you will do so properly, or I can assure you, you shall have me to answer to!"

"I only thought I should warn you."

"Now wouldn't that be ironic, me heeding a warning about the evils of women from someone with your reputation, Alfred?"

"Chandler Tate!" Eudora intervened again. "This is not at all like you."

"How in the devil would either of you know what I was really like?"

"They do say you can tell a man by the company he keeps," Alfred chuckled evilly.

"I can assure you both that if you truly did know me, you wouldn't approve of me any more than you do of Miss Murphy here."

"We have always believed you to be one of us, a well bred young man from one of the East's finest families," Eudora added. "Apparently we were wrong."

"Yes, apparently. If breeding means the possession of more arrogance than money, you could not have been more wrong."

"Well, I never!" Eudora huffed.

"No." Chandler smiled. "I don't suppose you ever have."

They all sat back in their seats as the gas footlights dimmed. The curtain rose. The play began. But Chandler was distracted. As his anger began to recede, he thought how Tessa had maintained such grace, even in the face of sudden and cruel effrontery. It was grace with a spark of fire. Deep in her eyes Chandler had seen a kind of spirit that he was coming to believe could adapt to almost anything. Tessa Murphy had not really needed his help against Alfred Dunne, he mused delightedly. Not in the slightest.

"I really am sorry," Chandler said, looking at her across the carriage seat after the play, as they pulled back out into the cool, starry night.

Tessa tipped her head. "What could you possibly have to be sorry for?"

Chandler leaned back against the leather seat and took a breath. "For bringing you here, I suppose. For subjecting you to someone as callous as Alfred Dunne."

"You defended me against him," she said softly. "No one has ever done that for me before."

"I would have leveled him if he'd gone on a moment more."

"Yes," she smiled. "I got that impression."

"Would you think it strange if I told you that I never really felt the desire to do that for anyone before?"

Tessa considered the question for a moment as the horse clopped steadily back down Broadway. "I might wonder why, when we have known one another for such a short time."

"I really wanted tonight to be special for you," Chandler confessed a little awkwardly.

"And it was."

He looked across at her, trying to determine her sincerity. It was there, alive and glittering on her beautiful, softly freckled face. Just as he knew it always would be.

"Very well, then. We shall speak no more about it."

"Good," Tessa smiled.

"So tell me," he smiled, too, "did you enjoy the performance?"

"Well, it was terribly sad," she said honestly.

"True. But then many of Shakespeare's greatest works were tragedies."

"I just don't understand why they both had to die. If they loved one another so much, why didn't they just run away and leave everyone else behind?"

Chandler considered the question thoughtfully, seeing how much the story had touched her. "I suppose everyone becomes a victim of their own circumstances, at one time or another."

"Even someone like you?"

Her question, and the direct manner in which she asked it, caught him off guard. Strangely, it made him want to be honest with her. It had been such a long time since he had been entirely honest with anyone. That was a risk he had not been willing to take before he met Tessa.

"I suppose so, yes," he replied cautiously, remembering his wife and the hopeful way things had begun between them, then the devastating way they had ended. "But I never felt I had to take my own life to remedy the situation. There is always another way, if one is clever enough to find it."

"Or desperate enough," Tessa added, thinking for the first time that evening of her own situation, of her father, and mostly of Brian Sullivan.

They lingered at her front door for a long time, Chandler not seeming to want to let her go. He was leaning his sleek, elegant body against the doorframe, one hand thrust casually into his coat pocket. An exchange between them followed. He said something that must have sounded entirely foolish. He was not certain what. She had said something in reply. But the words did not matter. He simply found that he wanted desperately to keep her there, not allowing the evening to end.

"What is it?" he asked when she began to frown.

"Only that I have spent an entire evening with someone who, to my surprise, I find to be more of a mystery now than he was when the evening began."

"I'm sorry to disappoint you, but there really is no great mystery, Tessa. There really isn't all that much to tell."

"You know I don't believe that. After all, I heard what you

said to the Dunnes about what they would think if they really knew you."

"It was spoken in the heat of the moment."

"Very often those are the greatest truths."

"Let's just say that I find you far more interesting than I find myself," Chandler countered, leaning softly forward. "You're different from the other women I have known."

"I'm certain that's true!"

"Tessa, I meant it in the most favorable way," he said deeply, slightly seductively, as he leveled his eyes on her. "For example, I believe that something inside of you presses you toward the truth, with little concern for leaving the right impression."

"I have my moments," she replied, trying not to think too much of Brian and the great truth of her feelings she had chosen not to tell him.

"You certainly knew how to handle the Dunnes. And you did so with great honesty and grace, I might add. I've been waiting for a decade to see someone get the better of that pompous lout and his very judgmental wife."

"Then I didn't embarrass you too much?"

"Embarrass me? Tessa, I cannot remember when I've had such fun."

She fought a smile. "Truthfully, neither can I."

As they stood close in the shadows beneath the hiss of the single gas lamp that lit the porch in glowing amber, Chandler felt an overwhelming urge to kiss her—or perhaps it was more a desire to touch her, to assure himself that she was real. But even as the thought crossed his mind, he had already decided that it was too soon.

When she raised her eyes—those innocent sea-green eyes—candidly to his face, Chandler knew that in spite of what he felt his decision had been right. He must tread carefully with her. Patience with such a brilliant jewel was essential. Li Kao Chen had taught him that.

"I really did have a lovely time," she said softly.

Realizing that, with her comment, Tessa Murphy was about to turn, walk back through that door, and go out of his life forever, Chandler caught her slim wrist and took it up between them.

"It needn't end, you know," he said huskily, still aching to touch those perfect, rosy lips of hers in spite of his resolve. Instead he settled for a chaste kiss pressed formally on the back of her hand.

Tessa's slim copper brows rose, and as her lips parted, she drew in a shallow breath.

"What I mean is, I would like to see you again. Tomorrow, if you are free."

"I thought that you were taken up with business."

"I would rather see you."

"Why?"

The muscles in his throat suddenly constricted. Why indeed? his mind repeated as her eyes glittered up at him in the light. No matter how much he was drawn to her, Chandler certainly couldn't fall for her. No, that was out of the question. There was no room in his life for a mix of love and secrets, not the heinous, unforgivable ones he was forced to keep.

"Because I enjoy your company, Tessa," came the words, quite in spite of himself, in spite of everything that was against them.

"All right then," she said, so simply that he was thrown off balance. Silently he struggled beneath her gaze to regain his footing. "Have you something in particular in mind you would like to do?"

"Only to spend time with you. Beyond that, you may decide what would please you."

"Often when I need to think, I go up to Central Park and lose myself there among the trees, the woods, and the lake. That place helps me to take stock of things. Perhaps you could use a place like that for yourself."

"Relentless, aren't you?" He smiled.

Tessa reached up and gently pressed at the small furrow in his brow that had not left him all evening. "No"—she smiled back—"just observant. It gave you away from the beginning."

"I'll have to watch for that in the future."

"You need watch for it with me only if you plan to make a habit of keeping secrets."

"I shall consider myself warned."

"Central Park then?"

"Central Park it is."

It was at that moment that Chandler realized he was still holding her hand, and she had not uttered a single word of protest. The realization unleashed in him an intensely sexual sensation, stronger than anything he had experienced for a very long time.

"Shall I call for you at two?" he asked, trying to release the hold he had on her as gently as possible without revealing the intensity of what he was feeling.

"I shall be ready," she softly replied.

As her color rose a little, she lifted her chin against the powerful attraction building between them. In her response, Tessa had forgotten about everything else, her curiosity about this enigmatic man, and her questions. Most especially, she had forgotten about her commitment to Brian Sullivan.

Chapter

12

CHANDLER TATE SHIFTED THE VELVET DRAPERY AWAY FROM THE grand window in his hotel suite and gazed down to the street below. Sleep would be beyond him for a good while longer this night, with Tessa Murphy still so fresh in his mind. He ran a large, firm hand through his tawny-gold hair, thinking how he had never met anyone quite like her. As he loosened his ascot, Chandler let the pleasurable thoughts of being near her steadily carry him away.

Tessa warmed his heart and stirred his blood in a way that no one else ever had. There was sensuality in even her most innocent expressions. His mind trailed over the image of what that gorgeous mane of copper hair must look like brushed out long across bare shoulders. When the image was at its most vivid, he could feel the desire within him begin to stir again. He was so caught up in the tide of his romantic daydream that at first he did not hear the short, insistent rapping on his door.

"You called for a messenger, sir," said a young, eager man who stood facing Chandler once he opened it.

Chandler strode across the room to a table where a book lay beside a neat stack of fresh paper and two gold pens. Quickly, he scrawled a note and handed it back to the messenger. "I want you to see that this is delivered tonight," he said. "The address is written down."

"But that is quite a distance, sir." the messenger said with surprise, seeing that the address was all the way downtown.

Chandler handed him the elegant leather-bound volume of Shakespeare's Comedies, tooled in gold. "Young man, I would pay you to take it to the ends of the earth," he said tartly, "if that was where the young lady lived."

Tessa leaned against the closed door as the messenger's boot heels clicked away, then faded away into the night. As she held the volume up to the light, her heart began to thump with an unsteady rhythm, forcing the breath out of her in disbelief. Again she read the note; her hands trembling.

Just to prove that not all love stories need to end sadly.
Chandler Tate

"So tell me, lass," Charlie asked his daughter with a wry, self-satisfied smile. "Now do ye still think he is just bein' kind?"

Chapter

13

AT TWO O'CLOCK THE NEXT AFTERNOON, TESSA STOOD BEfore the mirror in her bedroom trying vainly to call up the lovely creature in satin and beads who had met her there the night before. He would be at their door any minute, she thought with a sharp jolt of panic. Then Chandler Tate would take one look at the ordinary immigrant girl she was and he would be gone in a very brisk whirl of excuses.

For the fourth time, Tessa nervously smoothed the folds in her best forest-green skirt, then straightened the cameo pinned to the white cotton blouse at her throat as the crushing weight of disappointment stifled her shallow breath.

She wasn't at all certain why it should matter so much. Soon, Chandler would be returning to Boston and she would set a date to marry Brian. She was playing with heartbreak by expecting the situation to come to more than that. When she heard her father's short strides down the corridor outside her room, Tessa's heart stopped.

"He's here, lass," Charlie Murphy called through the door to her.

Tessa glanced back at her own face, trying to pinch some color into her pale cheeks. She had stayed up half the night reading from the book he had sent her. It really was the most extraordinary volume, more exquisite than anything she had ever owned. The leather. The gold-edged pages. She loved the rich, heady smell of it. It was pure elegance.

Downstairs in the parlor, Charlie Murphy once again entertained his wealthy guest with requested descriptions of the Ireland he remembered while Tessa kept them waiting.

"Of course I cannot imagine why a man like yourself would want to know all of that," said Charlie, leaning back in his chair and crossing one short leg over the other, secretly glad that someone like Chandler Tate showed an interest.

"I would like to know everything about your daughter. Her heritage is part of that knowledge."

"I'm certain my Tessa is not at all like the other young ladies you have known."

Hearing that he meant to make a point, Chandler shifted in the opposite chair, then settled back against it. "No sir, she's not. But she is very special indeed. It hasn't taken me long at all to discover that."

"Ye know, Mr. Tate—"

"I would be honored, sir, if you would consent to call me Chandler," he interrupted in his silken voice.

Charlie nodded. "Chandler it is then. Me daughter has a heart the size o' this whole splendid country, and it is a heart that has never been broken. Except by the death o' her dear mother."

"Perhaps you should simply say what you mean."

Charlie Murphy leveled his eyes at Chandler. "Whatever does or does not happen between ye, take care with me daughter's heart."

"I understand that you don't know me well," Chandler said, shifting again, "but I am not the sort of man who goes around breaking the hearts of young ladies, Mr. Murphy."

"If I thought that ye were, rest assured ye would not be escortin' me only child across this room today, much less through Central Park," Charlie said firmly. His eyes held the same directness and candor as Tessa's.

The bedroom door swung open soundlessly above them. Tessa came down the stairs and into the parlor, stopping their conversation. Chandler rose to his feet, straightening his shoulders.

"If such a thing is possible, you look even lovelier than you did last evening, Miss Murphy," he said, thinking how simplicity became her.

The sound of her laughter in response to his compliment was as soft and sweet as music.

"Why Mr. Tate, I believe that is the first time you've lied to me," she said sweetly. Chandler was quite certain she had no idea how sensuous her voice sounded. "And when I was just about to thank you for that wonderful volume you sent."

"I'm glad it pleased you," he replied with a courteous nod. "But I can assure you, that I have never spoken anything but the truth to you."

"I'm glad to hear it," she smiled.

Charlie puffed up, beaming as he watched their interaction, seeing the attraction this well-heeled Bostonian businessman had so quickly come to feel for his daughter.

"Well then," said Chandler with a sparkling smile, "shall we go?"

Tessa turned back to her father. "We're going to the park, Da. I'll be back before supper."

"But first," Chandler nodded to her, "I have a little detour in mind."

"Detour?" she asked, raising an eyebrow. "Where?"

"That's a surprise."

"How lovely," Charlie intervened, his gray eyes suddenly twinkling. "Me daughter loves surprises."

"I'll keep that in mind," Chandler chuckled.

"May I at least have a hint?" Tessa asked, glancing down at her simple attire and fearing, after last evening, that perhaps she would not be dressed appropriately for whatever it was he had in mind.

"Not a single one," Chandler rocked back on his heels. "Trust me, Tessa, you'll not be disappointed."

"I plan to keep you to that!"

They rode in the same splendor as they had the night before, along with all of the other elegant carriages up Broadway. Tessa leaned back breathless against the carriage seat marveling at how easy it would be to grow accustomed to such luxury. She casually pressed a finger along the leather seat cushion beside her and thought how Chandler seemed so at ease, so in command. He really was the most dashing man she had ever met. So completely different from Brian.

She was so taken up with the luxury of the ride that Tessa did not even realize when their carriage stopped outside the grand Italianate building that housed the fashionable Lord & Taylor department store.

"I've been by here a dozen times," she whispered in awe, remembering all of her fanciful strolls back up from the poverty and hopelessness of Hester Street to the riches along the Ladies' Mile. "But I've never dared to go inside."

"Well," said Chandler, with his most charming smile, as they both gazed up at the elegant cathedral windows. "There is a first time for everything."

Holding her hand firmly, he led Tessa inside the largest, most magnificent building she had ever seen. All around them, amid the crush of well dressed shoppers, were lovely bonnets, gloves, and shawls, arranged in mahogany cabinets beneath crystal chandeliers. Above it all, the store was crowned with a magnificent glass roof flooding the building with light.

"It's magnificent," Tessa uttered, her hand limp inside of Chandler's.

"Now," he smiled back at her, taking a gold watch from his vest pocket. "Time to do some serious buying."

"I can't afford any of these things."

"Perhaps not," he agreed, "but I can."

Tessa shook her head. "Oh, Chandler, I don't think—"

"You have half an hour."

"For what?" she asked, afraid to hear the answer.

"To buy everything you can carry," he smiled, genuinely pleased with his surprise.

"I couldn't possibly."

"I have found in life that nothing is impossible, Miss Murphy," he replied, pressing her hand into the crook of his arm. "Not if you want it badly enough."

"But *I'd* feel dreadful if I let you."

"And I'd feel positively dreadful if you didn't. Believe me, Tessa, I have always had far too much money and never enough fun with it. Please let me do this," he sincerely bid her.

Having agreed to buy a single modest item, Tessa moved through the store slowly, bewildered by the array of merchandise. All of the other women moved purposefully around her, completely accustomed to such a large selection, and such daunting prices. But Tessa was overwhelmed. It was too grand.

She stepped tentatively to a counter topped with gloves. There was brown leather. Black. Blue lace. There was even purple silk. Tessa fingered the back of a pale yellow kidskin glove with embroidery around the wrist.

"May I help you?" an authoritarian voice suddenly boomed at her from behind.

Tessa dropped the glove back onto the counter, whirled around, and came face to face with a barrel-chested old woman in drab gray, whose snow-white hair was pulled up into severe, unornamented bun.

"I was just—"

"Yesss?" the condescending woman cut her off.

"I was just looking at your gloves."

"Well, they are to be sold, young woman," she said tersely. "If you wish to look, kindly do so with your eyes, not with your fingers."

119

Chandler advanced from a table of scarves nearby and stood beside Tessa. "Is there a problem here?" he asked commandingly.

"Oh, not with you, sir," the saleswoman said with the greatest deference.

"And with my friend?"

The woman looked at Tessa, then back at Chandler Tate, not bothering to hide her amazement. "She is your . . ."

"Yes, madam, Miss Murphy is with me, and we are going to be purchasing quite a few items here this afternoon."

"Oh, yes sir," the clerk smiled politely as Chandler pushed past her to another woman behind the counter. "And, we are going to be buying them from this young woman over here."

Tessa raised a hand to stifle a smile as Chandler picked up the gloves she had been holding. "Shall we take these to start with?"

Tessa could only nod her approval for fear of laughing out loud.

"Fine. And why not add these and these as well?" he asked, piling two more pairs on top of the first. "Now perhaps you, miss, would be good enough to show us to ladies' hats."

With his request still heavy in the air, Chandler took Tessa's hand and turned away from the clerk who had dared to be rude to the most splendid young woman he had ever met. They walked away together, leaving her standing, stunned and speechless, as a rush of other customers whirled around her.

"That really was the most fun I think I have ever had," Tessa said with a breathless smile as they climbed back into the waiting carriage.

"More fun than last evening?"

"Oh, by far."

"You agreed to keep scarcely anything from all that I bought. Most women would have taken far better advantage of your circumstance."

"If that's the case, I would not be much inclined to know them."

"Now that you mention it," he smiled a pleased, relaxed sort of smile, "neither would I."

Chandler gazed across the seat at her. He was trying to keep his burgeoning feelings at bay but it was becoming more and more of a challenge.

"So then. Is it on to the park?" Tessa asked.

"Dear lady," he said in reply as he took up her hand. "Today, your wish is my command."

Central Park.

It did not take long for him to see why she liked it here. Quiet. Peaceful. The sound of birds chirping in the trees above them. Thick branches dappling the ground with sunlight. It was exactly like being in the country, he thought. Nannies pushing big wicker baby carriages. Couples lounging on the shaded grassy knolls. In all of his trips to New York, Chandler had believed himself too busy to enjoy this sort of an outing. He had never taken the time to see what Tessa saw. Until now.

"Everyone comes here," she said as they walked through the gates and down a lush, densely planted path. "I suppose that is why I like it. In the park, there are no classes. Everyone is allowed in, just the same. Young or old. Rich or poor."

Chandler's heart gave a little tug, as he considered what she meant. It was something he had never had to consider. He took Tessa's hand in his own as they crossed over the grass toward the arching elm-lined Mall.

They strolled up past the collection of wild animals. Monkeys. Tigers. A very restless lion. They watched children feeding the elephants, and Chandler bought Tessa a bag of peanuts so that she could feed them too.

There was another enclosure with several deer, and Tessa stood leaning against the fence for a long time, gazing in at them. "They're such gentle creatures," she finally said, her voice tinged with sadness. "They don't deserve this."

"But they are here so people can enjoy them."

"It shouldn't be that way," she looked back at him. "This is not a proper home. Nothing should be penned in like this."

"Life isn't always fair, Tessa."

He leaned against the fence with her and took in a steadying breath, sensing the urge to confess mount inside of him like a tidal wave. "I feel that way sometimes," Chandler said. "As if I am trapped by life, by convention. The only time I can remember in a very long time that I haven't felt it has been when I am with you."

When she looked away, he brought her face back with a single finger. "I mean it, Tessa. You make me feel so entirely free from all of the ugliness in my life."

Before he could betray himself further, Chandler took her hand again and led her across a small foot bridge and through an arc of trees. After rambling along a maze of paths, they sat on a bench and watched a group of well dressed little boys playing ball beneath the watchful eye of a stiff-lipped governess.

"I really have to thank you for what you did for me today," Tessa said, watching the children play and listening to their laughter.

"I do wish you would consent to keep a few more of those things I bought."

"What I meant was for the way you defended me to the sales clerk," she said, turning toward him suddenly. "It appears to be becoming a habit."

"You really should have let me report her for her insolence."

Tessa quirked a smile. "It was far more fun to see the expression on her face when you gave your business to someone else."

"Yes it was, wasn't it?" Chandler laughed.

At the same moment, he thought what a freeing feeling it was to laugh like this, so unpretentiously, from the soul. To feel like being with the same person, not caring what you are doing, as long as you were together.

Chandler wanted to tell her. He wanted to confess that already his feelings for her were so strong that he would defend her against anything. He wanted to tell her that protecting her seemed somehow more right to him than anything else had in a very long time.

But he knew she was not ready to hear that. Not when, really, they had only just met. And yet to Chandler, it felt as if he had known this girl all of his life. She could not have known that her laughter and her spirit were already changing him. Instead of telling her, he decided finally to kiss her. Chandler's practiced hands framed her small face. Her warm, sweet breath stirred the tips of his hair. His gaze fell to her smooth, moist lips. He moved closer. His heart was hammering as a rush of pink stained her cheeks and he steadily lowered his mouth onto hers.

They were suddenly torn apart by an unnerving wail. The cry of a little child. As he looked up, Chandler saw a little girl in a white pinafore and neat black button shoes with her hands before her eyes. Between her heart-wrenching sobs, she was calling out for her mother. He wanted to help, but it was Tessa who sprang to her feet first and dashed without the slightest hesitation toward the child.

"There, there, little one," Tessa soothed her, scooping the child up into her arms. "We shall find your mama. Don't you worry. I promise you."

As Tessa caressed her golden spiral curls and held her close, the child ceased her crying and, after only a moment, looked at Tessa with clear wide eyes set in a tear-stained face. Chandler saw that the little girl instantly trusted Tessa. He was touched by Tessa's gentleness with the child—her complete command of the situation—and he began to wonder if there was anything to which she set her mind that this bright young woman could not do. But for the moment, what *he* must do was find the child's mother.

Chandler looked behind trees, circled a lily-pad-covered pond, and ran down what seemed an endless maze of paths until finally the sound of a woman's frantic voice calling, "Mary Rose! Mary Rose!" deepened and drew nearer.

Chandler led the frantic mother and two other children through the trees to a clearing and a bench where Tessa sat with the giggling little girl on her lap.

"Oh! How can I ever thank you?" Tessa surrendered the child to the well dressed woman in smart blue velvet with a ribbon-tied bonnet.

"She's a beautiful child," Tessa replied. "No thanks are necessary."

"Just the same," the woman pressed, surveying Tessa's simple clothes, hairstyle, and lack of a proper bonnet, as she perfunctorily drew a few coins from her purse, not bothering to count them. "I am certain you could make good use of this."

Tessa recoiled as though she had been stung, clasping her hands behind her back. "I don't want your money, Madam! To know that you will watch her more closely the next time shall be payment enough for me."

"I know what my own governess earns, my dear, and you would be wise to take it. And speaking of watching children, where might your own little charges be? Perhaps you should take a bit of your own advice."

Before Tessa or Chandler could counter with the truth, the woman brusquely returned and forced some coins in Chandler's hand. "Well, if you won't take it from me, perhaps your employer here will accept it on your behalf, and speak some sense to you about it later. It is a difficult world to bear such pride, my dear."

The condescension in her voice hung in the air between them as she turned and began to walk hand in hand with her children back down the tree-lined path.

"Well, so much for my belief that people are all free to be the same in Central Park," Tessa said as she sank back down onto the bench. She gripped the end of it with both hands and gazed at the woman's silhouette and her children's as they grew smaller in the shimmering afternoon sun.

"You really were marvelous with the child," Chandler said, feeling the pain with her.

"Not so with the mother."

"The woman was thoughtless."

"She was truthful. She thought I was your servant. Just like the sales clerk this afternoon, and your friend at the theater."

Chandler sank onto the bench beside her and took up Tessa's hand, feeling compassion and affection leap inside him like a candle flame.

"I would gladly be *your* servant," he said in a husky whisper.

Then, with infinite tenderness, as they gazed at one another, Chandler reached up and cupped her chin in his hand. Without warning, he pressed his mouth smoothly yet commandingly onto hers, drawing her into an exquisitely sensual kiss.

As his arms moved down to encircle her back and bring her closer, Tessa felt her heart begin to hammer. Nothing could have prepared her for this powerful sensation. It was nothing she had ever experienced with Brian. But then, Brian had never touched her in quite this way; slowly, deftly, commandingly. She knew that she should pull away. She knew that she was placing her own romantic feelings above her allegiance to Brian and to her father for this fleeting and forbidden connection to a fantasy. Yet she wanted nothing so much as for it to go on forever.

Chandler's lips parted hers, and Tessa felt the bold pressure of his tongue in her mouth. As his hand played at the nape of her neck, a jolt of overwhelming desire surged up through her trembling body, weakening her further still. Thinking of nothing but this moment and this man, she surrendered, melting slowly and completely against him.

When he finally pulled away, Tessa sat on the park bench, flushed and shaken. To her surprise, Chandler Tate did not apologize for the liberty he had taken in the broad light of day.

"You must never listen to what others believe," he said, brushing a strand of windblown hair from her flushed cheek. "The only thing that matters at all is that you be true to yourself. I paid a great price to learn that lesson."

"Now you sound like my father."

"Wise man, your father."

They were still so close that Tessa could feel his warm breath on her skin. She found, as her composure began slowly to return to her, that she was glad they were in a particularly deserted area of the park and that he had not completely abandoned all etiquette. The way he had kissed her in public really was scandalous. Yet, in spite of the impropriety, Tessa found herself wishing he would do it again.

"It's late," she said, rising up onto legs he had made soft as butter. A warm breeze stirred the hair near her face and on her shoulders. "We'd better be getting back."

Chandler grasped her hand commandingly. "You know that I really don't want to do that."

"I think that we'd better."

"Very well then," he acquiesced with a lazy smile, "but say you'll have supper with me."

"I have plans," she said faintly, pushing past the ardent haze which still held her captive, and forcing herself to remember Brian and the private evening she had promised to spend with him.

"Break them."

"I can't."

"You and I both know there is nothing you cannot do when you put your mind to it."

He was still holding her arm, and they were facing one another, still a breath apart. Tessa tried not to look up at the aristocratic bearing or at the firm jaw that held that beautiful smile because when she did she could not think.

"Is it another man?"

When Tessa nodded that it was, he added with a smile, "Then you must definitely change your plans."

Chandler then freed his hands and ran his fingers teasingly up her arm. "Must I convince you to break them?" he asked seductively.

"Oh, I wish you wouldn't," she whispered in breathless

anticipation, knowing no matter what she said, that he was going to kiss her again.

"I don't believe that," Chandler replied, the tone of his voice now as gentle as a caress. "Nor, I think, do you."

This time, his mouth opened over hers with hungry insistence. Tessa quivered as he kissed her in what seemed an endlessly sensual surging and probing. There was the firm pressure of his hand bracing her back. His thigh was pressed against hers. As before, she felt helpless against the raw power between them. She had wanted Chandler to kiss her again. This man she would never see again. God help her, in spite of the impossibility of her dreams, Tessa wanted him to touch her like this and never stop.

"Now say you'll have supper with me," he breathed with velvety insistence, dragging his lips from hers and bracing his hands firmly on her shoulders.

"What will people say? You, dining with a milkman's daughter?"

"Don't you know by now, Tessa, that I really don't give a damn what people say?"

"All right then," she agreed, feeling overwhelmingly limp and yielding. "I will."

"You will have dinner with me?"

She nodded again and Chandler smiled, feeling as excited and eager as he had as an idealistic young man of eighteen. A man who had brought back priceless blue silk from a trip to China and saved it for a woman he would one day find to love. A young man he thought he had lost forever.

"Splendid!" he said, smiling.

Feeling on top of the world, Chandler stood then, offered Tessa his hand, and lead her back down the secluded little path to the place where it joined the main walk.

They were strolling together back into a swiftly moving crowd on Fifty-ninth Street when Tessa suddenly stopped. Chandler took two more steps, then stopped when he did not feel her beside him. He turned and walked back to her.

Before them, alone on the corner, sat a shabbily dressed little boy with a dirty face, stringy dark hair and a missing front tooth. No one else stopped or even seemed to see him sitting there on an empty crate in threadbare blue knickers and a jacket several sizes too small. Across his knees, he held a broken fiddle.

Pain pierced her heart when Tessa thought that this child was no older than the wealthy little girl they had just encountered in Central Park, and here he was out here, trying to play for money. Like hers and Chandler Tate's, the circumstances of these two children's lives could not have been more different. What an irony to encounter this, she thought. Today of all days.

"Do you have that woman's money?" she asked pointedly. "I think I would like it after all."

Seeing what she meant to do, Chandler hesitated. "Oh, Tessa, I don't think—"

"She wanted me to have it, didn't she? As I recall, the lady was quite insistent."

"Well, yes she was but . . ."

"Then it is mine to do with as I wish, isn't it?"

Chandler stifled a defeated little grin. "It is at that," he acquiesced, pulling forth the coins from his breast pocket and handing them to her. Just as he had suspected she would, Tessa gave all of it, without hesitation, to the boy.

"I know what you're thinking, that my father and I could have used that money. But it wasn't meant for me, you know," Tessa said as she turned back to Chandler with a satisfied smile. "I knew where the dear Lord meant for it to go the moment I saw that poor child."

Then, as if she had just given away pennies and not a rather significant sum, she strode across Fifty-ninth Street with her head held high. Chandler was a pace behind her and becoming steadily more enchanted than he had ever been in his life.

Chapter
14

WHEN SHE WAS FINALLY ALONE AND CHANDLER WAS ON HIS WAY back to the Hoffman House, Tessa slumped, weak-kneed against her bedroom door and felt a dizzying burst of confusion.

On her night table was the volume of Shakespeare he had given her. It was the most thoughtful gift she had ever received. Certainly it was the most costly. In two short hours, Chandler Tate would be back on her doorstep, looking more magnificently handsome than ever. And then what?

Trying not to think of his kiss, commanding and urgent, Tessa struggled to pull her shoes off, then flung herself down onto her white iron-frame bed. Oh, but his firm hands, how they had taken possession of her body. The sensation of his sculpted chest against hers . . .

"Stop it!" she cried aloud, tossing her head back defiantly.

Tessa covered her lips with the back of her hand as she tried to slow her racing heart. Whatever he had made her feel, to dream, it was wrong, and she would only despise herself more than she already did once he left her to return to Boston.

Besides, there was Brian still to consider, she thought guiltily. He wanted to marry her. Tessa had promised to find a way to meet him in the attic, their secret place, for a picnic supper this evening. He would be anxious to know what she had told her father about their engagement. And so the choice was plain. Hurt one man she once had loved and agreed to marry, or spurn another who excited her as no one ever had. A man who, in a week's time, would have entirely forgotten her, she was sure. But even as the question came into her mind, Tessa knew the decision had already been made.

A soft rapping at her bedroom door brought her to her feet. When she opened it, Mary Gallagher was standing before her holding out an oval box covered in textured burgundy fabric.

"This just came for ye, lass. A most impressive lookin' delivery man in full livery brought it."

Tessa shrank back, knowing who the box was from and knowing also that she could not accept a single gift more without being entirely swept away. Self-protection forced her to ask Mrs. Gallagher to open it for her.

Both women gasped in surprise as they gazed down at the delicately embroidered topaz-colored shawl decorated with tiny ivory beads. It was a perfect match for the elegant evening dress Chandler had given her to wear to the theater.

Tessa pressed the shawl to her chest and leaned back against the wall, wishing with her whole heart that Chandler hadn't done it. Wishing he wasn't so terribly charming. Unbeknownst to him, he was making her care for him with these gifts, with his passion, and with his kind, kind heart. The life without love to which she had consigned herself would be difficult enough to bear without continuing to wish for dreams that could not possibly come true.

It will be all right, she tried silently to convince herself. *It's only one supper. The fulfillment of one small fantasy. He will be gone in a few days, and then everything will be back to normal. I will marry Brian Sullivan and that will be that.*

"Ye've come to care for Mr. Tate already, haven't ye, lass?" Mrs. Gallagher asked kindly, seeing confusion on Tessa's softly freckled face.

"There are a hundred reasons not to," she whispered in reply.

"And yet ye do, just the same."

"The dear Lord help me."

Tessa collapsed onto her bed, the springs squeaking beneath her weight as she drew her knees up to her chest. "He is the kindest, most handsome, most gallant man I have ever met. I have never felt so happy as I do when I am with him. He is like something out of a book."

"And ye're just an ordinary immigrant girl with nothin' to offer a man like that."

"That is only part of it," Tessa glanced up.

Mary Gallagher sat down beside her on the edge of the bed.

"What if he knew the whole truth about me? That I don't spend all of my time like a lady, reading at the library and trying to improve myself, as my da likes to boast."

"That ye help an old midwife bring babies into the world."

"I am certain that it would not be considered a proper pastime for a lady by someone like him."

"Do ye know that for certain?"

"What I know is that he is a real gentleman, used to ladies with breeding and culture."

"Gentleman or not, I would think he would consider himself quite honored indeed to know ye, Tessa Murphy, and the young woman of purpose and conviction ye truly are."

Tessa looked up, pure vulnerability softening her expression. "Chandler will be going back to Boston in a couple of days. Back to his life, to the sort of people he is accustomed to, back to what he knows."

Mrs. Gallagher held up the exquisite shawl, examining it.

Her heavy gray brows lifted in an expression of consideration.

"I've lived a long life, lass, and these old eyes have seen far
more than perhaps they should have, so I can tell ye that this
shawl doesn't look any more like a farewell gift than any o'
these other fine things he bought for ye," she said, glancing
at the window seat filled with expensive gloves, shoes, and
hats that Tessa was going to give away.

"Well, whatever it is he thinks he feels, I cannot care for
him," Tessa countered firmly. "I have made my decision. I
have made promises."

Chandler tossed the room key onto a marble-topped table
near the door and walked through the late-afternoon sun
and shadows to the pitcher and basin of water across the
room. His breath finally now was less ragged, his loins a
little less tight. But the remembrance of Tessa Murphy still
whirled in his mind like some sweet, seductive perfume that
would not quite let him go.

He tossed his jacket across the bed and rolled up his shirt
sleeves as the thoughts drifted back relentlessly, making the
taste of her lips real again. The sensual way she had opened
them to his probing tongue. God, how he wanted her! He
was not certain he had ever wanted anyone so much. Not
just her body, although pressed against him as she had been
she had ignited a fire in Chandler that nothing but having
her would quell. But it was much more than that. It was her
proud, gentle sweetness he wanted to possess every bit as
much as the voluptuous silken curves and that shimmering
copper mane of hair. Never in his life had one woman
warmed his heart and sent a fire of lust through his veins so
furiously.

*You shall find her. You have only to look for her with your
whole heart for it to be so . . .*

Chandler cooled his ardor with splashes of water on his
face and neck until he could breathe again. Then he dried
himself with a towel and glanced up. It was then that he saw
it. On a silver tray in the center of his writing table near the

ink and paper and correspondence lay a telegram. He moved across the room to read it. The communiqué was short, three lines in all.

Beg forgiveness, brother. Return home at once. Company in terrible state.

Daphne

It was only then Chandler realized that in the last three days, days in which he had spent time with Tessa Murphy, he had not thought of his sister or of B.W. Tate & Company. Not even once.

Chapter

15

SHE HAD BEEN UNFAITHFUL.

It was what Tessa believed of her actions with Chandler Tate in the park that afternoon. Especially since she could not keep herself from the overwhelming desire to have him kiss her that way again tonight.

When she opened the door to the attic and walked in, the shame Tessa had been battling since Chandler had left her returned with a vengeance. Brian looked up at her across the shadowy room with such love and trust in his eyes that she felt as if she were going to be ill.

"I've missed ye," he said, tipping her chin up for a kiss that was as familiar to her now as breathing. "When I came home from work last night, yer da said ye had gone out. He wouldn't explain, though. Are ye all right?"

Tessa let him kiss her again, trying vainly to think of what to say in reply. She knew that no matter what she said, if it contained an ounce of truth, she was going to have to hurt him.

"Brian, I have something to tell you."

"I certainly hope it is that ye have finally confessed things to him."

"I did," she said carefully and watched with a sickening sensation of betrayal and a surge of nausea as his eyes lit with hope.

"Splendid!" he said, drawing her closer. "Finally now there's nothin' to keep us from bein' together. And wait til ye see the fine supper I've set for the two of us. I was hopin' you'd be makin' it a celebration. Now I'm not disappointed."

"Brian, I . . ." Her words trailed off when she saw the small table for two set with what she knew was his mother's best china brought out from a steamer trunk that he opened only on special occasions. There were also candles and neatly folded linen napkins beside each plate.

"Is it all right?"

"It's lovely . . . But I can't stay."

Brian's lips parted and as they did, did, he let go of her. "What do ye mean, ye cannot? Now that Charlie knows the truth—"

"It's not my da."

"Who then?"

Brian saw the answer and the self-recrimination in her eyes before Tessa lowered them. "Not that stranger from the other day," he gasped in disbelief.

"It's not what you think, Brian. Chandler doesn't know many people here in New York and—"

"Chandler, is it?" he asked tautly. "You call him by his given name?"

"Brian, please. Don't make more out of this than it really is."

His powerful body was suddenly rigid, his lips set in a firm line. "Then perhaps ye should tell me, lass, just exactly what it is."

"You asked where I was last evening."

"I did."

"Chandler took me to the theater as thanks for what we did for him the other day."

"Good Lord above! You're a woman engaged to be married!" he snarled, slapping a palm against his forehead. "Do ye not think a word o' thanks would have been quite enough?"

"I wanted to go," she forced herself to confess. "I've never been anywhere like that before. And I probably never will be able to again."

Brian was struck by the sincere longing in her eyes that followed the admission. It gave her away completely. Brian slumped, crestfallen, onto one of the dusty trunks that cluttered the attic floor.

When I was young, I used to dream of being a grand lady swept away by a handsome prince . . . Those words had haunted him since the day Chandler Tate had come so unexpectedly into their lives. Now he thought how portentous they truly had been.

In the silence, Tessa could hear him breathing. She could see the expression of real pain on his face. Pain she had caused. Finally, he looked back up at her.

"So now why can ye not have dinner with me tonight?"

"You know why," she replied with as much tenderness as she could enlist.

Their eyes were fixed on one another. "I want to hear you say it, Tessa."

"I told Chandler I would have supper with him."

"And exactly where does that leave us?"

Tessa's eyes filled with tears. "I didn't want to lie to you, Brian. You are the best friend I have in the world, and you deserve better than deception."

"I thought I was a good deal more than a friend."

"He will soon return to Boston."

"And things will simply go on between us as if nothing had ever happened?"

"I hope so, with all of my heart. This is just something I must do."

Brian came back up onto his feet and exhaled another breath. He had been in the parlor long enough that first night to see the attraction between the two of them, and that scene had played over and over again in his mind ever since. After all, the man was rich, handsome, and commanding. He was every young lady's fantasy. Brian knew he could not hope to compete with that. All that he had to offer Tessa was his heart.

"Ye were a child when ye first told me ye loved me."

"I was fifteen."

"That is very young to give yerself to only one man without ever knowin' any others. I suppose after I fell in love with ye, I let myself lose sight o' that," he said painfully, then pressed a kiss onto her forehead.

"Go with him tonight," Brian said in a whisper as he pulled himself away from her. "If we're to be, I want all o' ye as my wife, Tessa Murphy. I'll settle for no less than that."

Tears spilled onto her cheeks, but she wept silently as he tried for a moment to give her a smile. Then his face grew harsh again.

"Now go," he said. "I really cannot bear to speak about this a moment more."

Chapter
16

THE CARRIAGE PULLED TO A STOP IN FRONT OF DELMONICO'S. As he had the night before, the formal coachman extended a gloved hand to help Tessa out into the warm night air. Beautifully dressed ladies, all escorted by distinguished-looking gentlemen filed in and out of the bronze doors before them, laughing blithely and conversing as if this famous restaurant were just any ordinary place in the world to dine.

To live this way all of the time, Tessa thought, shaking her head as, once again, Chandler firmly took her hand. And yet she could not quite imagine it. To her, these places, the theater, the department stores, and now this, would always be fantasy.

"Mr. Tate, how nice to see you again, sir," the poised, gentleman, dressed in crisp black and white, said welcomingly. "We're quite busy this evening but I have saved one of our best tables for you in the public dining room facing the avenue."

"Thank you, Philip," Chandler nodded and casually pressed a hand to the small of Tessa's back so that she would know to precede him and follow the host.

As Tessa and Chandler walked beneath the glittering spray of crystal chandeliers, they passed table after table of diners dressed in the finest silk, ornamented with rubies, diamonds, and emeralds. Dowagers. Debutantes. Fine gentlemen in dark cutaway coats. All of them were sipping wine from the finest crystal. As she glanced down at her own classic gown, Tessa wondered what they would think if they knew how scandalously mismatched were this couple coming in among the polished wood and satin-draped windows.

"Here we are, Mr. Tate. Will this table do?" the host asked tentatively, holding out for Tessa one of the chairs covered in elegant yellow satin.

"This is splendid. Thank you, Philip."

Chandler glanced over at Tessa and, with only the slightest hint of a nod, she understood that he meant for her to be seated with the assistance of the man who had led them to their table.

She had never been to a restaurant before, let alone to one as famous as Delmonico's. Oh, she had passed by them, known that people frequented them for the privilege of paying someone else to prepare a meal. But never in her wildest dreams had she expected such luxury inside. She watched Chandler cautiously, intent upon making no mistake that might embarrass them both.

"Shall we have champagne?" he asked, as a waiter quietly took the folded napkin from the table and placed it neatly across her lap. Tessa's heart skipped a beat, thinking she had already done something wrong by not removing the napkin from the table herself. But then the waiter proceeded around the table and did the same thing for her escort.

"I don't know," she replied softly, trying to catch her breath. "I have never had champagne before."

"Then by all means," he smiled handsomely, leaning back. "We shall begin with a bottle of your finest."

Chandler said something else to the waiter in a language Tessa did not understand. The man nodded and left. "So, Tessa, how do you like Delmonico's so far?"

"I'm not certain," she said truthfully. "It's grand enough, but it's awfully bright. I've never seen so many shimmering lights."

Amusement danced in his eyes. "That is so none of these ladies in all of their finery shall have a chance of going unnoticed."

"They *want* people to stare at them?"

"Oh yes, indeed. They would consider the evening a dreadful failure if each one did not believe she was the center of attention upon her entrance and exit."

"Imagine that." Tessa giggled softly behind a graceful, delicately raised hand. "And it was the last thing I wanted as I came across this very long and very intimidating room."

"Oh, rest assured, Tessa, your entrance here was regarded with great interest."

Her eyes dimmed. "I didn't embarrass you, did I?"

"On the contrary. I suspect you have made me the envy of every other man in this room."

Their conversation was interrupted by the return of the waiter, who opened the champagne. In response to Chandler's nod, he poured them each a glass. Then, he ceremoniously laid a large red folder printed with gold letters beside each plate and left them once again. Tessa's eyes asked what it was before her lips could form the question.

"It is the menu," Chandler kindly explained. "I'm certain you'll find something in it you like."

"There is a choice?"

"Several," he replied with the same easy smile that had been able to put her at ease since the day they met. "But try your champagne first."

Mightily determined not to make any dreadful blunders on this last fantasy evening, Tessa carefully lifted her glass as she saw the woman at the next table do.

"Ooh!" she giggled, pressing a finger to her lips. "The bubbles tickle my nose!"

Chandler's smile widened in approval as he took a sip from his own glass. "You know, you're quite right about that."

Tessa felt a warm, calming wave pass over her as she sipped the champagne again. For the first time that evening, she felt her apprehension begin to fade.

"So, precisely how long do you plan to maintain this advantage you have over me, Mr. Tate?" she asked with a wry smile.

Her question now was reminiscent of the first words he had spoken to her from the sofa in her parlor, when he had opened his eyes and seen her staring at him. A surprised amusement lit his boldly handsome face at the suggestive tone in her question.

"How do you mean?"

She took another sip of champagne, feeling slightly more brave. "Well, I have told you about my family and where we come from. And you have met my father, who has told you everything he recalls about our homeland. But still we know almost nothing about you."

Chandler set down his own champagne glass. *What would you think if I really did tell you all about me, Tessa?* he silently wondered in the moment before he answered her. "Both of my parents are dead," he said instead, pushing away thoughts of true confession. "My father died most recently, less than a year ago."

"I'm sorry."

"He was a difficult man to understand. I don't believe I ever did, even though I spent a good many of my early years trying. Family honor was very important to him. I did know that," he divulged with a little spark of anger, recalling the codicil that had brought him here.

"Have you any brothers or sisters?"

"A sister," Chandler replied, exhaling a long breath as his expression became more formal. Daphne. Now that was another story entirely. And yet it was all part of the same miserable truth. A truth he could never risk telling anyone.

Especially this bright, beautiful girl with whom he was fast becoming enchanted.

"Daphne is married but has no children of her own, so she has, until quite recently, assisted in the care of mine."

Tessa's heart sank with a fast and heavy thud. So did her bright smile. She had been having such a lovely evening, such a lovely fantasy that, strange as it seemed, it had never once crossed her mind that Chandler Tate might actually be married.

"And your wife?" she forced herself to ask.

"I am a widower," Chandler replied, treading carefully on the jagged edges of the truth. "My children were in dire need of female influence after my wife's death, so Daphne helps me."

"That is good of your sister."

"She has her moments. But only when it suits her, I'm afraid."

Finally they were speaking a little bit about him, Tessa thought with relief. Finally they were tearing away some of the mystery. And yet she was surprised to sense a hint of tension beginning to build beneath the words of his explanation.

"That must have been a devastation, to lose your wife at so young an age."

"It was difficult on the children," he said coolly.

Tessa found it a curious reply, and he had given it in an even more curious tone of voice. She straightened, considering why he might have excluded himself.

"But certainly it was hard on you as well," she gently pressed. "You must have loved her very much."

"There was a time."

"What was her name?"

Tessa could see the small grimace of hesitation deepen the tiny lines around his eyes before he answered, as though she were coming too close to something.

"Her name was Cynthia."

"Since you're doing so well thus far, finally telling me

about yourself, I would really like to hear about your Cynthia. If you would like to tell me."

Chandler began to tense almost before the suggestion had left her lips. *Would that I could bare my soul to you, sweet Tessa,* he thought with a rush of longing. *But what, I wonder, would you think of me if I did?*

"It is a rather long story, Tessa." His voice cracked, but there was a strange sound of longing in the words as his smooth demeanor was suddenly gone again. Chandler shifted uneasily in his chair. "I don't like talking about it . . . about her."

"I'm sorry. I had no right to ask you something so personal. I only thought that since we—"

"You could not have known. It's just that I have struggled rather valiantly these past two years to put that all behind me and I don't like to think about any of it now."

Any of it? she thought with a little jerk of something inside her mind that she could not identify.

"I would really rather talk about you anyway," Chandler smoothly added, finding his most commanding voice again, and coaxing Tessa from her thoughts with what was suddenly a relaxed and pleasant smile.

"That is what you said last evening, as well."

"It is still true today," Chandler smiled. "Truthfully, I find you fascinating."

"But there is certainly a great deal more to your life than there is to mine."

"That is not always a great advantage, believe me, Tessa," he said mysteriously.

He picked up the menu and she casually followed his lead. But, for the second time in as many minutes, Tessa's heart sank as she glanced up at the formal looking ecru-colored parchment inside the folder. So far this evening she had done well. She had been careful, more careful than she had ever been, not to embarrass either of them. But now she was truly finished. None of the words on her menu were written in English.

She slumped back against the chair, momentarily stunned as the anxiety wound inside of her and hardened like a knot. Tessa was certain to make a complete fool of herself now, and when he left for Boston, Chandler Tate's greatest memory of her would be one of disappointment.

As if he could actually read her mind, Chandler leaned forward and lightly pressed down the top of her menu so that he could see her eyes. As he expected, they were as round and vulnerable as a doe's eyes, and there was a flicker of panic lighting them.

"You know, the waiters are quite accustomed to a gentleman ordering for a lady."

"Oh, would you?" she asked, biting her bottom lip to hide the little rush of relief she breathed.

"I would be pleased to," he nodded as he flashed his dashing, ever-confident smile.

The supper that followed was a grand affair, full of new sights and aromas for Tessa. Oysters. Lobster salad. Terrapin. And more champagne. Her confusion did not end after Chandler had ordered for them in what she realized was French. But he had been kind enough to request the same dishes for each of them and she had only to follow his lead to enjoy what she was certain would remain the most extraordinary meal of her life.

Across the room, an orchestra was playing while they dined, and a small group of couples were dancing beneath the flickering gaslights. Men in their elegant, dark formal attire gracefully whirled and dipped ladies in their brightly colored silks and satins. As she sipped her champagne, Tessa was mesmerized by how smoothly they moved to the music. It was not the noisy, raucous jigs and reels they danced in the streets around Mrs. Gallagher's boardinghouse. This was something refined and beautiful.

"Would you care to dance?" Chandler asked between courses, seeing her interest.

Tessa leaned forward toward him, not wanting to be overheard. "I'm afraid I don't know how to do anything but a jig," she painfully confessed. "And at that, I'm forever stepping on my father's toes."

Chandler held out his hand, nevertheless. "Come. I shall teach you."

She glanced around the room again, a swell of panic rising up suddenly from the pit of her stomach at the mere prospect. The smooth, effortless movements of the other dancers was like nothing she had ever seen before. They seemed to be floating. No matter how splendid a teacher he might be, Tessa was quite certain even Chandler Tate could not help her dance like that.

"Please," she stiffened. "I would rather not."

"As you wish," he relented, leaning back in his chair and studying her as the formally clad, white-gloved waiter laid another plate before each of them. "But, I do believe that you could do just about anything to which you set your mind."

Tessa gazed down at the lovely-smelling gravy-laden steaming dish upon a delicate white and blue china plate. His compliment had fallen beneath this latest culinary challenge. Nothing about this world, she thought, was anything at all like the one in which she lived. Not the sights. Nor the sounds. And certainly not the food. This curious-looking concoction might just well put an end to her determination.

"Ris de veau," the waiter announced with apparent pride then bowed and turned from the table.

"Sweetbreads," Chandler whispered in explanation, with a hand cupped casually around his mouth.

"You'd never know it to look at it," Tessa countered.

A flash of humor crossed his face at her expression and the way she had spoken that last declaration. The pure innocence in her voice made him chuckle. He could not help it. She was like a breath of fresh air in some great, stuffy old place. That place, Chandler had steadily come to realize, was his life.

"You're not laughing at me, are you?" She stiffened in defense.

"No, Tessa," he replied with an engaging chuckle. "I am merely laughing, and I can say with all honesty that it is the first evening in a very long time that I have felt like doing that."

He watched her poke at the sweetbreads for a moment more and then set down her fork defeatedly. "Tessa," he said, seizing the moment, certain he would lose his courage altogether if he did not speak the words now. "I have something to ask you."

"Oh?" she said, still blissfully ignorant as to the enormity of what he was about to suggest.

Chandler took a long swallow of his champagne, then settled back against the chair. "You, Miss Murphy, are without a doubt the most thoroughly charming and enchanting young woman I have ever had the fortune to know."

In the silence, he drew a small velvet-covered box from his pocket and, after setting it on the table between them, opened it for her. A huge, square diamond set in silver caught the light and glittered like a thousand bright stars.

"Tessa, I would be honored if you would consent to become my wife."

Through sheer determination alone she had maintained her composure, but now it was all lost as she sat in the echo of his unexpected proposal and in the sight of the most spectacular piece of jewelry she had ever seen.

"I know I am a modest girl from the sort of world you know nothing about, but I assure you, that I do not take kindly to being insulted in this way."

"And I assure you I am quite sincere."

She looked quizzically at him. "But we come from such entirely different worlds."

"I was hoping that we could make our own world."

"We barely know one another, Chandler."

"I know what I feel when I am with you," he said with an easy confidence. "Something I have not felt for a very long time. And now I am not certain that I ever really felt it at all before I met you."

146

"I still don't understand," Tessa said, glancing around the room. "I am nothing at all like these other ladies."

The corners of his mouth turned up again into a faint smile. "Precisely."

Chandler finished his champagne, knowing that it was better to give her a moment to try and digest what he was suggesting before he continued to plead his case.

"Shall I order another bottle?"

"No, thank you. My head is spinning already."

Tessa was gazing at the ring, trying not to stare, but he could see how overcome she was. Never in her life had she seen anything so magnificent, and now this handsome aristocrat quite unexpectedly was offering it to her. This afternoon she had prepared herself for the fact that this was the last time they would ever see one another. And now this!

"Do you . . . love me then?" she asked cautiously.

Her gaze was earnest and wide-eyed. It was one of the things he had loved first about her. Her refreshing ability to be nothing but entirely honest. She would be good for Alice and James. And she would most assuredly be good for him.

"I'm not certain I know what that means anymore," he said truthfully in answer to her question. "But what I do know is that you make me happy, Tessa. Truly happy. You excite and surprise me like no one else, and I know that I don't want to live the rest of my life without you."

He took a breath, trying to gauge her response but for the first time all evening, he hadn't a clue what she was thinking. Chandler had certainly felt the way she had responded in his arms earlier that afternoon; the way she had molded against him and let him kiss her without protest in the intimate way that lovers kiss.

And yet he knew, perhaps better than anyone, that passion was not love. He needed to ask what she felt as much as she had needed to ask him. But, when he saw a shadow of doubt cross her face, and her lovely green eyes begin to dim, Chandler knew that he was pushing too hard. He was forcing her to decide something so monumental too quickly.

"I cannot possibly take this seriously."

"I have, Tessa," he said softly. "So can you."

"It's just not that simple. There are other people to consider. Promises I have made."

"Promises?"

"There was another offer of marriage, and I have already accepted it."

"It's that Sullivan fellow, isn't it?" he asked with deep-voiced self-assurance. "He's the one you were supposed to be with tonight instead of me."

She tried not to look at the handsome and yet frighteningly mysterious man before her who was quite successfully trying to sweep her off her feet.

"I had things all planned."

"Whatever you have promised him, Tessa, you don't love him. You know that."

"But there is more to a commitment like marriage than love."

"There shouldn't be. Believe me, if you marry for any other reason, noble or otherwise, you will live to regret it."

She pressed a hand to her forehead. "I can't decide something like this right now. I need more time."

"I want you, Tessa. We belong in one another's lives."

"Please."

"All right then," he agreed, leveling his eyes upon her and covering her hand with his own. "I must return to Boston tomorrow. There is trouble with my company that won't wait."

"And I must have some time," she said desperately.

"Then you shall have it. But I mean to make this happen for us. I have not waited for you all of my life to let you marry another man just because you are trying to help your father."

Tessa's face reflected her surprise. "How did you know that?"

"Because I have seen the sort of woman you are. Because there is no length to which you will not go for someone you love. I could not help but notice that your father's health is fragile. You want to provide for him when he can no longer work."

Tessa glanced around the room. "I have no right, even to consider such a thing as your proposal."

"You have every right. You know I care for you, Tessa, and after today, I have every reason to believe you care for me."

"This is such a terribly grand decision, no matter how I feel."

"It was not an insignificant one for me either," he said, squeezing her hand. "After all, I have my children to consider."

Children, Tessa thought wildly, as her mind whirled with conflicting emotions. Not only was he asking her to become his wife, but she would be called upon to mother two children she had never even had the benefit of meeting. And it was all offered under such a thick veil of mystery that was more confusing the more she learned about him.

"Could you please see me home?" she asked, moving to stand.

Chandler could see her shaking as she gripped the edge of the linen-covered table. "Perhaps if you had a bit more champagne, and we could talk a while longer."

"I'm sorry. Everything is lovely. This place is lovely. But I really do have a great deal to think about."

Chandler did not contest further. He could only imagine what she must be thinking. He knew how absurd it all sounded, and he told her so to reassure her. It had even sounded a little preposterous to him that he could have come to care for her so quickly. But it had happened, nonetheless. When he was with Tessa the future seemed bright and full of promise, and he was not about to lose this exquisite, unpolished gem to the risky convention of a long courtship. And perhaps to competition. Not now when he had only just found her. It had happened just as Li Kao Chen had said it would.

The ride back toward Tenth Street was silent and long. They sat, this time, on opposite sides of the carriage, both of them listening to the faint tinkle of the horsecar bells in the distance. Tessa was careful not to meet Chandler's gaze. Instead, she watched the strollers. She pretended to see the stars and the streetlamps, which lit her face in flashes of soft gold.

Chandler found her, strangely, even more beautiful by this evening light, even though she would no longer look directly at him. Beautiful and proud, he thought. Yes, it was a fierce Irish pride that ran in her blood, even if it was the thing leading her to marry a man she did not love. It was all a part of her spirit, he reminded himself, and that spirit was part of her charm.

"No matter what my decision is," Tessa said as the coachman once again held open the carriage door. "I will say honestly that you are a very persuasive man."

"Persuasive enough, I hope," he said with an easy smile, but Tessa simply turned away from him and lifted the hem of her skirt, preparing to leave the carriage.

Chandler caught her wrist just as she was turning away, and she sank down onto the seat beside him. "Please promise me that you will really consider what I have proposed. I will return in ten days for your answer."

She did not argue. Her head was too full of fantasy. And uncertainty. Instead, she nodded, then waited for him to relinquish the firm hold he had on her arm.

"Tessa," he whispered. "God, how I love the sound of your name."

As he had done earlier in the park that day, Chandler took her chin commandingly in the palm of his hand. Then his long index finger caressed her cheek as his lips slowly descended upon hers, devouring their softness.

The heat of their connection pulsed through her veins, and Tessa succumbed to his kiss completely. She was shocked at the eagerness of her response, but powerless to struggle against it as Chandler pulled her against the taut length of his body. When he finally drew back, setting her free, Tessa sank against the seat, her lips still parted.

"I thought it wise to give you something more than my ring to contemplate while I was away," he said with velvety smoothness, as a half smile lingered on his mouth. Then, he drew her wrist to his lips and kissed the tender inside with the soft seduction of a whisper.

"After this afternoon," she replied, the taste of his mouth still warm upon her own, "you know that really wasn't necessary."

"I'll not lie to you, Tessa," he said in a husky whisper. "I am a man of passion, and what I feel for you may sometimes take over my good sense."

"If we were to marry, I would expect that to continue for the rest of our lives."

Chandler smiled. "Direct as always."

"I'm afraid I know no other way to be."

"I plan to hold you to that."

"My head is still spinning."

"Good," he replied, the handsome smile broadening.

Chapter

17

WHEN TESSA CAME INTO THE PARLOR, EVERYONE WAS COLLECTED near the unlit fireplace hearth. Their faces were strained. Mary Gallagher was whispering something to Brian that Tessa could not hear. The Baldwin sisters both were weeping. A tall, unfamiliar man dressed in black stood among them.

Her heart began to bleed before the final wound had been inflicted. It bled because she knew what they were about to tell her. Tessa felt their pity heavy on her, like a shroud. She saw it reflected in their eyes.

"It's my da . . . isn't it?"

The stranger, an angular man with dark, muttonchop sideburns and a thick mustache, took a single step forward. He was holding a small black bag. "There's nothing more I can do for him, Miss. It's his heart. I'm afraid it's just giving out."

"Who is he?" Tessa mouthed, looking over to Brain.

"I called for Dr. Bennett, lass," he said gently. "He came as quick as he could."

"Ye must be brave," she heard Mary Gallagher say.

"Is he—" Tessa's voice broke off as she scanned the room full of familiar faces. But it was the stranger who answered.

"He has not expired, no," he said calmly. "But, frankly, he doesn't have much time. I would make these last few moments count if I were you."

Tessa reached out, feeling as if she would faint, blood pouring from her heart like the flow of a river. She could not stop it. There would never be anything to stop it. This was her father. Her da.

Brian braced her from behind, large firm hands on her shoulders. "Do ye want me to go up with ye?"

The ache began. She missed him already. "No," she said softly. "I need to go alone."

Charlie Murphy opened his eyes and tried to smile at his daughter when he heard her come in. This wasn't supposed to happen, Tessa thought disjointedly as she moved slowly toward him in the dimly lit bedroom. The ache deepened. It began to throb. It roared in her ears. She had never felt a pain like this. A deep, dark chasm of grief. She was going to marry Brian. They were all going to live together. Her love was going to save him. She had it all planned.

"I'm glad ye're here," he struggled to say, lifting a shaky hand for her to take.

"Isn't this going a bit too far just to see that I have no reason left to marry Brian Sullivan?" she asked in a soft, jesting tone, sinking down onto the bed beside him. She leaned over, close to his face and took the hand he held up to her.

Tessa wanted so desperately to see that smile of his again. The sound of his laughter. The sweet smell of his pipe smoke. Those were the things about him that always told her everything was going to be all right.

"'Twas not in me mind, lass," he answered weakly. "But now that it is in yers . . ."

"Don't do this, Da. Please, you can't leave me."

Charlie Murphy closed his eyes for a moment, weary even

from breathing. Then he opened them again, glazed now and distant.

"It seems the good Lord hasn't left me much choice in the matter."

"But I need you."

"What ye need . . . is to be happy," he said between labored breaths. "Like water to a flower . . . ye've no way to bloom without it. . . . Mr. Tate is one who knows that."

In all of the commotion she had forgotten completely about Chandler's proposal. Part of her mind urged her to tell him. She knew that it would make him happy. Another urge was stronger. She wanted to take these last few moments all to herself. The need willed her toward silence. Chandler Tate really didn't matter now, anyway.

"Please, me darlin' child, be happy."

"Not without you."

"You're stronger than ye think."

Her mouth trembled. "But you're all that I have."

"And ye'll always have me," he said, reaching out to touch her heart. "In here."

Tessa curled on the bed beside him. The ache was making her numb. Everywhere but in her heart.

"What will I do without you?"

"Ye'll have a glorious life," he whispered, "and yer ma and I'll be watchin'. I miss her, lass. I'm a happy man to be goin' home."

"No," she said pleadingly, nestled against him.

"Let me go, darlin'. . . . I'm ready now."

She wanted to hold him and never let him go. She wouldn't let him go. They had so much left to do. So much left to share. As she held his hand, feeling it grow limp in her own, Tessa closed her eyes and remembered her father as he had been when she was a little girl. Strong. Forceful. His smile, as bright and warm as the summer sun. Full of hopes and dreams. For his Tessa. For them both. And it was possible, he always said, all of it, here in America.

Chapter

18

"HE'S HERE! OH, THANK THE DEAR LORD!"

Daphne Tate Forrester stood at the drawing-room window and watched the familiar black carriage lurch to a halt before her brownstone townhouse on fashionable Louisburg Square. Chandler had come after all.

Her heart began to beat wildly as she whirled back around and called frantically for her butler. Everything must be perfect, Daphne thought, if she were to make amends for what she had tried to do and to win him back to the company's helm.

She nervously touched her elegantly coiffed golden hair, then pressed her hands down along the line of her royal blue gown. She had pleaded with Lincoln to be here with her today when she humbled herself before her brother. She needed her husband's support. But he had declined. It was a predicament into which she alone most unwisely had gotten them, and alone she would have to see them out again.

Daphne's eyes shot around the room checking one last

time to see that everything was in place. A fresh decanter of her brother's favorite Scotch had been set out. She had had her cook make ginger cakes earlier that morning so that the whole house would be filled with one of the favorite aromas of their childhood.

Finally, she had strategically set a small picture of their mother on a small rosewood table beside the chair in which he always sat. Eleanor Tate had been the family's most powerful mediator and Daphne was not above using her dead mother. Especially now. She had always been shameless about getting what she wanted, and what Daphne wanted desperately now was for things to be as they were.

Chandler took four purposeful strides past the stiff-lipped butler toward his sister's parlor. He had refused the offer to be relieved of his hat and cane and leaned a shoulder in the arched doorway, arms crossed over his chest.

Her face wreathed in a welcoming smile, Daphne strode quickly across the priceless Chinese carpet with outstretched hands. "At last, you've come home!" She pressed a kiss on his cheek.

"I believe you have something to say to me," Chandler countered coolly.

Daphne stepped back, her smile fading only slightly. She could not afford to let him see what she really felt. But it was far worse than she had expected. He was going to make her work for this.

"I've had cook make your favorite ginger cake," she said blithely. "Come. We'll sit and have a slice while we talk."

Instead of heeding her invitation, Chandler took a gold watch from his pocket. "You have exactly five minutes, Daphne," he informed her, refusing to move into the room or to avail himself of her contrived version of hospitality.

"So what's it to be then?" she bristled. "A pint of blood? A pound of my flesh perhaps? Very well then," she continued when he did not reply. "Leave us, will you please?" she instructed her butler with a cursory nod, and waited for him to close the parlor doors.

"If you want me to say it, I will. I was wrong to urge father

156

to write the codicil, and I was wrong to threaten you with it."

"Go on."

"I know that perhaps I did not use the best judgment, but it is only that I want so badly for things to be as they should be."

"You have three minutes twenty-five seconds. I would suggest you concentrate on the apology and not the excuse."

"You are determined to make this difficult for me, aren't you?"

His brows lifted with reserve. "Can you think of one reason why I shouldn't?"

Daphne was on the verge of some biting retort. The muscles in her gaunt face tensed in anger at her brother's harsh demeanor as his sharp words rang in the air between them. But she must remember why he was here at all. Why she had sent the nauseatingly pleading telegram. She needed him. The company needed him.

"Chandler, you know as well as I do that all along father meant the business for you."

"True."

"Lincoln and I know nothing about it, really."

"Apparently you know enough to believe you can run things without me."

Daphne grimaced. "Wouldn't you like a nice glass of Scotch? I have your favorite just over there on the—"

"One minute forty-five seconds."

Daphne walked across the room and picked a piece of paper up from a shiny mahogany table. Chandler recognized it as the codicil. With purposeful snaps and not the slightest hesitation, she tore it into bits, never once breaking her gaze from his. "I am so sorry for trying to blackmail you into marrying Felicity. It's just that—"

Tasting another excuse on her lips, Daphne checked herself. "I need you, Chandler. The company needs you, and I promise I will never again mention my friend's name and marriage to you in the same breath."

Daphne waited in the silence to see even a sign that her

prideless apology had worked, but Chandler just stood there, seeming to study her and the surprisingly penitent words she had spoken. Then, without so much as a nod, he dropped the gold watch back in his pocket, turned around, and gripped the door handle, giving it a turn.

"Wait!" Daphne cried. "Chandler, you cannot possibly leave. We haven't come to terms yet."

"I said I would give you five minutes," he replied without inflection. "And I have kept my word. I shall let you know when I have decided what to do."

"But the company!" she pleaded more desperately than he had ever heard her. "What about that in the meantime?"

Chandler fought to stifle a victorious grin as he pivoted back around, still holding the door handle. "Well, if you mean what you say about being repentant, I suspect you and Lincoln will be working quite hard until I have made up my mind, won't you?"

Chapter

19

"PROPOSED?"

The word lingered on his lips as Brian stood before her, intense astonishment lighting his strong, square face. Tessa had caught him entirely off guard. They had buried her father that morning, and she was not thinking clearly enough to have been more gentle with her confession.

"I don't understand it." Brian shook his head, and tried to catch the breath that had just been knocked out of him.

"I'm not certain I understand it myself."

Brian leaned against the closed attic door for support, still dressed in his best dark suit. Beneath them in the parlor they could both hear the sound of mourners still murmuring their condolences. "Well, what did you tell him?"

"I said I needed time to think, and I needed to talk to you."

"Then ye're actually considerin' it?"

Her silence was his reply, and he gave her a sidelong glance of disbelief. "The man doesn't love ye, Tessa. My God, how could he? He barely knows ye."

"He says that he cares for me," she countered in a low, apologetic tone. "He told me that I am entirely different from anyone he has ever known."

"I'm certain he spoke the truth about that!" Brian roared bitterly.

The harsh words on his lips doubled the ache in her heart. No one was more aware than Tessa of the vast differences between her and Chandler, but in the days since her father's death she was trying her best to honor Charlie Murphy's memory by being truthful with herself. And the truth was that she had fallen in love with Chandler Tate. Still, she felt bound by her commitment to Brian.

"Brian, please. I am not saying I'm going to accept him. It is just that everything is so different now and I thought you deserved to know the truth."

In the gray evening shadows that blanketed the attic, Brian raked a hand through his unruly russet hair. He slumped against the closed door, not caring any longer who might hear them.

"What does Mary say about all o' this?" he finally asked, trying desperately to push the wounded pride from his already brittle voice. "I'm certain ye've confided in her."

"She approves. Like my da, she thinks of it as the life I was meant to have, and all of that."

"And what do ye think?"

"I have always planned to marry you," she said with a wide-eyed sincerity that threatened to destroy him completely if he looked at her a moment longer. "You know how long I have wanted that."

"Aye, but ye've also wanted things I can never give ye. Things this Tate fellow easily can provide."

She sat down on one of the dusty trunks and after a moment he sat down beside her. "You know that money is not that important, Brian."

"I recall someone who told me once that she used to dream of bein' a grand lady, swept away by a handsome prince."

"That was a little girl's dream. I never really expected

160

anything like it to actually happen. I wanted to be your wife, have your children."

Even with the great conviction in her voice, Brian knew her too well to believe that she had not been changed. He squeezed her hand, then brought it to his lips and kissed it. "Little girl's dreams can sometimes come true," he calmly countered.

"I wish I had never met him," Tessa achingly declared. "I hate him for complicating all of our lives this way."

Brian smiled lopsidedly and brought her close against the firm, broad expanse of his chest. "Hate is not what ye feel for the man, Tessa. I think we both know that."

The memory of her stolen kisses with Chandler leapt out at her, and Tessa averted her eyes. She felt a potent mixture of betrayal and self-loathing as if, by what he saw in her eyes alone, Brian could see straight through to her soul. Tessa was certain that she could almost feel his heart splinter into a million tiny pieces.

"Don't hate me for telling you the truth about this," she whispered. "You know how very much I despise secrets."

"It would be so much easier if I could hate ye," he answered in the same kind but strained voice, feeling the relentless pressure of fate heavier on him than anything he had ever felt in his life.

Chapter
20

CHANDLER WAITED A FULL TWO DAYS MORE BEFORE HE DECIDED Daphne had learned her lesson. Having extracted the required promise from her never to meddle again in his affairs, Chandler confidently reclaimed his place at the head of B.W. Tate & Company. He quickly found that an incredible amount of damage had been done in little more than two weeks.

To revive his company and to purge Tessa Murphy from his mind until he could return to New York, Chandler plunged headlong into work. He was quickly overwhelmed by the stack of unpaid bills and the volumes of correspondence that Daphne and Lincoln had allowed to accumulate. But even at that, Tessa was never very far from his thoughts. Nor from his fantasies.

At the mere recollection of her, a sensual tidal wave overcame him, whether he was conducting a meeting or tossing in his big heavy poster bed. The honey-sweet taste of her mouth. The sweet fragrance of her hair. The feel of her ripe, innocent body pressed longingly against his own.

Curious as it seemed, even to him, after all he had been through with Cynthia, Chandler truly wanted to marry her.

Making Tessa his wife as quickly as possible was the only way to wash away all of the bad things the past had brought him. And, in spite of the other proposal she still faced, it would happen for them. He knew it was *meant* to happen.

But until he returned to New York to claim her, Chandler filled his evenings with tedious social engagements as he filled his days with work. Were it not for his ritual periods of meditation to cleanse his mind each day, it was a pace he was quite certain he would not have been able to maintain.

He still detested the frivolous suppers, dances, and card parties, as well as the innocuous banter that defined them. But now he had someone else to consider. It would be far easier to introduce Tessa into society if he hadn't alienated everyone who could make her assimilation into Boston society easier for her. Their hurried marriage, if she accepted him, would incite enough gossip as it was.

And there would be such a great deal for her to learn, coming from so different a world. But if anyone could do it—Chandler grinned, remembering all of the enchanting little things about her—Tessa Murphy certainly could.

The evening before he was to return to New York, Chandler even sat through a dinner party attended not only by Lincoln and Daphne but by Felicity Pettigrew. Suspicious of her presence from the first, Chandler kept his distance, speaking most of the evening instead to his brother-in-law. But surprisingly true to her word, Daphne did not make the slightest overture to try and push them together.

Chandler did not really believe that his sister had changed. As a man of the world, he was not so naive. But the stand he had taken had frightened her into submission. At least where business was concerned. And at least for a while.

He had paid little attention to the uncomfortable silence in which the supper party progressed in dull, candlelit splendor. He participated in very few of the conversations going on around him. Instead, as he sipped his wine and pushed the food around on his plate, Chandler thoughtfully considered the current state of his life and the sort of existence into which he would be bringing Tessa if she agreed to marry him. It was only at times like these that there were any doubts at all anymore. To push them away, everything he had done since returning to Boston, he had done for her.

And through it all, never once did Chandler find himself compelled to call upon his former mistress, Lydia Bailey. Sensual a man as he was, with needs and desires that he was not in the habit of denying, Chandler felt that by even considering such a move, he would be betraying Tessa.

After supper was concluded, he stepped into the glittering, opalescent parlor and Lincoln Forrester followed behind him. Both men stood, each holding a snifter of brandy in one hand and a long, tawny-colored cigar in the other, gazing contemplatively into the chilly evening's fire.

"It was good of you to return," Lincoln said, the first to speak. "The company was truly in a state."

"I almost didn't."

"I suppose it would have served her right."

Chandler arched a brow of surprise and looked over at his brother-in-law. "Then you didn't go along with her blackmail scheme?"

"Good Lord, no!" Lincoln barked in reply. "But you know as well as I that your sister listens to no one."

Chandler exhaled a snowy puff of cigar smoke and leaned against the mantel. "Then let me tell you personally that I am sorry for leaving you in the lurch as I did. But there simply wasn't any other way."

"I am her husband, Chandler ol' boy. Reprimanding her occasionally goes with the territory. I only hope you didn't find things in too dreadful a state upon your return."

"I did." Chandler smiled, taking a slow sip of brandy.

"I was afraid of that. But I believe Daphne has finally learned her lesson about it and, if such an unbelievable thing is true, I would think it might have been worth the price."

Chandler glanced back into the fire, his wistful expression abandoning him. "She's helped me a great deal with the children these past couple of years, Lincoln. It was extremely difficult at first and I owe her a bit of leeway for that."

"Well, she really does adore you and, in her own way, I do believe your sister actually believes she is acting in your best interest. Not, of course, that I am trying to make an excuse for her about any of it."

"Of course," Chandler nodded and then looked back toward the fire again. "So then you think she may well have changed in all of this, do you?"

"Well," Lincoln tipped his head in consideration, "insofar as change is possible for Daphne."

"Good. Because there are going to be a great many changes around here in the near future, and things will go a lot more smoothly if I am not battling with her at every turn."

"Changes?" Lincoln asked, flicking his cigar ashes into the fire.

"I have been thinking of getting married again," Chandler announced with a wry look of self-satisfaction.

Lincoln Forrester touched his gleaming black hair at the forehead and his crimped lips parted in surprise. "You're joking. Don't tell me Felicity has finally won you over after all."

"Hardly," Chandler laughed. "No, the two women could hardly be more different."

"Great God, man, who is she? I had no idea you were even serious about anyone."

"Quite honestly, neither did I."

"Well?" Lincoln anxiously pressed as he twisted the corner of his thin, dark mustache.

"Nothing is settled yet."

"But you are seriously considering it."

"I have been considering nothing but," Chandler said truthfully.

"Are we at least to be told her name? Is she someone from

Boston? I can't imagine who. You've never shown the slightest interest in any of the women around here."

"All in good time, my friend," Chandler replied, setting his empty snifter onto the mantel as the other men filtered into the parlor behind them, each lighting up his own cigar. "All in good time."

"Now for the big question," said Lincoln, lowering his voice an octave.

"What's that?"

"Does Daphne know?"

"My sister knows nothing."

"Definitely better for your health. And for the health of your intended," Lincoln snickered. "The fewer weapons she has against you, the better. You know that she isn't likely to treat anyone but her precious friend Felicity with the slightest bit of favor."

"True enough." Chandler smiled, thinking of Tessa, her indomitable spirit, her fire, and how much he missed her already. "If I have my way, before long, I will have a powerful new weapon of my own."

"'Tis a miracle!" Mary Gallagher laughed.

She danced around Tessa's golden, lamplit bedroom, and her laugh was a deep, rolling sound that came up from the old woman's chest. "A genuine miracle, it is! Our Tessa, a real lady! Oh, lass, if ye only knew how long yer dear father prayed for such a thing—dreamed of it for ye!"

Finally, stopping long enough to sense Tessa's misgivings, she sank down onto the corner of the bed beside her. "Ye don't look like a lass about to claim the grand prize," Mary said more thoughtfully.

"I'm still not certain that Chandler Tate is such a prize."

"'Tis blarney, surely! Don't be tellin' ol' Mary here, Tessa Murphy, that ye've gone and lost yer mind. Mister Tate is a man who is rich, kind, and handsome to boot. Surely ye cannot deny any o' that."

"No," she agreed hesitantly. "He is all o' those things."

"And there is a spark of something splendid between ye. You've admitted as much."

"There is."

"Then why is that sweet face so long? 'Tis not only the loss o' your da that's done that."

"I'm not certain I know what it is, Mary," Tessa softly confessed, as she brushed two copper strands of hair from her forehead contemplatively.

"Would ye try to tell me?"

"There is something about Chandler that is too . . . mysterious. Actually, Mary, it frightens me a little."

"How'd ye mean?"

"For one thing, he won't speak about his wife."

Mary Gallagher's gray eyes widened. "The dear woman died, lass. Havin' lost my dear Francis the same way, I can tell ye, 'tis not a subject easy to bring across the tongue."

"But, unlike Chandler, you don't go out of your way to avoid telling a person who asks how it was that he died! That in itself brings up questions. I don't know, Mary." She shook her head. "There is so much unanswered still between us. When you come right down to it, we know so little about one another."

"'Tis not a great deal ye need know to fall beneath the spell o' love. Ye do love the man, don't ye?"

Tessa flinched at the truth and turned away, wrapping her arms around her waist.

"Tell me, lass," Mary pushed her to be honest. "When ye kiss him, when he touches ye, is it the same as when ye're kissin' Brian Sullivan? Can ye look at me and say it is?"

"No! All right? Is that what you want to hear?" Tessa cried, pivoting back around, her green eyes glinting in the lamplight. "When Chandler kisses me it is like nothing I have ever felt. I am entirely lost in his arms! But he is no shining knight, Mary, come to take me away! He is an aristocrat from Boston and a man with too many well-kept secrets!"

"Oh, I believe he is every bit your shinin' knight and if

ye're honest with yerself, I believe ye know it too. Why not take a bit o' risk for love, lass? I'm sure he'll come to tell ye everythin' that's important in time."

"And what of Brian?" Tessa softly asked. "How can I hurt him like that?"

"Better to hurt the lad a wee bit now than consign him to life with a woman who doesn't have him in her heart."

"That's something my da would have said."

"'Tis indeed. Honor his memory, Tessa, by followin' yer own heart. Not Brian Sullivan's."

Tessa turned back, her eyes stinging with sudden tears. It was what her father had wanted desperately for her. It was his last wish that she find a better life. One full of happiness and love. It had come from dreams he had kindled and nurtured, and shared with her mother a long time ago back in Ireland.

Of course she loved Chandler. She loved him with all her heart. But how could such a thing ever last? No matter what his ardor had lured him into believing, they could not be from more different worlds. No matter how respectably he dressed her up, or what she could manage to learn if she studied hard, Eudora Dunne's observation would always ring true. Murphy was an immigrant name for an immigrant girl. It was that simple. She would be better off as Brian Sullivan's wife. It would be a safer life. A more settled life. After all, she had accepted him and was there not something to be said for honoring that?

Brian's hands clamped down onto the dark wood banister outside Tessa's room. His body grew rigid, as if he were waging a silent battle against the words he had heard her speak to Mary. Against what those words had implied.

He was feeling more ill with each beat of his heart. Tessa belonged to him. She had pledged herself to him years ago, and he had taken it entirely for granted that, when the time was right, it was he whom Tessa would marry. He saw now that he had waited too long. He had let her grow up. She had become a woman with needs he could no longer fulfill.

Like an echo in the silence, the sound of her voice haunted him now. Again and again, Brian heard Tessa's description of her dreams. He remembered her eyes as she had gazed longingly at a window full of hats he could not begin to afford. Hats he cared nothing about. In a painful collage of images, he recalled all the times she had tried to tell him about the book she was reading or the play she wanted to see. Things he could not begin to appreciate. He was not at that moment losing Tessa to that aristocratic stranger. It had been happening for a long time.

"Let her go, lad," he heard someone whisper. In the silent darkness, he was certain that the voice belonged to Charlie Murphy.

Brian bounded down the stairs two at a time, suddenly needing to get away, desperate to escape what he knew was the truth. He stumbled along the street seeing nothing but images of Tessa through the years: a child who had become a woman before his eyes. Those sweet images mixed with the sour vision of her in the arms of that other man.

He refused the thoughts when they became too vivid. His heart leapt, bidding him to go against what he knew he must do. The knowledge of what lay ahead stabbed at him like a blunted sword, and he leaned against a lamppost helplessly surrendering to the anguish, the bitter ache of losing her forever.

A man stopped and pressed a hand into Brian's back as he gripped the lamppost like a lifeline. "Hey, Mister. You all right?" the unfamiliar voice asked.

"Nothin' a good dose of arsenic wouldn't cure," Brian bitterly rasped in reply.

Chapter

21

Brian Sullivan had risen early.

It was so early that he knew they would not be disturbed in the little pastel breakfast room. Tessa still rose before dawn, as she had done every day of her life, when her da had been there needing breakfast. His death was still so new, so fresh, that she had not been able to bring herself to change her routine. To do that would have been to let go of that last little piece of their life together to which she needed to cling.

Brian was standing in the pearly gray morning shadows, leaning against the doorframe, when she came in. Tessa could not see him bracing himself on the oak sideboard behind him. This was the most difficult thing he had ever had to do in his life. But it must be done. For her.

"What a surprise," Tessa smiled, flinging her arms around his neck. "How lovely to have someone to breakfast with again. It's been so lonely down here since—"

"I'll not be havin' breakfast," he said harshly, using every ounce of strength he possessed to peel her away from him.

Tessa looked up at the remoteness in his eyes and her

heart lurched with confusion. "What is it? What's the matter?"

Brian slammed the door so forcefully that it shook on its hinges. "Tell me somethin', Tessa. What was it I said that made ye feel I had given ye license?"

"I don't know what you're talking about."

"Oh, come now," he laughed cruelly. "Did ye really think I wouldn't discover the truth eventually?"

"What truth?"

"Have I to spell it out for ye as well?"

"I really have no idea what you're talking about. Has something happened? Has someone said something?"

He shot her an icy glare. "A fair guilty question, don't ye think, for a lass who claims to have no idea what I mean?"

"Brian, please, you're scaring me," Tessa said, pressing a hand to his chest only to have it flung away.

"Is that what ye said to him too? 'Please'? Did ye plead with him to touch ye, to kiss ye, even to lie with ye?"

"Brian," she swallowed dryly, and searching her mind for what he might have heard or seen. "It's not true."

"Enough! 'Tisn't anythin' I want to hear!"

Tessa recoiled at the command as though he had struck her. In all of the years she had known him, Brian had never once raised his voice to her. She wrapped her arms around her waist, barely breathing, amid the strained silence.

"His kiss is like nothing I have ever felt or will again? Is that not what ye said?"

Her face blanched. "God, forgive me."

"I am entirely lost in his arms . . ."

"Please, Brian, don't go on!" she pleaded, pressing her hands to her ears.

Tessa felt the tears sting her eyes and she gritted her teeth so that she would not sob out loud. How had he found out? She had never so much as looked at another man until Chandler. And when he did come along, she had forced herself to be completely honest with Brian, knowing that even the pain of the truth was better than a lie between them.

Wounded by his cruel accusations, and yet at a loss to defend herself from what they both knew to be true, Tessa searched Brian's face for even a sign of the familiar sweetness that had won her so completely as a child.

"I didn't want it to happen, Brian."

"If that is so, then ye're more of a trollop than I thought. I'm only glad I discovered it before I saddled myself with ye for life."

"Please don't say that. I didn't . . . I never—"

"Ye never what?" he jeered. "Ye never let him touch ye? Kiss ye? Save your lies! I heard ye tell Mary Gallagher otherwise with my own ears!"

Tessa squeezed her eyes and turned away from him, valiantly willing the tears and the shock away. "Ye gave him somethin' sacred, Tessa Murphy. Somethin' meant for yer husband alone. So now ye best make do and accept his offer. Mine is hereby withdrawn!"

She whirled back around, her willpower completely abandoned as the tears streamed down her softly freckled cheeks. "You don't mean that."

"Oh, but I do. I don't love ye, and I certainly don't want to marry ye now."

Brian did his best to keep the hostility, which he had worked so hard to convey, at a fever pitch. Cruel as it was, it was the only way to set her free. But standing here, seeing her shock and confusion, he wanted nothing so much as to sweep her into his arms, kiss away her tears, and tell her it had all been a dreadful mistake. That he still would marry her with only a single word of encouragement.

Fighting the surging nausea in the pit of his stomach, and the jerk of self-loathing for inciting the first lie ever to come between them, Brian stalked toward the door.

"Take his offer, Tessa," he said coldly. "Now that he has compromised ye, it seems the least he can do."

Brian was still shaking as he leaned against an iron hitching post behind a waiting phaeton, and vomited in the street. He felt as if he had vomited every bit of good inside himself. He despised himself for how he had hurt her. But he knew even now that it was nothing like the torture that life would be without her. Oh, Christ! He had been forced to alienate her just to save her!

But what about Brian? How can I hurt him like that? It was what she had asked so earnestly of Mary Gallagher. Those were the only words that gave him any little bit of comfort now that he had done the right thing. Tessa did not love him. She would never love him. Her heart belonged to someone else.

He tried to focus through tear-filled eyes and past the gut-wrenching pain of losing her. Struggling to stand upright, he looked back up at the window to her bedroom, knowing that after Chandler Tate returned to New York today, Tessa would be lost to him. And he tried desperately to make himself believe that he could live with that.

"Have a happy life, my sweet lass," Brian mouthed, looking up at her window one last time.

Chapter

22

"I WISH I COULD TELL YOU HOW VERY SORRY I AM," CHANDLER whispered as he held Tessa against his chest, his arms firm around her slim shoulders. "I didn't know him well, but I saw enough to know that Charlie Murphy was a splendid man."

"He was that."

They stood together a moment more, alone in Mary Gallagher's sunlit parlor. Tessa was more pale than he remembered her, and she was thinner. He knew that her father's death had been difficult. He had seen for himself the closeness between them. He longed to say something that would be meaningful to her. Something that would help even a little. In that, his heart silently battled with his head.

Tell her something, whispered his heart. *Give her a little piece of yourself, something to hold on to*, it urged. *But not too much*, a darker voice quietly warned him. *Even a little knowledge can be a deadly thing when there are secrets like yours.*

Chandler tenderly brushed a strand of hair back from her

eyes, trying, for the first time in a long time, not to listen, only to feel.

"I miss him so much," she said softly, and the sound her voice made was so vulnerable, like a heartbroken child's, that he actually ached for her.

"But you have so many good memories. Keep those," he said, intent for this single moment, on casting caution aside, on baring a piece of his soul. "And cherish them. They're as rare as jewels, believe me, Tessa. My own memories of my father now amount to little more than betrayal, first his of me, then mine of myself because of it. I made so many mistakes, trying to hurt him for how he had hurt me. It took me a lifetime to recognize what I truly wanted and to go after it, not giving a damn what anyone else thought."

Tessa did not know what to say. She was moved. After all of her gentle coaxing to get him to tell her something of himself, here he had finally begun to do it, and freely. In this single admission about a father by a son, Chandler had torn away a layer of the mystery about how a privileged life had been for him. Why he was here, yet again, still wanting to make a poor Irish girl from New York his wife. This one confession gave her hope that, as Mary believed, he might well tell her everything else. In time.

She studied him for a long moment, feeling the charge between them even now, wanting to cry for the bittersweet sensation welling up inside of her. She felt a terrible loss over her father, and yet, here before her in the form of Chandler Tate, was the hope of renewal. How complex he was, she thought. How terribly confusing to any woman who dared to try to understand him. And yet, if she dared, risked, how splendid might that challenge be?

"I do wish I had been here for you," he said.

"I had Mrs. Gallagher."

"And Brian Sullivan?"

"Brian cared for my father," Tessa replied, gazing up at him with tear-brightened eyes. "And I didn't know if you were really coming back."

"I told you that I would."

"People say a great many things."

"What I say, I mean, Tessa."

She tried to smile at his bold, reassuring tone. "I'm learning that about you."

"Good." He smiled in return, and it came as that dashing, slightly dimpled grin that was so much a part of him, for a moment before he fell serious again. "Is there anything I can do? Any arrangements still needing to be made?"

"Thank you, no. It has all been done. My da was buried on Thursday."

He brushed a gentle hand across her cheek. Without his meaning for it to be, it was a sensuous movement, one that made her body stir. Deep down, a fluttering sensation, like the wings of a caged bird, tried to escape against the barrier of her ribs.

When she did not pull away from him, Chandler felt his own passion awakening. He put his arms around the small of her back, pressing his firm hands into the fabric of her dress.

She moved to say that they really shouldn't, that this was neither the time nor the place, but the words would not come.

"I still do so wish I could have been with you," Chandler said.

"He's with my ma again. I believe that he's happy now."

"I said the same thing when my own father died. It makes it easier to believe it, I think."

He was ashamed of the way the vaguely stimulated feeling inside of him quickly ripened to passion. His own smoldering body surprised him as it began, quite suddenly, to burn out of control, the inappropriate lust roaring through him as his hand moved down along her spine, first in consolation, then in ardor. Chandler was, quite simply, possessed now with the need to be as near to her as possible.

Close as they were, he watched the color stain her pale cheeks, and he knew that, even at this awkward moment, she felt what he felt. Oh, the power of that! What had been kindling between them, almost since the first, had ignited and then burst into a bright, all-consuming blaze of desire.

Chandler's arms tightened reflexively around her, arousal ripping through him. The blood burned in his veins with the same heat as the fire inside the rest of him, and he could feel himself grow hard in response. He was so ready for her that he ached. But the time was not right even to kiss her, especially when she had not given him her answer yet.

"Can we go somewhere?" he asked huskily.

"Come with me," Tessa simply bid him.

"Anywhere."

But when they stepped from the house and out into the baking afternoon sun Chandler was surprised. "Might I ask where you are taking me?"

"Ah, now sure you don't believe you're the only one who can create a little mystery?" she said with that sunny, Irish laugh.

Tessa insisted that they forego his elegant carriage for a regular hired hack, in which they rode together through the Lower East Side. It was an area of New York into which a Tate had never ventured. An area Tessa Murphy, however, knew well.

Mrs. Gallagher was busy with another birth on Hester Street and, in the meanwhile, she had asked Tessa to go alone to visit another woman. This was a part of her life she could not easily explain. Despite the intensity between them, Chandler would have to see for himself how truly different their worlds were. Then it would be he who would have a decision to make.

They rode together silently into a neighborhood that grew steadily more dense, steadily more shabby. She could only guess what he must be thinking. Children with unwashed faces and hollow eyes were everywhere. Most of them wandered aimlessly up and down the crowded streets filled with women in ragged shawls and drab-colored skirts, their tanned faces drawn and networked with wrinkles.

Chandler was silent as they stepped into the narrow entrance hall of a ramshackle, soot-stained tenement. Nor did he remark, in the midst of the oppressive summer heat, about the quiet, miserable moans coming from the floors above. He seemed to trust her to show him what she meant to, and in her own time.

Tessa knocked softly on the battered, weather-worn door of a third-floor apartment. She ignored the two emaciated gray rats that scampered past them as they waited for someone to answer.

"Mrs. Gialli?" Tessa called softly after a few moments, when no reply came. She waited a moment more before twisting the dull brass knob and proceeding inside. Chandler followed soundlessly behind her.

The one-room apartment was the filthiest, most vile place Chandler Tate had ever seen, and he fought with every ounce of strength he possessed not to shrink back or to let Tessa see his disgust. The stench was foul. The room was stifling.

On a bare cot, in the restless sleep of starvation, lay a young woman wrapped in a blanket, her face turned into her hand.

A newborn baby lay in the cleft of her breasts, trying to nurse. Around them were boxes of rubbish and dirty wadded rags. A small stove, the room's centerpiece, held pots caked with dry food around which flies endlessly droned.

"Good Lord!" Chandler muttered in disbelief, but Tessa ignored him, kneeling down before the young woman and brushing a long strand of moist ebony hair from her eyes.

"Giovanna," she called to her softly. "Giovanna, can you hear me?"

When the young woman made no move to reply, Tessa glanced back up at Chandler. "Get me some water, would you? There's a common sink just outside the door," she said in complete command. "Bring enough back for tea. And give me a few moments. I need to check for infection."

Having no idea what he would possibly have said in

protest, even if he could have forced the words past a throat entirely constricted by heat and shock, Chandler turned and went back out into the dim and sweltering corridor.

Reluctantly returning ten minutes later, he found the girl sitting up on the cot, her back braced by a stained un-cased pillow, and the baby suckling at an uncovered breast as Tessa pulled the blanket back down over her dirty feet.

"You're much better," Tessa said in a slow, clear voice, indicating to Chandler that the girl spoke little if any English. "Did you bring the water?" she then asked, without looking up at him.

"What shall I do with it?"

"Set it on the stove and light a fire. I've some herbs I need to add before it boils, to make her a special tea."

Tessa reached into her skirt pocket and withdrew a small fabric pouch and brought it to the stove without looking at him. Chandler saw that her moves were methodical, studied. She wasn't paying particular attention to him or his reaction to this place.

When the woman had drunk a bit of the tea, Tessa went to her sack and brought out some bread, cheese, and a bit of corned beef, then stood watching the woman devour it hungrily. They stayed an hour, tending to the woman and her child with no words exchanged, except for the few instructions she had given to Chandler.

When they finally did return to the crowded street outside the tenement, Chandler's mind was whirling with so many unanswered questions that he could not seem to push one past his lips before the others. Never in his privileged life had he seen anything so horrible as this. The division of classes in Boston was so rigid that he was entirely protected from this side of life into which Tessa had now so boldly brought him. And she had done it intentionally. Forced him to look at the squalor and misery without even an explanation.

"Have you nothing to say then?" she quietly asked as they walked up Mulberry Street.

"Were you not prolonging the misery of that poor woman

179

and her child by giving her food?" he finally asked, struggling to find his voice again.

"Perhaps I am," Tessa considered after a moment's thought. "And then again perhaps I am showing her the one bit of human kindness she has seen in this country."

"But there are so many in need all around here."

"True. And I cannot help them all. But if I can help even one," she said looking up at him, her jade eyes glittering with conviction, "then, for me, it will have been worth it."

The high-pitched sound of a young boy's fearful pleading tore them from their conversation. Both Tessa and Chandler glanced down an alley between two sagging brick buildings.

The afternoon clouds and shadows acted as a cover, but not so much that they could not see three adolescent boys cruelly dragging another by the scruff of his neck. To Tessa's horror, they were kicking him savagely. And they were laughing. A stream of blood ran in bright vermilion ribbons from his nose and lip, and it was clear to them both that the beating he had endured was not over yet.

"You there!" Chandler yelled as he sprinted into the alley. "Let the boy go!"

Tessa was a pace behind him, but it did not take long to recognize that the boys before them were part of a dangerous street gang. She knew from Mary Gallagher that they were the sort to be avoided at all cost.

Each of them was more ragged and menacing than the other; all in soiled shirts, pants and suspenders. The one who appeared to be the leader wore a dirty blue cap pushed back on his head. For effect, he scowled as he held the butt of an unlit cigarette at the corner of his mouth.

"Let him go," Chandler repeated with an absolute firmness that, for an instant, made them stop their pummeling and turn toward him.

"Yeah?" the leader laughed, as another boy held their victim firmly by the collar. "And who's gonna make us?"

"Oh, be careful," Tessa murmured urgently behind him, her heart pounding like a bass drum.

"I don't believe you understand," Chandler said in an even-toned voice, but one that had a hint of danger. "That was not a request. I will say it only once more. Let the boy go."

They laughed evilly at him and whispered something amongst themselves as one of the boys grabbed an empty bottle and smashed it against the brick wall. Broken glass glittered to the ground as an instant weapon was fashioned.

The boy crouched down, head lowered, eyes raised, the rest of the jagged glass suddenly poised at Chandler and glinting in the afternoon sun.

Tessa pulled at his sleeve. "I know you come from an entirely different background," she whispered frantically, "but you must trust me when I tell you that these are not the sort to be challenged!"

"Nor am I."

The dirty boy with the cap and squashed cigarette hunched over further. His rangy body was suddenly taut, his dirty face blazing with anger, as he prepared to strike out with the makeshift weapon.

It is finished, Tessa thought frantically. *First they will cut that splendid face and then beat him to a bloody pulp. If he survives, Chandler will despise me for having been the one to bring him to this sort of neighborhood. What on earth was I thinking,* her mind reeled, *testing an aristocrat this way, a man so ill prepared to protect himself against street urchins. He could never be a match against something like this. Never!*

"Chandler, please, let's go."

"Not without the boy."

Tessa stifled a horrified gasp with a hand pressed against her mouth, fingertips biting into her own flesh. But Chandler did not flinch. He leveled his eyes at his opponent and a blue-hued cord stood out in his neck. Then he fell absolutely still.

Even in the sheer terror of the moment, she was shocked to see a curious concentration building inside him. She looked quickly, then looked again. Chandler reminded her of some wild jungle animal preparing to strike. This, she was certain, was far more than self-defense.

The unlikely combatants stalked one another slowly, the street youth clearly perplexed by the lack of instant grappling, the sort of scrappy dog fighting to which he was accustomed. Tessa was awestruck that, by his lack of movement alone, Chandler had already thrown his opponent off guard.

"Fight me, ye lout!" the dirty-faced boy called out. Then, tired of waiting, he lunged suddenly forward with the shiny shard of glass.

In response, with a single sharp, scissor-like movement, Chandler kicked the weapon from the boy's hand and it tumbled into the alley with an echoing *clink.* When he bent to retrieve it, a second jab fell on the youth himself. The powerful kick was almost graceful as it landed beneath his dirty chin, catapulting him up and onto his back in a grunting, moaning heap.

But even though his movements were calm and artfully studied, Tessa saw a sudden flash of raw fury glittering in Chandler's eyes when she looked again. It shocked her almost as much as this amazing ability to defend himself.

Something boundless and exciting twisted inside her until it became a small, hard knot. Woven through it, she realized a moment later, was a single, annoying little thread of warning that she tried hard to dismiss.

Yes, what a complete contradiction was this man, she thought again as her heart thundered beneath her dress. So refined on the outside, so worldly wise. Yet inside, at his core, something dark and mysterious burned. It was what she had seen traces of all along, but what she had been unable to name.

He may have been handsome and rich, capable of incredible kindnesses, but Tessa was certain of it now that she had seen it: Chandler Tate also had a dangerous side.

"Who will be next?" he asked, his tone quiet, deadly.

The remaining youths, their eyes spiked now with shock and with fear, glanced down at the broken shard of glass, then back at their opponent, wisely shrinking from a form of battle against which they knew they could not win.

A moment later, they tore down the alley in the opposite direction.

"Hey, mister. Thanks," the bloodied boy muttered as he dusted himself off, then turned and slowly limped out of the alley himself.

"Oh, God, you're trembling," Chandler said when he looked over at Tessa.

Without asking for her permission, he brought her firmly against his chest, folding her tightly into his arms.

She thought of objecting. She tried, as she had earlier, in the parlor, to put a voice to her reserve. After all, they were in public, her mind tried to say. And it was daylight. But, once again, her throat was as dry as desert sand, and the words did not come.

They did not come because Tessa wanted him to touch her. She craved this deepening sensuality between them now, and the truth was that she did not care any longer when or how or where.

She could feel Chandler's chin settle on the top of her head. After a moment, she felt him press a gentle kiss into her hair. With his arms around her like this, the feel of his lips above her, his legs and hips pressed close to hers, Tessa felt like a raw mass of senses. So near to him, everything about her felt tingly and swollen.

Tessa strained silently to keep her mind from spinning off into the blackness that steadily drew her when they were together.

"My," she mouthed, trying to say something clever, as her heart still hammered and the words caught in her dry throat. "You certainly are full of surprises."

Having felt her stiffen, Chandler took a step back and let her go. He picked up his hat from the alley, dusted it off, and tapped it back on top of his head.

"After today, it seems I could say the same about you," he replied, an unexpected smile playing at the corners of his mouth, until she had no choice but to smile back.

Being with him was a little like trying to outrun a cyclone, she thought when he looked at her that way, and then finally realizing there was no choice but to give in.

But he did not press his advantage. Not yet. Instead, Chandler simply led her out of the alley with a hand pressed firmly against the small of her back.

"Might I ask where you learned to fight like that?" she inquired, her body still trembling with a curious combination of fear and exhileration. "It was the most unusual thing I have ever seen. More like dancing than fighting."

"In China," Chandler said simply as they merged into the steady stream of shabbily dressed shoppers.

"You have been to China, too?" she gasped as they stood on the street corner waiting for a loaded dray to pass before them.

"The first time it was my initiation into my father's import business. He sent me there alone to seal a deal with a silk merchant with whom he was having a good bit of difficulty."

"How long were you there?"

"He sent me for three months. I stayed nearly a year."

"And the fighting?"

"The Chinese use it for meditation, and as self-defense if the need arises."

"What an exotic place that must be."

"Much of it is. It is as big a part of the man I am today as anything. China was where I first learned that there really would be someone out there for me to love, if I just waited and believed." He leveled his eyes on her, warming her. "One day, I would love to show you Hangchow. There is a wise old gentleman there named Li Kao Chen who would take great pleasure in knowing that he had been right."

Tessa's heart leapt as he shared even more of himself. That small thread of warning she had felt earlier began to unravel in her mind before it had a chance to become anything important. A moment later, it was gone completely.

"I thought last week, you made it very clear that you

believed this sort of boy to be beyond help," she said with her own sly grin once her heart had slowed enough to consider what had just occurred. "You discouraged me from giving my money to one of them, if you recall."

"I do."

"So why did you risk your life defending another of them now?"

"Because it was three against one," he replied simply. "Most unsavory odds, I would say. And because you hoped that I would."

"I didn't ask you to do it."

"No . . . but your eyes did. And, also, I really cannot bear to see anyone who has been made the underdog." *Not since my youth, when I was made one myself by my father.*

"No one has ever gone to such lengths for me," she said quietly. "You remind me of a storybook hero."

"Oh, I'm no hero, Tessa. I am just a man. Believe me."

"At the very least, a quite wonderful man."

Looks can be deceiving, his mind taunted him to say.

"I'm happy you believe so," he said instead.

They were on First Street near a small tree-covered square before he said, "All right then, your turn. Since I have been honest with you, suppose you tell me what coming down here was all about."

Tessa led him to a bench beneath two arched trees, trying to choose her words carefully so that he would understand what had driven her. As they looked at one another a warm wind moved the tips of their hair.

"When we were together last, you took me into your world," she began tentatively, her voice catching on the words. "Today, I wanted to take you into mine. I thought it only right that you know exactly the sort of girl you had asked to marry you. Not the one you dressed up and who pretended to fit into society, hoping to please you."

Chandler's brows arched. "Is that what you thought I wanted you to do? Pretend?"

"I'm not certain," she answered, looking away from him, as the little wisps of copper hair near her eyes shimmered in the filtered sunlight. "But what I do know is that I am not just Tessa Murphy, the Irishman's daughter from Tenth Street. Nor am I only the grand girl I saw in the mirror dressed up for the theater. To these unfortunate people I am Tessa, the girl who helps the midwife."

She took a breath but she could not bring herself to look back at him. She was vulnerable now and she must not look into those eyes until she had told him everything.

"I have helped bring babies into this world, and lately, I have helped to bury others. I have tended the sick at Mrs. Gallagher's side when they could afford no one else. And I have watched them die when no amount of her herbs or prayers could save them."

Finally, Tessa gathered her courage and looked over boldly at him, defiantly, almost. This was what she was, and she had told him. Openly. Honestly. "It is hardly the background of a proper gentleman's wife."

"I don't give two figs about what is proper, Tessa!" he declared hotly, clutching her shoulders with two, vise-like hands and making her face him. "And I am certainly not ashamed of what you have done to help those less fortunate than yourself. As a matter of fact, it makes me rather ashamed of how little I have done."

"I suppose I could have spared you this afternoon," she said reflectively, "but you may as well know now that I despise secrets. Something like this would not be right hidden between husband and wife."

Chandler's eyes were suddenly bright with surprise. He had heard the words, words he was not certain she would ever speak in relation to the two of them. Perhaps because of his surprise, he did not hear the conviction with which she had spoken them.

Perhaps, he thought later, it was because he had not wanted to hear.

"Then you have come to a decision?"

"It is one thing to know something about a person, Chandler. It is quite something else again entirely to see it for yourself. I wanted you to come here with me first and then to give you a chance to withdraw your proposal if the truth of my life was all too unbearable."

"I have no intention of withdrawing it. If anything, today I've realized how much I want you in my life," he said firmly. He took her hands and kissed each one of them gently. His lips were moist and warm and wanting.

"You asked me once if I loved you."

"And you said you were not certain if you knew what love was anymore."

"Well I am certain now."

Tessa tipped her head as she looked at him. "So you do love me then?"

"Quite hopelessly."

In the silvery shadows of the setting sun, with a gentle breeze blowing between them, Tessa reached into the deep pocket in her skirt and withdrew the grand betrothal ring he had given her. It glinted and sparkled in the fading amber sunlight as she handed it to him.

"Put it on for me?"

Chandler's lips lengthened into a smile as he took her hand. "You'll never be sorry about this, Tessa," he murmured. "I promise you."

Then see that she never discovers the truth, the dark voice in his mind echoed back.

Chapter

23

THE TRAIN CLATTERED OVER THE TRACKS AS TESSA GAZED DOWN at the new gold wedding band on her finger. Less than an hour before, in his suite at the Hoffman House, surrounded by Mary Gallagher, the Baldwin sisters, and the hotel manager, she had become Mrs. Chandler Tate. Already she was having trouble believing that it had actually happened.

Tessa closed her eyes and lay her head back against the crisp piece of white linen draped over the top of her crimson velvet-covered seat. She was glad it had happened. It was what she had wanted more than anything in the world. She just hadn't counted on missing everyone so soon.

Inside of her small carpetbag was her mother's pendant, two cotton handkerchiefs from the Baldwin sisters, and a pouch of herbs from Mary Gallagher. "Take these to remember your life here," she had lovingly bid her. "Perhaps one day there will be someone in Boston you will know how to help."

"A penny for your thoughts."

"Oh," Tessa sighed, trying valiantly not to cry again. "Today, they're worth far more than that."

"You miss them, do you?"

She twisted the new gold band around on her finger and looked over at him. "It is really so silly. I've been gone such a short time."

"Time has nothing to do with feelings," he said kindly, as shiny tears misted her eyes. "And you are the sort who loves with your whole heart."

She tried her best to smile. "How do you know that?"

"Because I know the sort of woman you are. But even if I didn't before now, it would be plain enough to see at this moment on that lovely face of yours."

Tessa gazed around the opulent train car as it swayed rhythmically through the countryside. For a moment, she forgot the pain she felt, still in awe of the plush ruby seats, the shiny mahogany, and the velvet draperies tied away from the window with gold-fringed tassels.

She ran her hands nervously across her lap smoothing away the wrinkles in her beautiful new topaz-colored traveling costume. Chandler was trying his best to be understanding, but today her life had been changed forever, in a sweeping, fairy-tale ceremony, and the reality of that quite scared her to death.

"Would you like a taste of brandy?" he asked, seeing how pale she looked, and how frightened. "I've a flask in my coat pocket."

"I don't think so."

"It really is all right to be nervous, you know," Chandler assured her, gently covering the hand with which she was gripping the arm of her seat. "Can I let you in on a little secret?"

Thinking of all the secrets she knew that he must have— about his life, about China, about the wife who had died mysteriously—she said, "Oh, I do wish you would."

"I am actually quite apprehensive myself."

"What could *you* possibly have to be apprehensive about?"

"This is quite a life change for me as well, you know. My children do not expect me to return to Boston with a wife."

Tessa gasped, and her copper brows arched. "Didn't you tell them that you had met someone and proposed marriage?"

By the startled expression on Chandler's face, the slight widening of the eyes, she knew the answer. "Your sister doesn't expect you to return with a wife either, does she?"

"Daphne had her own plans for me where marriage was concerned."

"There was someone else she wanted for you?"

Better she knew now, Chandler decided wisely. "For some time, my sister has been pressing me to marry," he confessed, "but the young woman is not someone I care for."

Tessa paused for a moment contemplatively, then lifted her chin and boldly met his gaze. "Does this young woman love you?"

"I'm not certain if people like Felicity actually love anyone other than themselves, and that is not at all the sort of influence I want for my children," he answered truthfully. Then he turned away from her as a sharp jolt of guilt tore through him. Chandler gazed out of the window at the blur of lush hills, farms, and stone fences passing by.

The guilt came from not having confessed the whole truth, the dark secret that he and Daphne shared. He wanted to tell Tessa. She deserved that sort of honesty. He simply couldn't. Not yet.

But Daphne knew the truth and she had gone on to use it as leverage against him at every turn since that one dark and terrible night two years ago. With any luck at all, his sister had learned her lesson about trying to manipulate him at last, and the things he kept pressed down in his heart were truths that Tessa would never need to know.

Tessa stepped from the train and onto the station platform with unsteady legs. She had one of Chandler's arms for support. Her smooth face was ashen once again and her lips were dry. A lump of apprehension closed her throat and she longed for a single glass of that wonderful champagne to steady her frayed nerves.

It had been such a long and hot ride to Boston. Hours of swaying and clacking and ceaseless vibration. And there was still so much ahead of them that would have to occur before this day was through. She had Chandler's children and his sister yet to meet.

"Are you all right?" Chandler asked with a note of concern as they moved together into the crowd of people all rushing around them, some with valises, others with tickets held up in their hands.

"I shall be fine," she answered, trying to convince herself as much as Chandler with the tone of her reply.

Out on the street in a shower of pink, late-afternoon light, they were met by a shiny midnight-blue carriage, as sleek and elegant as the one in which they had ridden to the theater and Delmonico's. A spindly little man with a receding tawny hairline, bushy mustache, and beady, dark-rimmed eyes limped toward them, one leg shorter than the other.

"Ah, there you are, Douglas. Right on time," Chandler said with an offhand wave and an easy smile as the man approached.

"Good to have you home again, sir."

"Thank you, Douglas. And you shall be the first to meet the new Mrs. Tate. Tessa, this is our driver, Douglas Cramer."

The coachman stepped back and then breathed a little whistle of surprise. "Does Miss Daphne know about this?" he asked cautiously, his hat in his hands.

"No, Douglas, she doesn't. And I'll thank you not to go ruining the surprise."

"Oh no, sir," he huffed a sigh of relief. "She'll hear nothing of it from me." After he had helped them up, Douglas tipped his head inside the carriage and added, "I shall retrieve your baggage now, sir, if that will be all?"

Chandler simply nodded. Once they were alone again, and the door was closed, he heard Tessa's quick intake of breath. "You have your own carriage and driver?"

"No, Tessa," he smiled, a smile full of masculine confidence as he covered the back of her hand with his own. "Now *we* have our own carriage and driver. Everything else that I have now is yours, too. To be a Tate, you need only to feel like a Tate. Remember that."

"There are so many new things to remember," she replied and he could feel her hand trembling beneath his.

"And there will be a good deal more of them before this week is through. Of that we can be certain," Chandler said, now patting her hand to try and calm her. "But you shall grow accustomed to all of it soon enough, I promise. Remember, I have great faith in your ability to handle all of this."

"Does that include your sister?" Tessa asked with a wary smile.

"You mustn't be afraid of Daphne. I'm certain that, at first, she will bluster as she always does, but in no time at all you will have all of Boston eating out of that lovely little hand of yours."

"And if I don't?"

"Then I shall be there to protect you until you do," he countered in a deep, resonating tone of complete assurance. "And the devil take anyone who tries to interfere with that!"

When he saw a reluctant smile turn up the corners of her mouth, Chandler grazed them with his own warm lips. He longed to do far more. But tonight, he thought, would come soon enough.

"More than anything, my sweet bride, I want to make you as happy as you have made me," he said huskily. "And I have every intention of making you forget there was ever a time when you did not have me in your life."

"That may prove a very difficult task," she countered softly, still feeling the sting of guilt for what she had done to Brian.

Chandler pressed a kiss onto her cheek and then lingered there a moment, near to her, wanting her to remember what he had been unable to forget: the touch, the sensual charge between them.

"Nevertheless, I believe that I am up to that task," he said with confidence. "And now we have all the time in the world to find out."

Beacon Hill was a rolling, elegant warren of red brick, ivy, and sparkling gas streetlamps in the setting sun as their carriage made its way steadily up Charles Street. Tessa gazed out of the window in awe at the stately townhouses with their graceful ironwork and their pillared porticos.

As closely built as they were, Tessa could see that each lavish house had its own distinctive flair. There were those with classical touches: tall drawing-room windows and formidable stone steps leading up to a variety of grand entrances. Some even had stylishly formal gardens in front. Finally, as the sun set completely on the graceful hill, their carriage turned into a sweeping drive and cobbled carriageway.

The red-brick house before them was twice as grand as most of the others, shuttered in elegant black lacquer and ornamented in green ivy. Lights shimmered from its long windows.

"You live here?" she gulped, pressing back the utter shock as the carriage lurched to a halt.

"All of my life."

"Welcome home, Mister Tate," an elegant portly man said, dipping into a formal bow before he reached up to take Tessa's hand.

"Thank you, Jennings," Chandler replied with an easy smile. "Jennings is our butler, darling," he explained in a whisper as they stood in the carriageway before a black-lacquered door at the top of three steps.

"He will be indispensable in helping you learn all that you will need to know in these first few weeks. He can be gruff, but once you make friends with him, and I have no doubt that you will, Jennings is a friend you shall have for life."

After the black-and-white-clad butler had helped the coachman with their luggage, both servants returned to stand formally before Chandler.

"Is my sister here?" he asked, and for the first time all day, Tessa heard a crack in his usually deep, confident tone.

"She is indeed, sir," Jennings replied. "And if I may say so, sir, she is in quite a state. It seems that the children have been firing stones at passing carriages from the knoll to occupy themselves this afternoon."

Tessa stifled a grin, happy to learn that not everyone in Boston was without a sense of humor or a spark of mischief. The double tempo of her heart began once again to slow.

"Well, I would just as soon you hear it from me, as somewhere else," Chandler proclaimed. "Tessa, here, and I were married this morning."

"Congratulations, sir," the butler nodded, but not before he exchanged a worried glance with the coachman, who stood beside him. "But if I may ask, what about Miss Pettigrew?"

"I am a married man now, Jennings," Chandler said firmly and with what Tessa thought was a hint of pride. "The status of Miss Pettigrew is no longer a concern of mine."

"Of course, sir."

"And Jennings," Chandler said, with a hand placed firmly on his butler's slim shoulder. "As you might imagine, the new Mrs. Tate will be needing a good deal of patience and understanding during her period of adjustment here. Especially these first few days. I hope that I may count on you."

David Jennings, a stout man with a pasty ivory face and full burgundy-colored lips pressed into what appeared to be a permanent pout, gave Tessa a cool, appraising look.

"Why, of course, sir."

The inside of the Tate home on Mount Vernon Street was like a vast, elegant mausoleum, Tessa thought as she moved slowly behind Chandler across the polished wood floor and into a grand two-story entry hall with a sweeping mahogany staircase as its focal point. Her eyes could barely take in the splendor.

Spread across the floors to warm them was a rich Brussels carpet, centered with a polished cherrywood table and a huge bouquet of freshly cut flowers. Olive-colored velvet draperies hung on heavy brass rods closing out the rest of the world, and the remaining bit of afternoon sunlight. The world closed off to her was one that Tessa missed already.

Just then, two small, impeccably dressed children and a huge gray scruffy dog scampered down the staircase. Both children were blond with wide blue eyes. The boy wore a navy suit with brass buttons and knee pants. The girl was in a flouncy dress of robin's-egg blue, and high black button shoes.

"Papa!" they cried in unison, charging into his arms as the dog barked and whimpered.

Tessa watched the little girl with her perfectly curled rings of golden hair climb onto Chandler's one bent knee and wrap her arms around his neck.

"Aunt Daphne was going to make us go to bed without seeing you, but James and I refused."

"Yes, I've heard you have made your Aunt quite cross with you this evening," he replied, fighting a smile.

Alice averted her brilliant blue eyes guiltily, hiding the mischief there behind mock repentance. "It really wasn't so bad as all that, papa," she said sweetly. "We were just having a bit of fun."

"The way you did at Regina Caldecott's expense? And Winifred Davis's before her?"

"What did you bring us, Papa?" asked the little boy, who stood beside his older sister with a wild tousle of golden hair and a small nose full of freckles, shining up at Chandler.

"Well," he beamed, and drew in a breath. "This time I brought you both a very big surprise."

Alice tried to reach into his coat pocket, the customary hiding place for the trinkets he often brought home to them. "Oh no, darling," he chuckled. "You'll not find it in there."

Both children looked around him and Alice slid from his

knee, her smile fading into a quizzical expression. Chandler stood back up, slipping his arm around Tessa's waist in a show of support for her.

"This is *our* surprise, children. This wonderful lady beside me has become my wife."

At the very moment he spoke the words, they all became aware of the formidable gaunt figure looming in the parlor doorway. The imposing woman in wine-red satin very intentionally cleared her throat with a tiny cough. A chill of silence fell over the house. Tessa was certain she heard the coachman who stood behind her gasp and sputter as though his very breath had been cut off.

A faint thread of terror wound through her, too, as they all gazed up in silent surprise at the woman whose slim face bore the sternest, most disapproving expression Tessa had ever seen. She felt impaled on the woman's steady gaze, and fought not to shrink backwards toward the door.

"What a surprise, indeed," the woman finally said with a brittle, yet absolutely inflectionless voice, as she twisted a long white rope of pearls at the end of reed-long fingers.

Chandler's arm tightened protectively around Tessa's waist. "Daphne," he said coolly, formally, "I expected you to have gone home for the evening."

"Oh, I'm certain you did. But I wouldn't have missed this for the world," she said arching a single dagger-sharp blond brow disapprovingly.

"You're our new mother?" James asked, suddenly ripping a jagged hole in the mounting tension.

Tessa glanced down at the matching wide-eyed expressions of surprise on the two small faces. In spite of the cold knot that was tightening in her chest, she managed to smile.

"You can call me Tessa if you like," she said sweetly, bending down to their level. "And who might this lovely creature be?" she asked, stroking the face of the dog who licked her palm and wagged his shaggy gray tail in canine approval.

"This is Mayflower," James replied. "He never likes anyone."

"But I think he likes *you!*" Alice chimed gleefully.

"Chandler, if this is some sort of joke to get back at me after our last conversation," Daphne said as she advanced into the foyer, silencing her niece and nephew.

"I assure you this is no joke, Daphne," Chandler answered with urbane reserve. "Tessa and I were married in New York this morning."

"Then you really are our new mother!" Alice smiled up at her, clearly enamored by the beautiful young woman and seemingly unaware of the tension mounting between Daphne and Chandler.

"Tessa?" Daphne's voice rang with disapproval. "What sort of a name is that?"

"Irish," Tessa replied directly, not missing a beat. "And so is Murphy, my family name, if there is to be a question of that."

The memory of the expression on Eudora Dunne's face that night at the theater had left her little option other than defense when faced now with the same sort of assault.

"I think we had better get you children ready for bed," Jennings intervened, shepherding both of them from the mounting tension and back toward the staircase.

With one foot on the first step, Alice pivoted back around. "Will you be here in the morning, Tessa?"

"Oh, she will be here, darling," Chandler smiled. "That is a promise. Now off to bed with both of you!"

Daphne turned on her heel, her skirts fanning out around her, once the children were out of earshot. "Chandler, I would like to speak with you privately," she said, more a command than a request, as she disappeared into the parlor with the expectation that her brother would follow.

Once again, Chandler put a hand to the small of Tessa's back as if to suggest that she move forward. "Oh, no," Tessa gulped. "She wants to speak with you alone."

"Anything my sister has to say, Tessa, now can be said in front of you."

"I don't know." She shook her head and whispered urgently, "she looks awfully angry."

"Believe me," he said, nudging his new wife slightly forward, "one way or another she will get over it."

"Come in and close the door," Daphne commanded, and her stern voice was like the crack of a whip.

She stood at one of the long windows, holding back the green velvet drapery, gazing down into the lamplit street below. When she heard the tall doors close, she spun around, her wine-red satin gown sweeping the floor.

"I said privately."

"If you have something to say, Daphne, I suggest you say it."

Chandler's sister moved toward them slowly, viciously, like a panther stalking prey. Tessa was taken aback by how formidable a woman she appeared, in spite of her shiny blond hair, sapphire eyes, and ivory skin. She had difficulty now believing that Daphne and Chandler were even related.

Daphne's perfectly featured face was pinched, and her honey-colored lips were pursed as though in perpetual frustration. Her eyes were not even the same brilliant sapphire as Chandler's. They were unresponsive. Cold. Ice blue.

"What are you trying to prove with this, Chandler?"

"I believe I made myself quite clear on the subject of your interfering in my affairs."

A sudden flush mottled Daphne's cheeks, and she pressed a palm to her forehead at his reply. "What on earth could you have been thinking? Dear Lord, how long have you even known the girl?"

"No matter what I offer by way of explanation," he countered with a seething calm, "the result will remain the same."

"Oh!" Daphne sputtered behind a row of pearl-white teeth. "Did you do this just to spite me for trying to see you and Felicity together?"

"I married Tessa for love, Daphne. A concept it is most unlikely you will ever understand."

Her body tense and constricted, Daphne stepped toward

Tessa. It was an unexpected lurching movement that caught Tessa entirely by surprise.

"Murphy, was it?" Daphne asked her, pressing her cruel tone into the deathly cold. "I believe I have a seamstress with the same name as that. Chandler, this girl is no more suited to be your wife than any of the rest of our hired help."

Chandler's face turned to stone. "Get out of my house!"

"I am trying to save this family!"

"By destroying me?"

"By helping you out of your mistakes, just as I have always done. Wasn't one disastrous union enough for you?"

"I warned you not to push me!" he declared, as the vein pulsed in his neck and his face filled with hot, angry blood. "I told you that you would never win. My life is my own to live as I choose, no matter what you or anyone else thinks! Now, get out!"

"From the kind-hearted little child you once were," Daphne countered, "you have really turned into a terribly selfish man."

"I learned from the best," he shot back scornfully.

Tessa was certain her legs were about to give way. She barely moved, her lips parted in fascination and disbelief. This had been the longest day of her life already and quite clearly it was not over yet.

In all of her young years she had never seen such cruelty or animosity between siblings and it was seemingly all because of her. Suddenly, she felt a masculine hand on her shoulder that did not belong to Chandler.

"We did not ring for you, Jennings!" Daphne spat bitterly.

"I merely thought, ma'am, that Mrs. Tate has had a long journey and perhaps she would like to be shown to her room while you and Mr. Tate conclude your . . ." he stumbled on the word intentionally, "your discussion."

"We do not pay you to think, Jennings!" Daphne chided. "And furthermore, I shall thank you to remember that since they were only married this morning, she is not, thank the good Lord, Mrs. Tate yet!"

Chandler's reply was to turn back toward Tessa. She could see that his expression had changed. It was full of more anger and resentment than she had ever seen displayed on anyone. "Perhaps it would be best if you went with Jennings, darling. It has been a dreadfully long day and you will want to freshen up, I'm sure, before we retire."

He brushed his lips lingeringly across Tessa's cheek and then took her hands in his. Chandler was trying his best to stay his rage enough to be tender with her.

"I shall be up in a little while, hmm? Go ahead."

In the midst of such confusion, and such hostility, Tessa was only too willing to acquiesce.

She let the courtly butler lead her from the parlor, grateful to be out of the fray. But not before she heard her new husband say to his own sister, "I want you out of this house now, Daphne. Tonight, I cannot stand the sight of you!"

After they had climbed the winding staircase, the corridor down which they passed was long and dark. Only two of the old-style wall sconces had been lit, but Jennings strode at a firm pace past their flickering light, leading the way.

"Thank you for that," Tessa said when he stopped to turn the brass knob on a heavy white door.

"The master requested that I look out for you," he said, with straight-faced formality, his chin tipped upward. "I was merely doing my job, ma'am."

"Kindness is kindness, Mr. Jennings," she said sweetly and then let him lead her inside.

The bedroom to which she was shown was bigger than both her father's and her own put together back in Mrs. Gallagher's boardinghouse. Her eyes took in with amazement the magnificent canopy bed draped in pale blue and dressed with crisp lace-edged linen that was its centerpiece. The rest of the room was equally impressive.

There were lacy white undercurtains beneath blue draperies. The wallpaper was French, with scrolls of blue and gold on a white background. A large bureau and washstand and a chair covered in blue-and-salmon-colored silk completed the room. Beside the bed was a dressing table topped with beautiful glass bottles, a hair brush, and a gold-framed mirror. An elegant blue and green Turkish carpet warmed the floor and tall, paned windows ushered in the golden glow of the streetlamps below.

Beside the bed, a young woman in black, with a pert white cap and an apron tied in a bow at the back, bobbed a curtsy then stood with her hands clasped neatly at her waist. The faint hint of a smile was on her full mouth. Like Tessa, her hair was red. But the shade was paler, less vibrant, and there were no golden highlights to brighten her small, round face. When Tessa approached, the girl nodded properly.

"This is Kathleen," Jennings informed Tessa in his sturdy baritone. "She will attend to all of your personal needs. Tomorrow the rest of the staff shall be presented to you formally. It might also comfort you to know," he added, "that Kathleen, too, is Irish."

Tessa was surprised by this second show of kindness, especially after he had just been so curt. She smiled appreciatively up at him for it. But as quickly as he had lost his reserve, it had returned again.

"The bath and wardrobe are through there," he said coolly, indicating a small, white-painted door near her dressing table. "And beyond that is the master's bedroom."

"Mr. Tate has his own—" she began to ask, but her voice broke off when she saw the disapproval lighting the butler's cool, gray eyes. "Oh."

It was clear by his scolding expression that she was not to address such matters as had crossed her mind, at least not in the presence of a male servant. There was so much to learn, thought Tessa, wondering how on earth she would ever survive this.

"Mister Tate takes his breakfast at nine," Jennings informed her, swiftly changing the subject as he moved back toward the open door. Then, placing his hand firmly on the brass knob, he turned back around. To Tessa's great surprise, there was another flicker of kindness in his eyes.

"It might also serve you well to know that Mrs. Forrester

does not arrive to help with the children until shortly past ten each morning."

"Thank you for that, Mr. Jennings," she said with a weary smile for the gift of time he had just given her. She had seen something far more important. In spite of his great reserve, he was offering to help her, and in his look there had been the first spark of friendship between them beginning to form.

Chapter

24

"SO YOU'RE SURPRISED THAT SOMEONE LIKE ME HAS MARRIED THE master," Tessa said plainly to the maid as she moved across the room and sank down onto the edge of the grand four-poster bed.

"'Tis only that we always thought if anyone was goin' to capture him, it was goin' to be Miss Pettigrew."

"Yes," sighed Tessa, fumbling at the soft coil of hair atop her head until it tumbled onto her back and shoulders in a copper cascade. "Apparently there is a great deal of that particular sentiment going around."

Kathleen blushed. "Forgive me, ma'am. I only meant—"

"It's all right, Kathleen," Tessa said, managing a weak half smile. "You won't have to tiptoe around me. If you have something to say, say it, and we shall get along just fine."

"Yes, ma'am," she curtsied again.

As Tessa rubbed her tired feet she gazed up at a face that was pixieish, with a small, slightly pink, button nose, wide blue eyes with long dark lashes, and ruddy round cheeks. It was a sweet face to match the young maid's disposition.

"And you need not do that for my benefit either," Tessa said of the deferential curtsy.

"Oh, but I must." Kathleen's face blanched. "'Tis what's expected o' the hired help here, ma'am."

"My father, who was very wise, always said that the task does not make the man, Kathleen. Character does. I assume that applied to housemaids and milkmen's daughters as well. You'll not need to curtsy to me in this house. At least not when we're in private."

The young maid moved toward Tessa a little more freely, the corners of her mouth lifting into a slight smile. "Shall I help ye prepare for bed then? Ye must be tired after such a long journey."

The clock on the marble fireplace mantel at the end of the bed ticked steadily toward the hour of eight, but to Tessa it felt far later. In the space of a single day, her life had been altered completely. She recalled Jennings's remark that tomorrow she would meet the rest of the staff. Already there were three, she thought in complete amazement. One to oversee the house, one to care for its inhabitants, and one to take them wherever they wished to go. How many more could a family, even a wealthy one, possibly need above that?

She had known there would be challenges ahead in her new life. But no matter how she tried, faced now with the startling reality of that life, Tessa could not help feeling entirely overwhelmed. It was such a grand place, the walls of which were lined with priceless tapestries and daunting gold-framed portraits. A home where her bedroom was as big as the entire first floor of Mrs. Gallagher's boarding-house. One thing was certain. A milkman's daughter would never grow accustomed to this sort of opulence. Never.

"So, how many of you are there?" Tessa asked of Kathleen as she unfastened the back of her beautiful topaz-colored traveling costume.

"Servants, ma'am?"

"Yes, servants."

Kathleen stepped back, lifted up her hands and proceeded

to count on her fingers in a whisper as Tessa sat back on the edge of the bed in her stockings and chemise.

"There are that many that you need to count?" she asked, her sleepy eyes widening in disbelief.

"There is Jennings of course, cook, cook's helper, the parlor maid, chamber maid," she paused a moment, her eyes cast upward in studied calculation. "There is the laundress, the sewing woman . . . and me. We haven't been able to keep a governess for the children for long. I suspect that is why Mrs. Forrester spends so much time here these days."

"Nine? There are to be nine servants who work only in this house?" Tessa asked incredulously.

"And 'tis true enough," Kathleen smiled and lowered her voice for what she was about to say, "that Mrs. Forrester keeps everyone of us busy, and then some."

After Tessa had washed with cool water and the most wonderfully sweet-scented soap, Kathleen moved to help her change into a long white nightdress. When Tessa stiffened at the maid's nearness, Kathleen stepped back.

"It'll only be a bit easier if I help ye, ma'am," Kathleen said tentatively.

"I've been dressing and undressing myself since I was a child. I certainly have never needed anyone's help before."

"Things are done differently here, ma'am. There's an order to everythin'."

"Apparently so."

"Do ye still wish me to leave ye to do it yerself then?"

Tessa inhaled two sharp breaths and looked back at the kind face of the maid, who still stood holding up the nightgown. She felt a little foolish for having been so harsh. But this was really too much and all of it was coming so quickly.

"I can undress myself, but I would be glad for the company while I do it," she muttered, her lips lifting slightly as she moved the two steps nearer Kathleen and the nightgown.

Once she had changed, Tessa took her single carpetbag

and carefully began to withdraw her own personal items, laying them on the dressing table, which was already decorated with expensive silver-topped scent bottles, a mother-of-pearl calling-card box, and a silver comb and mirror set.

To that, she added her own old wooden hairbrush with some of the bristles missing, two hair combs, a painted metal box, rusting at the hinges, and filled with hat pins. Beside it she gently placed her parents' wedding picture, set in a chipped oval frame.

It took no more than a moment to see the mistake she had made.

Only a spasm of surprise had crossed Kathleen's face when Tessa looked up at her, but that had been enough. Mirrored back at her was how meagre and out of place her things were here amid the grandeur, and she was embarrassed for having brought them out at all.

It was not likely that she would ever be mistaken for a grand society lady, she knew that. But Tessa had come away from New York with great hopes at least of blending in.

Carefully, and without showing any emotion at all, she packed each of her things back into the bag and closed it.

"There'll be time enough for that later," she said.

"Yes, ma'am."

Kathleen then led her to the turned-down bed. "I'm certain Mr. Tate will be comin' up any time, ma'am," she offered kindly. She could see how weary the master's new bride was, how out of place, and she could only guess what a shock it must have been to come all the way from New York only to have been faced with her bridegroom's very formidable and most unwelcoming sister.

"Shall I be brushin' yer hair until he comes, then?"

Tessa's mind jerked from the haze of fatigue and embarrassment. With those words, she was jolted into remembering that she and Chandler were man and wife, and very soon it would be time for her to *submit,* whatever that meant precisely. She would be called upon to do her duty.

Mrs. Gallagher had explained to her only that a man had certain physical needs, a desire for closeness with his wife.

And that, from the wedding night on, that duty, vague and frightening as it sounded, was part of the commitment of marriage. Mary had not been able to bring herself to elaborate further upon what exactly was going to happen.

Tessa thought about the idea of closeness and physical needs. It made her think of the way it felt to have Chandler touch her, the foreign, wonderful feelings it always kindled inside of her. A little tingle of desire crawled up her spine as she remembered the taste of his tongue in her mouth. She could almost feel his body pressed against hers, strong arms linked around the small of her back. How submitting to that little bit of ecstasy could be a duty, she hadn't a clue.

When Tessa nodded approval, Kathleen took up the long, silver-handled hairbrush and began the slow, rhythmic one hundred strokes she had been taught to do by the last Mrs. Chandler Tate. Her hand followed the brush down the thick, cascading red-gold mane and in no more than a moment, Tessa felt her eyes once again begin to weigh heavily. She sat still on the bed feeling utterly exhausted and entirely incapable of movement.

Until the hinges creaked and the door opened.

Kathleen stopped her brushing. Tessa's weary eyes snapped open. "I'll be leaving ye now, sir, if there's nothin' else," the maid said with another of her little curtsies. She made her way with soft, quick steps to the door, which Chandler had left ajar.

Once Kathleen had seen herself out of the bedroom, Chandler came to Tessa, who was still sitting on the edge of the bed. The brief interlude of calm she had felt exploded in a thundering wave of anticipation.

"Are you all right?" Chandler asked, looming tall and handsome over her, his rich voiced filled with concern.

"Just a bit tired."

"I shouldn't wonder."

By the soft golden lamplight, she had a kind of cameo loveliness reserved for works of art, he thought. His new wife was genuinely exquisite, not like the other women he knew who worked so hard at the presentation of their beauty. And yet beneath her graceful reserve was still that spark of fire. It was that same spark that had given her the courage to stand up to the Dunnes at the theater in New York, and to Daphne tonight. Chandler must take great care never to underestimate that heady combination, he reminded himself, with a wry twist of his lips and a jolt of pure desire for her.

"You handled yourself splendidly with my sister," he softly said. "But then I knew you would."

"You could have warned me."

"Would you still have come away with me if I had?"

"Probably not," she shook her head.

A smile lurked at the corners of his mouth, those soft dimples digging into his cheeks, and Tessa felt her heart lurch. For a moment, she had lost herself in Chandler's dangerously handsome face, so much so that she had forgotten that she was sitting here before him in nothing more than a thin cotton nightdress. But Chandler gazed admiringly at her. His eyes alone said she need not be embarrassed. That this was right and natural between them.

Tenderly, Chandler reached out and ran a single long finger across her shoulder, covered with the clinging white cotton. Through it, her flesh was warm. Smooth. He felt her respond to his touch. Saw her eyes flutter to a soft close as her head tipped back slightly. God, he had waited such a long time for this.

He fought a tempestuous battle inside of himself not to press her back against the pillows right then and there. Not to kiss her until they both ached with the longing. Not to mold her tightly against the length of his own steadily aroused body until she cried out to him for the full force of his ardor. This was her first time, he reminded himself, and she deserved more tenderness and patience than that.

The tight expression on his face softened, but he was still trying desperately to quell the lust that had surged up powerfully inside of him. He struggled to catch his breath.

"Over all, I think things went quite well tonight with Daphne, for a first meeting."

"You call that well?" she sputtered, recalling the glacial silence and the alternating anger that had marked her arrival on Beacon Hill.

"Considering my sister," he replied, unable to hide a grin, "yes I do."

Tessa shifted on the bed. Chandler's eyes followed her. Her face tightened in anticipation of something more that was yet to come. Chandler saw her shiver as he sat down on the edge of the bed beside her. I will be tender and gentle, he thought as his heart slammed against his chest, his body quaking with desire. More gentle than I have ever been, and the pain she fears shall last no longer than a heartbeat.

At first she was every bit as rigid in his arms as he was hard and aching. But his hand curved around the nape of her neck and the caress of his tongue became soft and languorous between her lips. He coaxed them gently apart, pressing her to kiss him back.

When at last he could feel her soften and begin to respond, Chandler reached around her, his arms moving down, tightening across her back and pulling her closer, until she relaxed enough to let him press her back onto the satin coverlet.

"Oh, my beautiful angel bride," he murmured against her lips. "You are everything that is right in my world."

His kiss deepened then and became urgent as his pliant fingers moved down the length of her, then slid back up to her breasts, touching every rise, every curve of her splendid young body. Pure lust roared through Chandler at that moment, and he pressed himself hard against her, wanting her to feel the full weight of his desire against her trembling thighs.

For Tessa, at first, the sound that followed was dull and distant as her body began slowly to melt beneath Chandler's. But after a moment, she recognized it as a soft, insistent rapping at the hallway door.

Panicked, and remembering Chandler's formidable sister, Tessa bolted upright on the bed, nervously pressing the opening of her nightdress, which Chandler had parted, back down over her chest.

"It's only Jennings, darling," he said raggedly, trying to temper his straining body in the face of her fear. "Come in," he called out and moved back to the edge of the bed.

"The champagne you requested, sir," Jennings said formally, bearing forth a silver tray with a green glass bottle of champagne and two crystal glasses.

"Thank you, Jennings," Chandler said, looking reassuringly back at his wife. "That will be all for this evening."

"Very good, sir," Jennings replied with a little nod. He turned and quietly left the room.

"I took the liberty of having this brought up. I hope you don't mind," Chandler explained as he poured each of them a glass. "I recalled how much you enjoyed it at Delmonico's, and I thought it might help. Today could not have been an easy one for you."

She drew in a long, steadying breath as he handed her a glass and lifted his own. Crystal glinted in the lamplight. Perhaps if they could just talk a while, he thought, and she could drink her champagne, then his sweet young wife could relax enough to chase that hint of fear from her eyes and the apprehension from her body.

After all, Chandler was not even certain if she knew precisely what was about to happen between them and he so wanted this first time to be perfect for her.

"I know that it seems a bit disconcerting now, but you will grow accustomed to having servants soon enough," Chandler assured her.

"I don't know about that." Tessa climbed off of the bed and glanced around the room with a timorous, shy expression. "This was your wife's room, wasn't it?"

"Yes it was. But that was a long time ago."

"You told me two years."

"A lifetime," he replied evenly, then averted his eyes. But not before Tessa saw how his blue eyes had grown suddenly remote.

She despised that. Any talk of Cynthia Tate seemed to

force a kind of wall between them. But she was not going to be so easily put off. Not now that she was his wife. Not when she had a right to know, and knowing could only bring them closer.

"What was she like? Cynthia, I mean."

"That is not exactly the sort of subject I was hoping to speak about on our wedding night," he bristled.

Tessa saw his face change. The wall grew more impenetrable.

"I don't mind, honestly," she said, fingering the full glass, desperate to find a way to make him feel safe enough to share the most intimate parts of his past now that she was his wife. "Have you any pictures?"

"Not one," Chandler snapped, sounding unexpectedly harsh, feeling his own skin break into gooseflesh.

What Tessa saw was his square jaw tighten. "Not even for your children?"

He drew in a short, difficult breath and looked back at Tessa, pushing away the memories that came to him each time he was forced to consider the past. They were dark memories that, like a thick caldron of poison, had been already stirred once tonight between him and Daphne.

"You needn't avoid talking about her to spare my feelings, you know."

"Rest assured, that is not what I am doing."

"But no pictures, no memories for Alice and James?"

His face became as stark and blank as a mask. "My children had a difficult time with the loss of their mother, Tessa, and I see no reason now to agitate them with constant reminders."

"Perhaps if you were to tell me—"

"Damn it, Tessa! Why must you push this? Can you not see that I have put that chapter of my life behind me?"

He saw her face flush at his angry tone and he nearly choked on the words of truth that tried to claw their way out of his mouth. She was his wife now, and he wanted her to know the real reason he was being forced to protect two innocent children with his silence. But, determined by old promises, and by the shame of the part he had played in so horrendous a crime, he pushed back the confession.

"I'm sorry. I didn't mean to pry," she calmly said. "I was only hoping that we might begin our marriage with honesty between us, and Cynthia is the one subject you never seem able to be entirely honest about."

"No one is entirely honest about every aspect of his life," he replied quietly, his heart aching for the chasm of distance he was forcing between them. "We all have our secrets."

In her eyes was a hurt, angry look that he had put there. "I don't," she said.

Chandler glanced up at the mantel clock, looking any place but at those eyes. His ardor quickly cooled. Like a douse with icy water, Tessa's questioning had made him suddenly want more than anything to leave this room, to be away from the shame of the past she was determined to rekindle. He was not ready to risk the truth, or to risk losing her to it.

Chandler pressed a chaste kiss onto her forehead then rose from the bed.

"You'd better get some sleep."

"But I thought you would want—"

"Get some rest, Tessa. You are likely to need all of your strength for tomorrow."

When he had disappeared through the door to the dressing room that joined their two rooms, Tessa let out a confused, exhausted sigh, trying to subdue her hurt. She had expected many things of this evening. Their wedding night. The way it had ended so abruptly between her and Chandler had certainly not been among the scenarios.

She glanced dazedly around a room which, even after two years time, was still filled with the woman who had occupied it first. Lacy undercurtains on all of the windows. The scent of dried flowers from sachets that had filled all of the drawers. An alabaster-colored pillow, tossed on the daybed, embroidered in crimson with the word Mother.

Tessa slid from the bed, suppressing a shiver. In the dark

of night, alone like this, she found the room almost eerie. It felt to Tessa as if the ghost of Cynthia inhabited it still, or at the very least, that at any moment she would walk through that door, just as Jennings had done, and reclaim it as her own.

Tessa had known she would be dealing with Chandler's past on some level. She had accepted that when she agreed to be his wife. But before she had come here to Boston she could have had no idea at all the depth that was involved.

On unsteady legs, Tessa moved to the small carpetbag, back now at the end of the bed, and filled with those few treasured possessions she had brought from New York. Yet they were far more than simply possessions. What she had taken away with her, she realized now, were memories of a life that was gone forever. These few things symbolized so much in the world that she knew or cared about. But, in all of their simplicity, they did not belong here. At least not yet. At least not until she gained her footing.

Until then, she would put them away where they would be safe from eyes likely to be far more disapproving than Kathleen's.

She would start with the two plain cotton handkerchiefs given to her by the Baldwin sisters. Then her hairbrush, hair combs, and the framed picture of her parents. Next she drew out the pouch of medicinal herbs given to her by Mrs. Gallagher. In spite of what Tessa had said to thank her, there was little chance that she would ever have need of them here, no matter how surefooted she became. Not in a grand house, so full of servants, brimming with every imaginable convenience, where doctors were likely to be at Chandler's beck and call.

She gathered up the items, wrapping them in her old shawl, and glanced around the room, searching for a suitable place to conceal them, her few precious, private things. Tessa needed to find at least one small place for herself, free from well meaning, ever-present servants and from the eyes of a sister-in-law apparently already set against her.

Drawers were not safe. Neither was the wardrobe closet, or even the dressing room between her room and Chandler's. Beneath the bed they would certainly be discovered.

She sank down for a moment onto the window seat trying to take in the overwhelming grandeur of this room, it's many places. The fabric-draped dressing table. The gold-framed mirror above it. That day bed, covered with a spray of small, lace-trimmed pillows, the high mahogany bureau, and two watercolor paintings hung from blue satin cords.

No place here in this entire room seemed safe. She was tired now and disappointed at what had happened earlier with Chandler. Her heart began to sink as she gripped the edge of the window seat. It took her a moment more to realize that the seat itself could be raised.

Tessa rose slowly, turned around, and saw the darkened brass hinges. Of course, a window seat. She smiled, feeling the slightest hint of relief.

She lifted the lid slowly. The creak was very slow and high, like a cat's cry. The dank, musty odor that followed came at her as thickly as a cloud and she knew the window seat was a place that had not been opened for a very long time. Perfect, she thought.

Inside there was a stack of blankets and an extra bed pillow. Pushing them aside for just the right place to conceal her bundle, Tessa was surprised to feel the smooth coolness of a handle. It was a compartment. That would be a far better place to conceal her own secret things than just beneath a few blankets.

Tessa slipped her finger through the brass ring and pulled. The wooden lid came away with a firm tug. But the compartment was not empty. The room now was full of shadows and she could not quite make out what had already been put there, so she carefully reached inside.

She pulled a piece of fabric out into the light. When she saw it, shock roared through her like thunder. The breath hitched in her throat and she gasped.

What she held before her was a woman's crumpled shirtwaist covered in hard, dry, rust-colored blood. Carefully placed beside it in the bottom of the window seat was a pistol.

Her hand trembled, and with trepidation rolling through her like a great hot wave, Tessa lifted out the weapon. Engraved on the oak stock were the initials C.T.

Chandler Tate.

There was a roaring in her ears as Tessa lay the pistol carefully on the nightstand and took a step back, trying to help her mind process the discovery. Guns. Duelling. A lady's honor. Angry men at twenty paces, facing off, as they did in her books. Blood. Death. Chandler's face just before he'd beaten that hoodlum . . .

The weight of foreboding was pressing down on her, threatening to crush her, like a very heavy stone. It meant nothing, she told herself vainly, trying to calm herself, to push away the weight, as her heart slammed against her ribs. That it looked this bad was purely circumstantial. Many men had weapons. Hunting was a sport. When one was powerful there was also self-protection to consider. She had even read that collecting them was sometimes a hobby among wealthy men.

For why her new husband's gun, with his initials so prominently engraved in the stock, was here, hidden away, with what, in all likelihood, was his dead wife's bloody shirtwaist, there must be a plausible explanation.

Dear Lord, her mind reeled, whirling into blackness. Please! Let there be an explanation!

But already it was too late, and she was far too exhausted for reason. From the moment the darkest thought had been given a spark of life, it began to breed, fast and furiously. The images and the possibilities swooped down on her like a hawk taking her captive.

Her mind began to pummel her hard with unanswerable questions. The bloody garment must have belonged to Cynthia. This had been her room. But, what had happened? Had it happened with this, Chandler's gun? And dear God in his heaven, was it actually Cynthia Tate's dried blood she held now in her hands?

Tessa's heart would not allow her to hear the answers that logic was hammering into her head. No! She pushed them down and held them with every bit of strength she possessed. *And still, it would explain so much,* a small, dark voice cruelly said, as it bled through her resolve. *Why he never spoke about his first wife with anything but the greatest contempt. And why he became so angry tonight when you tried to press him about her.*

Had Chandler despised his first wife so much for something that had happened between them that he had actually been driven to . . .

As heavily as her own mind pelted her with the possibility, Tessa forced it back again with a Herculean determination. No! He could not possibly. In spite of his unsettling behavior earlier that evening, and that way he had of cutting himself off from her, Chandler Tate was still the kindest, the most sensitive man she had ever known.

He simply was not capable of something so heinous.

Exhausted, disappointed, and with sickness churning inside her, rising up like bile, Tessa carefully placed the gun and the bloody shirtwaist back where she had found them. Then she flung herself onto the bed.

Of course there was a logical explanation. Yes, there simply must be. She loved him too much to assume otherwise without so much as an explanation. She would ask him tomorrow when she had had some sleep and when what had happened between them tonight had been forgotten. Yes, tomorrow she would press this issue with him, stubbornly even, for the good of their marriage, and this business of Cynthia would all be out between them at last.

After all, this was not some faint-hearted society girl he had married and brought home from New York, Tessa reminded herself, feeling a spark, just a spark, of the old spirit, the firey determination inside of her bleed through her exhaustion and all of this surprise. This was Charlie Murphy's daughter from Tenth Street! A force with which to be reckoned. Faced with that, Chandler Tate and his secrets, whatever they were, didn't stand a ghost of a chance.

Chapter

25

IT WAS NEARLY DAWN WHEN HE RETURNED.

The cover of darkness was the only thing that could have given Chandler the courage to enter her bedroom unannounced. Although he had tossed and turned between his own cool linen sheets for most of the night, he could be certain now, so near morning, that his beautiful Tessa had found her way to the peace of sleep.

He moved back into the room soundlessly, careful not to wake her. Just as he had thought, she was asleep. Her long copper hair was draped loose around her face and her dark lashes gently fluttered beneath closed eyes. She lay on top of the covers, just as she had fallen asleep, with her hands clasped below her breasts.

The thought that he had left her so harshly earlier that evening, on their wedding night of all nights, tore now at his heart. He knew she did not understand it. Perhaps he did not understand it himself. He had wanted to tell her about Cynthia. Confess it all. But that he could not do. He could

217

never tell anyone. His children's happiness depended on his silence. And on Daphne's.

As he gazed down on his bride, sleeping so peacefully now, Chandler thought how he had never known anyone even remotely like her. She really was the most exquisite creature. So free. So natural. So unsuspecting of the darker side of life. The things to which a person could actually be driven.

He surrendered himself quietly to the chair beside her bed. He wanted simply to watch her. The gentle rise and fall of her breast was hypnotic to him. He felt a little embarrassed being in here like this. But not enough to cause him to leave. No matter what Daphne thought, he knew that he had captured something great in Tessa Murphy. Now he wanted nothing so much as to be worthy of her.

As he watched her, as he touched her robe, which lay over the arm of the chair, Chandler began again to imagine what it would be like to lie with her. It was not the first time he had the fantasy. The passionate kisses they had shared in New York had begun the curiosity. The touch of her bare skin tonight, so close to his own, had touched off the yearning. He had been foolish to leave her like that. Foolish to let the past get the better of him when he had found so much in the here and now.

He thought of Li Kao Chen, the old man he had not seen for nine years, but whose wisdom and kindness had remained a bright flame of hope inside of him ever since. "You will find her," Li had said with complete assurance, of a woman he one day could love. "You have only to look for her with your whole heart for it to be so."

Chandler sat silently beside that woman for nearly an hour more, until a mellow pink sun began to arch over the horizon and then pour softly through the space between the heavy velvet draperies and light undercurtains that covered the long windows beyond her bed. He sat like that, perfectly still. Watching. Imagining. Completely content for the first time in a very long time. And quite to his surprise, falling more desperately in love with Tessa than he was already.

Chapter

26

TESSA WOKE THE NEXT MORNING TO SUN STREAMING IN THROUGH a crack in the heavy blue velvet-draped windows and lace undercurtains. She lay there not moving, realizing that yesterday, and last night, had not been a dream at all. She was actually married. She was farther from home than she had ever been, and she was installed in a house where a gun and a bloody woman's garment had been most carefully concealed.

She raised the covers over her head, wanting to sink back into the safety of sleep, until she saw four crystal-blue eyes gazing up at her over the polished rosewood footboard. A scruffy gray tail wagged in the air behind them and a child's sweet giggle suddenly broke the silence. Tessa bolted upright in her bed and put her hands on her hips in mock disapproval.

"So then. Are you to be my welcoming committee this morning?" she asked with a laughter-tinged voice.

Alice stood up, a little girl with long golden pigtails tied at the ends with neat pink ribbons. Seeing that Tessa was not angry for the clandestine invasion of her bedroom, the little girl came slowly around the side of the bed and poked her nose over the thick covers.

"And who else have we over there?" Tessa asked, when James, the more timid of the two, made no move to join his elder sister.

"Do you like prunes?" Alice asked with a note of suspicion edging her voice, and Tessa could hear that it was a test.

"I am afraid I don't know," she said truthfully, cautiously. "I have never tried them."

"Well, we don't like them at all, and Aunt Daphne is always trying to force us to take them. She says that they are good for our constitution."

"We're hiding from her," James confessed in a whisper, suddenly springing to his feet and coming around the bed to stand beside his sister.

Daphne, Tessa thought as she glanced up at the clock. Half past ten. Jennings had warned her and now she had missed the only opportunity she would have to speak privately with Chandler for the rest of the day. It was the only time she would have had to ask him about what she had found.

"Where did Father find you?" Alice asked, hopping up onto the edge of Tessa's huge bed.

"I am from New York."

"Is that in Europe?" James asked earnestly. "Father has been to Europe."

"No, silly!" Alice laughed at him but Tessa smiled kindly.

"It is not really all that far from here. And yet," Tessa let out a little sigh, reconsidering the statement after the events of last night, "just now it seems a million miles away."

The children looked at one another, not comprehending what she meant, but deciding collectively that it did not matter.

"You're pretty," James announced with childish authority, then lowered his blue eyes bashfully.

"Why thank you, kind sir," Tessa smiled down at him. "I do believe that is the nicest thing anyone has said to me since I set foot in Boston."

"Do you have any children?" Alice asked.

"No. I'm afraid I don't."

"That's good," she replied with a quick smile of approval, "because Aunt Daphne says we're enough by ourselves for anyone to handle."

James smiled, too, and stroked Mayflower's shaggy, long-haired back. "She said once, when she was really angry, that that was why we didn't have a new mother, because no one else but Miss Pettigrew would marry father, since he had two such unmanageable children."

Tessa's heart surged with anger. Not only was Chandler's sister unwelcoming and overbearing, but she had a cruel streak with little children as well. Suddenly the sound of shoe heels on the floor outside the bedroom door began to grow louder as someone neared. Alice and James exchanged a sudden worried glance.

"That's her!" Alice whispered frantically, her face suddenly pink and alive with panic. "She's come to find us and make us eat our prunes!"

"In there," Tessa whispered, pointing to the dressing room. "Quickly!"

A fleeting expression of comradery passed across Alice's small face and then deepened into a relieved smile as she led James and Mayflower into the impromptu haven. At the same moment that the dressing-room door closed, the bedroom door opened.

Daphne Tate Forrester stood in the arch of the door dressed in sweeping honey-colored silk. Her bony hands were on her slim hips, and there was a maliciously feline glint in her eyes.

"Still in bed, are we?"

"Perhaps things are done differently in Boston, but in New York, I was always taught to knock," Tessa countered, trying to keep her voice from cracking.

"I saw my brother leave an hour ago so I felt sure there would be little harm in—"

"What can I do for you, Mrs. Forrester?" Tessa coolly asked, not letting Daphne finish her sentence as she pushed the feeling of complete intimidation behind her own hauteur.

"I am looking for the children. They've left the breakfast table without my approval again."

"Why would you look in here?"

"They are very good at hiding where one would least expect it," Daphne countered, her voice dripping with velvety contempt.

They were combative with one another, Tessa quickly matching Daphne with every velvety, rude nuance of voice. Her ability to spar so easily after last night, and in the company of such formidable opposition, surprised them both.

"But then, we both know that the real reason you have come bursting in here is not my husband's children, is it?"

Tessa had cut to the heart of the matter with rapier-like precision, and her ability to do so had startled her opponent. Daphne took a step back and tipped her head to one side, studying her brother's young wife.

"I am quite certain I don't know what you mean."

"Just because Chandler loves me, doesn't mean he can't still love you, too. After all, you are his sister."

"Yes I am," Daphne said sternly. "The one who has known him, and the sort of things of which he is capable, for a far sight longer than you."

"Well, apparently I make him happy, and I would say that is certainly something."

"My brother amuses himself with Mayflower, too. That certainly doesn't mean the poor creature could hold his interest forever."

"I wonder how many people have had the courage to tell you that you could do with a bit of grace."

"Only those without the breeding to know when to hold

their tongues or the wisdom to know that they should never, ever try to go up against me."

There was silence as Tessa lifted her chin with a hint of sprightly Irish pride, daring Daphne to speak one word more. Kathleen's sudden appearance was a well-timed reprieve.

"Well. As you can undoubtedly see, there are no children in my bedroom, Mrs. Forrester. So, since we are apparently not going to be able to come to terms this morning, I hope that you will excuse me, I would like to dress."

"I'm sorry I'm late, ma'am," Kathleen said in English heavily laced with an Irish brogue, "but I thought after your long journey yesterday a bit of extra sleep would be in order."

"Thank you, Kathleen," Tessa said, swinging her bare feet out from under the covers and around to the side of the bed and tossing her auburn mane of hair with the firmest note of indifference she could enlist. "That was very thoughtful of you."

When it was clear that their discourse was over, Daphne Tate Forrester tugged on the rope of pearls around her neck sounding a little indignant huff. Then, thwarted in her attempt to remove this interloper from her brother's home by intimidation alone, she turned on her heel and went out into the corridor, not bothering to close the door behind her.

"You'll grow accustomed to her soon enough," Kathleen sweetly offered.

"I shall never get used to someone like that. I wouldn't want to," Tessa firmly countered as she walked across the room to close the door herself, then crossed back to her dressing room. "All right, it is safe. You can come out now."

Slowly, Alice and James and Mayflower filed out like three guilty suspects in a far bigger crime than prune evasion.

"So you were here!" Kathleen chuckled in surprise. "Ye little hooligans. Mrs. Forrester was lookin' everywhere for ye."

"To make us eat those awful things!" James said defiantly,

wrinkling his nose at the thought. "Besides, who are you to say a word? Aunt Daphne says you're only just a servant."

Tessa recoiled at the condescending tone from the mouth of such a young child. But before she could speak her disapproval, Alice moved toward her. She was looking up, as an expression of gratitude and approval sparkled like jewels on her sweet, round face.

"Thank you, Tessa. I really am glad father didn't marry Miss Pettigrew and chose you instead. You really are so much nicer."

She gazed down at the children one at a time, both of them so in need of a firm hand. In need of direction. So open and eager to love her.

"Would you like to go to the park with us?" James asked bashfully. "Mayflower loves it there."

"Don't you both have lessons or something today?"

Alice and James exchanged a gleeful glance and then burst into laughter with curled hands before their mouths. "It is Saturday, ma'am," Kathleen explained with her own note of amusement.

Tessa's confusion stemmed, in part, from hearing that Chandler had already left for work. "Mr. Tate works even on Saturdays?" she asked.

"He has for some time, yes ma'am. Told me once that he was married to the company."

"Not anymore." James giggled.

"Well then. I should love to accompany you to the park, if that would be all right with your aunt," Tessa said, glancing up at Kathleen for tentative approval.

"Jennings usually takes them for a walk since their last governess left us. But I'm fairly well sure he would be glad for the reprieve." Kathleen cupped a hand around her mouth. "He hasn't much of a way with children, ye see."

Tessa lowered her eyes again to two of the sweetest faces she had ever seen, and wondered what it was about them that had caused everyone, including their own aunt, to label them difficult. Having been an only child, Tessa adored all children and she steadfastly believed that a firm hand and a good deal of love could win even the most unruly among them.

"Would ye like for me to see to it with Jennings for ye, ma'am?" Kathleen offered.

"I appreciate that, Kathleen," Tessa smiled, "but I have the distinct impression that when dealing with these people I am far better off doing it directly."

"True enough."

"And I must begin somewhere, mustn't I?"

Kathleen nodded to hide a little smile of agreement.

When she went into the dressing room to collect Tessa's ensemble for the day, both Alice and James settled back onto the unmade bed, with Mayflower following in a burst of flying fur and wagging tail and hindquarters.

"Tell us how you and father met," Alice asked with a wide, happy smile, curling her arms around her knees.

"Yes, tell us," James seconded.

Tessa stood at the foot of the bed, still in her nightdress, wondering how she might make so whirlwind a courtship sound respectable to two impressionable children. But their faces were so wide and happy, so inquisitive, that she reluctantly found herself searching for a plausible reply.

"Well we . . . I . . ." she sputtered, running a hand nervously across her scalp.

"I bet father fell in love with your hair," Alice guessed, watching the way it rained down onto Tessa's shoulders like a cascade of fire in the morning sunlight. "It's an extraordinary color."

"Yes, extraordinary!" James parroted his sister as he stroked Mayflower's head. "It looks like the color of ruby jewels. Like the ones mother used to wear."

A blush of embarrassment painted Tessa's cheeks when she recalled the way Chandler had changed last night, how rigid he had become at the mere mention of their mother. It was the first time Tessa had ever seen that side of him and it had confused her. The sight of a pistol hidden so carefully, and bearing the initials C.T., had only heightened the confusion to a level just beneath fear.

"Your father stepped out in front of my carriage and I nearly killed him," Tessa uneasily confessed, realizing that no story she devised could be as unbelievable as the truth.

Their shared happy expressions grew suddenly intense with interest. "Is that why he had that nasty gash on his forehead when he returned home?" asked Alice, her lips parted in curiosity.

"I'm afraid it is. My own father and I felt dreadful about what had happened, so we invited him home for tea."

"And father fell madly in love with you then and there!"

Tessa smiled at how dreamily Alice had finished the story and she could not bring herself to correct her. How else could she explain it to children who wanted so badly to believe in the possibility of happy endings?

"Something like that," Tessa softly concurred.

"I always knew he would find someone special again, even though nearly every day after mama died, he said he didn't need love anymore."

"Children!" Kathleen gasped as she stood in the dressing room doorway holding the same elegant traveling costume in which Tessa had arrived in Boston. "Ye must come down from that bed at once!"

All three faces turned toward the sound of her censure. "What is the matter?" Tessa asked.

"They mustn't be allowed to climb about like a couple of wild animals once they've already dressed, ma'am! Mrs. Forrester would have my head if she saw them like that."

"They're not harming anything," Tessa smiled.

"Oh, but ye don't understand, ma'am. Mrs. Forrester favors everythin' just so around here. It really is the law with her since she took over."

"Well," Tessa huffed, pressing her hands onto her hips and smiling confidently. "There is a new mistress in this house at the moment."

Alice and James perked up and both of them began to applaud the courage of their new stepmother against an aunt who seemed to like nothing better than to thwart them and stir up fear at every turn. Mayflower, too, barked his approval.

"Shh!" Tessa swallowed a laugh and sank onto the bed with them as she pressed a finger to her lips. "We wouldn't want her to find you in here now. Not when you have only just found the most splendid hiding place in the house."

"Kathleen will tell on us," James said seriously, as fear darkened his wide eyes. "Servants are servants, Aunt Daphne always says. You cannot trust the lot of them."

Tessa looked across at the maid, who stood stiffly with her hands clasped before her. There was a tentative moment of silence in the sun-washed blue bedroom as they waited for Kathleen's reply.

"Mrs. Forrester shall learn nothing from me," she finally vowed and then joined them in a conspiratorial smile.

It was then that Tessa noticed the traveling costume that her maid was still holding. "Oh, I cannot very well wear something so grand as that to the park, Kathleen! Bring me one of my everyday dresses that I brought with me."

"But ma'am." Kathleen nodded. "It is the sort o' thing all fine Boston ladies wear on the Common or in the public garden. Ye really cannot be seen in your other—"

"The Common?" Tessa asked as Kathleen's words trailed off awkwardly.

"Boston Common, Mrs. Tate. The park just down the hill where the children take their dog. All o' the people who live around here take their children there. Mrs. Forrester always says it is the best place to be seen in Boston."

Tessa's heart sank a little with disappointment. It was disheartening to realize that the outing she had agreed to was not intended to be the carefree excursion she had in mind for two such spirited children as these.

An hour later, Tessa came alone down the sweeping mahogany staircase. She was dressed in the traveling costume and the matching shoes and hat. Now, as she clung fast to the banister, in the muted light of day, she had her first real opportunity to take in the unbelievable splendor of the Tate family home.

Priceless oil paintings and imperious-looking portraits adorned every wall. Heavy, floor-to-ceiling olive green draperies were tied back with gold cord.

There were huge emerald palms set in grand blue-and-white Chinese vases. Above the foyer, a magnificent brass chandelier sprouted from an intricate plaster medallion that, on the previous evening, she had missed entirely. A niche beneath the staircase contained a beautiful bronze bust.

The parlor in which she had stood in weak-kneed shock beside Chandler the night before, noticing little of this opulence, now in the light of day seemed almost stuffed to bursting with elegant furnishings.

Tessa's eyes darted now in amazement at the chairs and sofas with buttons and fringe, some covered in soft leather, others in velvet. Tables, topped with silver-framed photographs, antique snuff boxes, and delicate lace fans, were draped with Lyons silk and tapestries. Beneath her small feet, the vast floors were overlaid with oriental rugs and dotted with more potted palms than she had ever seen, giving the house a green, garden-like appearance.

"You have missed the master, ma'am," a crisp baritone rolled matter-of-factly behind her. "It is eleven o'clock."

"I know that, Jennings," Tessa replied, turning slowly around. "I came down here to find you."

The stiff, portly butler arched a silvery eyebrow and ran a gloved finger over a small glass-and-gold-leaf cabinet near the door. "Oh?"

"Yes, Jennings. I should like to take the children to the park myself this morning."

Jennings stopped; his hand froze along the side of the cabinet. "You, ma'am? In this house that is a job customarily reserved for the staff."

"On the contrary, Jennings," Tessa smiled confidently, pushing the hint of a tremor from her voice. "It *was* a job customarily reserved for the staff. Alice and James have invited me and I should very much like to accompany them."

"Respectfully, ma'am," Jennings frowned slightly, yet spoke with all proper civility, "I don't believe you know what you would be getting yourself into with those two. They are not like other children."

Tessa looked at him calmly, trying her best to disregard his objection. "Those two, as you call them, Jennings, are my husband's children. You would do well to remember that."

"Mr. Tate himself is the one who made those arrangements, with his staff, ma'am."

"Well *Mrs.* Tate—the new Mrs. Tate that is—is altering those arrangements, and you may hold me accountable."

Reminded by the insistence in her voice of the disparity of their positions, Jennings acquiesced. "Would you object then if I accompanied you all, at least this once, until I have spoken with the master myself?"

The sudden change in his tone filled Tessa with a great sense of power. Putting her chin up, she smiled victoriously. "I think, Jennings, that would be quite lovely."

They strolled together down the steep grade of Walnut Street, Tessa, with a hand linked in each child's, and the Tate family butler walking behind them on the steep, cobbled street.

In the light of day, this part of Boston was far more charming than Tessa had expected, with its tall gas lamps, wrought-iron railings pressed against red brick, and shiny brass knockers centered on doors of lacquered green and black. All of it lay beneath bristling bursts of blossoming creepers and great leafy trees. Tessa marveled at each of the neat street-front houses, some of them with lovely purple window panes that glistened like jewels in the morning sun.

"Those purple panes are really lovely," she remarked to Jennings as they crossed Beacon Street. "I have never seen anything quite like them."

"They actually weren't supposed to be like that," Jennings

explained, marking his steps with a ivory-handled walking stick as the children and Mayflower skipped on ahead toward the gates to the park. "The color is the result of sunlight bringing out the imperfections in the imported Hamburg glass. Having made the best of it, however, people now regard them as quite fashionable."

"Come on, Tessa!" James called out to her from behind the tall black iron gate. "Let's play hide-and-seek!"

"All right!" she called back. "I shall hide but you must find me."

"Oh, ma'am," the Tate butler snorted. "It really isn't a good idea. It is one thing to let children frolic and play, but that sort of thing just isn't done here by Boston's fine ladies."

"Nonsense, Jennings!" Tessa chuckled in reply. "Don't people here in Boston have any fun at all?"

"Not that sort, no, ma'am."

Tessa stopped and faced him. "It is my understanding, Jennings, that those two beautiful children have had a difficult last two years. Isn't that true?"

"True enough, ma'am."

"And wouldn't it be lovely just to see them carefree and happy again, and someone enjoying that happiness with them. At least for a little while?"

"But Mrs. Forrester would—"

"Mrs. Forrester is not here now, Jennings, I am," Tessa countered with only a slight edge to her voice, still buoyed by the response she had garnered from him earlier. When she saw that it had the same effect now as before, her firm expression was quickly replaced with an easy smile. "Now, I shall hide, and you shall help them look for me."

"Very well, ma'am. If you say so," he said, letting out a deep sigh of resignation as he started off toward the two, eager-faced children.

While they counted to ten, Tessa dashed quickly down a winding path and into the depths of the elm-dotted park, all of it alive with the sweet fragrance of summer flowers. Slowly, their childish laughter and pattering feet faded beneath the chirping of birds and the scampering of squirrels. But she must be careful not to go too far or too fast, Tessa thought. After all, they were only children, and if they were anything like their father, they had grown accustomed to winning.

The memory of his abrupt and unexplained departure from her room the night before was still etched in her mind, because there the questions had begun to multiply.

As she had lain against the pillow, nearly asleep, Tessa had searched her mind for an explanation of what she might have said or done that had provoked such a change in Chandler merely by bringing up Cynthia's name. "We all have our secrets." She heard the echo of his angry tone even now as she ran down a shady incline across a soft expanse of grass.

Her new husband was a mass of contradictions. Smooth, elegant, thoughtful. Even compassionate. Yet at a moment's notice, he could turn introspective, even cool.

It was only another moment before she heard the giddy laughter of both Alice and James, and Mayflower barking behind them. She leaned against the tree and held her breath.

"Tessa!" Alice called out, only a few feet away. "Where are you?"

"I think she's over here." James called to his sister as she headed toward the vast, rippling frog pond.

"No, Master James!" Jennings called out with a tone of panic, yet at too much of a distance to make them stop. "You must not go near the—"

His words were halted by a little cry and then a huge splashing sound. Tessa darted out from behind the tree to the sight of Alice leaning over the pond and water still lapping near its edges. She and Jennings surged forward into the pond, neither seeing James, both fearing the worst. Thinking it was all part of the game, Mayflower paddled into the water after them, happily splashing everywhere as Alice moved in up to her knees to try and stop him.

Only then, as both Jennings and Tessa frantically searched

with grasping hands and legs beneath the surface for the little boy, did his childish laughter bring them to a halt. The sound was coming from the tree branch above them.

"Oh! You know better than that, Master James." Jennings scolded angrily as the little boy quickly shinnied down the trunk and into the water with them. It had been a huge stone cast into the water, not James, that had made the frightful sound.

"Someone might have been harmed, or far worse than that, killed!" Jennings barked.

"I was just having a little of fun," James countered in a seemingly repentant tone, now up to his waist in murky pond water with them.

"I ought to skin you alive myself!"

Tessa glanced down, seeing now that the water, up to her hips, had entirely ruined her new dress and shoes. On top of that, Mayflower was shaking himself off gleefully and spraying all of their faces with muddy brown water.

"Oh! You bloody beast!" the butler roared as Alice and James erupted into laughter at the sight of all of them reduced in an instant to a pack of drowned rats.

Tessa gave the butler a little smile, that stopped him in his tracks just as he lunged for the dog. "Really, Jennings, no harm was done now, was it really? And you *do* look silly standing there wet and muddy."

A reluctant smile touched his lips as he paused to examine the two of them. Tessa's hair was wet and matted, her hat, still on her head, was tipped off-center, the gold braid dripping limply. Her gown clung to her in soaking folds just as his black suit did to him.

"Respectfully, ma'am," he choked on a laugh, "I have never seen anything quite so ridiculous as you just now."

"That's the spirit!" Tessa laughed.

Everyone was mudcaked and soaking wet. They were all giggling as they stumbled back into the house. But the happiness and the laughter ceased when they came face to face with the stiff and very formidable Daphne Forrester.

* * *

"What, in the name of heaven . . ."

The unfinished question boomed from Daphne's mouth, and the entire house seemed to quake with her fury.

"It is my fault, ma'am," Jennings admitted grimly. "The children were my responsibility."

"This is positively scandalous! We are sure to be the laughingstock of all Boston when word of this gets around."

Tessa stepped out in front of Jennings, her head held defiantly high. She was a pitiful sight in her soaking gown, with her hat still askew, water dripping from the twisted braid that hung from its brim.

"I insisted on taking them to the park," she confessed. "Jennings only accompanied me. If there is anyone to blame here, it is I."

In the deafening silence, no one else moved as Daphne descended the last few stairs and approached her new sister-in-law with the most frightening look of contempt any of them had ever seen.

"Young woman, this is unacceptable!"

"Please, Aunt Daphne," Alice intervened. "We were only playing a game."

Daphne ignored the child, gaining strength from the knowledge that Chandler was safely at work and was not here to defend his young, ill-bred new wife.

"Have you any idea at all the sort of harm to which you have subjected these children with your little game?" she charged, ignoring Alice and scrutinizing Tessa's mud-splattered face and the complete ruin of her dress.

"Perhaps I am not certain of how things are done in New York, or whatever place you have *really* come from, but here in Boston, we behave with dignity and decorum befitting our stature, and this is absolutely unacceptable!"

Tessa drew a shaky breath and proudly righted her dripping hat. "Mrs. Forrester, our falling into the pond was nothing more than an accident."

"Young woman, we do not *have* accidents. We Tates take great care to avoid them at all costs. You have been here less than twenty-four hours and yet have managed to plunge this family not only into the frog pond but into certain degradation and embarrassment as well."

"I see that I have arrived just in time to referee."

The words came from a tenor voice, filled with staid calm.

Tessa whirled around and saw a man with slick, gleaming black hair and a carefully clipped black mustache and beard leaning casually against the doorjamb.

"Lincoln, this is hardly the time to try to be clever," Daphne chided the stranger. "Can you not see I have a potential catastrophe on my hands here?"

"Catastrophe?" Lincoln asked appraisingly, stroking his bearded chin. "It appears to me that what you have on your hands is a little competition," he drawled, sizing up Tessa.

His eyes moved next to the wet and shivering butler, then to James. "Go for a swim, did you, my boy?" he asked good-naturedly, trying to wedge a bit of levity into the tension-filled foyer.

"I fell in," James defended himself as the atmosphere around them grew thicker by the moment. "Tessa only tried to save me."

"Another new governess you and Alice decided to test?" Lincoln asked, his lips quirking mischievously.

"Father's new wife!" Alice countered proudly.

Lincoln Forrester's crimped mouth widened into a genuine smile. His murky, olive-black eyes were strangely welcoming. "Lucky devil," he chuckled beneath his breath.

"You cannot seriously find anything remotely attractive about her." Daphne sputtered incredulously.

"Can't I?"

"Her voice! Her very manner!"

"Seem perfectly charming to me," Lincoln interjected, glancing at Tessa. "I hope that you will pardon my wife. She is only angry that her brother appears to have gotten the better of her yet again. Second time in a month, isn't it, my dear?"

"That is preposterous!" Daphne huffed.

"Oh, you know perfectly well you had poor Chandler's

life entirely mapped out with Felicity. You're only angry because his heart took him elsewhere."

"Elsewhere, indeed." Daphne stifled a condescending laugh behind her hand as her eyes played over the wet and muddy hat and limp copper strings of hair that had entirely overtaken Tessa's beautiful face.

"Where on earth was it that my brother found you?"

"In New York," James answered for her, eager to defend the woman who promised to be his mother, the woman who had saved them from Felicity.

"Shall I take Master James and Miss Alice upstairs for a change of clothes, Mrs. Tate?" Jennings asked, trying subtly to deliver them all from this inquisition.

"You do that, Jennings," Daphne intervened coolly. "And then you may march yourself down to the basement, pack your things, and vacate this house at once."

At his wife's startling directive, Lincoln Forrester let out an audible groan. Jennings had been a loyal employee of the Tate family for more than twenty years.

"Mrs. Forrester, I know that I have erred but—"

"Precisely, Jennings," Daphne sniffed, cutting him off sharply. "You well know what is required in this house in the governing of these children and I simply will not allow so flagrant an act of insubordination because of some young, pretty face who has trotted her way into my brother's bed. I tell you, I'll not have it!"

"Mrs. Forrester, you musn't blame him. It really was my fault," Tessa declared, taking another brave step forward, trying to intervene on Jenning's behalf.

"How well I know that," Daphne snipped, not even bothering to look at Tessa. "And, no matter what I must do to convince my brother of your unsuitability for this family, rest assured, you shall be the next to go."

Tessa stared at the coldest, most heartless woman she had ever met, and a fresh onslaught of tears began to well up behind her eyes. She had no idea what more she could say. There could not, after all, be any reasoning with a woman who did not appear to possess a single grain of human kindness.

"You heard me, Jennings. Do not make me repeat myself. See to the children's change of clothes and then I want you out of this house."

"If anyone is leaving this house, Daphne, it most certainly will be you. Preferably over your husband's shoulder with your backside in the air!"

This firm pronouncement was followed by a full, masculine laugh. Tessa whirled around, the wet, cold gown clinging to her hips and legs. In spite of the many distrubing questions she had for Chandler, never before had she been so glad to see or hear anyone in her life. A tiny breath of relief escaped her tightly pursed lips.

"What on earth happened to you?" he asked with an expression of genuine amusement, looking over at Tessa, his children, and their butler, all of them still dripping water onto the priceless carpet.

"It was my fault," Tessa explained in a strained voice. "The children wanted to go to the park and—"

"And James dashed a rock into the frog pond from his favorite tree," Chandler said in a knowing tone, finishing her sentence.

"H-How did you know that?"

"Oh, this is not the first time my son has taken a summer tumble into the pond. It seems he enjoys the attention he gets from having people scramble frantically after him. And Alice, little actress that she is, is only too happy to play along. I am sure she was quite convincing."

Tessa glanced at the children in disbelief. Then she looked back at Chandler, trying to comprehend his words. "But your sister said there were no accidents in this family."

"Daphne wasn't aware of their specific escapades with the last two governesses," he calmly explained.

"I thought . . ." This time the words died on her lips as she realized that the children, who only just this morning seemed so desperately in need of her, had orchestrated all of it out of nothing more than a great fondness for mischief.

236

"I'm sorry, Tessa," James volunteered, seeing the disappointment flushing her pale cheeks. "I never wanted you to get in trouble. I only wanted us all to have a laugh. Everyone is always so sour around here."

"I think you had better go upstairs with Jennings, son," Chandler directed, struggling to keep a straight face. "You too," he added, glancing down at Alice.

When the children were out of the foyer, Chandler stepped up beside his new wife, doing his level best to stifle a booming laugh, one that threatened to explode at the slightest further provocation.

His heart surged with unexpected affection as he looked at Tessa, so completely bereft of her defenses and yet so adorably proud. He had returned home unexpectedly to collect some papers, angry at himself all the while for having forgotten them. But he could see quite clearly now that it was fortunate for them that he had. Perhaps Tessa needed him after all.

"Now, now, sister dear," Chandler quipped as he stepped out protectively before Tessa, seeing his sister still glaring at her. "Your envy is showing."

"My brother, the white knight."

"I can only hope that Tessa finds me so."

Daphne stared at her brother, desperate and angry. "How long is this vendetta of yours going to go on? Can you not see what havoc she has already managed to wreak in this house?"

"What I see," Chandler firmly countered, taking Tessa's arm just above the elbow, "is a young woman with a peculiarly refreshing zest for life, one mirrored brightly in the reflection of the bitter crone that you have become."

Then he turned to lead Tessa back upstairs, quite content to leave his sister standing there, utterly speechless.

Tessa stopped trembling only when she was seated on the daybed safe in her own bedroom. She was not frightened so much as confused by everything that had occurred. Her hands were braced on the cushions beneath her, and Chandler was bringing a basin of warm water and a cloth to her side.

"That really isn't necessary."

"Turn about is fair play," he said in a quietly seductive voice as he knelt before her. "I let you tend to me in New York, didn't I?"

As he moved the warm, wet cloth over her forehead and chin and along her nose in gentle strokes, the handsome, cavalier stranger she had known in New York began to return.

He pressed the cloth over her lips and then down her slim neck, and Tessa fell completely motionless. She felt paralyzed, as if she had fallen to the power of a spell. The touch of his hand, the warm water, were sensual. Unlike the night before, she did not want him to stop.

She watched silently as he wrung the cloth in the water and lifted it back up, pressing it against her skin once again. His gentle, rhythmic strokes fell across her chest down to the cleft of her breast near the bodice of her soiled dress. Mud caked her smooth ivory skin.

As he continued to wash her, a kind of primitive urge built inside of Tessa. It was a powerful force, which frightened and confused her after the events of last night. Chandler deftly unpinned her limp, mudstreaked hair and watched it tumble onto her shoulders in long, copper streamers. He tenderly ran a cloth over her hair again and again.

When he finally drew back and sank onto his heels, Chandler said nothing. He seemed to be treating the charged situation as if it were the most natural thing in the world to have touched her in so intimate a manner. He mysteriously demanded nothing more.

"I'm really very sorry for stirring up problems with your family," she whispered, "and for creating trouble for Jennings."

"Daphne is looking for an excuse to cause trouble," Chandler said softly in reply.

"Your sister has made it quite clear that she would like me out of your life."

"You are the first person I have seen stand up to her in a very long time," he said proudly.

"Except you, of course."

Chandler's mouth lengthened into a slight smile. "She really does detest it when anyone gets the better of her."

"So it would seem."

"You and poor Jennings did look a sight. I can only imagine the expression on her face when she first saw you. In all the years I have known him, I have never seen Jennings with so much as a hair out of place."

"What will happen to him?" Tessa asked with genuine concern. "None of it really was his fault."

"Nothing will happen to Jennings," Chandler assured her with such easy authority that she instantly believed him.

When she lowered her lashes, Chandler tipped her chin up by the power of a single finger so that she was looking at him again. "Daphne does love to bluster. It is the only power she really has."

"Then why is it that you bear her insults? Why is she such a presence in this house?"

Chandler stopped, his mind full of a lusty haze. He ran a hand through his own hair and drew in a breath, considering her question. "There is a great deal I owe her, Tessa. It's a long story," Chandler said, then seductively touched her neck again with a single, long finger. "I'd rather not go into it at this precise moment in time."

"If not now, when?" she lightly pressed, remembering the gun and wanting so much to ask him and to hear a plausible explanation for what she had discovered.

"I have told you all that I can, my darling wife. Please let that be enough."

"At least tell me, does it have something to do with Cynthia?"

Chandler felt the calm slipping from his grasp again as she pushed. His reason was slipping, too. As it had the time at the Moores' garden party, when his father had drunkenly dared him to level a blow on him to prove who was really the stronger Tate. "But you'll never do it," his father had boasted loudly before their friends. "My son's not man enough!" "Stop it, father." He had tried to turn away. "What? Too much like some damn Chinkie now?" his father had cruelly pressed.

He was always doing that. Pushing him. Pressing him. Trying to humiliate him into the Benjamin Tate perception of success. "Gone to the Orient for a year and now he's better than the rest of us! Happy to be led around by the nose by that alley cat he married."

And so he'd hit his own father, hard. His fist coiled tightly with years of rage. He had slammed it into that satin-covered paunch, soft by then, vulnerable with too much rich food and easy living. The guests had thought it had been on Cynthia's behalf. But the blinding fury had been entirely his own. It had been coming between them for a very long time. He remembered that feeling now. Felt it again. The pressing, the needling . . . the rage . . .

His voice cracked. "My first wife is my past, Tessa, and I mean to keep her there. Please don't continue to push this."

Only a mere moment before, there had been such tenderness and intimacy between them. Now Chandler's tone was harsh. Tessa recoiled from the slight. He had secrets. Grand secrets. Something involving Cynthia. And Daphne. Tessa saw the pistol in her mind. Her own blood ran cold.

"Chandler, I cannot bear the secrecy. A person's mind can conjure up the most dreadful things. Just let me ask you about—"

"No! No more questions!"

He rose back onto his feet with the wash basin in his hand and strolled back into her dressing room with it, not answering her. When he emerged, his handsome face was stony, his seductive smile gone. He moved to the door in four long strides, eager to be away from her questioning.

"I am not discussing this any further, Tessa, and that is final."

"Please don't leave," she weakly bid him from across the room.

He turned back with his hand on the brass doorknob. "I

will be home at six," he said with a straight-faced firmness, and yet trying to soften his tone. He added, "I shall see you for supper."

"By six o'clock, there may well be nothing further for us to speak about."

"That would make me very sad," he said sincerely. "But, no matter what, I trust that I have made myself clear. The subject of Cynthia is closed. Permanently."

The sound of her name burned on his lips. Chandler could think of nothing but Tessa as his carriage swayed, rolling steadily back to the Tate offices on Summer Street. It was all closing in on him. It felt like a great wave, drawing him under. Trying to drown him. Everything he thought he could handle when he had decided to marry her. The balance he had thought he could keep. But what else could he have told her? He tossed the forgotten papers onto the opposite carriage seat in frustration.

But he had cut her off cruelly, yet again. He knew that, and already he despised himself for the look of disappointment he had seen on her beautiful face. But if he had stayed in her room a single moment longer, Chandler knew that to silence her questions he would have taken her in his arms, pulled her against himself, kissed her, and confessed the whole dark, unbelievable truth. He wanted to give her the world. But on one point he must remain firm.

Confession was not possible.

Tessa glanced down at her betrothal ring and tried to examine the quickly changing circumstances in which she found herself. *If he does not trust me enough to share his secrets with me, how can I believe anything but the worst? And if I believe that, how can I possibly stay?*

She had been fighting the notion of leaving since Chandler had left her, yet again, alone in her room—Cynthia's room. But with every pounding beat of her heart, she was being forced to consider a dark and awful possibility about the man she had married.

She glanced at the note she had left for Chandler explaining everything: what she had found, the suspicions it had raised, and her unwillingness to live amid so much secrecy. After reading it, he surely could not begrudge her leaving. She took the diamond ring from her finger and lay it beside the note.

"I've come to apologize," said a tiny, whispered voice from beyond the door. The pleading tone pulled her from her own miserable thoughts. "Please, may I come in?"

Tessa crossed the room and opened the door to find James's wide-eyed, repentant face gazing up at her. Alice was standing behind him, slightly taller, with her hands placed firmly on her brother's shoulders, as though to steady him. "We've both come, Tessa."

Neither child could contain his shock at seeing that she had changed into a simple day dress, one that she had brought from New York, and that near the bed, lay a stuffed carpetbag.

"You cannot go!" James cried as the pair moved into her bedroom and closed the door. "Not on my account!"

Alice's expression was desolate. And Tessa felt that same pang of tenderness she had felt earlier that morning. They hadn't meant to hurt her. They were simply children being children, innocent needy hearts without benefit of direction.

"I am not leaving because of you," she said very gently, stooping down before James, who was now on the verge of tears.

"Then why?"

"Because I don't belong here and I see now that I made a dreadful mistake in coming."

"But you married Papa," Alice countered. "A wife cannot leave her husband."

"It is more complex than that, sweetheart," Tessa said, reaching out to take the girl's hand. Alice drew it away sharply.

"You're just leaving us like all the others. I thought you were different, but you're just the same."

"The others?" Tessa asked.

"There were four governesses who tried to like us before you. And there was mother of course. But even she left us."

Tessa felt little satisfaction when Alice lowered her eyes. These children needed so much. More than she had to give. "Please try to understand. It's not your fault. My leaving has nothing to do with either one of you."

"Does Father want you to go?" James asked, knowing that his father had returned to work and now could not convince her to stay even if he had wanted to.

"Look," Tessa tried to smile and to change the subject. "You both are very special. I could see that from the first."

"And Mayflower?"

"Mayflower, too," Tessa smiled her soft smile.

"But we need you!" James pleaded. "You can belong to us. You are an awful lot of fun and you won't make us eat our prunes."

They were far too young to understand, Tessa thought, stifling a sad little laugh. "You can write to me in New York and I shall write back. I would really like that."

"You needn't bother," Alice said ruefully. "That is what our last governess said and we never heard from her again."

Never in her life had Tessa Murphy given up anything without a fight. But after her last unnerving encounter with their father, and all of those between Daphne and herself, she had felt like a butterfly trapped in a jar. Her single thought had been of escape.

No matter how much she loved Chandler, it had been a mistake to marry someone about whom she knew so little. And at least if she left him now, before things progressed any further between the two of them, annulment would be a clean and simple matter.

"Can't we say anything to change your mind?" James asked desperately.

"I'm afraid not. But in spite of what you or anyone else may think, I had fun in the park this morning and I think Jennings did, too. Don't give up on him yet. There is a streak of fun in that old boy there somewhere." She shooed the children from her room before she had time to change her mind.

Tessa left the grand house on Mount Vernon Street, carpetbag in hand, careful that no one should see her. She was not at all prepared to face a glib parting line from Chandler's sister who, for all she knew, was still waiting in the parlor to bait her further.

She walked quickly down the hill along the same path they had taken that morning to Boston Common, with absolutely no idea how she was going to get home. She had no money of her own and not the slightest idea how to get to the train station. The only thing of value she had in the world, her ring, she had left behind.

Tessa sat alone on one of the park benches, trying to collect herself. A warm afternoon sun glinted through the trees, dappling the ground around her. She gazed blankly down at the emerald grass and then watched a squirrel scamper up the thick trunk of the same tree behind which earlier that same day she had hidden. She needed to catch her breath. She needed to develop a plan. All Tessa had known, as she sat in that opulent and cold bedroom facing Chandler's stubborn refusal, was that she wanted to leave. Whether or not she could actually go through with it was an entirely different matter.

Chapter

27

"SO I UNDERSTAND CONGRATULATIONS ARE IN ORDER."

Chandler glanced up from his carved mahogany desk, sprayed white with papers and ledgers. His face was crossed by a stream of golden sunlight that came through the office window. Propped casually against the doorjamb of the Tate office, arms crossed over his short, broad chest, Nelson Winthrop stood flashing a lazy, good-natured smile.

"Well? When do we get to meet your new wife?"

"And where did you hear about that?"

"Oh, really Chandler." Nelson lifted a single mocking brow, then added glibly, "You know how quickly news travels in our circle. Even for one so very much on the fringes as I."

Our circle. How much Chandler hated that phrase. The small minds. Exclusive expectations. People like Felicity. Like Cynthia. Oh, Cynthia! How had he ever married someone like that? Believing he had loved her, when Tessa had been out there all along.

Chandler stifled a grin. He sprang to his feet, pressing the thought of a life he would never again need to live from his mind as he moved across the room. The two men then lunged into a back-slapping embrace.

"When did you get back in town?"

"Just last night." Chandler smiled at his former Harvard roommate and his dearest friend.

"Well, I guess I don't have to ask you how New York was, do I? Daphne must be livid."

"As usual," Chandler drawled and slipped back into his desk chair as Nelson sank into the red-leather chair facing him.

"So what is her name? You must tell me absolutely everything."

"Her name is Tessa Murphy. Mrs. Tate, now."

Nelson frowned slightly and raised a hand to stroke his chin. "Hmm. Don't know any Murphys. None that I can think of. Who are her people?"

"Good God," Chandler groaned. "You sound just like Daphne. I thought Sylvie had had more of an effect on you than that."

"Well, people *will* ask."

"They can ask all they like. I will still tell them only what I wish. Tessa was sent to me like some sort of angel and how it happened or where is really no one else's business."

"All right, all right," Nelson held a firm hand up to still Chandler's defense. His opposite arm rested comfortably across the chair back. "The rest of Boston be damned," he chuckled. "But of course you will tell your oldest and dearest friend all about this mystery bride of yours."

Chandler sank comfortably back in his desk chair and breathed a sigh, steepling his fingers and resting his elbows on the padded arms of the chair. He was in the presence of someone who could be trusted.

"We met a few weeks ago in New York when I left to teach my sister a lesson."

"And you've married her already? Quite a whirlwind, I'd say."

"She stole my heart the moment I saw her."

"This Tessa really must be something to have softened an old chestnut like you."

"She is that."

"Well, when do Sylvie and I get to meet her?"

"My wife is a bit nervous about being here in Boston," Chandler confessed. "She wants very much to make a good impression with my friends."

"So then you've abandoned the safe route and found yourself a gem like my Sylvie," Nelson declared with a pleased expression.

"What makes you say that?"

"What lady of means do you know who would lack the confidence to make an impression here in Boston, even at a moment's notice?"

"You've got me there," Chandler smirked.

"So then, if she is not one of us exactly, I suppose there are a great many things you will want her to learn."

"Learn?" Chandler asked.

But he knew what Nelson referred to: the sort of things Tessa needed to know if she were to fit into Boston society. Nelson Winthrop had never concerned himself with these things as they applied to his own wife, because everyone in Boston already knew her background. But for Tessa to fit in the way Nelson meant, there would be dancing lessons. Posture. Diction. The social graces. The array of subjects she would need to master to be assimilated smoothly into society was staggering.

But even if her unmistakable poise and bearing needed only a bit of direction, it was not what Chandler wanted for her. Or for them. He had no desire to mold Tessa into the sort of woman one found here in Boston. He had fallen in love with who she was, a young woman with a mind of her own and a thoroughly disarming zest for life. She was the girl Li Kao Chen had promised he would one day find.

"I don't want to change a thing about her," Chandler declared, tapping a pen against the desk. "Tessa is perfect just the way that she is."

"I'm sure."

"No, I mean it. She is. You'll see."

"Well, what is there to learn really?" Nelson smirked. "They are all a lot of stuffy opinionated old fops and crones who will make their judgments no matter what the poor girl does to charm them. How well I know that."

The fact that Nelson meant it in jest did little to ease Chandler's trepidation and concern for the sparkling lamb he had knowingly led toward a society slaughter. "Be that as it may," he countered firmly. "I suspect it will be a few weeks, at least, before Tessa feels ready."

"Does the same hold true for a private introduction for your oldest and dearest friend?" Nelson pressed with a clever gleam glinting in his hazel eyes. "A friend with a wife who could use a friend as much as yours undoubtedly could."

"Give us a few days," Chandler answered, dropping his pen onto the mound of papers as he leaned forward. "I would like at least a bit of privacy with my new bride before she dazzles all the rest of you."

"That good, hmm?" Nelson smirked.

"Better!" Chandler countered.

Tessa sat alone on the edge of the same park bench. A late afternoon breeze stirred her loosely coiled hair. Tessa was so dazed with confusion that she was not certain how long she had been there when she felt someone sink down onto the bench beside her.

"I thought I might find you here."

She lifted her head slowly to see David Jennings sitting beside her in a fresh black suit and white shirt, leaning on his ivory-handled walking stick. His expression was not punitive or even condescending. Rather, it was surprisingly gentle. Chandler Tate's butler was the very last person she ever expected to see again, and his calm presence here beside her threw Tessa entirely off guard.

"How did you find me?"

"That is not so important, is it?"

"But I left no trail. I told no one."

"Where else would you go in an unfamiliar city?" he asked knowingly.

"I . . ." the words sputtered past her sudden sobbing so that she could barely speak them. "I have left him, Jennings."

"I know," he countered in a deep, compassionate tone. He helped Tessa to her feet and then took her elbow firmly, seeing how frightened and vulnerable she was. "Let's walk a bit, shall we?"

"I can't go back there, Jennings," she protested weakly as her eyes continued to fill with despondent tears and they ambled along one of the winding paths. "No matter what you say, you'll not convince me to stay. That's why you've come, isn't it?"

Jennings plucked a clean handkerchief from his breast pocket and handed it to her. "I was merely going to say that I had not judged you to be the sort to run away without a fight."

"Perhaps you can give me one good reason why I should stay in a house choked by a mystery that my husband refuses to reveal. A mystery of which his sister is well aware."

As Tessa dried her eyes with his handkerchief, Jennings paused reflectively, watching two squirrels play at the base of a thick elm tree.

"The Tates have always lived by a kind of credo, believing that family is everything," he thoughtfully divulged. "Whatever the mystery is between them that has kept things so on edge these past couple of years, I can tell you that Mr. Tate and his sister are honorable people."

"How splendid for them," she shot back angrily. "But for an outsider, those people and their honor have created a hornets' nest of secrecy, and I cannot think of one good reason to subject myself to it."

"That you love him with your whole heart is not enough?"

When she did not reply, he looked back directly at her, as if he knew her as well as she knew herself.

"Very well, my dear young woman. Then I shall venture to tell you another reason why you should remain his wife.

Because Mr. Tate needs you desperately. You are young and spirited and, if I might say, he has waited a lifetime for you."

"He has a very peculiar way of showing me that."

"I can also tell you with great authority that beneath the tortured facade you see now lies a good and decent man. A man who has been through the fires of hell. Now, perhaps that is not reason enough for your heart, but perhaps for your conscience . . ."

Tessa's expression turned suddenly vulnerable. "But I am afraid that he has done something terrible. I have . . . found things."

David Jennings's eyes glowed with sincerity as he looked down at her. "Do not convict him, my dear, not without knowing that for certain."

They both stood silently for a while. His kindness and sympathy were like a warm blanket suddenly spread around her, making her feel safe with this unlikely new ally.

"Tell me how you know so much about Chandler."

"I have been with him since he was a little boy. Sometimes I believe I know him better than he knows himself."

"I don't feel I know him at all." Tessa shook her head and a stray copper curl dangled across her forehead.

"That sort of knowledge and trust between two people takes time," Jennings said thoughtfully.

"Did he have it with Cynthia?"

Tessa watched Jennings flinch at the sound of her name. "I'm sorry," she said before he could reply. "Perhaps I shouldn't keep prying about her when everyone seems so intent on keeping the truth about her hidden from me. It's just that I detest secrets so."

"If you ever tell him I said this," Jennings drew in a deep, contemplative breath, "I shall deny it wholeheartedly."

"Of course I wouldn't."

"The truth is that their relationship hurt him very deeply. Scarred him permanently in many ways."

"How?" Tessa asked carefully.

"They were both so very young and, I believe, foolish with one another's hearts."

"Do you mean that they were unfaithful, Jennings?"

"All I can tell you, ma'am, is that the image they presented to the rest of the world was not the reality that existed between them in private. But Mr. Tate went to great lengths during their years together to make a happy home for his children. I always respected that about him."

"Did he love her?"

"In the beginning, I believe so, yes. But that was a long time ago, and a great many things happened between them afterwards."

"Before she died," Tessa clarified.

"We are not to speak about that, any of us," Jennings answered as kindly as he could manage. "But I can promise you one thing. Chandler Tate is a kind and honorable man. There is none finer. Believe one thing if you believe nothing else: Whatever you may have found, you need not fear him."

Tessa softened as she inhaled a steadying breath. "Even if I wanted to give it one more try, which I'm not saying that I do, I left my ring and a note behind. Surely Chandler has come home and seen it by now."

"Are you referring to this note and ring?" Jennings asked, pulling her engagement ring and the crumpled missive from his breast pocket.

She gasped, watching the magnificent stone sparkle in the muted light as he took her hand and gently slid the ring back where it belonged. "Leave because you and Chandler cannot find a way to make a life together, not because of something your imagination has led you to suspect about him."

Tessa watched him take a gold watch from his breast pocket and flip it open. Then he looked back up at her. "There is still time to return to home. Mr. Tate does not customarily return until after six."

Jennings saw the hint of hesitation in her eyes but continued undaunted. "Speak with him tonight, my dear. If, by tomorrow morning, you have not found your own reason to stay, I shall drive you to the railway station personally and pay for your ticket myself."

Perhaps Jennings was right, Tessa told herself. She never

really had given him a reason to believe she wanted to know about Cynthia for any other purpose than curiosity.

In the space of time it took to walk around Boston Common, Tessa had decided to stay one night more. She told herself that in spite of her fears, she had made a commitment to him. But her heart whispered back to her that it was something far more than that. She was still desperately in love with the man she had married, and more than anything, Tessa wanted to believe he was not capable of committing a crime.

"All right then," she quietly said, determined to try one more time. "Tonight it shall be."

"So then, can I at least count on your bringing your new bride to the house by the end of next week?" Nelson asked as he and Chandler walked out to the street to hail a cab. "Sylvie will have my head on a platter if you don't."

"I don't see why not," Chandler replied, craning his neck for the sight of a single hack where usually there was a string of them. "Where in the devil are all of the cabs?"

"It's the epizoöty," Nelson answered woefully, referring to the devastating influenza gripping Boston's horses. "It has gotten much worse while you were away. Still killing off dozens of the poor beasts every day."

"Haven't they a clue what is causing it?"

"Not a one, and I don't mind telling you, after the great fire in Chicago last year, I'm getting a bit nervous. There are not nearly enough horses left even to pull the fire wagons. If something were to happen here in Boston like that, it really could be a dreadful catastrophe."

"Nothing is going to happen to Boston," Chandler smiled. "The good Brahmin families here simply wouldn't have it!"

Chapter
28

TESSA WOKE LATE THAT AFTERNOON TO THE SOUND OF WATER being poured from a pitcher. She had forgotten where she was, and in a burst of panic she sprang from the bed, pulling the loosely draped quilt with her.

"Who's there?" she called into the soft, golden light coming from her dressing room, her voice brittle with panic.

"'Tis I, ma'am," came a soft Irish voice, as Kathleen walked out from the light holding a basin of water. "I was thinkin' ye might be wantin' to freshen up before supper."

Tessa strained to see the gold mantle clock above the marble hearth across the room. She tried to focus. Hunger dominated her body to the point of pain. She was disoriented and tired. As her maid drew back the heavy velvet draperies, Tessa began to remember. It was not a dream. It had all really happened. The gun. The mystery. Daphne's cruel chiding. And yet she had returned here to Beacon Hill because the truth of the matter was that she desperately loved this enigma called Chandler Tate and she wanted to believe in the goodness of the man who had swept her so entirely off her feet and taken her away from New York.

After she had washed, she blotted her face with the towel, then gave it back to Kathleen. As she did, Tessa was comforted by the sight of the sparkling betrothal ring, back on her finger as though it had never been gone. She felt a twinge of guilt now, as sharp as the sting of a bee, at the memory of having given it up so impetuously. Thank the good Lord for the kindness and common sense of David Jennings.

Her maid moved a step nearer. "Might I help ye dress then?"

Tessa ran a hand through her thick, unbound hair. Her eyebrows lifted, then merged in a slight frown. "I know it is part of your job to keep asking, Kathleen, but I've been dressing myself for a long time, and I mean to continue."

"As ye wish," Kathleen bobbed a tentative curtsy, unable to control the well-worn reflex. "Ye remember that yer wardrobe closet is through that door."

"Thank you, yes I do."

But Tessa was far more concerned with the supper tonight than with whatever there might be for her to wear. Especially when she considered the prospect of dining in so grand a house beneath the watchful gaze of servants, and even children, all of whom were accustomed to what was expected of the ritual. Would she select the right fork? Drink from the appropriate glass? Take too much food from the serving platter? There were so many things to consider even when engaging in a simple meal.

Tessa recalled the baffling array of silver and dishes that night at Delmonico's, when every course, every bite, had felt like a test. But Chandler would help her this evening, as he had before, she silently assured herself. He certainly had not brought her all this way to see her embarrassed.

Neatly hung now beside a selection of far more elegant dresses, were the few garments she had brought with her from Mrs. Gallagher's boardinghouse. The others must have belonged to Cynthia. The only things Tessa possessed that came even close to any of them were her traveling costume and the dress she had worn to the theater and to Delmonico's. One of those, wherever it was, was dripping with muddy water from Boston Common's frog pond. The other, even she knew, was far too elegant for an evening meal at home. Even on Beacon Hill.

Glancing back into Cynthia's wardrobe closet, Tessa was confronted with the most beautiful array of colors and fabrics she had ever seen. Lace and beads. Silk ribbon and cord. Enough of everything elegant to take her breath away. As she lightly fingered one after another, her smile slowly faded. No matter how beautiful these things were, no matter how they beckoned her to try them, they did not belong to her.

Carrying her own simple forest-green skirt and white blouse, and trying her best to do it proudly, Tessa moved barefoot across the room. She lay the clothes across her bed and sat down at the dressing table. Then she gazed up at her reflection in the mirror. What she felt as she picked up the silver-handled hairbrush, surprised her.

In spite of their last miserable encounter and the harsh words spoken between them, Tessa now found herself eager to see Chandler again. She wanted so much for him to explain away her silly suspicions. And tonight he would. He would set all of her fears and misgivings to rest. She must believe that.

Chandler gazed down at the ruby necklace in its velvet-covered box as it glittered in the lamplight. It was an exquisite piece of jewelry. A fitting apology for last night. It was also excellent recompense for the scare Tessa had endured because of his children this morning. They meant well. They were precious children. But the loss of their mother had taken its toll. They needed Tessa in their lives almost as much as he did.

"So, Jennings, what do you think?"

"Lovely, sir," the butler replied, holding up Chandler's dark jacket, duly impressed by the large ruby surrounded by a spray of smaller diamonds, all of them set in gold.

"But do you think Tessa will like it?"

"I'm certain she will adore it, sir. What new bride wouldn't?"

"Precisely what I thought." Chandler smiled and shrugged into his jacket. "If a few jewels make this whole disagreeable transition easier for her then so much the better."

Chandler was smiling confidently until he glanced down at his butler whose expression was a curious mix of hesitation and reserve.

"All right, Jennings," he frowned, "out with it."

"Well, sir. It's only that I believe a young woman like your Tessa may well need reassurance of a different sort than expensive gifts."

"Nonsense!" Chandler scoffed and straightened his necktie. "All women adore jewels."

Jennings thought how easily Tessa had been willing to part with her betrothal ring, as he said, "Not all women, sir."

Chandler turned away from the mirror with a deeper frown creasing the light skin between his brows. "Say it, Jennings."

"Well, sir." Jennings breathed a little sigh. "It would seem to me that this has all been fairly traumatic for her. A new city. A new family. Not to mention your sister. Women far more accustomed to the social whirl would be equally daunted."

Chandler sank onto the fringed brown-velvet daybed, still holding the box. "I see what you mean. But what more can I do? It was the loveliest, the costliest piece of jewelry they had available on short notice. I had really hoped to sweep her off her feet with it. And frankly, Jennings, I needed to make amends for more than Daphne."

The courtly butler—Chandler's friend—sat down on the

edge of the daybed beside Chandler, then turned at an angle to face him. "Do you want to tell me, sir?"

"Last night," Chandler said in a suddenly vulnerable tone that was barely above a whisper, "she wanted to know about Cynthia."

"Oh dear."

"Then this morning, too. I'm afraid I didn't handle either encounter very well."

"And that means what, precisely?"

"I ruined the evening last night by leaving her room rather unceremoniously."

"On your wedding night? No wonder she—" Jennings sighed, recalling the forlorn young woman who had been desperate enough to leave her husband the day after their marriage.

Before now, Jennings had thought Tessa's reasons for wanting to leave Boston were based mostly on some vague suspicions, the impetuous act of a young bride. Not so, he realized now, knowing how clandestine, to the point of anger, Chandler could be about what exactly had become of the first Mrs. Tate.

"Perhaps you should tell your wife what she wishes to know and be done with it. It seems to me that the fastest way to make another woman an issue between you is to maintain a mystery. Be out in the open and be done with it, I say."

"I know you mean well," Chandler sighed, raking a hand through his oiled and tamed blond curls. "But it's not that simple. There were circumstances that even you don't . . ."

His words trailed off.

"She really is a spirited, splendid young woman, sir. Full of such fire. I would hate to see you lose all of that for a—"

"Who said I was going to lose Tessa? We may have a problem, but she's my wife now. And my wife she will stay. That I can assure you."

"I am only suggesting that you take care with her," Jennings countered knowingly before Chandler cut him off again, growing more agitated.

"Well, don't. She has made a commitment. We both have. Tessa is the sort who would never go against that."

He closed the velvet box with a snap and shot back to his feet, buoyed by his own confident declaration. The frown he had worn only a moment before was now replaced by an easy, confident smile.

"Oh, don't look so worried, Jennings," Chandler chuckled suddenly. "You'll see. One way or another, I'm going to make this work. Tessa is my own angel from heaven and I have absolutely no intention of ever losing that."

Chandler sprinted downstairs, surprising himself by how eager he was to see his bride. It had not even been a full day, and yet he had missed her. That bright smile. Those green eyes sparkling up at him. Deep, unending eyes. He had never known that kind of love, his heart said. Nor that kind of trust, his conscience reminded him.

"Good evening, brother dear."

The bubble of Chandler's imagination burst with a snap at the grating sound of Daphne's voice coming at him the moment he reached the parlor.

"What the devil are you still doing here?" he asked irritably. "My wife and I are both at home now. The children are in good hands. So you are free to leave."

"So much for pleasantries."

Crossing his arms over his chest, Chandler leaned against the fireplace mantel. "Very well, Daphne. What is it now?"

"We really must speak about this."

"What I told you last night I meant completely."

"Chandler, please. It is still not too late to put an end to this entire ridiculous charade."

"The charade was my life before I met Tessa."

"Oh, she doesn't know the half of it, does she?"

Chandler's eyes quickly darkened at Daphne's lightly veiled reference. There was a small charged pause, but Daphne continued undaunted.

"She's coarse as table salt and every bit as common. There is not a single thing about her that makes her worthy to have become your wife. Just listen to her speak. No matter how in the name of heaven she managed to charm you, that dreadful sound tells everything."

"She's my wife, damn you!"

"No one knows that yet, Chandler," Daphne pushed, coming toward him desperately. "You don't want to marry Felicity or anyone else I choose. All right, then. I understand that now. You have made your point about that in grand style. But, for the love of God, Chandler, let Lincoln and me see to an annulment for you first thing in the morning. We will make a settlement on the girl and then you can choose a bride from a suitable family. Anyone you like. I will stay out of it. You have my word."

"That is the way you deal with everything, isn't it?" Chandler snapped, his eyes blazing with sudden contempt. "Buy them off."

"Money does have its privileges."

"And it's curses."

"The Tate wealth has certainly rescued you from one serious scrape I can think of. I must say I didn't see you ridiculing family intervention then."

Chandler glared at her as his body stiffened. His sister at last had crossed the line. Mentioned the unspeakable. The past reared up at him with a vengeance.

In the seconds before his reply, Chandler fought silently to vanquish the dark images. It was the same valiant attempt he had made the night before when Tessa sought to bring out the truth between them.

Chandler's voice was a growl. "That was very different, and you well know it."

"Lies are lies, Chandler. Even the white ones."

"This taunting of yours is going to stop," he said fiercely, picking up one of the priceless crystal brandy glasses from a table near the front window. He held it up to the light and then glanced over to the fireplace hearth to gauge the distance. "And it is going to stop right here and now."

"Chandler, no!" Daphne cried out in a panic, springing to her feet when she realized what he was about to do. "Those glasses are—"

Crystal shattered like rain against one of the elaborate andirons. "—a hundred years old," he said, finishing her sentence.

"They have been in our family nearly that long. How could you have so little regard?" she gasped, looking at the hearth and then back at her brother, her anger replaced entirely by shock.

"I want to be very clear on what material things and social position mean to me, Daphne. How dare you still continue to try to control me? To insult Tessa? I alone decide my fate. Not you! Not anyone else!"

"Dear Lord, Chandler. B.W. Tate and Company is our heritage. All of this, even those glasses, are our heritage. I have only ever had your best interest at heart."

"Tessa is my best interest!"

"I'll tell her the truth, Chandler. I swear I will!"

At that precise moment, with the air still thick with their cruel dispute, Tessa entered the parlor in her starkly simple skirt and blouse.

Her hands were clasped lightly before her waist, her translucent skin glowing in the lamplight. But in her hand she held a pistol. The pistol she had pulled from the safe haven of Cynthia's window seat. It was all that either of them saw. The weapon glittered in the lamplight like an evil enemy come back to haunt them both.

"Tell me what?" Tessa asked.

Chandler moved forward swiftly, still brimming with the anger that had been roused by Daphne. Suddenly he could see nothing, think of nothing but the gun. "Where did you find that?"

"I was only going to ask you—"

"Never mind," he said dismissively, charging across the carpet toward her. "Give it to me."

Reflexively, as fear wrapped around her heart and her throat so that she could not breathe, Tessa shoved the gun behind her back. Apprehension pulsed through her like a shock.

"As much as I would love to stay and see this particular

little scene played out," Daphne said smugly, moving in slow steps toward the door, "this time, brother dear, I'm afraid you're on your own."

The bitter aroma from Daphne's perfume lingered in the parlor after she had gone. Tessa felt as if she might choke on it. And on the shock. She had been stunned by her husband's tight, bloodless face and by his response.

She moved a step nearer forcing herself to believe that what Jennings had told her was true. Needing desperately still to believe, if she could only ask the question.

"What is it, Chandler?" she finally asked with an impossibly dry throat. "Please tell me what it all means."

"Give me the gun, Tessa."

"But I—"

"Give it to me!"

Angry with his shockingly harsh tone, and with his command, she pushed through her own fear and lifted her chin a fraction.

"Well, I for one have had quite enough of this! If you are not going to tell me then I might as well just—"

As she turned toward the door, Chandler gripped her elbow. She felt his hand like a vise pressing into her skin. Tessa spun back around like a spring.

"Let me go! You're hurting me!"

Their eyes met. They were a single heartbeat, a breath away from one another. Chandler saw the fear behind the thin veil of anger. He loosened his grip just enough.

Free from his grasp, Tessa dashed up the stairs, her green skirt sailing out behind her. It had all been a dreadful mistake. Trusting Jennings. Trusting Chandler. Loving him.

"This is not settled, Tessa!" Chandler shouted at her heels as he dashed after her to the top of the stairs.

"It is certainly settled for me!"

She stumbled over her hem as she sprinted down the long corridor. Unable any longer to catch her breath, she was surprised to feel warm tears on her cheeks.

Tessa tried to close Chandler out of her bedroom with her best hard thrust of the door. He was stronger. He pushed through it with such force that she stumbled backwards, nearly losing her balance altogether.

"God! The sight of that thing makes me want to vomit," he raged. "And in your hand!"

"Chandler, please. What is the matter with you?"

They had barely passed through the door to her bedroom when he thrust his arm out once again, lunging for the gun. But, in his fury, he caught Tessa's sleeve instead. With a single powerful jerk, he tore the fabric so boldly that it came away from her arm and even her chest with a long rip.

Instinctively, Tessa pressed what was left of the fabric against her chest and shoved the pistol stubbornly behind her back. They were both panting, each staring into the other's eyes.

"Why are you doing this?" He brayed the question, his face shimmering now with a sheen of perspiration.

"Why am *I* doing it?"

"I warned you to leave it alone. Not to push."

"Chandler, you're frightening me, really. I only wanted to ask you why I should have found something so shocking beneath the window seat last night."

She fought to catch a breath in the shadowy, dimly-lit bedroom. Fought to finish her explanation as she looked into eyes that were fixed and glassy. Eyes that seemed no longer to belong to Chandler.

"I was only trying to find a safe place for some of my things in a room I was told was now mine."

Her heart drummed achingly in her chest and in her ears. She looked away, eyes darting frantically around the room. Heaven help her, the door was too far across the room for her even to escape. And at this precise moment, she honestly feared him and his blasted secrets enough to want nothing so much as that. Escape.

"All right! Go ahead!" she shouted defiantly, tears streaming down her cheeks, when she could see that she had been cornered. She thrust the gun at him. "Do what you will with it, and with me! I'll not live with secrets!"

Everything went suddenly still—quiet as death—once he realized what she had said.

Turning away from the fear in her eyes, which branded him like a hot iron, Chandler shuffled a few short steps to her bed and sank down on the edge of it. His head dropped between his shoulders. Finally, he clenched his eyes and surrendered his ravaged face to his hands.

"Oh God, I am so sorry," he murmured with gut-wrenching remorse. And then there was silence once again.

Tessa did not move at first. Her heart hammered in her chest and she fought to catch the breath he had frightened out of her. She was trying to quiet her own sobbing. But finally, as she watched him so full of this sudden and confusing contrition, she felt a wave of tenderness rise up from the deepest place inside her heart.

Through her anger and frustration at what was actually occurring here, she heard Jennings words echo through her mind. *Whatever you may have found, you need not fear him.*

Slowly, Tessa moved the few steps that brought her to the bed before him. Not thinking, only feeling, she reached out her hand. In response, Chandler clamped his powerful arms around her waist, burying his head against her flat stomach.

"I don't know what made me do that. I wouldn't hurt you. I could never hurt you."

Tessa swallowed hard, forcing the words past her strained throat. "But you did"—her heart skipped a beat—"hurt *her,* didn't you?"

It took a moment for Chandler to comprehend the accusation. As he looked up at her, his eyes widened, his blond brows arched.

"You mean Cynthia?" he mouthed in disbelief. "You think I killed my wife?"

Tessa took his softly whiskered chin in her hand and spoke just above a whisper. "I want to know what happened, Chandler. Please, finally, won't you help me to understand how it all ended?"

His throat burned with the words he could not force

across his lips. There was still, and always would be, danger for his children in speaking the truth aloud. But the reason to stay silent had become so much more than that.

This sweet Irish paragon of pride and honor was too principled ever to understand the lengths to which he had been driven. She would never be able to accept that there once had been a darker side to him, one capable of committing such a heinous crime.

If you knew the truth about me, Tessa, he wanted to say, he ached to say, *it would be the end of everything that is good between us. And heart of my heart, that I could not bear.*

He expelled a ragged breath as the pain plunged deeper down into his chest. "I cannot tell you what you wish to know," he said instead. "But I did not kill her. That, I swear to you with everything that I am, Tessa. I swear it!"

Tessa sank down before him, lowering her head onto his knees and letting him stroke her hair.

"You can trust me, darling," he whispered desperately into her hair. "I need you to trust me. I will never hurt you. I would rather cut out my own heart than hurt you."

Before she could respond, Chandler pulled her up crushingly against his chest, wanting to show her with more than words the proof of what he said. In what felt to her like one urgent and yet fluid movement, his mouth came down on hers and he plunged his tongue inside of her mouth.

One hand pushed past her corset and played at her hardening nipple as he reveled in the taste of her passionate groan. The other hand moved down the length of her spine.

He felt the straining pressure in his loins, the ache to fully join his starving body with hers. His kiss grew more insistent, until he could no longer catch his breath, and that he could not, did not matter.

"Tell me that you believe me," he muttered between conquering kisses.

"I want to believe you, Chandler, I do."

"Then believe it. Lord above, I could never hurt you!"

Tessa was locked beneath him, her body and mouth

bound by his desperately growing desire. Chandler pressed her back into the bedding. Forcefully, he drew up the firm, coarse fabric of her skirt and made his way through the tangle of petticoats and drawers to touch the place between her thighs.

He had wanted it to be more like lovemaking than desperation between them this first time. His own hunger to possess her however, and his need to blot out the pain of the past, had become a demand. He surrendered to it. There was nothing more for him than the sensations that her body conjured. Skin. Mouth. Fingers. Perspiration. He parted her thighs with his knee without even waiting to see if she was moist enough to receive him. Tessa struggled as he began to thrust at her, his hands bracing her shoulders roughly back against the bed linen.

"Chandler, please!" She tried to struggle from a place somewhere between desire and fear.

"Don't fight me, Tessa. It shall hurt for only a . . ." His words trailed off into breathing that was fast and ragged.

Tessa gasped, then cried out as Chandler entered her fully. She tensed against him, not prepared for the pain. His jaw was clenched as he gripped the long tendrils of hair that lay across her shoulders.

The kind, gentle man she had married was completely lost to her. In a daze of confusion and heightened senses, she tried to surrender to the surging, probing mass of raw fury crushing her now with his need. He would have his way, and they both knew it.

Swiftly, Chandler's fingers moved beyond her hair and were digging into the soft flesh of her shoulders. His powerful body was like a vise, keeping her steady as he thrust into her again and again. Her mind spun with a sensation that was not quite pleasurable and yet no longer filled with pain.

Suddenly, and with no warning at all, Chandler began to shudder. Then he let out an earthshaking groan, as if he had been wounded. Yet still he did not release her body. He moved down to her breasts, drawing on them with his lips. First one and then the other as he rocked against her. As he continued to thrust.

A moment later, his heart still beating furiously, Chandler dragged himself from her and fell onto his back. His eyes tightened to force back the sheer agony he had felt even in release.

It was wrong. She had deserved better than to be used by him like this. In the silence, his gasps for breath came between them, short and hard. "I'm sorry," he said in a quaking whisper. Tessa turned to see the torment still rigid and exposed on his handsome, lamplit face. "It should not have been like this between us," he said.

"You needn't apologize," Tessa tried to reassure him with a voice that sounded shaky and vulnerable to them both.

"But you deserved more tenderness the first time between us."

"I want all of you, Chandler Tate. The good and the bad. Don't you know that by now?"

He waited another moment, then turned onto his side. He drew up a knee. He must tell her the truth, if only some small fraction of it. She was the love of his life, and she deserved that much.

"My marriage to Cynthia was a mistake," he admitted with an edge to his voice, as his heart finally began to slow. "Most of the time it was sheer hell for us both."

Jennings's words came back to her as confirmation: "Believe me, he has been through the fires of hell."

"The fact of the matter is that I didn't love her and she didn't love me. But we had the children and—" His voice broke off again.

"And you tried."

He ran a hand back through his hair. "How I did try."

"But the gun. Your initials are right there on the stock."

"C.T. stands for Cynthia, not Chandler, Tate." He took a breath. "For me, that pistol of hers is just a symbol of all of that. Of the fighting. The constant anger. And even the violence. She shot a squirrel with it once and brought the

ANGEL BRIDE

poor dead thing into the house, cradled like a child, just to try to shock me."

"Which explains the blood on her shirtwaist."

"Sadly," he said. It had been the truth in part. But the blood on that gun and on the garment around it had not come from a squirrel. It was human blood. "It was just such a shock to see it again."

"Your marriage was not a happy one," said Tessa, believing she understood, at last. "That is the reason you don't wish to speak of it."

He ran a hand across her cool, bare shoulder where the torn fabric had come away from her skin. "But can you ever forgive me for frightening you? Dear God, to have suspected me of murder and then for me to have behaved as I did about a gun!"

"If you have been truthful with me at last," she said with conviction and a new surge of love for this complex and tormented man, "then there is nothing to forgive."

"I have," he said.

Liar, his mind echoed in return.

After Tessa had fallen asleep, Chandler kissed her forehead and then moved quietly through the dressing room between their two rooms. His own bedroom was dark. No lamps had been lit. The only light came from a full moon through the lacy beige undercurtains on two tall windows. A silvery-blue glow.

Another letter awaited him on his bedside table. A wave of icy shock coursed through him, then stabbed at his heart. He didn't need to open it to know from who it had come. It had come from Paris.

Tearing it into shreds until there were nothing but tiny bits of white paper littering the carpet beside his bed, Chandler cursed the air trying vainly to control his anger.

"Damn you, Cynthia! Damn you to hell!"

Chapter

29

HE WAS WAITING FOR HER AT THE KITCHEN TABLE THE NEXT morning, as uncertain as a child. Chandler had asked Kathleen to bring his new wife here rather than to the breakfast room with the starched white linen cloth on the table and the row of priceless decorative plates lining the paper-covered walls.

Sun did not flood the kitchen in golden streamers as it did the upstairs rooms. And there was no fragrance of roses, of rich, fat blossoms coming in from the walled garden beside the breakfast room.

This place reminded Chandler of simpler times. Better times he had lived in this house. Times he wanted again now with Tessa.

Once the cook, housemaids, and Jennings were assured that these were truly the surroundings that the master desired for breakfast with his new bride, Chandler was left with a rack of toast, a fat blue ceramic pot of berry jam, and a pot of steaming tea. To your own devices, sir, Jennings had said after Chandler had winked at him. "Newlyweds," Mrs. O'Neil, the cook, had muttered grumpily.

A moment later, Tessa came alone down the narrow flight of stairs and into the kitchen. Chandler forgot to breathe when he saw her wearing the plain yellow-and-white-striped day dress that she had brought from New York. Her hair was neatly coiled on top of her head once again. Looking at her, so beautiful and so serene, it was as if the darker parts of last night had never even happened.

In a flash, he was on his feet feeling so repentent and so happy to see her that he forgot how awkward he felt.

"Oh, darling," he said, suddenly aware of both the simplicity of her dress and the nobility with which she wore it. Chandler rose and took the two short steps to meet her.

He tried to smile but it came out as a grimace. "I should have had a proper wardrobe seen to long in advance of our arrival home. I don't know what's the matter with me."

He sat down beside her and took up her hand. He kissed the delicate skin of her palm. Softly. Slowly. Then Chandler looked up at her again. "I have something I want to give you."

Her eyes followed his to the plate laid before her and to a ruby necklace glittering on it that was the most exquisite thing she had ever seen. "Chandler," she said breathlessly as she cast a glance back at him. "It is magnificent."

He kissed her hand again, then smiled. "No more magnificent than my bride."

Tessa fingered the stones with her other hand. She was in complete awe that something like this could possibly belong to her. "My own special golden things."

"What's that?"

"It was what my mother called this kind of thing."

"Something of great value."

"It was what they wanted for me some day," she said a little sadly, remembering. "It was why we came to America."

"You are what is golden to me," he said huskily, already

wanting her desperately once again. "And because it is so, what happened between us last night shall not happen again."

When her face flushed with knowing, Tessa turned away. But Chandler brought her chin back by the gentle power of his thumb and forefinger.

"Until it is what we *both* want more than anything in the world, I'll not lay another hand on you."

"I am your wife, Chandler," she whispered, but the words only came with great difficulty. "Such a promise is hardly necessary."

His face grew suddenly serious. "I don't ever want it to be out of duty that you lie with me, Tessa. I want more for us than that. Let me do this for you, darling. For us. Agreed?"

Her lips turned up into a slight smile, but she was secretly a little sorry that she would have to wait to feel that commanding power of his body above her like that once again.

"Now that it's settled, we shall speak of it no more, hmm?" Tessa let him pour her a cup of tea then he took a piece of toast and spread it with jam.

"I used to love to come down here as a boy," he went on, leaning over the simple oak table and taking up her hand between them again. "Things seemed so simple to me in this kitchen."

"I can imagine," Tessa smiled, considering its contrast to the enormity, and magnificence of the rest of the house upstairs.

"Tessa, this life's not all bad, though. Some of the grand parties and suppers we will attend together will actually be entertaining, if we go with the right attitude."

"The right attitude?" Tessa asked, nibbling on a piece of toast.

"It simply cannot be taken too seriously. You will find that most Bostonians take themselves far too seriously to have any real fun."

"Then we'll just have to make our own."

Tessa had assumed when she agreed to marry Chandler that some socializing was part of the agreement. But now the reality of it frightened her to death. She did not dance nor converse properly, and she even had difficulty using the appropriate utensil without Chandler's assistence.

"What is it?" he asked, seeing the easy smile leave her face as she stiffened in her chair.

"You know that I don't know how to dance. At least not in any way your friends would find proper. And I'm bound to slip up in a situation where any sort of lengthy conversation is required."

"The devil with them!" He slammed down his cup. "I didn't marry you to turn you into something you are not."

"But it is quite likely that I will embarrass you miserably if I don't learn at least a few things."

"Tessa, my darling," he kissed her cheek, "that would be impossible."

"Oh, you are wrong about that!" she said earnestly. "I may not have gone to school, but I have read enough books to know that there is an entire world out there I know nothing about."

"The sort of wisdom you have," he squeezed her hand and smiled his handsome smile at her, "is the sort of wisdom you cannot learn in school. It's inside here," he assured her, pressing her hand back across her own heart. "Trust that. Trust what you know and it will never fail you."

"You will say that until the first time we dance and I positively crush your poor feet."

Chandler laughed out loud and leaned back in his chair, more contented and relaxed than he had been in years. God, how he adored her ability to put him at ease. She could charm absolutely anyone just as she was. He was certain of it. But she was bright, eager, and willing, and so the rest would come easily enough.

As he sat gazing over at her, not certain he could bear to see a thing about her changed, he forced himself to ask, "Is learning what you truly want then?"

"Oh, yes, Chandler, could I?"

"Darling, I told you I meant to give you the moon," he chuckled. "A few lessons in etiquette will be easy compared to that."

The children came bounding down the stairs in their leather shoes, breaking the silence like a herd of wild elephants.

"Tessa!" James cried out, bounding into the kitchen and up to her lap. "You've come back! See Alice, I told you that she would!"

"I only went for a walk with Jennings yesterday," Tessa carefully explained, settling her teacup back into the saucer and wrapping both arms around the little boy.

"But you took your—" James began to say.

He was stopped in mid sentence by one admonishing glance from his sister.

"We must have misunderstood, that's all," said Alice.

"We really are so sorry about yesterday," James chimed in.

"Aunt Daphne sent us to bed without our supper," his sister confessed.

Tessa looked back at Chandler. "I don't suppose there was really any harm done, was there?"

Alice leaned against her father. "But you really mustn't play those sorts of dangerous games with people," Chandler admonished them. "Someone could have been hurt."

"But it was worth it to see Jennings dripping from head to foot and his hair all askew," Alice laughed. "Climbing out of the water he looked like a giant sheep."

Chandler bit his lower lip to keep from laughing out loud. "I must confess, I wish I had been there to witness that sight myself."

"And Aunt Daphne's face when we all arrived home looking like a ragged pack of immigrants! That is what she called us. A pack of nasty immigrants."

Tessa's easy smile faded first. Then Chandler stopped laughing. He cleared his throat.

272

"And what do you think immigrants look like, precisely?" Tessa asked.

"Oh, they're dreadfully ragged," James replied with great authority. "Their hair is always shaggy and they're miserably dirty."

"All of them?" Tessa pressed.

"At least that is what Aunt Daphne says. She made us promise never to talk to any of them when we are walking out on the Common or in the public garden."

"Well. I will tell you both something very, very important."

"Tessa, you needn't—" Chandler began, trying to halt an apparent confession.

"It is something I learned a very long time ago," she said, before he could continue. "You must never, ever judge a person by the clothes he wears or the place from which he comes. A person's good is not inside those things. It is here," she said pressing her hand to her heart. "Inside of you."

James and Alice both looked up to their father, their faces shiny and questioning. "She is right about that," Chandler confirmed.

"Besides, immigrants are only people who have come here to America from other faraway places. In their homelands, they would be just like everyone else, and it is you who would be the stranger."

"I never thought of it like that," Alice said, considering. Once again, she looked up at her father. He nodded in agreement, only this time he was smiling.

"Father, do we know any immigrants?" James asked with true interest.

"I'm certain that we all do, son. And, for that matter, Tessa is entirely correct. We must remember that they really are no different from you and me."

"Kathleen is someone who came to America with her family from another place," Tessa offered. "That makes her an immigrant. Perhaps today, you both could try to remember what we spoke about in your dealings with her."

Chandler pulled them to himself one at a time, kissing the tops of their heads with a show of tenderness that rocked Tessa's heart. He was such a splendid, devoted father.

"Father," Alice said, "do you suppose perhaps we might all go to the park together tomorrow afternoon? You, Tessa, James, and me?"

"I promise to be good," James said solemnly, crossing his heart.

"It really would be fun, Father. And it has been such a long time since you've come with us."

"Mayflower would like it, too," James added, stroking the dog who followed them like a shadow, tail forever wagging.

"I'm afraid that is out of the question, Son," said Chandler with a sigh.

"But why?" Alice asked with surprise.

"I simply don't have time for that sort of thing this time of year. Now is the very busiest part of the season for business."

But even as Chandler spoke the words, he knew how incomprehensible they must sound to children. They wanted only to spend time with their father, knowing little and caring less for the world of business into which he had purposely plunged himself after their mother's death.

Chandler sighed and watched Tessa, who made no move to reproach or argue as the children stood up and prepared to go back upstairs.

"I am really so glad you're here," Alice declared. "Father needs someone like you around to make him smile. He really does work so awfully hard. Perhaps you can help him to change that."

Chandler touched the child's smooth cheek and then chucked her gently beneath the chin.

"You know, on second thought, I suppose I could use a bit of a rest tomorrow. Perhaps a walk in the park would do me good."

The expressions of complete surprise on their small faces tore at his heart. They also told him that he had made the right decision. No matter what had happened in the past, no matter how driven he had been, it was time to start living again. And he was glad this new life of his would include this woman who was fast becoming a part of his soul.

"Do you think she will stay now?" James asked once they had reached the top of the stairs.

"I don't know," Alice whispered thoughtfully as they walked in tiny children's steps toward the music room. "But she did come back, and I do wonder what it was that changed her mind.

"Perhaps it was Father who found her and forced her to return."

"Perhaps," she agreed, linking her hands behind her back. "Well, he loves her madly. That much is certain."

"Since he agreed to come to the park with us on a Monday, he probably does love her quite a bit."

"I think he would go anywhere with her," said Alice.

The grand ebony clock in the foyer ticked five times before James asked the next question. "Alice, do you ever wonder how Mother died? He doesn't even talk about her and neither does Aunt Daphne."

"Sometimes," she answered truthfully. "And sometimes I forget about her entirely. After all, she's been gone for such a long time now."

"Well, I hope Tessa stays," James declared. "It would be so lovely to have a mother again."

"It would be even lovelier to have *her* as a mother," Alice corrected her brother, and they both nodded approvingly.

"What is all of this?" Tessa gasped the next morning, standing barefoot in her nightdress as the morning sun filtered into the room in long pink streamers. A line of strangers shuffled in around her carrying swatches of silk and satin, sketchbooks, and trunks full of hats, shoes, gloves, and shawls.

"This is Mr. Armistead, the dressmaker," Kathleen explained of the man who stood erect, arms loaded, at the foot of Tessa's bed. "And this is Miss Taylor. After they have taken yer measurements ye are to select the designs and the fabrics ye favor."

Tessa rubbed the sleep from her eyes, still not comprehending. It was barely eight o'clock and she had not been able to fall asleep until almost dawn. "I don't understand."

"The master's orders, ma'am. They were to be presented to you the very first thing."

"But no one works this early in the morning."

"Oh, they do if they're called for by Chandler Tate, ma'am."

A flurry of activity erupted around Tessa. One assistant led her to a full-length mirror by her dressing table and began measuring her waist and hips while a short, portly man opened a trunk full of exquisite hats.

"But I brought bonnets with me from New York," she said sleepily.

"Mr. Tate was very specific, ma'am," Kathleen explained. "The milliner's selection was to be included today."

"If these are not to your liking, Mrs. Tate," the woman interrupted respectfully, "I have these catalogues from which you may choose as well. And I will have any of them for you by week's end."

At the same time, a spindly little woman was opening another trunk beside her, packed with elegant evening slippers and soft, calfskin high button shoes and boots. She laid them in a neat row at the end of the bed as Kathleen helped Tessa on with a blue silk robe and neatly tied her sash.

"Chandler instructed all of these people to come?"

"I'm not certain I understand it myself," Kathleen shook her head earnestly. "But when I rose this morning, I did find Jennings supervising the removal of all of the late Mrs. Tate's things. I heard Mr. Tate tell him that not a stocking was to be left behind."

Tessa sank back down on the edge of the bed as one of the dressmaker's assistants held out her arm and began to measure the length from shoulder to wrist.

"So then, are any of these to your liking, Mrs. Tate?"

asked the pasty-faced milliner, as she held up a costly green silk-and-feather hat with one hand and one with blue ribbons in the other.

"Might we ask you to stand again for us please, Mrs. Tate?" the dressmaker inquired at the same time.

No sooner was she on her feet again than the assistants proceeded with more measurements beneath their dressmaker's watchful eyes.

"It is lovely," said Tessa.

"It also comes in gold and green. May I order it in those colors for you as well?"

"I have the perfect satin to go with the green," the dressmaker offered.

Tessa could only look blankly over at Kathleen, her eyes pleading for assistance. She felt a tiny rush of relief as her maid nodded and Jennings came in through the door amid the swirl of activity. His head was held high with the usual courtly pride, but his firm mouth hinted a slight smile. "May I help with anything?" he asked kindly.

"Oh, Jennings, would you? I really have no idea what would please Mr. Tate."

Jennings wound her arm in his, confidently, and then led her over to the rose-velvet daybed at a right angle to the fireplace. Then he sat down beside her. "You needn't worry, ma'am. You and I shall make some wonderful selections. You may leave everything to me."

In all, Tessa chose patterns and fabric for five new dresses, two ball gowns, and another traveling costume, all with shoes to match. With Jennings's encouragement, she bought six lace and linen nightdresses, a selection of stockings, and the fabric for eight new dresses. She also reluctantly chose six new hats. One she could not resist was exactly like the hat she had seen with Brian that night on The Ladies' Mile. A hat the likes of which she had never expected in her life that she might own.

"Are ye all right, ma'am?" Kathleen asked, once everyone had gone and Tessa sank back down onto the bed.

"He is just such a complex man," Tessa softly said, brushing the hair back off of her shoulders.

"It hasn't been easy on Mr. Tate, with losin' his first wife and all," Kathleen offered. "It's been an empty and sad place here since then."

"I can imagine."

"And I can tell ye another thing. There hasn't been as much joy on the faces o' those children in a very long time."

"That is sweet of you to say, Kathleen."

"I speak only the truth, ma'am. That way, ye need not try to remember what ye've said."

"Sage words."

"Aye. Me da's words. But that's another story. So tell me then, ma'am. Are ye feelin' up to dressin' now? Ye haven't much time, ye know."

"Time for what?"

"I'm to see ye readied by half past ten. Jennings said the carriage would be waitin' before Mrs. Forrester arrived."

"But I cannot go anywhere," Tessa protested. "We promised the children we would take them to the park."

"I'm told that comes after, ma'am."

"After what, Kathleen?"

"After your lessons, ma'am," she whispered and then lowered her eyes slightly. "The master said to tell ye that the moon goes on sale first thing today. Those were his exact words. I don't understand a word of it, but Mr. Tate said ye'd know what he meant."

Chapter

30

THE AFTERNOON WAS MAGIC.

The sun shimmered a bright golden glaze above, but the bristling trees spread a canvas of shade across the area where Tessa and Chandler sat and watched the children play. Mayflower barked joyously on the grass as the pair engaged in a spirited game of tag. They ran to their father and his bride.

"Your turn!" Alice laughed, tugging at her Chandler's arm as James pulled Tessa with equally great demand.

Chandler's reserve lasted only so long as his wife's. She was allowing a gleeful little boy to drag her from the bench and out onto the rolling green grass. "All right then," Chandler chuckled. "If it's a romp you want, a romp you shall have!"

"You're it, Father," Alice declared with a happy shout and then scrambled behind a tree as Mayflower jumped and barked.

Chandler crouched down and, in perfect imitation of a

madman, began to seethe and stalk toward his children, both of whom pealed with laughter between their screams.

He quickly caught James behind the park bench, tapping his back and exclaiming victoriously, "Ha! Now you're it!" before he darted out across the grass.

What the child lacked in speed, he more than made up in agility and in no more than a moment, he had caught his sister behind the tree, tapped her shoulder and run for cover expelling a long, infectious giggle.

Everyone was laughing and gasping for breath when Chandler was tagged a second time and began again to stalk toward the protective trees. But this time, his target was Tessa.

Her face alive with laughter, Tessa dashed quickly behind a stone statue, but as Chandler neared she was laughing so hard that she forgot to pick up her skirt. As he lunged for her, she tried to dash in the opposite direction. In an instant, she caught her skirt beneath her shoe and they both went tumbling onto the soft, spongy grass.

For a moment, they were both still laughing so hard and gasping that neither of them could move as Chandler arched over her, his arms pinning hers up near her head. He could feel Tessa's sweet breath on his face as James hiccuped a laugh and then made a sour face. As he and Alice watched their father with Tessa, Alice reached up and pressed a hand across her brother's mouth. But it was too late. At that very moment, someone standing behind them cleared her throat. The sound was like a dash of icy water, reminding them of propriety, willing them all back toward convention.

"Chandler Tate, is that you?"

He snapped back to his feet, brushing the grass from the front of his trousers and recognizing the stalwart woman before him as Horatia Wainright. Chandler gave the old society matron a jaunty grin, realizing that in spite of the terrible impropriety, he regretted absolutely nothing about his present circumstance.

No other woman had ever made him feel so free and so alive, and so reckless in his life. It was an entirely different sensation from what he had felt for the married Lydia Bailey, or even for Cynthia.

"It is indeed I," he replied. "How are you, Horatia?"

Mrs. Wainright stared at him up and down as she stood woodenly in green-and-white-striped silk. "Benjamin Tate's son rolling around on the grass in the broad light of day. It is positively vulgar."

"You and Albert really should try it some time."

"Out of the question." She sniffed. "We are far too well bred for that."

"Pity. At the very least, it would put a bit of that spring back in poor Albert's step."

"Mind your own step, my boy." She wrinkled her long, flat nose as she looked over at Tessa, who was being helped back to her feet by Alice and James. "I tell you I wouldn't have believed it if I hadn't seen it for myself."

"Happy I could accommodate you."

"Smug as always, I see."

"Just happy, Horatia. A state I am quite certain you wouldn't know if it bit you."

"What I am quite certain of, is that dear, foolish Lydia will not take kindly to having been cast aside for this new dalliance of yours, once you sufficiently ruined her reputation in this community."

"This, Mrs. Wainright, is not a dalliance. Tessa is my wife."

Mrs. Wainright's thick gray eyebrows arched severely and her color went from garnet to chalk. "Your dear father must be rolling over in his grave."

"Perhaps, since he never did care a bit for my happiness when it conflicted with his own reputation."

"Perfectly understandable."

"Why am I not surprised that you said that?"

"Well I am very much surprised at you. After that last ill-bred girl you paraded around as your wife, this is not a scandal that will easily die, Chandler. You will never live this down here in Boston."

He leveled his eyes upon her. "Well, at least I will be

giving them all something fabulous to gossip about at the card parties on Thursday afternoons, won't I?"

"Ach!"

"I would close my mouth if I were you, Horatia. There is quite a sizeable number of flies out today."

Horatia Wainright pivoted so forcefully that the edge of her skirt swirled around her ankles like a top.

"They'll never accept her into society, Chandler, any more than they did Cynthia. Mark my words. Never!"

He could not resist. "Oh come now, my dear Mrs. Wainright. Certainly you know what they say about never saying never!"

"The woman is a viper," Chandler seethed after she'd turned and stalked away.

Tessa wanted to speak in reply but her throat had completely closed. These emotional ups and downs were beginning to take their toll. The primitive sensation of fear still whirled inside of her like a hurricane. How could she ever be a match for women like that?

But no matter what she felt, she was determined not to let these people get the better of her. Not now that she knew for certain that she belonged here with Chandler and with his children.

"If you want to back out of the lessons and even the parties, Tessa, I certainly will understand. I find them dreadfully pretentious, anyway."

"Oh, not on your life. Especially when that is precisely what your Mrs. Wainright would like me to do."

Chandler's expression was one of surprise. He did not see that Alice and James were grinning. "But when the price of an introduction into society is unabashed cruelty—"

"Even that cannot last forever. Next month they'll have someone else to gossip about. Besides, when the risk is great, so is the gain."

Only a hint of a smile pushed past Chandler's indignation. "Another of your father's sage observations?"

"Charlie Murphy was a wise man," she smiled freely.

"A lucky one, too."

"Since we are doing so well, might I ask a question?"

"Ask away," he smiled as the children darted out across the Common, Mayflower behind them.

"Who is Lydia Bailey?"

After a moment's contemplation, Chandler took her hand, held it tightly, and then exhaled a heavy sigh as he led her to a bench beneath the protection of a low-hanging tree.

"Lydia and I were lovers before I met you, Tessa," he said directly. He studied her face in the silence, trying to gauge her response.

"So Horatia Wainright was telling the truth?"

"About that she was."

"And the woman is—" The words caught in her throat so that she could not speak them.

"Married," Chandler said evenly. "Yes, Lydia is married. To a much older man who can no longer provide—"

He checked himself rather than continue an explanation of something so intimate, which Tessa could not begin yet to understand.

"And now?"

"My beautiful wife," he breathed, bringing her hand to his mouth and pressing a kiss onto the smooth honey skin, "How desperately I do want to show you that there is no other woman in my life, or in my heart, but you."

Tessa took back her hand and looked across the Common at the children off in the distance.

"Why did you do it?" she asked, and Chandler was genuinely touched by her desire to understand.

"Oh, my beauty," he sighed. "People do curious things sometimes when they are hurt or lonely."

"And which one were you when you took up with Mr. Bailey's wife?"

"Both, I suppose."

"Because of Cynthia?"

"Yes."

"I really cannot bear the thought," she said, recoiling as he reached out to take her hand.

"You asked me to tell you the truth, Tessa," he said firmly, turning her face toward his with a powerful forefinger as he leveled his storm-blue eyes upon her. "Don't make me sorry for trusting you."

"You can trust me with anything. That doesn't mean I will always like what I hear."

"Point taken." He smiled, then stood again. "But in spite of the discussion that it led to, I am actually glad you found out."

"Why is that?"

"Because it feels good to begin with honesty between us. I've actually begun to imagine what that might be like all of the time."

Two days later, at precisely four o'clock, Chandler's carriage stopped before a modest brick townhouse on Chestnut Street. Tessa turned to her husband, pressing her hand into the crook of his arm.

"I really don't think I am ready for this," she said pleadingly as Douglas walked around to open the carriage door.

"Do you honestly believe I would bring you somewhere if you weren't?" he asked, his voice ringing with confidence and affection.

"But I've only just begun my lessons and there are so many things jumbling around in my head. I know that I shall never be able to keep them all straight."

Chandler covered her hand with his own. "You won't be needing any of that here. Here, we are among friends, Tessa. True friends."

Nelson and Sylvie Winthrop waited at the top of the landing in front of their open front door, a welcoming gesture that surprised Tessa. She and Chandler climbed the front stairs together but she hung back a step as he clapped the man's shoulder affectionately and then kissed his wife. They moved to the foyer before introductions began.

"Tessa, I would like you to meet two of the most splendid

people in the world," Chandler said, clasping a hand firmly around her waist. "The only two people who made my life bearable until I met you."

"It is truly a pleasure," Sylvie smiled genuinely and held out her hands as she spoke in a silky voice, heavily accented with French. "We are just so happy that Chandler has finally found someone to make him smile again."

"A sight I frankly never thought I'd see," Nelson intoned.

"Nor I," Chandler surprised everyone by seconding.

Tessa and Chandler followed their hosts into a parlor far more modest than the one in the Tate home. It bore a cozy, lived-in warmth that immediately set her at ease. There was fragile-looking blue paper on all of the walls and crisp white lace curtains hanging in front of the long street-front windows, which still brought in great crimson shafts of late-afternoon sunlight.

The pictures on the walls were not huge and daunting landscapes like the ones that graced the walls in Chandler's home. Instead, these were children's portraits. It was precisely what she would have placed on the walls if it had been her choice.

They all sat facing one another on two large, blue brocade-covered sofas, and Tessa felt herself slowly begin to relax as kindly, stoop-shouldered Mrs. Yates came in with a rattling tray of tea and fresh biscuits.

"So, Tessa," Nelson said as the housekeeper handed her the first cup of tea, "how are you finding Boston?"

"Bewildering," she said honestly, and her tone made him laugh.

"Pretty unfathomable, isn't it?" he chuckled, and his urbane humor set Tessa instantly at ease, as he draped an arm casually over the back of the sofa behind his wife.

"We haven't been out yet," Chandler explained, taking the delicate china cup that Mrs. Yates had handed to him. "As I mentioned to you last week, Tessa wanted an opportunity to acclimate herself first. She isn't at all familiar with how things are done here in Boston."

"I'm not certain that I am either, and I've lived here all of my life," Nelson chuckled, exuding a refreshingly genuine warmth.

"It seems that ol' Nelson here committed the unpardonable sin of falling in love with someone not considered appropriate for his stature," Chandler explained.

"I married my mother's lady's maid!" Nelson laughed blithely, being more direct.

When Tessa could see by his expression that what he had lost by doing so was far outweighed by what he had gained, she betrayed a slight smile herself.

"That must have taken a great deal of courage," she said.

"Not really. Sylvie is the one with real courage," Nelson countered. "She not only took me on, but she stood up to my mother in the process."

Tessa thought of Daphne and realized how much she and Nelson Winthrop's wife had in common. Chandler wanted her to know that in Boston there was at least one other person who was capable of understanding completely what this whole transition was like for her, another person who had come from the same humble beginnings and survived. She understood why he had been so insistent that they come here.

Tessa watched the way they all sipped their tea and she followed their lead meticulously. Only Nelson caught the little flinch of hesitation in the way she took a biscuit from the tray on the tea table between them.

"It may not seem like it now," he said kindly, "but it will get much easier."

"There are just so many things to learn," Tessa said, breathing a defeated little sigh at the progress she had thus far failed to make. She then felt free enough to add, "I'm not any more like you and Chandler than Sylvie is, you know."

Tessa felt a little spark of disappointment that neither Nelson nor his wife appeared to be surprised by her admission. "Apparently I have more work to do than I thought."

"I would be happy to teach you enough French to fool

even old Mrs. Wainright, who behaves as if she speaks it fluently."

"I doubt whether I am bright enough to learn all of that by next week."

"The Kennicotts' ball," Chandler explained. "I'm afraid we can't avoid it."

"Ah, a few well chosen words here, a clever turn of a phrase there, you will be splendid," Sylvie assured her, her own smile full and serenely wise.

"Well then, thank you," Tessa nodded. "Thank you very much."

Chandler smiled at his wife. "See what I told you? Nelson here is not such a bad sort."

"That's not what you thought when I first met you," Nelson countered to his friend, as one side of his mouth curled up.

"What do you mean?" Tessa asked interestedly, wrapping her fingers over her knees.

"Only that your sterling husband broke my nose the first time we met. I used to be far better looking than this."

"You deserved it," Chandler laughed.

"You were trying to make me break off with my girl," Nelson corrected in mock indignation.

Tessa looked at each of them. "Sylvie?"

"Oh, no," said Nelson. "This all happened much earlier, before I had developed an eye for real beauty."

Chandler turned to his wife. "We met at school. Lord, we were both so young and innocent then."

"There was not a single thing innocent about you, Tate," Nelson interjected, laughing now, too. "You'd seen half the world by then and I had never even been out of Boston."

"You held your own, as I recall."

"Only because I was bigger than you, and still you managed to permanently disfigure my nose."

"Bigger is not necessarily faster or better," countered Chandler, with half a grin. "And all that's left from our skirmish is that little bump."

"Skirmish? I tell you, he fights like some sort of exotic war lord. The strangest kicks. High and fierce like a dancer. Like nothing I have ever seen. Secretly, I thought him an absolute marvel."

Tessa's eyes were wide with adoration. "So did I."

They sat with the Winthrops, laughing and trading stories, until well after dark. When they rose to leave, Tessa could scarcely believe three hours had passed. She felt comfortable and safe with Nelson and Sylvie and a wave of optimism swept over her as she and Chandler bid their hosts goodnight from the carriage.

It surprised her, but slowly, ever so slowly, Tessa was regaining her balance. Today, thanks to Chandler, she had smiled, and she had even been able to laugh at the threats of someone as pompous as Horatia Wainright.

"Thank you," she said softly, sitting close to him on the same seat in the flickering glow of the carriage lamps.

"For what?"

"For caring enough to introduce me to the Winthrops. For the loving and patient tutors I face every day."

"My angel, I told you the day we married that you had made me the happiest man alive," he said, and his blue eyes shimmered with sincerity. "It is my fondest wish that one day soon, you shall be able to say the same thing about me."

A moment passed before Tessa spoke, breaking the powerful spell between them. "Who was that first girl in Nelson's life?" she softly asked.

Chandler flashed a toothy smile, remembering. "My sister, Daphne," he chuckled. "And, no matter what he thought at the time, I certainly was not about to see the poor boy subject himself to that!"

Chapter

31

THE WEEK AFTER JENNINGS HAD SECRETLY ENCOURAGED TESSA to stay in Boston passed quickly, as Tessa worked tirelessly with the coterie of tutors and instructors whom Chandler had provided for her. The process was slow but she had learned to tell a sauterne from a Bordeaux, how to walk with a book balanced on her head, and how properly to intone *merci* and *très bien*.

It was a complex world of privilege and opulence, which she could never have imagined even a month before. But now she desperately wanted Chandler to be proud of her. Tessa would attend the Kennicotts' ball with him at the end of the following week, and she was determined to shine there.

Throughout the long afternoons of memorizing French phrases and refining her diction, Tessa was surprised that she had also been spared further confrontations with Chandler's spiteful sister, Daphne. The woman who sought to undermine Tessa entirely was no longer a frequent visitor to the Tate family home.

Daphne's only appearances, ostensibly on behalf of her niece and nephew, were made each afternoon during the small window of time she had discovered that the new Mrs. Tate was mysteriously absent from her home.

But Tessa was far from being kept in the dark about these surreptitious visits. In her brief time as mistress of Chandler's Mount Vernon Street home, she had not only endeared herself to Alice and James, but she had quite quickly gained the loyalty of the household staff, as well, especially David Jennings and Kathleen O'Reilly.

Two days before the Kennicotts' party, Tessa paced evenly back and forth across the bedroom, carefully balancing a volume of poetry on her head, when there was a gentle knock on the door.

"Come in," she called out, catching the book as it tumbled into her hands.

"Ye called for me, ma'am?"

"I can balance it a bit longer every day. I suppose that's progress, hmm?"

"Congratulations, ma'am."

"Close the door, would you?"

Kathleen did as she had been instructed and then, when motioned to do so with a little pat, joined Tessa on the velvet-covered daybed near the hearth. When they were sitting together, Tessa pulled a large box out from beneath them and handed it to her maid. "Open it," she instructed, smiling brightly.

"But, what—"

"Go on, open it."

Kathleen pushed back the top of the box hesitantly and gasped as she gazed down at what she recognized as one of Cynthia Tate's dresses, a robin's-egg-blue silk, altered now into a far simpler, but still lovely style.

"But I thought Mr. Tate had all o' these disposed of when yer new things arrived."

"He did. Most of them, that is. I took the liberty of saving this particular one for you," Tessa explained, her eyes bright and alive with a mischievous twinkle.

Kathleen pulled the dress part way from the box and then stopped. The exquisite fabric lay limp in her hands. "But I cannot possibly accept this, ma'am."

Tessa demanded, "And why not?"

"Oh, it is far too fine a thing to be givin' to yer maid, ma'am."

"Better it should wind up in the rubbish heap along with all of Cynthia Tate's other beautiful dresses?" Tessa asked, arching a copper brow.

When they both realized how likely that had been, considering Chandler's lack of feeling for his deceased wife, they laughed like two great conspirators, and Kathleen stood and held the dress before her maid's uniform.

"I cannot imagine where I would wear something so grand."

"With these few alterations that have been done, I think it is just right to wear on your evening off, don't you? Perhaps to dinner," Tessa suggested, pulling five dollars from the pocket as though she were surprised to find it there.

"Oh, ma'am, ye're far too generous. I don't know how I can ever thank ye."

Tessa rose up now, too, and crossed the room with her maid, who had moved before the mirror and was holding up the dress before her.

"Kathleen, it is I who cannot begin to thank you for all that you have done since I have been in Boston. You have helped to make a potentially disastrous time bearable, and it really gives me great joy to pay you back in this small way."

"Ye make it easy, ma'am," Kathleen demurred, her ruddy Irish cheeks flushing as she crossed the room once again, this time to lay the dress carefully back in the box.

"Speaking of disasters . . . and of Daphne Forrester," Tessa said with a complicitous little grin, "suppose you help me select something from that grand wardrobe of clothes I now have that would be appropriate for her birthday supper."

"'Tis the reason for all the fuss downstairs, ma'am?"

Kathleen gasped. "You and Mr. Tate are havin' her birthday supper here, after everything she has—"

"The children pleaded with their father," Tessa explained simply. "It was very well rehearsed. Almost believable. I'm afraid Mrs. Forrester knows only too well that they are her brother's greatest weakness and she used them quite expertly."

"'Tis awful, what ye say." Kathleen huffed.

"Agreed. But the children do deserve to keep what family they have left and I'll not be the one to go against that."

"Ye're a brave woman, Mrs. Tate." Kathleen shook her head gravely. "Mrs. Forrester can be quite a frightenin' figure when she wants to be."

"I have certainly discovered that," Tessa replied.

Yet, feeling a fresh burst of confidence, she thought that tonight Daphne Forrester might well discover that her new, very disagreeable sister-in-law could actually be a rather frightening figure herself.

Whatever happened, it was bound to be a most interesting evening.

Chandler despised birthdays. But a birthday was the only event that could have possibly forced him to permit Daphne to dine again at his table after the inexcusable way she had behaved toward Tessa. She was his sister, she kept his secrets, and he gave her a certain amount of latitude for that. But, in spite of the fact that a single word from her could destroy him and his children forever, Chandler would not be held hostage. Not even by Daphne.

Supper, Tessa's first among strangers, was a heavily orchestrated affair every bit as confusing and fraught with possible mistakes as the dinner at Delmonico's had been. There were so many strange dishes and utensils. But Tessa learned quickly to take her lead from Chandler, never moving toward a fork or spoon until he had done so. He led. She followed expertly.

There was safety in mirroring his behavior at dinner. The same could not be said for the evening as a whole. In that, there was no safety at all. The only other woman at the table resented Tessa as an outsider and still made no attempt to conceal her distaste.

"Thank you. Thank you all," Daphne said with a sedate smile as she lowered her goblet onto the lace tablecloth.

Fanned out around her like petals on a rich rose were what was left of the Tate family. Lincoln. Chandler. His children. And his new wife.

Daphne sat at the head of the grand oak dining table. She sat at their father's place, her head high on its slim white neck, her back erect. She looked like a queen holding court. And it was precisely the effect Daphne Forrester sought.

She had just blown out the candles on her birthday cake and the children were perched on the edge of their chairs. They were awaiting their slices of the heavenly confection, their reward for having been proper and silent for what had become a very long and unpleasantly warm evening.

"What did you wish for, Aunt Daphne?" James asked with a gleeful smile, as Jennings leaned in to place a china plate of white cake and icing before his aunt.

"Oh, it's bad luck to tell, darling," Daphne said, glancing back across the table at Chandler, then at his wife, before she continued. "But I am quite certain your father knows."

"Is it bad luck to give us a tiny hint?" the small, curly-headed boy asked his aunt, having just taken his first joyous bite of the rich cake.

"That's quite enough," Chandler admonished. But with safety in numbers, Daphne ignored him.

"I don't suppose a tiny hint would do any real harm," she smiled acidly, "and after all, the wish is really not for myself."

"Do tell us," Alice pleaded.

Daphne laced her slim fingers and then propped her black, silk-draped elbows on the table. "Let me see. Well, I wished for the past. I can tell you that."

"Is your wish going to come true?"

"All of my wishes come true, my darlings, sooner or later."

Chandler surged onto his feet, intent on stopping his sister's not-so-subtle manipulation of an evening he had been against in the first place. But it was Tessa who caught his arm and pulled him back down beside her as the children continued happily eating their cake, blissfully unaware of the silent war flaring around them.

Daphne was a strangely bitter woman for one so young, and Tessa battled an overwhelming desire to see her new sister-in-law put in her place. She was, after all, Irish through to the core of her soul, and propriety would only hold her temper in check for so long. But these two precious children had endured enough.

Servants moved in and out of the silver-heavy dining room bearing coffee, and Tessa sat now, barely able to breathe in the stiff, restrictive corset, beneath the hissing gas lamps.

"I saw Nelson Winthrop today," Chandler forced himself to say civilly through the tension-thick, aroma-laden air.

"That fool?" Daphne sputtered. "Marrying beneath him like that. Such a disgrace to his family."

Lincoln countered his wife's attempts to keep the contest with her brother raging. "How delightful. How is he?"

"Marvelous, as usual," Chandler replied, the vein in his neck still pulsing with restrained fury. "Living without the great albatross of convention obviously agrees with him."

"Jennings, I believe I'll have a bit more of that wine now," Lincoln said.

Chandler leaned back in his chair, fingering the base of his goblet, mollified by this unexpected branch of support. He had never liked Lincoln Forrester. He had always believed him far too weak to ever handle his sister in any way that would make a difference. But he was wealthy. Far wealthier than the Tates. Heir to a great textile fortune. Benjamin Tate had assured his children that this was the only thing they need consider. Ten years ago, Lincoln Forrester had been the catch of Boston and Daphne had caught him.

"So then, will you and Tessa be going to the Kennicotts'

party at the end of the week?" Daphne asked with a condescending, insincere smile.

Chandler cast an adoring glance across the table at his new wife. "We wouldn't miss it. I shall finally have a chance to show off my beautiful new bride."

"It really is a grand affair," Lincoln told Tessa. "The Kennicotts have it every year during the second week in September. William and Eve have a splendid ballroom with a view of the Back Bay, and it is all done up in flowers and lights."

"It sounds lovely." Tessa tried to smile when she said it, but her mind whirled with all that she would still need to learn before she could attend a social event of that magnitude without making an utter fool of herself or of Chandler. It was less than three days away.

"I'm certain it will be like nothing you have ever seen before," Daphne quipped, shooting a poison-tipped barb through the steadily declining tension she hoped to revive.

"Let's change the subject," Lincoln intervened once again.

"Splendid idea," Chandler agreed, feeling more civil toward his brother-in-law than he had felt in the past ten years. Jennings poured a second round of coffee from a silver urn.

"Nelson tells me that the horse epidemic is no better."

"Epidemic?" Tessa asked.

"Yes, dreadful problem, that epizoöty." Lincoln shook his head. "The poor beasts are dying faster than they can bury them. If it keeps on like this, there won't be a single animal left in all of Boston."

"As it is, they're having to use oxen to pull the drays, and the fire department has had to pull engines by hand to their last few calls," said Chandler.

"It really would be quite a devastation if anything serious happened," Lincoln added.

Chandler took a sip of coffee. "I have had trouble getting a hack already. God willing, that won't be a sign of things to come."

"You shouldn't have had to resort to a public cab," Daphne sputtered in a low tone of disgust, vainly trying to stir the caldron of contempt.

"I enjoy it on occasion," Chandler countered, glancing at his children's cake plates and silently gauging how long it would be before he could send them upstairs and then give his sister a proper thrashing. "We could all use a bit of humility now and then."

"As you can see, humility is a quality my wife finds highly overrated," said Lincoln.

Disregarding her husband's slight, Daphne waited seven ticks of the clock in calculated silence.

"So, Tessa dear," she said frigidly, with a fork poised over her cake, "you must tell us all how you managed to capture this very illusive brother of mine so quickly when so many others have tried and failed."

"It was I who had the good fortune to capture her," Chandler interceded graciously as he lifted his crystal wine goblet in salute to his wife.

"Oh come now," Daphne pressed with an imperious smile. "There must be something more to it than that. Why just last month you exhibited a complete antipathy toward the state of matrimony. Your own as well as Mrs. Bailey's."

"Really, Daphne," Lincoln protested, his dessert fork clattering onto the china plate. "Haven't you said quite enough for one evening?"

"Well, you must admit, it does all seem rather suspicious when you had every eligible girl in Boston, and some not quite so eligible, at your fingertips. And he did you know," she said, suddenly directing her acid words at Tessa. "My brother could have had anyone, and yet, here he is, married to you."

"Daphne!" Lincoln gasped.

"That's it!" Chandler slammed his goblet onto the table so hard that most of the red wine sloshed onto the white table cover.

It was at that same moment that Tessa's firey Irish blood

finally got the better of her. She had endured all that she meant to. Children or no children.

Her movement was slight, so furtive that it really did appear to have been an accident. But in the same moment that Chandler's glass toppled, Tessa reached across the table and with a single flick of her wrist sent her own untouched plate of cake cascading directly into Daphne's black satin lap.

"Oh! You imbecile!" Daphne cried, springing back from the table, sending her chair tumbling. "You've completely ruined my dress! Jennings, fetch me a cloth. Quickly!"

"I am sorry," Tessa said, feigning sincerity and shaking her head. "How very clumsy of me. And it might have come out too, if there weren't so much sugar in the frosting."

Chandler covered his smile of complete surprise and glanced over at Lincoln, who was doing the same. Tessa could take care of herself, Chandler thought with amusement. Daphne had been asking for retaliation all evening and Tessa had now provided it so cleverly, in a way that could not be proven, yet was completely understood by every adult at the table.

When Daphne and two housemaids had blotted the dress all that they could, and a large stain still remained, Lincoln cast a surreptitious wink at Tessa, tossed his napkin onto the table and then stood.

"Well," he breathed with a contented sigh, and took a few steps toward the dining room door, "I believe I have had quite enough food and entertainment for one evening. Daphne, are you coming?"

"I am not going anywhere yet!" Chandler's sister snarled, shooting her husband a venomous glare. But to her complete surprise, for the first time in their marriage she was glaring at his back. Lincoln Forrester was prepared to leave Beacon Hill without her.

"Well, I am going home and I am taking the carriage. So unless you wish to engage in the apparently objectionable practice of calling for a hack at this late hour, I suggest you come along."

"She did that intentionally!" Daphne snorted, still peering down at the dark stain on the front of her dress. "Chandler, make her apologize this instant!"

"Make her?" He smiled, lifting a brow. "If you haven't discovered it already tonight, dear sister, my lovely new wife is a young woman who knows her own mind."

Buoyed by Chandler's firm support, Tessa rose as well, her green eyes glittering with confidence. "I really do hope they shall be able to save your dress. It was so lovely."

"Ach!" Daphne snapped indignantly, picked up the damp folds of her skirt, then turned on her heel and swirled out of the dining room with her nose thrust high in the air.

Lincoln, who had lagged behind, turned around again and gave Chandler a slap on the back as the two men broke out in a sudden uproarious fit of laughter.

"Chandler, ol' boy, I don't know when I've enjoyed an evening at your house more," Lincoln said beneath his breath. "And for the first time in years, tonight I actually envy you."

Looking back at Tessa, Chandler replied, "Tonight, my friend, I can see why you would."

While Lincoln and Daphne were being shown to their carriage by a secretly amused David Jennings, Chandler and Tessa led the children to their bedroom to bid them good night. When they were tucked safely into their beds, Chandler and Tessa blew out the lamp together and walked down the hall.

"You must be exhausted," he said, standing with her outside the closed bedroom door.

"Actually," she smiled triumphantly. "I'm rather invigorated."

"I'm really very sorry about my sister," he said sincerely. "Testing you as she has continued to do is really most unsavory. I tell you, if you hadn't stopped me when you did, she would have been most unceremoniously tossed out of this house on her very pompous little ear, children or no children."

"Apparently there was a great deal more about becoming your wife that you neglected to tell me in New York," Tessa said with a twisted smile. "It would seem I am discovering more all of the time."

"I wouldn't blame you if you wanted to leave me already," he surprised her by saying. "I will admit a trial by fire of this magnitude was not part of my proposal."

Tessa twirled the betrothal ring around on her finger and leaned against the closed bedroom door. She remembered how closely she had come to doing precisely that only a few short days ago.

"I have a bit of good Irish pluck left in me yet."

"I can certainly see that. You really were splendid." He began to chuckle, recalling the expression of complete surprise on his sister's face.

It seemed natural at that moment of intimacy between them, standing close to one another, almost touching, that when Chandler opened the bedroom door, they should go inside together.

"Then you weren't angry at my ruining her gown?" Tessa asked as they strolled across the floor and then stopped.

"Angry? I'm only surprised you did not wrestle her to the floor and press that piece of cake across her very smug face."

"Oh, Chandler, don't be silly," she laughed demurely. "Even *I* know when something would be going a bit too far."

Chandler laughed and, without thinking, suddenly gave in to the lustful urge he had been holding at bay for the better part of an hour . . . since the moment they had vanquished his sister.

He swept Tessa into his arms and his mouth came urgently down upon hers in the dim lamplight. The soft fragrance of perfume from her dressing table swirled around them. As it always did when he kissed her, Chandler's blood stirred, craving more. Much more.

"I want to stay the night," he whispered huskily against her lips, trying desperately to suppress the harsh need in his voice. "But you must want it, too."

"I do."

But the response of her body was not the same as the one he had tasted on her lips. Chandler felt her stiffen as he softly kissed her neck and the tip of her ear. Her body was telling him she was not ready. He had promised her that he would not press her. Not after the frenzied first time between them. Chandler Tate was a man of his word.

Besides, he did not desire the same sort of volatile and eruptive volcano of passion in this marriage that he had lived in the last. He wanted something pure, something kind. This was a marriage that was going to endure a lifetime.

His fingers moved lightly across her breast as he pulled away. He desired her so desperately that even the feel of a bit of her bare skin was torture. But he needed to give himself that much. As he dragged his hand away, raw need streaked through him, hardening him even more. Chandler kissed the top of her head as he held her face in his hands with a calm that surprised even him.

"You really were splendid tonight with my sister," he said softly, preparing to leave her. "Everyone at the Kennicotts' ball is going to love you almost as much as I do."

"But I thought that we—" she tried to say, still holding on to his lapel.

"When you are truly ready, my angel," he replied with a rich and understanding smile. "And not a moment before."

Chapter

32

BUOYED BY HER SUBTLE VICTORY OVER DAPHNE, TESSA PLUNGED herself wholeheartedly into her lessons. She found that even though she had been only two weeks in Boston, her life had already developed a pattern. Each afternoon, after she had accompanied the children to the park, seen to the menu for supper, and met Sylvie Winthrop to study her French phrases, Tessa was secretly readied by a complicitously quiet staff. Then she was whisked off to Chandler's office on Summer Street for the rest of her private lessons.

It was still frustrating for her at times, when she did not immediately master the waltz or when she continued to confuse her silverware. But after Daphne's birthday supper, a relentless and focused determination had been born. Tessa wanted more than anything to make her husband proud. Thoughts of returning to New York had steadily vanished.

In between her lessons, Tessa tended to Chandler's house with the same joy and care that she had devoted to everything else since coming here, hoping to add her own special mark to all that she touched.

"I really would like some fresh flowers in here," she said to Jennings, tapping a thoughtful finger against her lip and studying the parlor one afternoon after her lessons. "It is the height of summer, so you ought to be able to locate some lovely ones, don't you think?"

"I'm sure that could be arranged," Jennings agreed.

"And if that hassock is not some great family treasure, perhaps we could find a less *conspicuous* place for chartreuse velvet?"

"Very well, ma'am," he nodded, fighting a smile.

She had been here such a short time, Jennings thought, and yet she was changing everything. The house. The children. She was bringing Chandler to life again. She was upsetting a well-worn system that had been in place for decades. A smile cracked Jennings's formal demeanor. How splendid of her, he thought. And it really was such an atrocious hassock.

"And what about those draperies?" she asked, hands on hips, moving across the room away from him. "They're so awfully dark and heavy."

"They keep out the summer sun, ma'am."

Tessa lifted her chin a fraction. "They also keep out the light, Jennings."

There was a little silence, and he could see how pleased she was with herself. He had to give her a good deal of credit. After all, this was no small house to manage or to change, and yet in so short a time she had accomplished both. How delightful it was to have this drafty old place brought back to life. Until Tessa had come here, he had not even realized how much was missing. As always in her presence, and quite in spite of himself, Jennings continued to thaw.

As he followed Tessa into the dining room for the same cleansing scrutiny of that room, Alice and James scampered up from the kitchens and dashed past them, only to be stopped by Jennings's two very quick and powerful hands.

"Whoa! What have you been told about running in this house?"

Out of breath, and with an expression of genuine fear, James glanced up. "We had to get away!"

"Why was that?" Tessa asked, moving forward and bending down between them.

"Mrs. O'Neil said that we must take our prunes!"

Tessa glanced with surprise back up at Jennings. "Is that the cook's duty, to see to something like that?"

"I'm certain it was at Miss Daphne's directive, ma'am. Mister Tate's sister believes strongly in its effects on young systems."

Tessa rose back up again, her face spiked with concern. "But they're both healthy as a couple of new colts. Should children like these be forced to take something they despise in light of that?"

"Not in my opinion, ma'am."

"Nor in mine," she huffed. "I was never forced against my will to eat a single morsel of food in my life. I find Mrs. Forrester's opinion barbaric."

"Then we shall see that it is stopped at once," Jennings said simply, and with a faint smile of agreement.

Tessa's jade eyes widened. "Can we do that?"

"Remember, ma'am," he said kindly. "You are the mistress of this house."

A hint of smile touched her lips in the moment of silence. "So I am, at that," she said, placing her hands back on her hips.

"What do you say we go inform Mrs. O'Neil of the change in things together? In fact, I think I would quite like a nice piece of molasses candy just about now. How about the two of you?"

"Oh, yes!" they sang out in unison, then smiled happily back up at Tessa, each offering up a hand in return.

"Meanwhile, I will see to that hassock," Jennings called after her. Tessa turned back around, having, in the face of this new domestic crisis, forgotten entirely about the hassock.

"Thank you, Jennings," she said sincerely.

"My pleasure, ma'am," he nodded.

"There you are, finally!"

Sylvie Winthrop was waiting for Tessa in the little sun-room at the back of her house when she arrived an hour later. Sylvie looked up with a welcoming smile as two small children scampered and played at her feet.

"I wasn't certain that you were going to come today."

"Sorry I'm late," Tessa said, hurrying in with a French book under her arm. "There was an encounter that could not wait."

"With your husband, I hope." Sylvie smiled.

Tessa sat down in a black wrought-iron chair across the glass-topped table from her new friend and French instructor. "Only an unfortunate domestic situation."

"It is splendid how quickly you have truly managed to become mistress of that house, Tessa. I envy that."

"Don't envy me too much," Tessa said, as the children took their ball and dashed out of the sun-room, laughing gleefully. "I'm afraid I do a far more admirable job in the safety of our home than I will ever be able to do in public."

"What is it, *chérie?*"

"I'm just so terribly nervous about tomorrow night," Tessa confessed, fingering the binding of the battered grammar book, which she had set on the table between them.

"Tomorrow evening," Sylvie kindly corrected her. "Here in Boston, one would say 'evening.'"

"Of course you're right. I knew that. It was one of the first things I learned. How will I ever manage it? Two weeks of lessons and I'm still bound to embarrass myself and Chandler miserably."

"Not with your French, you won't," Sylvie assured her. "You have done remarkably well with the important phrases. Enough, if you are careful, to fool anyone. Besides, I think you could entirely fail the evening and Chandler would be more madly in love with you than he is now."

"Do you really think so?"

"Do you not see the expression in his eyes when he looks at you?" Sylvie asked with a soft smile. "I have known Chandler Tate quite a long time and I can tell you I have never seen that expression before."

"Not even for Cynthia?"

"Especially not for Cynthia."

Tessa propped her chin on steepled hands. "Tell me, Sylvie, what was the great mystery about her?"

"I am not certain I know what you mean."

"She was the mother of his children and yet no one seems willing to so much as mention her name without the most diligent prodding. Doesn't a woman whose greatest crime was dying deserve to be remembered a bit more favorably than that?"

"Unless of course, dying was *not* her greatest crime."

Tessa sat up on her chair. "Do you know something? Oh, if you do, you must tell me. Chandler has tried his best to be honest with me and we have made progress, but there is still something dark and hidden between us. I can feel it."

"I know only what I saw while she was alive."

Tessa covered Sylvie's hand desperately. "What was that? Please. I must know."

"Cynthia Tate was a woman who seemed far more interested in her own pleasure than in the well being of her husband or her children. That is really all that I can say. Anything more would only be adding to the gossip and speculation."

"There was gossip about her?"

"As there is about every member of Boston society, Tessa. But you are bound to learn that soon enough, no matter how much you change for these people."

"Jennings told me that he believed Cynthia and Chandler hurt one another quite badly during their marriage."

"That is not difficult to believe."

"But why? What was it about them that—"

"Please, Tessa," Sylvie held up her hand. "I can tell you no more than I have."

"You cannot or you will not?"

"Chandler is my husband's dearest friend, *chérie*. The only friend he has left in Boston. Don't ask me to endanger that."

"All right," Tessa acquiesed with a reluctant sigh. She opened the French textbook on the glass-topped table between them. "I'll not push you. But there is something more to Cynthia Tate's death. I can feel it."

Chapter

33

CHANDLER HAD CHOSEN THE FABRIC PERSONALLY.

After all, this was not for just any gown. This was to be for his wife's debut into Boston society, and he wanted her to feel like a queen. He had personally brought the shimmering bolt of lapis-blue silk from Hangchow. It had never seemed right to have it worked into a dress for Cynthia. Li Kao Chen had bid him to save it for the one. He would know her, the old wise man had said. And he had been right.

Until he had met Tessa, Chandler had locked it away, like his heart, where it would be safe.

This bolt of smooth, bright silk symbolized for him a young man full of hopes and dreams. And ambition. A young man who had gone off alone to China, inexperienced and unsure. One who had returned a confident young man. It was that bright star inside of himself that Chandler thought he had lost. Someone Tessa had helped him to recall.

If the dress had turned out half so lovely as he meant for it to, his beautiful Irish bride would shine more brightly than any other guest at the Kennicotts' ball tonight, and the rest of Boston would have little choice but to fall as madly in love with her as he had.

It was what he was counting on.

A moment later, Tessa slowly descended the curved staircase in a shimmering rustle of lapis-blue silk. It was the perfect complement for her pale apricot skin. Her hair tonight was swept up elegantly in a loose spiral and wound through with a string of blue beads. Chandler was waiting impatiently at the bottom of the stairs, tapping his foot in perturbed silence. Until he glanced up and saw her.

The expression froze on his face. She took his breath away. Tessa was every bit the goddess he had hoped she would be in the delicate Chinese fabric, cut so daringly low at the bodice. Fringe on the capped sleeves dangled against her smooth, bare arms, and Chandler clenched his hands again, determined not to look too long upon her tiny waist or the rest of her willowy curves. Nor would he admire too much how perfectly suited the special fabric was to her. He would save a confession about the exquisite silk for later, when they were once again alone. He wanted personally to make her understand its value to him.

"You look beautiful," he said as she descended the last two stairs.

"Beautiful for you."

"That dress is everything I had hoped it would be on you," he said breathlessly. He knew that she could not fully comprehend what he had said. But it did not matter.

Nothing mattered other than the fact that she was his wife, and tonight he was the luckiest man alive because of it.

The Kennicott house glittered like a brilliant jewel.

Chandler held Tessa's elbow, leading her up the brick stairs and into a grand foyer flooded with light and crowded with guests.

Supported tenderly by her husband, Tessa smiled radiantly. Full of determination to make this evening the most splendid of both their lives, they then moved in among the other guests as they stood beneath a blazing crystal chandelier.

"If it isn't Chandler Tate. Why, how splendid to see you, my dear." The woman had spoken the words convivially and sincerely, but with an uppercrust Boston accent that caused Tessa to tremble.

Chandler and Tessa both turned around. Her heart skipped a little beat as they faced a small, stout woman with a heavily lined face and a cap of impeccably twisted snow-white hair. On it, a diamond tiara glistened.

Chandler took the woman's hand and brought it to his lips in a courtly gesture. The woman was almost regal in crimson taffeta, with a long strand of diamonds and pearls knotted at her throat.

"Did you really believe I could stay away forever, Eve? Your parties are all people speak about for a month before and after."

"I'm afraid this year, darling, the gossip about you takes precedence," Eve Kennicott returned, surveying Tessa in a glance as her wrinkled mouth curled in amusement.

Chandler brought Tessa forward with a firm hand wound through hers, suddenly affectionate and supportive once again.

"In this case, Eve, everything you have heard is true," he smiled rakishly. "Eve Kennicott, may I present my wife, Tessa."

White eyebrows merged as their hostess took in every detail of Tessa's appearance appraisingly. "Oh, your sister was right, my dear. She is an extraordinarily lovely creature."

Tessa longed to say what a surprise it was that Daphne should have had anything pleasant to say about her at all. But she bit her tongue. After all, the old woman's ice-blue eyes said that Daphne had told her a good deal more than that, and there was still such a long, uncharted evening ahead.

After a few more pleasantries were exchanged, and they were bid properly to enjoy their evening, Tessa and Chandler moved slowly into the parlor amid the crush of guests, and into the center of what looked to Tessa very much like a museum.

The mix of imported European furnishings was staggering. A Louis XIV divan covered in crimson silk next to a table topped with ebony and ivory, both sitting on a lush oriental carpet. Dark art. Important art. All framed in heavy gold.

She had never seen so many fine things in one room, and only her relentless lessons had given her even an inkling of their possible value.

Chandler took a glass of champagne for each of them from a silver tray. Then he silently led her upstairs toward the second-floor ballroom. The mahogany banister of the wide stairs they climbed, like all of the doorways, was festooned with fragrant summer flowers. Stiff-backed, liveried servants carried elaborate hors d'oeuvres on shiny silver trays, as the orchestra began another waltz.

The second floor of the Kennicott home was cooler, Tessa found to her relief, and there was little need to use her new ivory fan. The vast wall of windows had been thrown open, bringing in the night sky.

Tessa sipped her champagne slowly and glanced around the room at the amazing display of richesse. The entire room had been lined with flowers. Table centers were filled with bouquets in delicate crystal vases. Others bore white roses, the stems cut short. The fragrance was sweet and pure. Everything sparkled. It was rather like a fairy tale.

Until she heard a voice that had become frighteningly familiar to her.

"Good evening, brother dear," Daphne drawled, leaning forward and taking Chandler's hand so he was forced to kiss her cheek. "It seems you're becoming something of a stranger to Lincoln and me. We've missed you."

"It has only been a few days, Daphne, and you know as

well as I why that is, and how to change it," he said civilly, then extended a slight smile and a more congenial hand to his brother-in-law. "Evening, Lincoln."

"You're certainly looking lovely, Tessa," Lincoln said, despite the reproachful scowl shot at him by his wife.

"Why thank you, Lincoln," Tessa beamed.

"That color really does become you. I must say though, I never thought I would see that ol' chap part with his precious bolt of Chinese silk after all these years. Not even for such an exquisite gown."

Tessa glanced down at her dress, fingering the folds of the elegant blue skirt with an unmasked expression of surprise. "I had no idea it had any special significance."

Chandler cleared his throat and stiffened. This was not at all the way he had envisioned Tessa finding out about her gown.

"Oh yes, your husband has been holding onto it for years," Lincoln continued. "Brought it back from the Orient himself ages ago. Always said he was saving it for something special." He arched a slim ebony brow, then cast a surprised glance at Chandler. "Didn't he tell you?"

"I *was* waiting for the right moment," Chandler said as Tessa's heart rushed to overflowing with love and surprise.

Lincoln shrugged his shoulders in apology, as Daphne reached for her brother's hand. "Dance with me? At least let's make a showing of family unity, shall we?"

Too much a gentleman to deny his sister publicly, Chandler led her with a firm hand out to the other dancers.

"Oh, dear. It appears that I have spoken out of turn." Chagrined, Lincoln shook his head when they were left alone.

"I am glad you did."

His gaze shifted back to her. "It's just that he hadn't brought it out to show anyone for such a long time. Kept it locked away, to preserve it. I just assumed that tonight he would be proud to boast about it since apparently he finally found the woman special enough to wear it."

"He certainly is full of surprises," Tessa said softly as they watched their respective spouses appear to waltz happily with one another.

"Surprises? That he is. It is a mysterious trait of the Tate family, I'm afraid. One to which you will need to grow accustomed sooner or later if you mean to survive."

"Daphne, too?" Tessa asked, shooting him a glittering green-eyed look of surprise.

"Oh, indeed. The complexity was what drew me to her in the first place. The challenge of it, I suppose."

"And the frustration?"

"My cross to bear," he declared with an amused little smile.

"And is she as secretive as Chandler?"

"Every bit," he confirmed. "Especially about each other. Fight like cats and dogs, they do. But when it comes to family secrets, they're fiercely protective of one another."

Tessa sipped her champagne thoughtfully. "Curious, don't you think? When most of the time they cannot bear to be in the same room with one another."

"I used to think so, in the beginning. But . . ." he stopped himself mid-sentence. "Oh, you'll think me foolish."

"No I won't," Tessa earnestly assured him. "I promise."

"Well, I've often suspected that there was some deep, dark family secret those two shared that kept them from ever giving up on one another entirely."

A sudden weight began to settle on her again and for a moment Tessa found it difficult to catch her breath. "What makes you think so?"

"Ten years of marriage and a considerable amount of experience with both of them."

When the waltz ended, and Daphne and Chandler had rejoined them, Lincoln terminated their conversation. But not before he had stirred that old sensation of foreboding inside of her.

Amid the lights, the laughter, and the flowing champagne, her new brother-in-law had just confirmed what she still suspected. There was indeed a Tate family puzzle. And it was deepening by the moment. But what was it? What were Chandler and his sister hiding? And did she really want to know any longer, even if she could unravel the truth?

"Tessa dear," Daphne said acidly, "why have you not waltzed yet this evening? Oh, you mustn't tell me that you don't know how."

She lifted her chin a fraction. "I have not danced yet because my husband has not asked me."

"Then by all means, take mine," Daphne suggested before her brother could offer. "Lincoln dances splendidly. He can make simply anyone look as if they have been dancing for years."

"I would be delighted, sister," Lincoln said with the greatest sincerity. He then bowed so gallantly before her that Chandler chose not to interfere.

Allies come from the most unexpected places, he thought silently. Lincoln Forrester could be formidable if he chose to be.

He watched Tessa let a little smile of relief curl her lips just slightly at Lincoln Forrester's offer. The music began again as he offered his arm and they moved together out onto the dance floor.

"So I see this evening is not to be a total loss, after all."

At the sound of another woman's studied soprano, Chandler turned his eyes automatically upon Lydia Bailey. She stood beside him, a slightly faded, yet still elegant rose in the palest pink.

But before he uttered a word of greeting, he felt the judgmental gazes and surprised whispers of a ballroom full of people who, thanks to Boston's very efficient gossip mill, knew precisely what these two had once meant to one another.

"Lydia," Chandler said with a defiant smile, and boldly pressed her hand to his lips.

She smiled in return. "Why didn't you tell your old friend Lydia Bailey you were getting married, hmm?"

"It was really all rather sudden," he replied, releasing her hand.

"Sudden is not the word," Daphne muttered, but her remark was lost beneath the rich strains of the music.

"You're looking wonderful as ever," Chandler smiled gallantly down on a woman who, quite unknowingly, had helped him through the darkest period of his life. A woman for whom he still retained the deepest affection, if not the attraction.

"And you are as spectacular a liar as ever."

"You cannot imagine," Daphne whispered snidely behind her hand.

"I understand that you met her in New York."

"Yes I did."

"It must have been very romantic, such a swift courtship. Was it love at first sight?"

"It was for me."

"I envy your Tessa," Lydia said, and her voice held a hint of longing for something that could never be again. "She is a very lucky woman, you know."

"Coming from you, Lydia," Chandler said kindly, "that means a great deal."

When the waltz ended, Lincoln began to lead Tessa back to her husband. As they neared the place where they had previously stood however, Tessa froze. Her legs would not carry her another step. She knew simply by the way they looked at one another, and by the way he still held her hand, the identity of the woman with Chandler.

Feeling the reluctance in the hand he held, Lincoln stopped and turned back around.

"That's she, isn't it?" Tessa asked in a pained whisper.

"Who?" Lincoln hedged, knowing precisely whom she meant.

"My husband's mistress."

His face blanched. "You know about that?"

"Try as he might," she sighed, "Chandler has not managed to keep all of his secrets from me."

"Well, believe me, Tessa, when I say that you have absolutely nothing to fear from Lydia Bailey."

"That's not what it looks like to me," she countered, seeing the closeness between them. Tessa could see that they were whispering and that Lydia Bailey's expression was unmistakably adoring.

A flicker of disappointment changed Tessa's happy expression, and she battled a sudden urge to race from the ballroom. She simply could not face that particular introduction. Not on her very first night out in Boston.

She glanced around trying to find something, anything else she might do to avoid returning to Chandler's side at the moment. At least until her husband's former mistress was gone.

"You know, I do believe I would like a bit more champagne," she declared to Lincoln as the other dancers passed by them.

"I would be happy to get you a glass, my dear, but are you certain you wouldn't mind being left alone? Especially since it is your first ball in Boston."

"Oh, no," she shook her head and tried to smile, already looking for a terrace or alcove, any place to which she could go until Chandler came looking for her. "I am fine. Truly."

"Very well, then. I shall come right back to this very spot."

"I will wait for you here," she assured him, with no intention of doing so.

Alone, Tessa quickly lost herself amid the crowd, free now to search for a secure place to wait out the threat of a woman who had shared more of her husband than even she yet had. Tessa found that place in a small, book-lined recess at the end of a dimly lit corridor beyond the ballroom.

In addition to leather-bound volumes and two red-leather chairs, there was a brocade-covered settee onto which she sank. Two small brass oil lamps lit the room in a warm bronze glow. It was a cozy little space, in spite of the elegance, and Tessa took two long breaths until she was certain she had beaten back the sensation of jealousy threatening to wrap its dark, powerful arms around her heart.

It was she whom Chandler loved, she told herself. She whom he had married. Still, the thought of him doing with a plump, middle-aged woman, someone else's wife, what he had done that night with her, forced tears to her eyes that she could no longer press back.

She pleated the blue silk skirt of her gown with trembling fingers, and tried not to sob too loudly.

"Whatever it is, it certainly cannot be worth the price of those tears on so lovely a face."

Tessa looked up, drawing a hand across her eyes. A slim young man stood before her, a handkerchief extended from his hand. His straw-colored hair was tamed with oil. His manner was easy and polished.

Uncertain of what to say—or more properly, what not to—and weary now of trying to figure it out, Tessa sprang to her feet. She tried to push past him but she was no match for his masculine strength.

"Since your face has temporarily paid the price of those tears, you certainly cannot go back to the ball just now. Here. Take it," he said kindly, offering his handkerchief again.

"But, I don't even know you," she said sniffling.

"A circumstance easily remedied. Call me Peter. And you, of course, are Tessa."

Her misty eyes widened. "How do you know that?"

"I know all of the Kennicotts' guests. Drearily predictable, I am sorry to say, and a hazard, I suppose, of having lived in Boston too long."

She sank back down onto the settee and the stranger sat down beside her as she wiped her eyes. "Have you a last name, Peter?" she asked in a small voice, touching the handkerchief beneath her nose.

"Yes of course. But mystery is so much more exciting. Don't you agree?"

"If I did agree, you would be able to maintain this disadvantage at which you have me."

"A circumstance any gentleman with eyes would desire to maintain."

He laughed softly, properly, when he spoke but the sound possessed a note of sly wit that put her instantly on edge. He was sitting too close, she thought. Speaking too familiarly. Suddenly Tessa wished that even one other person would come into the room, or at least pass by the door. She stiffened as he lowered an arm across the back of the settee behind her.

"I really should be getting back to my husband."

He stopped her from standing by placing a hand gently on her knee. It was a hand that, Tessa had no doubt, could grow more insistent in the space of a heartbeat. A lump of alarm swelled in her throat.

"Relax," he said coaxingly, his deep eyes glittering in the lamplight. "If you return now, Tate and everyone else will certainly know that you've been crying and you wouldn't want that on the evening of your big debut, now, would you?"

She had to agree that he had a point. But it was a bit unsettling how much this stranger knew about her when she had not even been out in public once before tonight. She would give it another five minutes, Tessa thought resignedly. But only five. And then, no matter what he said in protest, she was leaving this room.

"Even with a pink little nose, you know, you look incredibly beautiful in this light," James said softly.

"Lamplight is flattering to everyone," she countered.

"No, my beauty. Not to everyone."

His lips descended upon hers then suddenly. Ruthlessly. His arms dropped around her shoulders and held her fast against the settee. Tessa tried to struggle, but it was useless against such youthful force. His tongue was thrusting at her sealed lips, choking her with his insistence.

"So it has come to this, Peter, has it?"

Tessa heard the words as though from a distance. But she knew even so that the voice coming from the doorway belonged to Chandler.

Hearing it too, the young man pulled away from her quickly. But Tessa was shocked into silence to see that Peter was grinning, and his dark eyes were blazing with what looked like pure mischief. She pushed away from him and sprang back to her feet. Beside Chandler, Lincoln stood with an expression of pure shock lighting his long, gaunt face.

"Chandler, I didn't—" she tried to say, but she could force no more words than that past her lips for the shame.

"Tit for tat, I always say," Peter chuckled cruelly.

"Tessa has nothing to do with this, and you know it."

"Doesn't she? You take something of mine, I take something of yours. Quite simple really."

"Touch my wife again, and I will kill you without a second thought," Chandler said with an icy, even tone.

The young stranger, whom Tessa knew only as Peter, only laughed more deeply at Chandler's threat. "You would never do that to my mother."

"What is he talking about?" Tessa whispered in confusion, having rushed behind the safety of her brother-in-law.

"Come on, let's go get some of that champagne, shall we?" Lincoln suggested, taking her arm. But Tessa wrenched it away.

"Oh, that's right," the young man chuckled, suddenly looking at her again, clearly enjoying the mystery and subsequent conflict that he had set in motion. "I never did mention my last name."

"You refused to tell me," she angrily corrected him.

"My name is Bailey. Peter Bailey."

Her eyes widened. "And your mother is—"

"Oh, she's quick, Tate," he grinned like a cat. "My mother is your husband's mistress."

Chandler did not bother to argue. Nor did he ask for an apology. This had been building between them for months, and now Tessa was being asked to pay the price. The rage inside him reached a crescendo and Chandler struck out at the young man with a sharp blow to the side of the face. It possessed the thundering power of a cannon ball, and Peter Bailey doubled over. Then he fell back onto the settee, moaning.

It had not been the same exotic oriental movement Tessa had seen Chandler use in New York against the band of thugs. With this, a spoiled young aristocrat, it had been brutish. Raw. It had also been deserved.

Tessa looked over at her husband. Chandler's body was taut, like a tightly coiled spring. His face was a stony mask, the fury etched deeply into the turn of his jaw. His eyes were blazing.

"Get up, you little brat, and fight me then, since a contest between us is what you want!"

Peter Bailey stumbled back to his feet. In a half-hearted attempt to defend himself, he lifted his fists chest high, but his eyes, so full of malice only moments ago, were now spiked unmistakably with fear.

"Come on, Chandler," Lincoln intervened. "I believe you've made your point."

"Oh, believe me, I haven't begun to make my point!" he answered bitterly.

Chandler lashed out again at the boy, who fell beneath his fearsome blow a second time. He tumbled backwards, this time into a tea table, before he thumped onto the floor.

"Chandler, please stop this!" Tessa cried. "Oh, this is all my fault!"

"Mr. Bailey here has a few manners left to learn before we are finished with one another."

A crowd that included Lydia had started to gather outside the door. People were whispering and looking at Chandler's mistress. Then at his wife.

"I believe the young man here owes Mrs. Tate an apology," Chandler said coldly, his dark eyes drilling hate into Peter Bailey, who still lay slumped into a heap on the floor. The boy was snorting wildly, trying to reclaim his breath.

"I owe her my contempt," he spat, "as I do you!"

"Peter!" Lydia Bailey gasped, moving forward into the

fray. "If you have insulted the man's wife, apologize this instant!"

"I shall do no such thing, Mother! Not after what he has done to you!"

Again there was the buzz of whispered voices outside in the corridor and around the doorway. Until now, faced with Chandler's rage, Tessa had forgotten her earlier embarrassment and what had led her away from the ball and into this anteroom in the first place.

"You would be well advised to listen to your mother, young man," Lincoln warned. "Mr. Tate is quite skilled in—"

"I know very well what you are skilled in!"

"Peter Bailey!" Lydia knelt beside her son and looked back up pleadingly at Chandler. "The boy is drunk. It is all that I can say on his behalf. Please," she implored her former lover. "No more violence."

"She's right, Chandler," Tessa bid him softly as he coiled and uncoiled his fists several times, trying to stem his rage.

"And there really was no harm done." Tessa put her hand on his shoulder and gently squeezed it, hoping to change his mind. "Please. Let's just go back to the party."

He seemed to soften beneath the tender sound of her voice. Slowly, some of his reason returned. Harming the boy—Lydia's boy—further really would serve no purpose. Perhaps, in a way, he had this coming, Chandler thought. Peter was a young man trying to protect his mother. Revenge was the only way he knew how. Chandler finally stepped back and turned away, taking Tessa's hand.

"Let's go," he muttered hoarsely, "before I change my mind."

The ballroom they re-entered was already abuzz with whispered gossip. Though few had seen the actual confrontation, everyone seemed to know about it. There were stares and more whispers as Chandler led his new wife back across the crowded floor.

It surprised Tessa that he did not flinch beneath their castigating glances and their whispered words, when she felt an overwhelming urge to shrink from all of them. But he seemed unconcerned, holding his head high, like a Donatello statue, beneath the gold gaslights, as he smiled with a renewed confidence. The orchestra struck up another waltz, but no one moved.

"Dance with me, Tessa," he bid her suddenly, magnificently, his eyes alive with a devotion that overwhelmed her.

As he took her hand firmly and led her onto the dance floor, the rest of the guests remained at a standstill. Tessa felt as if she had been lifted onto a cloud. They were the only two in the world, as everyone watched them dance.

"My God, but you are beautiful tonight," he whispered and smiled down at her, his face bronzed by the light. He looked as handsome as she had ever seen him. "You are the dream of every man in this room."

"As long as I am still your dream," she whispered back.

"Rest assured, my angel, you shall always be that."

The words of commitment hung like sweet perfume between them as Chandler pressed his lips against hers for a deeply sensual kiss. Tessa surrendered completely to the quiver of excitement as his kiss deepened, and he ravished her mouth with the kind of mastery that left her weak.

When he pulled away finally, Chandler kissed the tip of her nose, her eyelids, and then each cheek, as though sealing the new level of intimacy between them. Her eyes met his. The rest of the world around them stilled.

"Let's go home, Chandler," Tessa said softly—and they both knew what it meant.

"Are you certain?"

"Very. I am ready to be your wife . . . in every way."

"Because after tonight, you know that I will never let you go," Chandler warned her huskily, still holding her in his powerful embrace.

"It is what I am counting on," Tessa smiled and let him take her hand.

The carriage ride back to Mount Vernon Street seemed to take forever and they could not climb the twisted mahogany stairs to her bedroom fast enough. In the carriage, Chandler had not been able to keep his hands from her body, readying her with his lips, hands, and with his masculine fingers, to give all that he so desperately wanted to have from her once they were alone.

No one had lit the lamp near Tessa's bed, since they had been expected to return much later, so the room was a soft silvery blue from the moon, as it shone through the open window.

Chandler moved with Tessa to the bed, then lay down beside her. "Tonight," he whispered, unwinding her hair and watching it cascade onto her shoulders like bright copper flames, "I give you my heart, as well as my body. I give you all that I am, forever."

"Does that mean that you finally trust me now?"

He moved on top of her and she could feel him hard through her gown as he pressed himself against her thigh. Chandler parted her lips, kissing her long and deeply. "With my heart and with my life," he answered her.

"I do worship you," he breathed instead.

The blood began to beat in her ears as he kissed her again and again, blotting out her questions and his answers. Her pulse raced as he rolled her to one side and began to unhook the precious Chinese silk. Expectation shot through her body as he touched her, as his warm breath stirred her hair.

She moaned as Chandler pulled away her little cap sleeves and buried his lips above her corset in the ample cleft between her breasts. This was what they both wanted now, she thought, even after that first awkward, frightening time.

Tessa felt his tongue move down toward her nipples as he worked urgently to free the tight, constraining undergarments. When they were tossed, abandoned on the floor beside the bed, Chandler removed his own shirt and trousers, then came back to her.

His lips brushed across the lobe of her ear as he arched over her. She shivered at the raw power of his body, knowing how completely in control he was. Yet she did not struggle against him when he seized her lips again and drew her tongue into his mouth.

He would not hurt her, he would never hurt her, he had sworn, and she believed him.

As he kissed her wildly, Chandler's body began to pulse against her with the same rhythm as his tongue, a seductive plunging and retreating that left them both flushed with passion and dazed with desire.

"Sweet Jesus," he murmured thickly against her lips as he touched her between her legs, "you're wet as moss."

It would be easier this way, he thought with relief, glad it would not hurt her this time. This time belonged to Tessa. With a determined physical effort, Chandler ignored the aching need for release that already was upon him. He took his time deliberately, determinedly. After everything that had happened between them, this night was far too special to rush.

Against her skin, he blazed a trail of tantalizing kisses, down between her breasts, across her stomach, licking, touching, exploring, until his lips found her sweet, tiny bud. Langorously, he drew back the salty-sweet petals with his tongue.

"Oh, you taste so sweet." He breathed the whispered words against this achingly sensitive part of her.

Tessa cried out as pure desire swelled then burst inside her. That anyone should touch her like this! Even more, that she should crave it, and that her body should respond with such an explosion, never once struggling against something so forbidden!

But as she teetered on the edge of this new ecstasy and pure oblivion, Chandler suddenly reared up away from her legs and plunged his tongue, still wet with the taste of her body, between her parted lips. He wanted this to last forever between them but the sweetness of her body would have been his undoing if he had not pulled away.

Restraint, however, and that powerful reserve of his, were useless as she wrapped her fingers around the nape of his neck, desperate to draw him nearer. His heart was racing. His pulse was racing. Blood and raw lust, everything that had been simmering inside of him, was now ripping a path, as clean and clear as lightning, downward in his body.

Helpless to stop what would soon be an instinctive reaction to Tessa's tender touch, Chandler rose up, bracing himself over her, and reveling in the pleasurable pain. At last, he pushed into her as gently as he was physically able.

But when she cried out again anyway, he felt that wild, primitive urge completely take him over. His arms and legs were taut as he lost the battle to hold back, wound in the magical feel of her slim, silky legs.

Chandler rocked and thrust against her, and she began to meet each movement until they felt to her like one body. Each was bathed in the sweat of the other, their breathing, between each bruisingly powerful kiss, was coming in mingled gasps.

Then, just as Tessa lay in the hammering, dizzying aftermath of what had been, tonight, her own fulfillment, a groan tore up from Chandler's throat and he began to drive full force inside her. He thrust against her fiercely, over and over, until finally she felt him shudder with his own powerful and blinding release.

She wanted this, all of him. Anything Chandler could give her. His powerful body as well as his heart. Never mind the risk. Never mind the secrets he still kept from her. She had laid herself open to him here tonight, given him all she had to give. She had trusted him with the most intimate parts of herself, yet again. Because she loved him. Desperately.

They lay against one another, Tessa's breath beginning gradually to slow and the blaze that consumed her body cooling to a smolder. She ran her hands down the length of his back, feeling as if she wanted to keep him and the way things were between them like this forever.

"Are you all right?" Chandler later asked in a husky whisper, dragging his head from her shoulder and brushing back the hair from her glittering eyes.

"If I had known it could be this splendid, I would certainly have insisted that we not wait so long."

"I'm awfully glad you didn't."

"And why not?" she asked with surprise, tipping her head to one side.

"Because you didn't love me then as you do now," Chandler quirked a sleepy half smile.

"Perhaps it was that I didn't trust you as I do now."

Chandler ignored the little prick of guilt as he kissed her again, hard and full. When they parted, Tessa moved onto her side with him, the two of them still joined.

"When was the first moment you knew that you loved me?" she asked, tracing a little circle on his chest.

"I believe I knew for certain the day you took me to Hester Street."

Tessa arched a single brow. "Now you're teasing me."

"No, I am quite serious. Before that, I had been enraptured only by your beauty and wit. But that day, I saw a completely honest and open woman, one full of complexities and nuances I hadn't begun to expect. I knew then that you were a woman who could captivate me forever."

His candor surprised her, and Tessa felt at this moment as if she were bathed completely in love, and that there was a new level of honesty between them.

Chandler pressed her chin down lightly and then gazed into her eyes with such sincerity that she felt like weeping. "I make a vow to you here and now," she said. "No matter what, I will never doubt your love for me again."

"And I make a vow to you," he said softly in return, "to try my best never to give you a reason."

"I love you, Chandler."

The intense rush of feeling, hearing her say it, the exhilaration, surprisingly, was almost painful to a man who had lived so long without such devotion. Chandler felt his body respond by stirring powerfully again.

No woman in the world had ever made him want her more, nor created such an overwhelming sensation of urgency to possess her. No other woman ever would. It was the pure honesty between them that had aroused him and hardened his body again already. It was the same thing, he knew, that had softened her reserve.

"Tell me again," he bid her silkily, stroking her cheek with the back of his hand.

"I love you."

"Again."

"I love you," she softly repeated. Then the words came with more conviction, for she meant them to the core of her soul. "I love you. I love you, Oh, how I love you."

Tessa sat on the edge of the bed watching him sleep. Chandler looked like a god in the hazy early morning light; sleek, bare, to her golden. His chest rose and fell with a gentle rhythm and she thought how she had never seen him look so at peace, so free of whatever it was that had tortured him.

His eyelids fluttered softly and she longed to reach down and kiss each of them. But Tessa could not bear the thought that her touch, no matter how gentle, might wake him.

She felt more in love with him by morning's light than she had ever imagined she could. Tessa wanted nothing so much as to be with him and to share all that there was between husbands and wives. The deepest intimacy. The greatest passion. There was nothing she would ever deny him. Nothing.

She moved from the bed and walked soundlessly across the room to where the silk ball gown lay cast across her daybed. Tessa fingered the glorious lapis-blue fabric and thought back to Lincoln's declaration that Chandler had brought it back from China. He said he had saved it all of these years for someone special. That someone was not Cynthia Tate nor Lydia Bailey. It was she.

Devotion for this curiously complex man and his children swelled inside of her, cresting like a wave, as Tessa sank down and pulled the gown across her lap. Although they had only just pledged their real love to one another last night, Chandler had been showing her the depth of his feelings in a dozen different ways since they first had met.

There was the betrothal ring. The other jewels. A wardrobe of more garments than she could ever wear. The lessons. And the relentless way he had defended her last evening. She would die loving this man. She knew it.

"Why are you so far away?" he asked thickly across the great chasm of her hazy sunlit bedroom.

Tessa looked up and saw Chandler propped up by a bare arm, gazing at her with a sleepy, contented smile. "How long have you been awake?" she asked.

"Long enough to see you admiring your gown."

"Is it true what Lincoln said last night, that you saved this fabric for all of those years?"

"Guilty as charged," he replied with a broader smile as he propped himself up on the pillows a little more.

"But why didn't you tell me?"

"Because, as I said, I was waiting for the right moment."

"Is it the right moment now?" she asked him, draped in the silk as she rose again and moved close enough for Chandler to grasp her hand and draw her back down onto the bed in a heap of smooth ice blue.

"Certainly good enough," he chuckled.

Tessa sank down beside him again and touched his face, the broad sweep of his jaw, wanting to make certain that this magnificent man was real.

"Tell me about this gown," she bid him.

"A wise man in China gave the fabric to me the day before I left. Li Kao Chen knew before I did that I would find you."

"He sounds almost as wise as Charlie Murphy."

"Almost." Chandler smiled.

"I would like very much to hear about China. About Hangchow."

"It is a beautiful country," he said more softly, as she let him fold her into his arms. "It is a world away from America and all of the pressures I knew here. Simple. Peaceful."

Chandler took a deep breath and closed his eyes. "Sometimes at dusk, if I am very, very quiet, it comes back to me. The sights, the sounds, all of it."

"Do you miss it?"

"Teahouses and lotus blossoms. The fragrance of perfumed oils in morning mist, a quiet gentility. I do miss it. But things change. I have you now."

"That you do."

Chandler dragged her steadily back beneath him, touching and kissing her breasts and her long, smooth neck.

"What made you come back?"

"Duty."

"To your father?"

"To my family. Daphne and I were infused with the concept, almost from birth. They needed me. The company needed me."

"And now?"

"Until I met you on that strange and wonderful afternoon, my father's company had become a substitute for everything else that was missing in my life."

Chandler brushed the smooth skirt fabric up along her cheek and then wound it down past her breasts and across her belly until he felt her arch beneath him. "That's it," he murmured hotly. "That's what I waited to see."

His lips descended on hers again, claiming her hotly as the precious fabric pressed between them. Chandler moved his own body back and forth, brushing against the gown, feeling the cool silk press over the willowy curves of Tessa's body.

Seeing what he meant to happen, Tessa tried to move out from beneath him. "Chandler, we can't!" she whispered frantically. "Kathleen will be here any minute to see to the bed!"

"Not likely," he countered, pinning her arms firmly over her head and hungrily devouring the sweet flesh of her neck. "Not once Jennings informs her that mine has not been slept in."

Realizing that he did not mean to be denied, Tessa tried to pull the costly dress out from between them. "Leave it,"

Chandler bid her huskily as he dragged his mouth from hers and arched up over her. "I want to feel it around you when . . ." His words trailed off into a groan as he entered her with a single furious thrust.

A moment later, his breath was already coming hot and fast and each stroke brought a jolt of sensation up from the core of Tessa's body. She wrapped her legs around him, gripping his shoulders with rigid fingers.

It was not at all as it had been the night before. Chandler this time was rough, insistent, as he pressed her wrists into the bed, his hands like two iron vises, and hammered into her with a force that drove Tessa steadily toward her own boundless, magical peak.

His perspiration dripped onto her neck and chest as another groan tore from deep in his throat and he continued even harder to drive himself inside her.

The silk was wound between them, a cool smooth contrast against the burning rigid shaft that dominated her body. Tessa shuddered, feeling a peak of hot tingling pleasure wash like a powerful wave up from her loins and pulse through her body in spiral after spiral of pure sensation.

Chandler felt her response and he thrust even harder, faster, as though he were trying to make her a part of himself. "God!" he groaned. "Oh, God!" gripping the silk gown and pressing it against her breasts as Tessa's body convulsed beneath his.

Tears were streaming down her cheeks, mingling with his sweat, and her head was rolling from side to side as finally Chandler's body tightened and, with spasm after spasm, he poured himself into her with a shuddering groan of pure ecstasy.

Tessa lay heavy as lead beneath Chandler for what seemed an eternity, unable to move, unable to completely recapture her senses. He made no move to release her. Both of them were still bathed in the silken sweat of their desire. Birds chirped from the elm tree that bristled outside her window. Beyond the door, they could both hear the footsteps of servants passing busily up and down the corridor preparing for the day ahead. But, where only moments before, that prospect had frightened her, Tessa now listened to the sounds of morning, and the creaks and groans of an old house coming to life, with a detached sort of peace.

"I had no idea," she finally whispered, "that it was supposed to be pleasurable for me as well."

Chandler lifted his head from the pillows and gazed down at her serene expression. That had been his final undoing, he thought. To have felt her respond as she had beneath him. It had been like that with Cynthia only in the beginning, when the whirlwind of passion between them had eclipsed his reason. After that, with him, she had done her duty, nothing more, as the love, and the marriage, had quietly slipped away.

He thought of confiding at least that much more of the truth to Tessa now, as a way of strengthening the bond between them. But right now, Chandler wanted no one else in this bed, least of all the phantom memory of his first wife.

"Mrs. Gallagher told me that I must submit. But I must not prepare to like it," Tessa smiled drowsily. Chandler pressed a soft kiss onto her cheek and smiled down at her. "I am awfully glad she was wrong."

"Oh," he grinned, "so am I."

"Tell me about Lydia and Martin Bailey," she said with a soft insistence which bled quite suddenly into the leisure between them.

It was a strange request at a moment like this, Chandler thought, but the trust and the closeness now between them had apparently given her the courage to ask.

"The last time we spoke about that, you were not particularly fond of what you heard."

After a moment, seeing by the determined expression in her eyes that she meant not to be deterred, Chandler pulled her against his chest and breathed a kiss onto the top of her head.

"Martin Bailey is entirely confined now," he said carefully. "He has been for several years. For a long time, he tried to convince Lydia to leave him, because he could no longer—" Chandler paused, choosing his words carefully. "Because he had also begun to lose his memory and the function of his mind."

"And she wouldn't leave him?" Tessa asked, braiding her fingers through the thick blond hair on his chest.

"Lydia refused even to consider it. Even when things turned bad. She stayed by his side nursing him through the worst of it. There were days when he did not recognize her. When he called her some of the most vile names imaginable and stole out of the house only to be returned hours later by policemen, half naked and weeping like a baby."

He took a difficult breath, then exhaled. "The strain on her was enormous. It is a blessing now, really, that he lives in a world of his own. Martin is completely unaware, not only of who he is, but of Lydia and Peter as well."

"Before that, did he know about you and his wife."

"He knew," Chandler answered quietly. "Martin handed her over to me after Cynthia died, saying that he would rather it be me than someone else. We had all been friends, and he knew that I would protect her until she grew strong enough to make her own way."

Tessa looked into his face and saw the troubled expression that the recollection had brought. "We had all been friends for a very long time," Chandler said in what was nearly a whisper.

She shook her head, understanding more of this brilliantly complex man than ever before. "I just thought—"

"I know what you thought, that I brazenly stole an aged man's wife out from under his nose. So did everyone else who knew about us. But two years ago, I was just confused enough and angry enough at the world not to care at all what anyone else thought."

"She really came to care about you, didn't she?"

"We cared about one another. We helped one another through the most devastating time in both of our lives. We took comfort where it was. Not particularly noble, but there you have it. The truth."

He looked down at her, still troubled by the sound of his own words. "So tell me, Tessa, does my idealistic and principled young wife despise me?"

"I could never despise you."

"Oh, don't be too certain of that," he said with a curiously somber tone.

"What's past is past. Besides, I adore you. Haven't you realized that by now?"

Tessa did not understand the expression on his face, which, instead of lightening, grew darker and more tormented with each beat of his heart.

"What is it, my love?" she whispered as they lay together. "Tell me."

"I have done some things in my life," he said haltingly.

"What sort of things?"

"Things of which I am not proud. Things that will surely torment me until the day that I die. But please do not ask me to tell you anything more than that just now, because I really don't believe we could survive more of a confession than I have already given you."

Tessa moved to kneel on the bed before him. She took his face into her hands and looked into his suddenly tear-brightened eyes. "If I could take away the pain you feel," she whispered, "you know that I would."

In reply, his mouth came down hard on hers and, with his own hardening body, he pressed Tessa back against the rumpled bed linen. "You can take it away. You are the only one who can," Chandler murmured against her warm lips. "I want you with every part of myself. The need is so powerful sometimes that it actually hurts."

"I know," she whispered.

"My God, how I adore you, Tessa," he said softly in return.

As he kissed her, Tessa drew his tongue into her mouth and wrapped her fingers around the nape of his neck in loving compliance, wondering if heaven could really be any more glorious than this.

* * *

When Tessa had finally coaxed her husband out of bed and sent him on his way to work nearly a full hour later, she dressed and then went down into the sun-filled blue-and-white breakfast room. But what she saw tore all of the fantasy from her mind with one powerful jolt.

Jennings glanced up with the good sense to wear an expression of apology, but Daphne did not even bother to acknowledge her. Between them, James sat strapped to a chair, ankles bound, socks tied over his hands.

Jennings was quite reluctantly directing him to eat as Mayflower would, by lowering his mouth into a bowl of cold stew. The entire disgraceful scene was taking place beneath the watchful gaze of the child's aunt.

"What the devil . . ."

"It is my family's belief that the punishment should fit the crime," Daphne replied stonily by way of explanation, as Alice stood in the corner silently weeping.

"What on earth has he done to merit this?"

"It seems that the boy kicked Mrs. Forrester squarely in the shin," Jennings said quietly as James began to gag on the last sloppy mouthful. Daphne seemed to have no intention of explaining the situation to Tessa.

"Merciful God, Daphne!" Tessa gasped incredulously. "He's a child!"

"Old enough to know the proper use of his appendages with regard to his elders, and a lady especially. And to see that he doesn't forget again, he shall lose their use for the most basic of functions for the rest of the day."

"Stop this!" Tessa cried out hotly. "Stop it at once! Jennings, take those restraints off the boy, and remove those socks from his hands!"

Daphne came slowly to her feet as James looked up, his mouth smeared with food, tears falling down his cheeks.

"Do not contradict me, Miss Murphy," Daphne hissed evilly. "Believe me, I have been at this far longer than you and I know what is best for my nephew!"

"The name is Tate, Mrs. Forrester," Tessa fumed. "And by virtue of that fact, these children are my responsibility now. They are no longer yours. Jennings, I said take off those restraints!"

"Jennings, don't touch them!" Daphne countered acidly without taking her combative gaze from Tessa.

"I have never seen anything so barbaric in my life!" Tessa raged. "If he kicked you, it was quite likely a matter of self-defense!"

"Plebeian sentiment from a cultureless immigrant."

The crack of flesh was hard and swift. Tessa had slapped Daphne so smartly across the cheek, and the assault was so unexpected, that Chandler's sister was nearly rocked off her feet. She gripped her flaming cheek and shot back a look of utter contempt.

"Why, you——"

"You should be absolutely ashamed of yourself, punishing a child so savagely," Tessa countered. "What could you have been thinking?"

The moment he was freed from his restraints, James bolted from the chair and into his sister's open arms. Daphne glanced coldly at Jennings, who had openly defied her. Then she looked back at Tessa.

"I have run this house quite efficiently for my brother these past two years and I have seen to his children with the same care."

Tessa's green eyes blazed with hot-blooded Irish contempt as she looked over at the shaken little boy. "You have the gall to call that sort of treatment care?"

"No, that I call discipline. Something in which you appear to be sorely lacking. But I can assure you, my niece and nephew shall not suffer the same fate. Not if I have a single thing more to say about it!"

"They'll not be tied to any more chairs, Daphne! Of that I can assure you!"

Daphne's small, perfectly round nostrils flared, and she slapped her hands onto her hips. "Just who do you think you are?"

"I know that I am your brother's wife and now mistress of this house."

"Oh, my dear young woman," Daphne chuckled acidly. "Do be careful of illusions. Things in life are not always quite as they seem."

"I don't suppose you plan to tell me what that meant," Tessa said, feeling suddenly cautious, sensing a trap set expertly by her malicious sister-in-law.

"Take it as you like."

"What I would like, Daphne, is for you to leave my home."

At that, Daphne tipped her head back and laughed. It was a cold, highly pitched sound with the feel of jagged glass. *"Your* home, is it? For someone so poorly educated, you certainly have worked my brother like a master."

"We may have asked you to come here to see us, Aunt Daphne, because we thought you were lonely. But you are not to speak to Tessa that way anymore!" Alice defended boldly, stepping forward with James still protected behind her.

"Don't you dare to give me orders, you ungrateful little churl!" Daphne snapped, as her head swiveled back toward the children. "Not unless you want another bar of soap pushed between those pretty pink lips of yours!"

"Another of your punishments to fit the crime?" Tessa asked with dry-lipped disbelief at the mere mention of such a thing.

"Just look at the open defiance you have already kindled in these two! If you have your way, no doubt, they'll be running around this house ragged and barefoot, bucking any show of authority, in imitation of a couple of ill-bred Irish savages!"

"You may be my husband's sister, but if you cannot behave with kindness and compassion when he is not here, Daphne, I will ask you again to leave."

"I do not take orders from you, and Chandler has given me no such directive!" Daphne countered defiantly, as they stood rigidly, no more than a breath away from one another.

"I would advise you to heed my request, Daphne," Tessa said with a commanding stare. "Unless of course you would prefer to be dragged out of here by the hair. After all, you know now, first hand, how violent we ill-bred Irish savages can be."

Daphne contemplated her options for only a moment and, finding none suitable for the refined sensibilities of a fine Boston lady, whirled on her heel in a great huff of lavender, satin, and lace.

Then she spun back around, her blue eyes ablaze.

"I shall never understand why you have come into this house and insisted on changing everything, things that have gone on fine for a very long time without you. Why you have sought to undermine and belittle me in front of these children, and in front of a staff who, until today, have always deferred to me."

"Call it one of life's little mysteries, Daphne," Tessa replied with just the slightest hint of a smile. As Daphne went storming out of the breakfast room, Tessa had the most extraordinary feeling that she might actually be winning this little war between them after all.

"Thank you, Tessa," James said shyly after Daphne had gone.

"Tell me. Did you really kick your aunt?" Tessa asked, trying not to smile as she gazed down at two earnest, round-cheeked faces.

"She kicked Mayflower in the ribs for lying on her new calfskin shoes beneath the breakfast table. She kicked him so hard that he wouldn't stop yelping." James looked away. "So I kicked her back."

"Seems like punishment to fit the crime to me," Tessa said, exploding with held-in laughter.

"Then you truly are not angry with him?" Alice asked, unable to mask her surprise.

"Seems to me it was just punishment for harming a poor defenseless dog."

"I should have known better than to ask her to come and see us." Alice shook her head.

"Do you think Papa will be angry that you sent her

away?" James asked grimly. "She has always been able to do around here precisely as she wished."

"Well, as your aunt pointed out, a great many things have changed around here since then," Tessa assured him, as she crouched down to his level and took both of his hands in her own. "And after today, I can see that they're not quite through changing yet."

Chapter

34

WHAT WAS DAPHNE STILL HIDING? WHAT WAS IT THAT SHE knew?

Tessa hadn't asked those questions of anyone this time. Not even of Chandler. But in spite of Tessa's little victory over her, Daphne's words, so venomously spoken, had rekindled that nagging curiosity that Tessa still could not quite put to rest.

Do be careful of illusions. Things in life are not always quite as they seem.

Tessa sat at her dressing table, which was lit by the yellow-gold flame of a crystal oil lamp, brushing out her long, nearly dry copper hair, the possibilities reeling through her weary mind.

Chandler sat beside her, propped up in bed, watching her brush her hair. Wanting her. Possessed by a need to have her almost more urgent than it had been the night before, because now Tessa was no longer just his fantasy. This woman sitting beside him, smelling of rose milk and looking like an angel, was really his wife now. In every way. God, how he wanted to drink into his own battered soul the purity of hers.

"It's getting late, darling," he said huskily. "Come to bed."

"I'm not really sleepy yet," Tessa softly replied, gazing back at her own reflection in the gold-framed mirror as she lay down the brush.

Chandler held out his hand to her. "Who said anything about sleep?"

Tessa rose up in her cotton and lace nightdress and sat down on the edge of the bed beside him. Warm night air came in across the room from an open window. The wispy ends of her hair fluttered like tiny copper flames around her face.

"What is it?" he asked.

"I don't know what you mean."

"I know we haven't been married very long, but I believe I know you well enough to see that you are just the littlest bit distracted this evening."

"It's really nothing," Tessa lied, as he touched her hand, then ran his own up the back of her arm. Chandler wound his strong fingers seductively behind her neck until her reason, and those relentless questions about the past, began slowly to drift away. His hand was warm. His breath shallow, as he pressed a kiss gently onto her creamy cheek.

"Was it my sister again?" Chandler asked, as his tongue traced down along the softness of her silky smooth chest. He gently untied the ribbons of her nightdress. "She was here again today, wasn't she? Trying to pretend she was still in charge, I'll wager."

Tessa's pulse was racing, beating like a dull drum in her neck, beneath his warm lips. "I'm beginning to believe I can actually handle Daphne," she murmured.

"Of that I have no doubt." He nibbled at her throat. "And, speaking of my sister, I think it's high time that *you* host your first supper party and we invite *her* as a guest."

The moment of passion was at an end. Terminated as swiftly for Tessa as if he'd dashed her with ice.

"You want to *ask* her to come here?"

Chandler gently touched her face. His mouth curved into a confident smile. "I was thinking this Saturday evening. Not a large gathering the first time. Perhaps Nelson and Sylvie and Daphne and Lincoln."

"I'm not certain I understand," Tessa said, trying not to grimace at the mere thought.

"What I want is for us to continue sending a clear signal that, like it or not, *you* are the lady of this house now, not my sister. I want her to see a united front from us in that. With that sort of formidable opposition, she's bound to wear down eventually."

She had begun to wear down already. Tessa had seen it. *Keep your friends close,* she remembered her dear father once saying, *and your enemies closer!* After the chink in Daphne's armor she had seen today, Tessa knew that it was absolutely the right thing to do. She waited only a moment more to respond. "I suppose wearing your sister down does have a certain ring to it."

His kiss now was sudden. Pure in its demand.

"You really are the most incredible woman," Chandler declared, pressing her back down onto the bed and then taking one of her nipples into the warm, moist hollow of his mouth. "Do you have any idea how much I want you at this moment?"

"After last night and this morning," she smiled. "I believe that I do."

Chandler clasped his body tight to hers so that she could feel his beating heart and the raw, male hardness between his legs. Her body tingled from the contact as he parted her lips and forced his tongue between them.

In a moment, the kiss became insistent, the pressure of his body over hers was crushing. His heart throbbed against her breasts as he arched up to spread her thighs with his knees.

"You're finally really mine now, aren't you," he muttered

hungrily in a way that craved no response above compliance. "All of you."

Tessa felt his kisses grow more insistent, almost punishing, against her neck, until he was biting her skin, pressing his fingers into her back, and drawing her quickly toward that same dark abyss in which she had been that morning.

"You'll not deny me then?" he whispered.

"Never," she moaned at the splendid sensation. And they made love again, this time forcefully, wantonly, with no restraint necessary, none desired, between either of them anymore. All that each craved and sought in the other's arms was intensity, passion, and fulfillment.

She did not try to move away from him, nor he away from her, for what seemed an eternity. Tessa was content instead to listen to the slowing rhythm of both their hearts still pressed together as if they were one body.

She wound her fingers in a little stray brassy coil of hair near his brow and tried to recall what had taken so much of her mind earlier that evening. Everything but this, what was between them here and now in their private little sanctuary, seemed unimportant.

"I didn't frighten you too much this last time, I hope," he said later when he had finally caught his breath.

"No," she whispered back, still eager for the reassurance of his touch.

"Because sometimes I frighten myself with the power of what I feel for you. Sometimes, when we're like that, I'm afraid I'll lose myself entirely. Do you know what I mean?"

"I'm not sure."

"I knew that I loved you in New York. I told you that. But there is such power in it now. It's like nothing I have ever had with anyone before. As if, just now when we were joined . . . well, as if I lost my very soul to you."

"Believe it or not," she said softly against his chest, "I felt the same thing exactly."

Chandler's mouth moved up into a weary, sated smile. "Do you suppose it will always be like this between us?"

"I certainly hope not," Tessa chuckled. "I'm quite certain I would never survive it."

A drafty night breeze came across the bed, cooling their two bodies. "About my sister—"

"Shh," Tessa quieted him with a finger to his lips, drawing up the bed covers and abandoning her curiosity. "Suddenly, not even Daphne seems all that important anymore."

Chapter

35

RATTLING CHINA WAS THE FIRST SOUND TO WAKE HER.

Tessa stirred beneath the mingled fragrances of sweet roses and fresh coffee. Next came the soft sound of children's laughter. She did not open her eyes at first. Her eyelids were far too heavy and her mind still held her head fast to the pillow, possessed by memories of an unfinished dream.

Then someone suddenly tore back the heavy velvet draperies, and golden morning light flooded the bedroom.

"Rise and shine," she heard Chandler's voice, soft and coaxing. But it had come from the foot of the bed, not from the pillow beside her.

When finally she opened her eyes and rubbed them with the backs of her hands, Tessa saw her husband standing over her with a breakfast tray crowded with steaming fresh biscuits, butter, cups, and a china pot filled with coffee. The sweet faces of Alice and James shone beside it.

"Breakfast in bed for the lady of the house," he said

formally, in imitation of Jennings, "and for the queen of my heart."

"Roses, too!" said James, shyly thrusting forth a small bouquet of sweet, ruby-red flowers. The crystal vase caught the sunlight and glittered like a jewel.

"We picked them ourselves in the garden," Alice proudly exclaimed, as Tessa sat back against the headboard and gave way to a sleepy smile.

"Well, my goodness. To what do I owe such grand service?"

Chandler set the tray on her lap and opened a white linen napkin for her. Then he took the flowers from his young son and placed them on the bedside table. The room was filled with their fragrance.

"Alice told me what you did yesterday for James," Chandler said.

"Then you're not angry?"

"Angry? Gracious, no. I'm not angry with you. But I am furious with Daphne."

"I asked her to leave," Tessa warily confessed, as he poured her a cup of coffee. "Actually it was more of an order."

Chandler smiled. "She must have been livid."

"You know," Tessa smiled, too, "I believe she was, at that."

Then his thick blond brows merged in a frown. "I don't know. Perhaps this supper party is not such a good idea after all."

"No, I've thought about it as well, and I think you are absolutely right. We should do it. After all, if we're united, and she sees that, what could it possibly do but help?"

Chandler shifted his weight slightly. "Well, I don't want her in this house while I'm away. You shouldn't have to face another scene like that. Not until I have had a chance to set her straight. Is that clear?"

"Very," Tessa nodded, trying to hide her relief.

"I shall give Jennings and Douglas the same instructions before I leave."

"You're going somewhere?"

"I must make a short business trip but I will be back on Friday. I forgot to mention it last night, having had so much else on my mind," he said, with a slight smile he knew she would understand.

"You will be gone two days?"

"I'm afraid it cannot be helped. There has been a problem with one of our shipments, and they're holding it, refusing to release it until the matter is settled."

"I wish I could go with you," she said, trying not to sound too pleading or insecure.

"You don't know how much I wish that, too."

"Tessa will be all right, Papa," said James, sensing his father's hesitation to part from his new wife. "I'll look after her for you."

Chandler smiled down at his young son sitting on the edge of the bed. The confident smile mirrored his own. "Well, I suppose you are the man of the house when I'm away at that, aren't you?"

"Yes, sir," James preened.

"And you'll not permit your Aunt Daphne to bind your hands again if somehow she finds a way back into this house."

"She'll have to catch me first!"

Chandler smiled. "All right then. It's settled. Tessa, I'll handle my sister personally when I return. But in the meantime, you have full authority, as if you needed it from me, in this house. Use whatever means you like to keep her at bay. And whatever you do, you are not to converse with her or let her bait you further with those idle threats of hers. Understood?"

"Clearly."

Chandler glanced back at his son. "All right now, James. I am counting on you to help see to the women while I am away."

"I won't disappoint you, Papa."

Chandler clipped James's shoulder affectionately with a gentle fist. "I know that, my boy. Now, you and Alice take

Tessa's tray back down to Mrs. O'Neil for me, will you? I would like to speak with her privately for a few minutes before I leave."

Alice came around and took the tray from Tessa's lap, smiling happily. "We sure are glad you're here, Tessa," she said in her sweet, child's voice. "This house hasn't been so happy in a very long time."

"I'm glad I'm here too." Tessa smiled as James climbed down from the bed.

"And son," Chandler called after him with a wry smile, "pull the door closed on your way out, would you?"

Chapter

36

"YOUR PARLORMAID SAID YOU WOULDN'T BE OUT MUCH LONGER. She suggested that I wait in here," Lydia Bailey said tentatively, rising up from the loveseat in a smart, rose-sprigged dress as Tessa and Jennings came in after a carriage ride with the children. "I hope you don't mind."

It was the first time Tessa had gotten such a close view of her husband's former mistress. She tried not to look too closely at Lydia's face, which she was certain Chandler knew by heart. Lydia Bailey was an attractive woman, with sharp, vivid features, a firm chin and curved, pink lips. Her skin was only slightly wrinkled at the corners of her bold, blue eyes. In her youth, it was clear, she had been quite a beautiful woman.

Tessa tried valiantly to be calm, the picture of civility that her lessons were teaching her to be. But her heart felt as if it were suddenly in her throat, and her mouth had gone bone dry. "I'm afraid my husband is not here, Mrs. Bailey," Tessa said, struggling to sound polite.

"Truthfully, I came to see you."

"Shall I bring tea, Mrs. Tate?" Jennings asked, returning to the required formality in the presence of others. In his voice was a cue. Above the rapid beating of her heart, Tessa was certain she had heard that an offer of tea, no matter how objectionable, was the socially appropriate and gracious thing to do.

"Thank you, Jennings." She nodded, and he closed the parlor doors on his way out, leaving wife and former lover alone. Together.

The parlor was suddenly warm. Tessa sank into the winged chair opposite the loveseat. She motioned her guest to sit down as well. "Well then, Mrs. Bailey, what is it that I can do for you?"

"I have come here to apologize."

A strange collection of thoughts paraded across Tessa's mind in the single moment after Lydia Bailey's reply. Did the woman actually mean to speak with remorse about the sinful relationship between herself and another man besides her husband? Or might the pretense of an apology actually be a reason to gloat about a man she had taken first into her heart and her bed?

"I wanted to apologize for my son's inexcusable behavior the other evening."

The sincere tone jolted Tessa and sent a shock wave through her. Tessa had not expected that, and she sank further back into the chair.

"That really isn't necessary," she managed to say.

"It is to me. My son is an angry young man, indeed. But that is no excuse for involving you."

"Chandler wanted to kill him."

"Justifiably so."

A bit of the old Irish fight returned at the sound of Lydia Bailey's last remark. After all, the boy's mother had engaged in an adulterous affair. Had he not had reason, Tessa wondered, to try to hurt the man who had shamed his father in the most lethal way he could?

There were different sorts of values here on Beacon Hill from the ones she had learned from her father, the values he had brought from a small town in Ireland, where times and lives were far simpler than the one she was living now.

Here was Chandler Tate's former mistress preparing to take tea with his new young wife and apologizing, not for her own scandalous behavior, but for the behavior of her son.

"You really needn't have come for that," Tessa said, unsuccessfully fighting to keep the icy tone from her already strained voice.

"Oh, but I did, my dear. It was only proper to do so, considering the circumstances."

"Proper?" Tessa asked, feeling as if any moment she might choke on the word, the irony of it. Jennings came back into the parlor with a full tea tray.

"I really would like us to be friends. Perhaps I can even call you Tessa. It is such a lovely name."

"Oh, I don't see how—"

"Yes, Mrs. Bailey," Jennings smoothly intervened, expertly cutting off Chandler's new, less experienced wife as he poured them their tea. "Just this morning Mrs. Tate was telling me that a person can never have too many friends."

"Especially when one is new in a town," Lydia agreed.

"Precisely," Jennings countered, ignoring Tessa's wide-eyed expression of surprise.

"I have come about something else, as well," Lydia said, as Jennings backed away. But this time he made no move to leave the room.

"And what might that be?" asked Tessa, managing to hold her cup without shaking, despite the anger she felt.

"I would very much like you to come to my home tomorrow afternoon. A group of us play cards every second Friday, and I thought it would be nice for you to become acquainted with some of them. They really are such a lovely group and it may well help to make your transition here in Boston a little bit easier."

"Oh, I don't think—"

"How delightful, ma'am," Jennings interrupted again, cutting Tessa off.

"Jennings!" Tessa snapped, with a gasping sound. She

moved to say more as he bent over her with a small silver pitcher poised artfully between them.

"Cream, ma'am?"

"No, I don't want any cream. I want—"

"Oh, of course. Forgive me. It has been a long day, Mrs. Bailey. Mrs. Tate would certainly have had me ask you first."

"Just a bit of sugar, thank you, Jennings," Lydia replied, holding out her cup. "So then, will you come?"

Tessa looked desperately up at Jennings, realizing that for some inexplicable reason, he wanted her to be more than cordial to Chandler's former mistress, and knowing that it was the last thing in the world she wanted for herself.

"Might I bring someone with me?" Tessa finally asked with a little smile, having found no civilized way to reject the invitation.

Lydia sat up on the loveseat with a relieved little smile, as she set her cup back into the saucer. "You've made a friend in Boston already?"

"Yes. As a matter of fact, I have."

"How splendid, Why yes, of course. Certainly. Bring her with you," Lydia replied, smiling graciously, not caring who it might be. Rather, she was pleased that the first awkward moments between them had now passed.

Like everything else in her life this past year, coming here had been for Chandler's sake. It was over between them, she understood that. But she still cared deeply for him. She would forever. And at the Kennicotts' ball he had asked her one last favor.

"Tessa could only benefit from someone in her life like you, Lydia," Chandler had observed at the Kennicotts' party. "It won't be easy for her here."

"It seldom is for outsiders."

"Unless they are blessed with kind assistance," he added in that commanding tone of his. He leveled his deep blue eyes at her in a way that would have made her promise him anything.

"Will you help my wife then, Lydia?" he had asked.

"There really is no one else with your influence that I can ask."

"What makes you think I would want to help the woman who took my place?" she hedged.

"Knowing what we meant to one another once."

That decided it for her. She would never have him again as she once had, but Lydia Bailey did not want to risk losing Chandler from her life completely. And she knew in her heart that she would have done far more if he had asked her to.

"If it is what you really want," she had said.

"It would mean a great deal to me."

And so she had come, humbling herself before a younger, more beautiful rival.

"We meet at two," Lydia said graciously, glancing one more time at Tessa's fine, smooth skin and lustrous copper hair.

"Two will be fine."

As they walked to the door, Lydia Bailey breathed a sigh of relief that the encounter was at an end. She had done what she had promised. "You will be happy to know that my son was properly chastised for his actions," she added as they stood together in the doorway. "He'll not be bothering you again."

"My husband will be most glad to hear it," Tessa could not keep herself from saying.

Jennings had come up behind them and now stood on the marble floor and was holding the door to the carriageway open for their guest. Lydia moved out onto the landing and then turned back around.

"Well then. I am glad that we had this opportunity to speak and I hope that in the coming weeks we shall come to know one another even that much better."

Tessa could feel Jennings's eyes on her, pressing her relentlessly to make one final civil comment in parting.

She extended her hands in a gesture of friendship, and Lydia took them both. "I really do appreciate your calling, Mrs. Bailey," Tessa finally said, her voice ringing now with all the sincerity she had squeezed up from the depths of herself. "And I shall look forward to tomorrow."

"Oh, by the way," Lydia said as an afterthought, as she stood in a stream of afternoon sunlight that rushed in through the open door. "I nearly forgot to ask. Who is it that you'll be bringing as your guest?"

"Oh, I'm certain you know her," said Tessa. "She's a lovely woman, though she hasn't many more friends here in Boston than I do. Her name is Sylvie Winthrop."

"You cannot possibly take her there, ma'am!" Jennings gasped.

Tessa spun back around after the door had closed. She was a little ashamed of how she was still glorying in the truly horrified expression that had taken over Lydia Bailey's once dignified face.

"I cannot?"

"It would be like sending a lamb to a pack of hungry wolves!"

"Sylvie can hold her own, Jennings," she said with newly won confidence. "And if not, she will have me beside her."

"All right, two lambs to the slaughter," he said bleakly.

"Really, Jennings," Tessa said merrily, completely ignoring the troubled tone in his voice. "I thought you had more faith in me than that. Why, just this morning, wasn't it you who said you thought I could face anything?"

"This, ma'am, is another matter entirely. Nelson and Sylvie Winthrop are considered unacceptable by society here."

"Because they married for love? How dreadful of them!" Tessa laughed. "That really is such nonsense. It is high time, Jennings, that people came down from the clouds and got over it. After all, considering her behavior with my husband, Lydia Bailey is no great paragon of virtue herself."

"True enough," he conceded.

"Besides, Jennings, I owe her. Sylvie has been an invaluable friend and confidante to me since I came here, and I think it is high time that the rest of society was made as aware of her worth as I am."

"She will never go through with it, you know," Jennings warned.

"Oh, of course she will. Sylvie is as anxious to have Nelson back among his old friends as I am to have them there. She only needs an avenue. Then we will be able to do things together in public. Go to balls and the theater with people I actually like. And can you imagine how surprised Chandler will be when he hears what I have done?"

"Oh, he'll be surprised, ma'am," Jennings said, finally coming away from the door with her.

"I think Mrs. Bailey took it rather well, actually." Tessa giggled with two fingers pressed to her lips. "After she picked her chin up off of our floor."

"Make no mistake about it, Mrs. Tate," he warned. "Lydia Bailey is someone to cultivate as an ally, not an enemy. She can make a great deal of difference to you here."

"I appreciate your concern, Jennings," Tessa said blithely, "and even your clever interference earlier. I know you only had my best interest at heart. But I will be fine tomorrow. After all, what can they possibly do to me now?"

Chapter 37

TESSA TOOK GREAT CARE IN DRESSING FOR LYDIA BAILEY'S AFTER-
noon of cards. She took suggestions from both David
Jennings and Kathleen O'Reilly as to the proper attire, and
the most becoming style for her hair. They settled on a dress
of green and black stripes and her hair worn up away from
her face in a loose knot, with only a modest string of green
ribbon wound through it.

Everything must be perfect, as much for Sylvie's sake as
for her own. She still had not told Sylvie where they would
be going by the time Chandler's brougham came around to
fetch her a few minutes before the hour of two. She didn't
want the Frenchwoman's fear to prevent her plan's fruition.

But Sylvie knew the house at once, with its commanding
brick facade and its pair of octagonal bay windows like dark
brooding eyes glaring at her. She grew rigid, sinking back
into the carriage seat as though she hoped it would swallow
her up entirely. "Tell me we are not planning to stop here,
Tessa."

"Relax," Tessa said calmly, taking Sylvie's trembling

hand and rubbing it gently. "You wouldn't want them to see your fear, would you?"

"You said we were going for a drive."

"And so we have. A drive to Lydia Bailey's house. I suppose I neglected to mention that you and I have been invited to play cards here this afternoon."

"Tessa, you have no idea what you are doing," Sylvie strenuously objected, her usually lilting French voice ringing now with alarm.

"I most certainly do. I am trying to pay you back for all that you and Nelson have done for me since I have been here in Boston."

"Believe me, Tessa, this sort of gratitude we can do without!"

"Oh, nonsense. And, after all, don't you owe my idea at least a chance? For Nelson's sake?"

Sylvie Winthrop gripped Tessa's hand tightly. Her normally friendly liquid brown eyes now were glazed with fear. "I know that you are new to this city, Tessa, but you truly do not understand. You cannot force these people to accept me. To Boston society, I will never be anything but Penelope Winthrop's maid."

"And what do you suppose that makes me?"

"Far better at hiding your past than I, for one thing. Really, Tessa. I would like to go home."

"After one game of cards," Tessa bargained. "Since we're here anyway now, and we're both expected."

"We?"

"Lydia Bailey knows full well who I am bringing."

"I cannot believe you told her it was I."

"Of course," Tessa swallowed a little laugh. "She didn't jump for joy, I'll be honest enough to tell you that. But she didn't object either."

"That is very odd," Sylvie said warily.

"They've just decided to put it in the past. After all, no one can hold on to anger forever, can they?"

"Oh, Tessa," Sylvie shook her head. "You obviously don't know Penelope Winthrop."

They stood on the brick landing in a sultry breeze, as Tessa pressed the brass knocker against the door with three small taps. Just beyond, they could hear the echo of feminine laughter, soft and muted, and the light chatter of ladies. It was an affectionless, tittering sound. As they waited, Tessa took Sylvie's still trembling hand again and squeezed it.

"Everything is going to be fine," she whispered. "You'll see. The first few minutes are the most awkward."

"Mrs. Tate, I presume," said a stiff-spined butler in a deep monotone.

"Yes. How did you know?" Tessa smiled up pleasantly.

"Process of elimination, madam," he countered dryly. "You are the last to arrive."

"And this is—"

"Mrs. Nelson Winthrop," he cut her off in the same disinterested tone. "Yes, I know. If you will both follow me, I shall announce you."

"You see?" Sylvie whispered frantically, as they moved together a pace behind the surly butler. "It is happening already."

The parlor of the Bailey home was grand, on a par with the one in the Tate home. There were the same heavy, gold-framed portraits, these ornamenting red-and-gold wallpaper. There were potted palms, enough to make a garden, and a general overabundance of furniture.

Brocade-covered settees sat beside silk-covered chairs, and most of them were occupied by impeccably dressed ladies who, at first, glanced up casually as Tessa and Sylvie were shown past the heavy velvet draperies into the room.

Tessa breathed a little sigh of relief when Lydia Bailey was the first to rise and come across the oriental carpet toward them. She was smiling now as graciously as she had been the day before, and her hands were outstretched.

"Mrs. Tate."

"Mrs. Bailey," Tessa countered, linking hands with her, as those lessons in etiquette had taught her to do.

"I am so glad you could come."

"Thank you for inviting me. And of course you know Mrs. Winthrop."

"Sylvie," Lydia nodded, her welcoming expression becoming slightly more strained.

A bitter hush fell over the room at the sound of Sylvie's name, and Tessa could feel the stiffening of spines all around her. Noses were thrust haughtily into the air. They both felt the sudden crackling tension in the room.

Great God! Tessa thought frantically as she glanced around. For all of my good intentions, have I really made an error in this after all? Surely these well-bred ladies have enough tact at least to tolerate Sylvie politely, as Chandler's former mistress and I are doing with each other, if not to welcome her into their midst. After all, it has been five years.

"Good of you to join us as well, Sylvie," Lydia finally condescended to say in a cordial tone that bore only the slightest trace of malice. "Please, both of you, do come in and get acquainted with the others. We're just having a few refreshments to fortify ourselves before we get down to the serious business of playing cards."

Tessa moved a few steps, with Sylvie glued to her heel. Both of them began to look around the room for a single friendly face as soon as Lydia Bailey turned away. What Tessa found instead was Daphne Forrester, who stood whispering to a striking young woman. Sylvie divulged that it was Daphne's good friend, Felicity Pettigrew.

So then Jennings was right. It is to be two lambs to the slaughter after all, Tessa thought, sadly realizing how badly she had miscalculated the afternoon.

"Tessa, I believe I could kill you for this," Sylvie murmured as they stood alone in the center of the room, all eyes upon them.

"I think it is going rather well, under the circumstances. Look. Here comes a kind-looking lady to introduce herself."

"That is not a kind lady, Tessa," Sylvie said, taking in a frantic gulp of air. "That is my mother-in-law!"

"Hello. I am Tessa Tate," she said pleasantly once again, and extended her hand. "And you know Mrs. Winthrop."

"My dear," the elderly, stony-faced woman with the platinum hair and vacant blue eyes retorted cooly, "*I* am Mrs. Winthrop. This girl is my maid. At least she was while she still possessed the last grain of sense."

Mrs. Winthrop examined her daughter-in-law as if she were a prize horse. Her expression, however, was one lacking great interest. "Sylvie, I always knew you were brazen, laying a trap for my son as you did. But I really would have thought you would have had more dignity than to try and come flaunting it like this."

"Mrs. Winthrop," Tessa said with a hint of her own building anger. "Sylvie is my guest here. She is no longer your maid, to be spoken to like that."

"Thanks to my son's more basic instincts," she cruelly growled.

Tessa was actually relieved to see, from the corner of her eye, Daphne and someone else approaching. At least with Chandler's sister, she knew what to expect.

"Oh, splendid," whispered Sylvie. "Now Daphne and Felicity Pettigrew can join the feeding frenzy."

The infamous Felicity, Tessa thought, studying her more closely as the two women approached. She was a striking beauty whose very bearing suggested sophistication. She had sparkling dark eyes, hair to match, and perfect ivory skin.

"Why Tessa," Daphne purred evilly, not wasting a moment to begin her attack. "What a surprise it is to see you here. Does my brother know you're out alone like this?"

"You know very well that your brother is out of town until later this afternoon."

"He doesn't know that you are here, humiliating yourself? I thought as much. You do seem to make a habit of getting yourself into trouble when he is away."

"So, you are Tessa," Felicity declared appraisingly with a

slightly less caustic grin than the one still lingering on Daphne's face, making it cold and hard and aged.

"I had wondered what you looked like. You're not at all as I pictured you and you're certainly nothing like the other women to whom Chandler has ever been drawn."

"From what my husband tells me, Miss Pettigrew, I have that in my favor," Tessa could not keep herself from saying.

The silence that followed was like death. For an instant, a short eternity, the room was cold. Then Felicity began to laugh. She pressed her fingers over her lips but the sound escaped anyway. Daphne turned to her friend frowning with a huff of reproach. But it was too late.

"It's no use, Daphne," Felicity smiled. "The girl is charming."

"She's Irish!"

"So are you and we have never held that against you."

"Third-generation Irish on my mother's side is hardly the same thing as someone whose family is barely off the boat," Daphne countered a little too quickly.

"Charm is charm, Daphne dear, no matter from where it comes."

"Oh, don't be absurd. You know you would have made my brother a far better wife than this."

"She won him fair and square. Come now, Daphne dear, after all, no one likes a poor loser. Besides, I plan to positively murder her at cards this afternoon. I am certain there will be some recompense for the bruise to my pride in that."

Tessa smiled, feeling a rush of relief she could not hide, surprised beyond words to find allies in two of her husband's former inamoratas. Life certainly was full of irony, she thought. Only Daphne and Penelope Winthrop, who still stood in their midst, her face twisted like an old prune, seemed to want to cling to past bitterness.

Lydia's welcome, followed by Felicity's apparent declaration of a truce, was infectious. Two more ladies, neither of whom Tessa recognized, rose from a red-velvet couch and drew near.

"Hello, Sylvie," said a short, plump woman with straight blond hair and a flawless peach complexion. "It has been a long time."

"Too long," the other said sincerely. She had the same smooth skin and blue eyes, but with hair as dark and shiny as a pot of ink. It was clear by their features that they were sisters.

Tessa could sense Sylvie's pure shock at the encounter without even having to look over at her. But Nelson's wife was not the only one aghast at the presence of these two young women. Penelope Winthrop sailed across the room, her thick lips rounded into an O of surprise.

"Christine! Elizabeth!" she bellowed.

"Really, Mother," said the elder of the two, with a hint of exasperation. "Hasn't enough time passed?"

"How is our brother, Sylvie?" the dark-haired girl asked anxiously.

"He is well," Sylvie replied carefully.

"And the children? Little Nelson must be—"

"He is five now," Sylvie cautiously divulged with a faint, yet still cordial smile. "Camille is nearly two."

Tessa was dumbfounded. Not only had Nelson Winthrop been deprived of his position in society by marrying for love, but his family had completely disowned him. Penelope was such a bitter old crone that she had grandchildren she had never seen. These people were family. They shared the same blood, a history, and yet the matriarch had selfishly cut them out of her life and her heart without a thought to anyone but herself. How could someone live with such bitterness, Tessa wondered.

Anger was not borne without a price. It was clear in the afternoon sunlight that Nelson Winthrop's mother was being slowly eaten away by an emotion she doubtless had nursed for years. Her face, obviously once lovely, was now twisted, dominated by a taut network of wrinkles.

Tessa was certain, standing here in the midst of this awkward family reunion, that she had never seen anything more tragic in her life. So much time lost, never to be regained. So much pain caused, never totally to be healed.

"Do you suppose Nelson would see us, after all these years?" asked the blond-haired sister. "It would mean a great deal to finally meet our niece and nephew."

"Christine Winthrop! I forbid you to say a single word more!" Penelope screeched bitterly.

"Oh, Mother." Elizabeth rolled her eyes. "Do be quiet, will you? If you want to keep up this absurd vendetta of yours for the rest of your life, so be it. But Christine and I are ready to get beyond it."

Having dared to speak against her mother with what was probably more force than she ever had used in her life, Elizabeth Winthrop looked invigorated as she glanced back at Sylvie.

"I only hope that Nelson does not believe it is too late for us."

The spell of anger and recriminations having been broken by the Winthrop sisters, the rest of the afternoon progressed smoothly by comparison. Considering the magnitude of what Tessa and Sylvie had gone up against, it was actually quite successful. Both of them were drawn, by invitation, to the same card table as Christine and Elizabeth, and then they were joined by Felicity Pettigrew. After a while, Tessa could see that Sylvie was actually beginning to enjoy herself. Between hands, she answered Christine and Elizabeth's questions about their brother and about the children. Both sisters seemed hungry for even the smallest details of the family members they had lost.

As the afternoon progressed, the whispering and surreptitious finger pointing from the other tables finally ceased. At the next table, Tessa even caught a glimpse of Lydia Bailey, her face bright in a ray of sunlight, smiling with an unmistakably pleased expression.

"I tell you, Nelson, we owe everything to Tessa," Sylvie said, still speaking excitedly as the three of them stood in the Winthrop foyer later that afternoon.

The explanation of events at the Bailey house had come tumbling from her lips, a cascading waterfall of briskly spoken English mixed with indecipherable French. She had not even waited until they were free of their hats and gloves before she had told her husband nearly everything.

"And Elizabeth and Christine both said they wanted to see me?" he asked.

"They did indeed. Stood up to your mother the entire time. You would have been so proud."

Nelson betrayed only the slightest smile as he stood in astonishment. "Better late than never, I suppose."

"It was really quite a shock to see," said Sylvie.

"You're right about one thing. It was better that I did not know where you two were going when you left. I would likely have come after both of you with a rope and a switch!" Nelson chuckled. "If I live to be a hundred, I would never expect to hear a story like that."

"Tessa somehow knew it was all going to work out," Sylvie said, looking back gratefully at her new friend and resting her head gently against her husband's vest. "I didn't want to go. That is certain. But she would not take no for an answer."

"Lord above," Nelson exclaimed, pressing a hand to his forehead in disbelief as his eyes glazed with emotion. "Is it possible that we are finally about to become yesterday's news?"

"It would seem that way," Tessa said brightly.

"It has been such a long time since anyone has done something so nice for me, or been so brave. It is difficult to know what to say."

"Seems to me that your sisters were really the brave ones. Now that I've met her, I know that it couldn't have been easy for them to stand against your mother."

"Well, you're right about that," he laughed, and his eyes brightened. "Formidable, isn't she?"

"Not all that different from Daphne," Tessa smiled.

"Nelson had given up hope of ever seeing any of them again," Sylvie confided. "They were so angry."

Tessa's bright smile faded a degree. "It isn't right for families to be apart. I'm just glad for what little hand I might have had in it."

"Sylvie and I owe you, Tessa," Nelson solemnly replied. "Believe me, I won't forget that."

Chapter
38

CHANDLER WOULD BE HOME ANY MOMENT. TESSA HAD NEVER FELT so much anticipation at the prospect of anything in her life.

She was surprised how much she missed her husband's touch after only two short days. The feel of his body pressed against hers. The musky smell of his skin, and the smile that could make her believe anything was possible. Her skin turned to gooseflesh thinking about what their reunion might be like.

When a knock sounded at the door, she came to her feet in a crimson velvet robe with a gold cord at her waist, her hair long and silky across her shoulders. As she pivoted around, Tessa's heart began to pound. Anticipation hardened like a knot in her chest.

"Oh, I've missed you," Chandler said as she fell into his solid arms, burying her head against the reassuring texture of his tweed jacket.

"Two days seemed an eternity," she whispered, giving herself over to the tidal wave of desire that had quickly engulfed them both.

His eyes, as he gazed down at her, were dark with passion. The feeling now that they each had someone to count on and to trust was stronger than it had ever been.

"Heart of my heart, I do worship you," Chandler whispered huskily, playing at the knot at her waist. "If I should ever lose you—"

"You never will," she assured him, looking up with an open, trusting expression just before he kissed her deeply.

The tall bedroom door squealed on its hinges but neither of them heard it at first. Then suddenly they looked across the room to see two sets of eyes, both blue and seeking, peering around the half-open door.

"Is it all right to come in?" Alice asked tentatively.

"Of course it's all right," Chandler chuckled. "Come here at once and welcome your ol' father home, both of you."

Gleefully, James and Alice bounded into the room toward him and skittered into his arms.

"So were you good while I was away?" he asked, kissing the top of one head and then the other.

"Very!" Alice nodded proudly.

"We saw the North Side with Tessa today," James added as he wrapped an arm around his father's shoulder.

Tessa could see Chandler tense and the easy smile leave his face. "What were you doing over there?"

"Jennings and I took the children out for a ride, and there was a detour. I hope that was all right."

There was an awkward little silence before he replied. "Of course. I'm sorry. It's just been a long day and a long ride and I would like to have a bath myself."

He smiled down at his children and they softened again. "It was so sad, Papa, really. But we gave money to some of the children."

"Yes," James seconded. "We tried to help."

"I don't suppose I would ever have thought to do something like that," Chandler's lips twisted slightly as he looked up at his wife.

"You know I don't believe that for a moment," she said,

gazing down adoringly at him. "I saw the honorable sort of man you were back in New York."

"I didn't win you over all that easily."

"Oh, don't be too certain of that," she laughed.

"If I recall correctly, there was the little matter of one Brian Sullivan who tried rather ardently to win you, too."

"I see now that there never was any choice to be made."

"Oh, you might want to check out my suitcase," Chandler smiled down at his children. "I believe there's a little something in there for each of you."

Alice and James scampered across the room toward the door to the dressing room connecting Tessa's bedroom to their father's. "It is on my bed," he called after them. "Ask Jennings to help you."

When they were alone again, Chandler pulled her to him forcefully and pressed his mouth to hers. She quivered at the punishing sweetness of his tongue against the back of her throat. The crush of his arms around her.

"I'll want far more than this from you, if we don't stop now," she breathlessly warned.

"Is that a promise?"

"Always. But Alice and James could come back through that door any moment and I don't think either of us fancies an audience."

"They have certainly grown fond of you."

"Well I have grown very fond of them," she said, tracing her finger across the line of his jaw. "Promise you won't laugh if I tell you something?"

"I promise," he said sincerely.

"I have come to feel sometimes as if Alice and James were actually my own children."

"Do you mean that?"

"I suppose it's foolish, since they had a mother, someone I am certain who loved them every bit as much as I do, and who should never be forgotten."

Chandler let go of his grasp and took a step backward. "Cynthia was not always the mother she should have been," he divulged in a tone of confession.

Hearing the sudden flicker of pain in his voice, Tessa was silent. "I need to try to tell you something. I *want* to tell you something," he said as he led her to the edge of the bed, then sat down beside her. "That place where you were this afternoon, the North Side, it holds a great many bad memories for me," he said slowly, holding fast to his reserve so that the entire ugly truth did not come rushing out.

"Cynthia," he began again, certain that he would choke on the bitter taste of her name, "she was . . . I found her there, a long time ago, with a gentleman. Although I am not certain *gentleman* is the appropriate word for the scurrilous sort of vermin he was."

"Was?"

"He was a merchant seaman. A big, foul man," Chandler described, catching himself. "There was really nothing of the gentleman about him at all. Beyond that, I only meant that he thankfully disappeared from Boston after that."

In part it was still a lie, but there was more truth in Chandler's words at this moment than there had ever been. And perhaps, just perhaps, he might find his way toward total honesty after all, if she could help him.

"I hated her, you know." He took Tessa's hand as he continued on in a pained, rasping whisper. "Not only for what she had done to my children. I discovered that she had abandoned them for him on a dozen different occasions. But I hated her for what she had done to me. To what I believed was the truth. She had destroyed it all, crushed it without a care, like something insignificant. Something meaningless."

Chandler took a breath, doing his best to gauge Tessa's response. What would she think of him if she knew all? Was their love really strong enough to withstand that?

"I felt as if she had taken my heart and cut it out with a blunt-edged knife. Wiped away my feelings. My ability to love. And I wanted her dead. God help me, all I could feel for the longest time was hate. Lord almighty, how I wanted her dead. . . ."

His voice trailed off. He did not continue right away. He

felt Tessa squeeze his hand as he tried to believe that it would still be all right between them once she knew.

"And since it would seem that I am in the mood for confessions today," he finally began again, "I may as well tell you that the merchant seaman was not the first man to turn my wife's head. It seems that there was a rather substantial line before that. A business associate of my father's was the first. And for a time, Cynthia rather favored our gardener. Suffice it to say that she spent a good deal more time collecting lovers than she did attending to the needs of our children."

Tessa pressed her fingers against her lips so that she would not gasp or put voice to the revulsion she felt.

"It was our gardener I caught her with in this very bed one afternoon," he continued painfully. "James was crying in the cradle beside them, entirely unattended."

Tessa swallowed dryly. "It is difficult for me to believe you could ever have fallen in love with someone who would be capable of such—"

"Yes, I know," he said quietly, not allowing her to finish, as he watched her face for a sign that he was safe enough in her love finally to continue, that his beautiful wife would still love him, no matter what more he said next.

"That is a horrible story," Tessa shook her head.

"Yes it is."

"I'm sure Cynthia believed she had her reasons, but I will never understand what people allow themselves to do, and the excuses they make for it afterward. For me there is right and there is wrong," she said proudly. "My da always said life was as simple as that."

"Sometimes things happen."

"Not that I will ever understand."

He felt a chill of reserve. Chandler stood and took her hands to help her back to her feet just as Alice and James came back through the door, each holding a small sack of candy.

He was glad for the reprieve. He loved Tessa with all of his heart. He would love her forever and he did not blame her for her convictions. But her firm assertion just now had told him what he needed to know. Total confession was still not possible. Not now, perhaps never.

"So, this is the business you were really out of town for?" Nelson Winthrop asked with a slow smile.

"Well, a man cannot buy the finest rubies in the world just anywhere, can he?" Chandler slyly replied.

The next morning, he and Nelson sat in the Tate study, which faced Mount Vernon Street. They were contemplating two sparkling sets of ruby earrings mounted in gold.

"Well?" Chandler asked, crossing his legs and looking over at his best friend. "What do you think?"

"I think they are breathtaking."

"But which pair best suits Tessa, do you think?"

Nelson's eyes narrowed on the exquisite jewels as he came forward on the velvet-covered chair in the contemplative silence. "When I first met your wife," he began thoughtfully, fingering one set and then the other. "I might have chosen the teardrops for their simplicity. But now, you know, I believe Tessa can carry something a bit more grand."

"My thoughts exactly."

"She has changed since she's been here."

"She has certainly changed me."

"That too," Nelson smiled. "But what I was referring to is the confidence she has gained. I am quite certain now that there isn't anything your wife could not face or conquer."

He looked at the jewels for another moment, then back up at Chandler. "I have seen the life she has breathed back into this old mausoleum of yours. And what she did at Lydia Bailey's card party was not the sort of bold move just anyone would have had the courage to make."

"I think Sylvie provided her with part of that courage. Tessa was only trying, in her own inimitable way, to pay your wife back for all of the French lessons and the friendship she has extended."

"The two of them do get along splendidly, don't they?"

"Probably much better than either of us could ever have dared to hope," said Chandler with a little wink, as he picked up the round ruby-and-diamond earrings. He watched them sparkle for a moment, casting a prism of color on the study wall. "Have you seen your sisters yet?"

"A meeting has been set for next Tuesday afternoon. And that I most definitely owe to your wife."

Chandler scooped up both sets of earrings. "Then I suppose we will just have to take them both."

"Now I know that you adore her, but what on earth will Tessa do with two sets of ruby earrings?" Nelson asked with a low chuckle.

"She will ask me to give a set to Sylvie."

"Oh, no," Nelson objected, putting up a hand. "I cannot possibly let you do that."

"Perhaps you can say no to me, old friend," Chandler said, as his smile broadened slowly. "But I wonder, would you want to risk the same with my very bold and beautiful new wife? Besides, Sylvie should have something appropriate to wear with her dress when you attend our dinner party tonight."

Nelson's eyebrows lifted. "We cannot possibly."

"Oh, yes you can. We are giving our first dinner and our best friends have simply got to be here. It will be a small affair. My sister Daphne has even agreed to extend herself," he said glibly. "She will come with Lincoln and you and Sylvie are to be the only other guests. I believe Daphne may be ready to make amends for her shameful behavior toward you and Tessa."

"And she did not insist on bringing her friend Felicity to act as moral support?"

"No, Daphne has taken this matter over and was quite specific that the only other guests this first time be you and Sylvie. Besides, Felicity has a new beau."

"Felicity Pettigrew serious about someone besides you?"

"About time, wouldn't you say?"

"Eh." Nelson twisted the tip of his chestnut-colored mustache. "Perhaps it is time for a great many things to begin changing at last."

"Look, Nelson," Chandler said seriously as he leaned forward in his chair. "I owe you an apology for not having done this sooner. There is no excuse for my not having been a better friend to you and Sylvie in this."

"We cannot blame you for our banishment from society, Chandler."

"Perhaps not. But, I blame myself. Those may have been bleak days for me but I am sure that there was a great deal more I could have done to defend you." Chandler leveled his hand on top of Nelson's briefly. "Come to dinner tonight and have Sylvie wear these as a gift from you. Consider them partial payment for all of the nights the two of you let me invade your home and cry on your shoulder."

"She really has changed you, hasn't she?"

"Frankly, I didn't believe it was possible."

"Now that you mention it," said Nelson as a corner of his mouth slowly rose. "Neither did I!"

The Tate house had been transformed.

Like everything and everyone else Tessa had touched since her arrival in Boston, this too had been forever changed. There were new, lighter draperies in the foyer and in the parlor, and there was a new, cool shade of apricot paint to replace the drab brown. The heavy, dark portraits that had always lined the stairwell and the walls had been replaced by watercolors hung in lighter frames. In addition, the sheer amount of furniture was reduced, making the home considerably less cluttered.

The new young mistress on Mount Vernon Street, about whose lineage everyone had cruelly gossiped only a few short weeks ago, had suddenly won the respect of every disapproving matron on Beacon Hill. Everyone, with the notable exception of Daphne Forrester, was a little in awe of her bold behavior at Lydia Bailey's.

Now, as Tessa shared a joke with Nelson Winthrop, even Chandler could not help but regard with surprise his own poised and beautiful new wife.

"Having a good time?" Chandler asked Sylvie Winthrop as he stood beside her, but not taking his eyes from Tessa.

"Better than I thought I might."

"Well, considering the circumstances, that is something, isn't it?"

"I must say, Chandler, I was a bit surprised there were not more guests invited. Or were there those who declined?"

"Those invited are all in attendance," he assured her. "It was my sister's idea to make it intimate. I thought it was rather nice that she is making an effort at last to get to know both you and Tessa."

They both watched Tessa tip her head back and laugh at something Nelson had said, her alabaster gown catching the light from the chandelier.

"Those earrings she is wearing are breathtaking," Sylvie said after a moment. "Almost as exquisite as my own."

Chandler looked at her, seeing that she knew. "Then you didn't mind?"

"That they came from you? No. Nelson was happier this afternoon, watching me try something this beautiful on, than I have seen him in a very long time. He has always wanted me to have something fine like these."

"Now you do," Chandler smiled affectionately at her. "You deserve them, Sylvie, believe me. I could not have asked for better friends than you and Nelson. Especially these past two years."

"Well, you are the *only* friend we have had these past two years, and actually looking back now, you were the only one worth having anyway."

Then they both laughed, and Chandler gave her a little hug. "You know, Sylvie, I do believe the three of us have made it through the fires of hell."

"It is certainly a world away from what you had with Cynthia. That much I can see."

Chandler stiffened slightly at the mention of her name. "I

was a boy then. I have no better excuse for my lack of judgment than that."

Seeing how his carefree expression had changed, Sylvie took his arm and gave it a little squeeze, as they looked back out across the room to Tessa. "But of course that is all in the past now anyway, isn't it?"

"Of course it is," Chandler replied, trying not to grimace.

Supper in the Tate's candle-lit dining room progressed with surprising ease. The intense heat of summer was gone from Boston but the snapping cold of winter had not yet replaced it. Tessa insisted that all of the dining-room windows be opened to catch the balmy autumn breeze. She could not fill the house with enough freshness.

The evening was a surprising success. Lincoln conversed intensely with the formerly banished Nelson Winthrop (everyone was surprised to see that), and Daphne even inquired of Tessa where she had purchased such a lovely shade of fabric for the new draperies. And Sylvie Winthrop's frequent laughter warmed the room.

But the biggest surprise was how animated Daphne Forrester had become, telling tales about when she and Chandler were children, as the other guests chuckled and listened intently. After his second glass of wine, even Chandler chimed in, embellishing one of his younger sister's particularly unbelievable stories.

"You were not ten," he laughed easily. "You were not even seven when you bribed our governess, convincing her to make *me* eat your entire plate of peas."

"Did she really?" Tessa asked a little in disbelief.

"She did, indeed. My sister never lacked for determination when she had decided there was something in particular she wanted."

"I can confirm that," Lincoln added, fingering the stem of his glass as he slumped back, relaxed, in his chair. "Daphne was positively relentless with me until she had me completely convinced that I could not live a single day more without her. Of course," he added with a mischievous, slightly inebriated smile, "Daphne was a far sight older than ten, and far more subtle with her powers of persuasion by then."

Everyone laughed, even Daphne, as the flames danced from tall white candles in their polished silver holders in response to the soft evening breeze. One servant poured more wine for everyone, while another cleared away the dishes.

Surprised as she was, Tessa had actually begun to enjoy herself, and even her sister-in-law. Perhaps the two of them would never be the best of friends, but at least it appeared that they were fast approaching something close to detente.

She was so pleased with the turn of events and the outcome of her first dinner party, that Tessa did not notice Chandler's startled gaze as someone at the dining-room door captured his sudden and full attention. Nor did she see his expression instantly change and his skin turn ashen as his blue eyes met those of the uninvited guest standing in the archway.

"Heaven above!" Lincoln Forrester muttered.

"Is it possible?" Sylvie Winthrop asked.

Chapter

39

"HELLO, CHANDLER," THE WOMAN SAID COOLLY.

Silence flooded the room like a wave of icy water as she moved forward, a striking woman with hair the color of highly polished mahogany, done up in a fashionable loose twist above a face pale and flawless.

She was tall and willowy, dressed in an elegant gray-green dress that matched her eyes. But they were not the lovely wide eyes of a kind woman. They were cold green with small gold flecks, mirroring a lethal calm.

Tessa surmised from the look that passed between this woman and Chandler that she and her husband were far from strangers. Tessa looked back at Chandler to see his face drained of blood, white as powder. A glance across at Lincoln and she saw he, too, was stunned. Only Daphne's lips betrayed the slightest hint of a smile when Tessa glanced across the table at her.

"Well, my goodness, Chandler. You don't look at all glad to see me," the woman said, her very controlled voice dripping with sarcasm.

Chandler bolted to his feet like a coiled spring, his face now as red and filled with ruthless fury as, only a moment ago, it had been pale and filled with shock. His brows merged in a frown and his lips pursed as tight as a bud. Tessa could see that the mere sight of this mysterious woman made him furious.

"How dare you come here?"

His voice was low but sharp as glass. He was angrier than Tessa had ever seen him.

"Oh, now Chandler, darling, is that any way to speak to me when we haven't seen one another in such a long time?"

Lincoln and Daphne were standing now, too, but Tessa remained in her chair along with her other guests, entirely uncertain of what to do. She was the only one who apparently had no idea of the identity of the woman before them.

Chandler moved a few steps toward the woman and gripped her arm firmly, preparing to take her out of the room.

"Before I have even had a chance to greet your sister and her husband?" she asked, jerking it free.

"Cynthia, dear," Daphne nodded, unable to contain a self-satisfied smirk. "You always did have such a grand sense of timing."

"Enough!" Chandler brayed, glaring evilly at his sister.

"Daphne," the woman said, unmoved by Chandler's hostility, "you're looking splendid as ever."

"As are you, for someone who is supposed to be dead." Daphne returned the compliment with a little nod.

Chandler yanked the woman's arm again, clearly more and more anxious to take her from the room, but she braced herself against his pull.

"Are you not going to introduce us?" she said next, staring down at Tessa, who wore her bewilderment as boldly as a placard on her sweet, unsuspecting face.

"I believe you have made quite enough of an impression," Chandler said coldly in response, as at last Tessa, too, came to her feet with a quaking inner reluctance.

"Introduce us, Chandler," Tessa darkly bid him.

"Let the games begin at last," Daphne muttered beneath her breath.

Chandler's face was like granite, his body ramrod straight. "Tessa, I don't think this is the time—"

"Who is this woman, Chandler?"

"Yes, Chandler," Daphne echoed with a quiet smile. "You really must introduce them."

Tessa extended a trembling hand when Chandler did not comply. "I am Tessa Tate," she finally said dryly. "Chandler's wife."

"What a coincidence." The woman smiled acidly back at her. "I am Cynthia Tate, Chandler's other wife."

Tessa grimaced. She did not want to believe it. "What does she mean?" Tessa uttered the question weakly, looking with desperation to the man she loved so dearly. She needed an answer that would not tear her life and her heart entirely apart.

"Oh yes, Chandler," Daphne chimed, "do explain it to her, and to the rest of us. Cynthia, you must know this really is quite a shock."

"That is it, I said!" cried Chandler. "All of you, not a single word more! Cynthia, I shall speak to you in the library! Now!"

"No!" The sudden conviction in Tessa's tone hung over them all like a thick, dark cloud. Everyone glanced at her in surprise. "Chandler, I want you to tell me what is going on . . . who this woman really is."

He seemed to soften when he looked at her. Chandler came toward Tessa and grasped her upper arm gently. "I will, darling. I promise," he said pleadingly. "Only not now."

"The poor dear does deserve to know whether or not the two of you are really married after all, doesn't she?" Daphne asked, shaking her head as she pushed her way into the strained silence.

"Oh, will you be quiet!" Lincoln admonished his wife.

Chandler only gave his sister an evil glare, then looked back at Tessa. Her startled gaze shot around the room to each of her guests, shock and embarrassment parading through her mind over any of her more rational thoughts.

"Is she telling the truth, Chandler? Is this woman your wife?"

He did not reply, but Tessa saw the unmistakable flicker of pain dart across his face. She fought her own sudden stabbing ache of betrayal as her body began to shake uncontrollably. Was it actually possible that he had married her knowing all along that he had another wife? Of course it was possible, her heart told her as she looked back at him. This, at last, was the truth. She had only to look at Chandler's face to see that.

She had been made a fool. Tessa had followed him to Boston, become part of his world, to make him proud. She had given herself over to him body and soul, believing finally that there were no more secrets between them.

Now Chandler had betrayed her.

"It isn't what you think it is. If you will just let me explain," he tried to say, as Tessa's knees nearly buckled beneath the weight of the shock. It was his tone that had chilled her to her very core, because she knew the moment that he spoke the words that the woman, this stranger, had told the truth. An unexpected flurry of tears filled Tessa's eyes but she fought them.

"You lied to me," she whispered brokenly, her throat suddenly dry as desert sand. "All of it from the very first moment . . . all of it has been one great continuous lie."

"That's not true," Chandler tried to say, but Tessa pushed past him, determined not to hear a single word more.

When she reached the door, Tessa whirled around on her heels. With tears shining brightly in her eyes, she surveyed the other guests, all but Daphne as visibly shaken and shocked as she.

Chandler lunged toward her, not caring that in a single miserable instant his reputation and the welfare of his children, which he had fought so hard to protect, had been ruined forever.

"Please, darling, you must let me explain!"

Tessa cast his hand off her arm with a powerful jerk. "More of your truths, Chandler?" she asked angrily before she rounded the corner of the dining room and disappeared.

"Let her go," Daphne pleaded, clutching her brother's taut arm. "It really is for the best."

Chandler raised his hand to her, which was curled into a powerful fist. "I swear to the Lord God, Daphne, if you utter one single word more—" he growled, but the words broke off just before he turned and charged out of the dining room after his wife.

The rest of the guests were too shocked to speak after what they had just witnessed. The only sound was of Chandler's feet pounding down the stairs, through the still open front door, and out into the street. And his softly muttered prayer that it was not too late.

Chapter

40

TESSA HAD DISAPPEARED WITHOUT A TRACE.

Chandler returned home, shaken and out of breath from running up and down the tangle of lamplit streets that comprised Beacon Hill. In the shock of everything that had happened, he had no idea even where to search for her. She was still so new here in Boston.

His face was covered with a thin patina of perspiration and his eyes glittered with white rage as he burst back into the dining room. Mercifully, the Winthrops had gone. Only Cynthia, Daphne, and Lincoln remained.

"If anything happens to Tessa," he raged at Cynthia, "so help me God, you will live to regret it!"

"Funny," she drawled back at him, taking up one of the goblets half full of wine from the table. "I don't recall such anger from you during our courtship or during those first blissful months of our marriage."

"Blissful, hell!" Chandler spat, collapsing into one of the dining-room chairs. "You changed the moment I slipped

380

that ring onto your finger, and being married to you from then on out was four years of pure misery."

"Strange how we managed to conceive two children in the midst of such *misery,*" she drawled.

"Don't you dare mention those two precious children to me!" he raged, thumping his fist against the table so forcefully that the crystal and silver rattled. "You never gave a damn about them either. Alice and James were nothing more than consequences to you and you know it."

"That's a lie!" Cynthia countered defensively. "I love them both."

"Really, Chandler, I know that you're angry," Daphne intervened with caution, "but this really is no civil way to speak to your wife."

"My *dead* wife, if you recall. And we paid her quite handsomely to stay dead, you and I," he reminded his sister before he glared back at Cynthia. "You have broken our agreement."

Cynthia took another slow sip of wine and twisted a little ring of her mahogany hair that fell forward near her face. "It is most unfortunate indeed, I agree, but it is a matter of finances."

"I paid you a bloody fortune."

"Well, money doesn't go as far in Paris as it once did."

"He left you, didn't he?"

"I have no idea what you're talking about."

"That French cretin bled you dry."

Her eyes suddenly darkened. "Go to hell, Chandler."

"I have already been there, thanks to you."

There was a crack in her well-tooled armor, and Cynthia slowly put down the goblet. "The fact remains, I am penniless. Quite destitute, actually. I spent the last of what I had getting back to Boston."

"You could have written."

"I did," she countered. "You never bothered to answer, and you know how I hate to be ignored."

Chandler stiffened, recalling the letters he had destroyed

381

without opening. He had refused to face the past in the midst of the joy he had found. "What do you really want?"

Cynthia rose and moved slowly around the well appointed dining room, enjoying center stage once again. She fingered the silver chafing dish on the sideboard and the crystal candlesticks beside it. "I want to see my children, for one thing."

"Over my dead body."

"Now there's an idea."

Chandler rose up to meet her. They were facing one another beside the sideboard. He was as tense and combative as a cornered lion. "It took them a long time to get over losing you."

"And whose fault was that, when it was you who railroaded me out of town?"

"Better to *believe* their mother was dead than to *know* she is a *whore!* And worse than that a—"

Cynthia slapped him hard across the face, cutting off the word. She had hit him so hard that when she pulled her hand away it left a bright-red imprint along the line of his jaw.

"You bastard."

"Spare me the great maternal show and come to the point of why you've really come back here so that you can get the hell out of my house," he said, gripping his burning cheek.

"What I want is enough money to return to Paris and to live there comfortably."

"Until the next handsome and penniless lothario turns your head and steals you blind?"

"Pay her, Chandler," Daphne intervened firmly at last. "This family, what is left of it, would never survive the next scandal she would involve us in if she stayed."

"How could you have been so cruel to Tessa, forcing her to find out like this?" Chandler asked Cynthia. "And Daphne, you enjoyed every moment of it."

"Oh, that's right. There is the little matter now of your having two wives." Cynthia smiled.

"You know perfectly well that I have only one legal wife!"

"Oh, now Chandler, darling, do try to see the humor in this for once in your life, would you? After all, it really is a rather delicious predicament. Here you are, the pillar of society, with one wife, who Daphne tells me is really an uneducated immigrant, and another wife who is mysteriously back from the dead."

Chandler stormed back across the dining room unable to bear the sight of her a moment longer. "Your great show here tonight has won you what you desire. You will have your money first thing tomorrow," he bitterly declared. "But if you so much as try to see the children, you'll not get a single penny. Faced with a choice like that, I am quite certain I can trust the weight of your great maternal instinct."

When he reached the door, Chandler turned back around as if with an afterthought but his eyes held a conviction that said he knew exactly what he meant to say.

"And now that you have finished the job you began two years ago of destroying my life, I want you out of this house. As far as I and our children are concerned, you are dead. You have been for two years, and you still are!"

Near dawn, Tessa sat slump-shouldered in the Winthrops' dimly lit kitchen, her entire body still trembling with the shock. The only stroke of good fortune she had had all night was that the Winthrops had denied it when Chandler came to ask if she had sought refuge there.

"We owed you a debt of thanks for what you did for us with Lydia Bailey. We told you that," Nelson reminded her. "You can stay here safely until you have decided what you want to do."

"Have you any idea what that is yet?" Sylvie asked her carefully.

"I don't know." Tessa shook her head, still mired by shock and disbelief. "I must get away from Boston."

"Perhaps you should at least give him a chance to explain."

Pain streaked across her face. "Explain what? That he lied

to me? That everything he ever told me, from the day we met, was founded on lies?"

Sylvie's heart ached for her. Her beautiful face was swollen, and tears dried in long ribbons on her pale cheeks. "What can we do?"

"I want to go home. But I haven't any money. Only the jewels," she said, offering up her betrothal ring and the ruby earrings with an expression of such complete devastation on her tear-stained face that Nelson felt his heart squeeze.

It was the first time in his life he could ever remember disliking Chandler Tate. No matter why he had done it.

"That won't be necessary," he said softly, closing her fingers back around the gems. "You keep them. Sylvie and I will see you back to your family."

Chandler lay on top of her bed, fully dressed. Her velvet robe with the gold cord was wound across his arm. Finally now, near dawn, he felt the numbing pull of sleep. They had searched through the night without so much as a trace of Tessa. He would begin again at first light even though he knew in his heart that there was no use in it. His wife, his love, was really gone and she meant to stay that way.

Tears swelled behind his eyes but he could not cry. This was his own fault. Every last awful bit of it.

"You are a fool, Chandler Tate," he muttered hoarsely, gazing up at the dark ceiling. "You asked for this to happen and now, God help you, you have gotten what you deserve."

He taunted himself with a vengeance, forcing himself to recall her face as she stood before Cynthia earlier that evening. The expression of betrayal in her eyes. Then the anger. The pain of remembering it was beyond any sort of torture he had ever known.

Chandler's eyelids grew heavier still. Wound in her robe, he reached across the coverlet as he had done a dozen times before, as if he could actually reach out and feel her beside him in those last few moments before he fell asleep. But all he felt now was cool, crisp, empty linen.

He had forced himself to come in here instead of going to

his own room. Here he could think of her. Every sight, every smell, reminded him of Tessa. And all he had lost. He expelled a ragged breath.

How could he have kept the truth from her when she had pleaded with him so many times for honesty? He had tried to make up for the charade he was living by pampering her, by sharing everything he had to give. Everything but the truth. Now his beautiful spirited Irish angel quite likely despised him. And for that, Chandler Tate had no one to blame but himself.

Chapter

41

Two blinding, grueling weeks passed without Tessa. On the fourth day, Boston society columns reported that Mrs. Chandler Tate had returned to New York City to visit relatives. Jennings had given them the details in hopes of keeping the gossip mill from the truth—that no one had the slightest idea where Tessa had gone. Or if she would ever return.

In her absence, the house on Beacon Hill began to haunt Chandler, who saw now, in aching detail, how much of herself his young wife had left behind. It was in the newly reupholstered furniture. The new, lighter fabric of the draperies. But mostly it was in the faces of the children, who still could not comprehend why Tessa, too, had gone away.

When the meditation he had learned in China no longer brought him any peace, Chandler threw himself into his work. He hoped to keep his mind from the agonizing thoughts of her. Thoughts that haunted him whether awake or asleep. Even when he was drunk, Chandler saw her face, so full of betrayal as she had faced Cynthia and another more damning piece of the puzzle.

Trying to forget Tessa was futile. She was always there with him. The sweet sound of her laughter. The silky soft touch of her skin. In a few short days, Chandler had lost everything that had ever mattered to him. His wife, the love of his life.

Night after endless night, numbed with liquor, his own mind tortured him with the pleading echo of her voice as Tessa bid him over and over again to tell her the whole truth. He had tried, but in the end, he had betrayed her. And he had betrayed their love.

As he propped an elbow against the fireplace mantle now, unshaven and dressed only in an open shirt and yesterday's black trousers, Chandler was so deep in thought that he did not even hear Nelson Winthrop enter the parlor.

He strode across the oriental carpet after Jennings had shown him in, hoping that a visit from an old friend might help. For the past two weeks, Chandler had neither seen nor spoken to anyone, steadfastly refusing all visitors. He had especially refused Daphne who, in spite of her pleading, he would never forgive.

"You look like hell," Nelson declared, his hazel eyes warmed by an uneasy boyish smile as he placed a firm hand on Chandler's hunched back.

"I'm not receiving guests this afternoon, Winthrop," Chandler slurred, his tongue already thickened by a liberal blend of Scotch, wine, and brandy.

"Well, I'm not a guest. I'm your friend," Nelson persevered. "And, as such, I feel it is my duty to tell you that you smell even worse than you look. When was the last time you washed?"

Chandler did not reply. Instead, he turned away, lifted a glass of Scotch he had been holding limply and emptied what was left in one swallow.

"Well, are you not at least going to be hospitable enough to offer me a drink, if you're not in the mood for conversation?"

"Help yourself," Chandler replied flatly as he nodded toward a silver tray that held three crystal decanters. "And get me another while you're at it."

Nelson looked back at him, seeing through the mask of nonchalance he was trying so unsuccessfully to put forth. He could see through it because they were friends who had shared their pain before. Now it was raw and unmistakable in Chandler's dim unfocused eyes.

"Don't you think you've had enough?"

"There isn't whiskey enough in the world," Chandler replied thickly.

Nelson came back reluctantly with two glasses and handed one to Chandler. It had been against his better judgment to come, after what Chandler had done to Tessa. But Sylvie thought perhaps there was more to the story. He finally relented.

Like everyone else in Boston, he too had believed the story of Cynthia Tate's sudden, if somewhat mysterious, death. He had even mourned with his old friend two years before, never once suspecting such a complicated ruse. Through the worst of times, they had been honest with one another, or so Nelson Winthrop had believed until that evening two weeks before.

"Have you had any word from her then?"

Chandler's bleary eyes widened suddenly, as though he had been dashed with icy water. "Do you know where she is?"

"Under the circumstances, if I did, I doubt that I would tell you," Nelson could not help himself from saying.

In blinding desperation and an alcoholic haze, Chandler lunged forward violently, losing his balance. The two men careened backwards into the sofa as Chandler gripped Nelson's collar. "Tell me, damn you! If you know, tell me where Tessa is!"

"What the devil is wrong with you, man?"

"Tell me, Nelson!" Chandler raged, pummeling his defenseless friend on the chest until they were both gasping for breath, and Jennings and Douglas came scrambling into the parlor to intercede. "Tell me!"

"She's gone home to New York!" Nelson cried out as the two servants worked together to pull Chandler from him.

"Damn you! Damn you!"

"Sir! Please!" Jennings pleaded as Chandler collapsed onto the floor, his head and body still heaving with the effects of blinding, impotent rage. "Sir! Mr. Winthrop is your friend!"

Kathleen and Mrs. O'Neil stood in the parlor doorway, their Irish faces full of concern, both covering their mouths with their hands. But Chandler saw no one past the still bright image of Tessa.

"It's all right now," Nelson finally rasped, wiping a bright red stream of blood from the corner of his mouth and wincing as the two servants propped him up against the leg of the sofa. "Leave the two of us alone, please."

Jennings gray brows narrowed with concern. "Are you quite certain that is a good idea, sir?"

Chandler's face was in his hands as he sat slumped beside Nelson. It had been building for two long weeks. He could see that now. He also knew that the worst had passed.

"I'm certain," Nelson quietly replied.

A tense silence followed when the two men were alone again. Nelson did not press him. Instead, he rose, grabbed the decanter of whiskey and two fresh glasses. Then he came back to the place on the floor where Chandler remained, handing him a glass of the amber liquid.

"Here. I think we could both use one of these."

Chandler took the glass but did not drink from it this time. "She is . . ." His ragged voice caught on the words. "She is gone for good."

"My God, Chandler. The poor girl has discovered that you are still married to someone else! A dead woman, to be precise. How the bloody hell did you expect her to react?"

"Tessa took a vow," he repeated agonizingly. "We both did."

"I don't understand it," Nelson shook his head. "Why you never told her . . . Why you never told any of us that Cynthia was still alive."

"It's a long story," Chandler replied, slowly sobering.

"No story is that long, Chandler."

"This one is."

"Why don't you try me? You've got to tell someone before it eats you alive."

Chandler took in a deep, difficult breath and exhaled as he raked the tousled blond hair back from his forehead. "I'm almost drunk enough to do it."

"Good. I'll get us the rest of the bottle if it'll help," Nelson declared, staggering back to the silver tray and bringing back the nearly full decanter. Motioning for Chandler to drink his untouched glass, Nelson refilled his own as he sat back down on the floor beside him.

"I just don't understand how you could tell everyone that Cynthia was dead. Why would you lie about a thing like that?"

"She might as well have been dead," Chandler said flatly, "for all that happened."

"Such as?" Nelson asked, raising an expectant brow.

"Such as murder," Chandler replied, looking up with an icy calm. "Now are you satisfied?"

They sat together in the silence drinking their Scotch as the clock ticked endlessly over the fireplace mantle. Nelson was about to say that such a comment was in truly poor taste. Then he saw the sudden deadly calm on Chandler's classically featured face.

"Murder? Good God, Chandler," he mouthed. "Who?"

"A foul, useless merchant seaman. I never even knew his name."

Nelson gulped a swallow of the liquid to press back his shock. "How could you have done it? What could have been worth murder?"

"My wife."

"Cynthia?" he asked incredulously.

"The bastard, it seems, was having an affair with her. They were carrying on in the seediest tenement you could imagine. And he wasn't the first."

Chandler took a slow, deliberate swallow of his drink, hoping to numb the pain enough that he might continue his confession. "It began shortly after we were married. There was our gardener and the Carlsons' driver before that."

"Heaven above," Nelson muttered, brushing a hand across his face. "I had no idea."

"Nor did I at first."

Nelson felt the anguish in Chandler's admission when the image of his own wife passed across his mind. In the short silence he wondered to what lengths he might have been driven had Sylvie betrayed him in that way.

"I spent a lot of time at first," Chandler continued, "asking myself, and Cynthia, what I had done. Trying to make things better between us. I even forgave her the first few times. For the children's sake."

He took another deep, contemplative swallow of the drink and, for a moment, closed his eyes waiting for it to take effect.

"But things steadily worsened to the point where she began neglecting them. It all came to a head one afternoon when James was just a baby. He had a cold and I came home unexpectedly to check on him. I found him crying in his cradle by her bedside, and our gardener skittering out of the room through the window, trying to pull on his pants."

He looked up blankly at Nelson. "She hadn't even bothered to remove the child from our room before—"

"Good Lord, how dreadful. How heinous of her. But murder? I still don't see how you could have brought yourself to that."

Chandler looked up again with the same icy calm. "I could have done it, Nelson. I tell you I wanted to with every fiber of my being." He exhaled a breath sharply. "But I didn't."

Nelson Winthrop exhaled his own audible breath and leaned back against the base of the sofa. "So, who killed him, then?"

The doors to the parlor parted just as he spoke the question, and they both looked up like two guilty schoolboys. The air of tension and the anticipation of an answer was broken as Jennings stood in the shadows looking in on them. He was still afraid of what, in his absence, they might do to one another, afraid of what the quiet signified.

"Go on," Nelson waved him away. "It's all right."

Jennings hesitated a moment more, as though trying to make up his mind. "I only thought—"

"Leave us, please," Nelson said firmly as he finished the rest of his Scotch. "We're fine. Really."

When the doors were closed again and they were alone, he looked back at Chandler, on whose face a pained expression had returned with the confession he was forcing himself to give. Nelson hated to press the question again. But still he had to ask it. He believed he must know the truth. And Chandler needed to tell it all at last.

"If you didn't kill Cynthia's lover, who did?"

Chandler stared straight ahead, gripped now by the powerful memories he had fought so valiantly to forget. He held up the crystal glass, twisting it in a golden splash of sunlight.

"It really was the perfect crime," he said in an eerie monotone. "We worked it like true Tates. Daphne and I took over entirely . . . covered every trace of what had happened. We had to do it. . . . She convinced me we had no choice."

"I still don't understand, Chandler. I thought you said you didn't kill the man."

"I didn't."

Nelson Winthrop's mouth went suddenly dry. "Was it . . . Daphne? Good Lord, not your sister!"

Chandler did not reply, bound now by the gruesome story he at last had begun to confess. "I went alone. I knew where

392

she had gone because I had followed her there before. She hadn't come home that night and I was full of rage. I remember thinking, You can tear out my heart if you will, but you'll not do this to Alice and James! Not again! You will be there to have breakfast with your children if I have to drag you back by the hair!"

Nelson was almost afraid to ask. But they had come this far. "Did you and this merchant seaman . . . did you do battle over her then?"

Once again, Chandler made no move to respond. His eyes were gray and glazed. His face unshaven. "There was so much blood," he began again disjointedly, seeing the scene in his mind. "I had never seen so much blood. It had spattered onto the walls, the bed, even Cynthia was covered with it."

Nelson was not certain that he could bear to hear a single word more of so gruesome a tale. But he was compelled by friendship to hear the whole sordid story to its last detail.

He nervously filled Chandler's glass again, and then his own. Each man took a liberal swallow in the silence, until Chandler collected himself enough to continue.

"She just sat there huddled beside his body, rocking back and forth like a child, with that blasted gun in her hand. They had quarreled, she said, and it had gone off accidentally. She kept muttering that she hadn't meant to do it. She said the same thing over and over again, almost repentant for having just murdered a man in cold blood.

"So many things went through my mind as I stood there, looking down at her. Looking over at him, his body limp and naked, sprawled on the unmade bed. I thought to myself at first, Finally. Finally it is over between us. They will lock her away for the rest of her life, and finally I shall have my retribution."

Nelson's face blanched with the horror of what he comprehended at last. "Cynthia? Dear God! She killed him herself?"

Chandler tipped his head back, resting it on the sofa

cushion, spent now from the horrid confession. He closed his eyes but even so Nelson could see the effort it took for him even to breathe at that moment.

"Can you imagine? My first thought was not even what it would do to our children to know what she had done. It was that she would pay. . . . And I have despised myself for that ever since."

Nelson tried to clear his throat of the dry lump that had formed there. "Oh, I don't know, Chandler. Under the circumstances—"

"There was no excuse!" he snapped. "Only after feeling the relief did I think, What would this do to two small children who hadn't even had a chance yet in life? Their own mother an adulterer . . . and worse yet, a murderer!"

He raked both his hands through his hair nervously now, his voice accelerating. "From there, I just seemed to function without thinking. I covered Cynthia's face and my own coat so that we would not be recognized, and I led her home once I was certain no one had seen us. Daphne came up with the rest of the plan. 'The children cannot be expected to pay for this,' she kept saying. And I agreed."

His eyes were suddenly full of tears. Two turbulent blue oceans of tears. "I had to protect them, Nelson. God, no matter what Cynthia had done to me, she was their mother and she had killed her lover in cold blood! How could they ever have risen above the truth of that? Their lives would be ruined because of her."

Nelson put a solid arm around Chandler's shoulder and felt him tremble. Suddenly it all made sense. His old friend had not been cruel or selfish in the secrets he had been forced to keep. Nor had he really betrayed Tessa. What he had been forced to do that awful night could only be seen, by anyone who knew the truth, as the noble act of a desperate father for the love of his children.

"Daphne and I stayed up that night while Cynthia slept," Chandler muttered out the last few details, "trying to decide how to do it."

"You couldn't risk her being caught and charged with murder, so you sent her to Paris."

"I made a deal with the devil to protect my children," he said blankly. "For her freedom, Cynthia agreed to divorce me quietly and to go to Paris. We had eloped to Philadelphia, so a quiet divorce there was not difficult to obtain."

"You told everyone she died in Philadelphia," Nelson said, remembering. "When she went with you there to buy fabric. I believed it completely."

"So did everyone else. Everyone, of course, but Daphne. She and I told Cynthia we would give her enough money on which to live if she would agree to let us tell everyone, including the children, that she had died unexpectedly."

"She got off rather easily for all that she put you through."

"I knew it was wrong. I knew that she should pay for what she had done. But I didn't see a choice. I wasn't the only one who had seen her go down into that awful neighborhood, or who knew why," he rasped. "People had already begun to whisper about her."

"I know," Nelson said sadly. "I heard some of the rumors myself. But never in my wildest dreams did I think . . ." He stopped himself, then began again. "So you sold your own peace of mind to save your children's futures?"

Chandler looked up through a haze of tears and regret. "There was nothing I would not have done to save them."

"But you didn't murder anyone."

"No," he shook his head.

"And you never found a way to tell any of this to Tessa?"

"Tell her that the man she loved and trusted had knowingly covered up a murder? Worse yet, hidden away the murderer?" Chandler's voice quaked with emotion. "What would she have thought of the man she had come away to marry then, do you suppose? When I fell in love with Tessa, I naively believed I could at last put that whole dark period of my life behind me, and God help me, I wanted it to stay that way."

"Well you must go to her," Nelson resolved.

Chandler wiped his eyes with the back of his hand. "Don't you think I want to?" He took in a shallow, painful breath. "I just can't."

Chandler hung his head, his emotions spent now by what he had kept hidden for so long, what he had finally confessed. "The dream is over for us. I realize that is the chance I took in keeping the truth from her. Quite frankly, I don't deserve to get her back." He looked up suddenly, his eyes now dry and full of the old conviction. "Tessa is gone, Nelson, and there is no reason on this earth to think she will ever return."

Chapter
42

"YE REALLY MUST EAT SOMETHIN', LASS," MARY GALLAGHER pleaded. Yet she took care not to push too hard.

"I'm sorry," Tessa tiredly replied. Her face was gaunt and gray in the shadows, her expression was as stricken now as it had been that first night she had come back here from Boston two weeks earlier. She sat forlornly on her unmade bed.

"Why not write to him, lass? Wouldn't a note make ye feel better? I'm certain yer husband would at least be overjoyed to hear that ye're all right, if nothin' else."

"I cannot."

Mary put the tray of biscuits and tea down on the bedside table. "I don't believe he meant to hurt ye, lass."

"Lies always hurt somebody, Mary," Tessa said in a soft voice.

"'Tis true enough, I suppose."

Mary had never seen anything like the transformation of Tessa in the two weeks she had been back in New York. Her vibrant skin was gray, her cheeks growing hollow. Green eyes that had sparkled so brilliantly when she had last been a part of this house were vacant now and rimmed with dark circles.

She lay on her bed, arms wrapped around her knees. She looked as fragile as glass. It was the restless ache that had done it to her, a reminder of the lie that had torn at the fabric of her tender heart.

"There simply must be somethin' more to all of this," Mary said, finally breaking the silence. "Some reason why they did not simply engage in an amiable divorce and have done with it."

"For the same reason the Tates do everything, it would seem," Tessa sighed weakly. "To avoid scandal. Easier to be rid of an unfaithful wife and pose as a grieving widower than to admit being a cockold."

"Dreadful thought if it's true, but I do so hate to hear ye sound so bitter, lass."

"I made a horrid mistake marrying him," Tessa suddenly declared, trying to convince herself as much as Mary of the truth of what she had said. "Chandler Tate is a wicked, wicked man and I don't ever want to see him again."

"I don't believe that, lass. Nor do you."

The unexpected voice had come from the doorway. The sound of it was as comforting and familiar as an old quilt. And yet Tessa could barely believe that it was him. Not until she looked up and saw for herself that he stood in the doorway.

Tessa leapt from the bed and dashed into Brian Sullivan's open arms. She pressed her head against the solid, reassuring expanse of his chest. He had avoided her since she had returned to the boardinghouse. This was the first time he had allowed himself the sight of her since her marriage.

"'Tis about time," said Mary beneath her breath as she moved to withdraw from Tessa's small and simple room. "I'll be leavin' the two of ye to yer reunion."

Brian and Tessa stayed like that, beside the door, in one

another's arms, until she could catch her breath. As he held her solidly, letting her weep, Brian's mind drifted back to the girl so full of joy and promise that Tessa Murphy had been before her marriage. The difference in her since summer was startling, and he fought the urge to go to Chandler Tate and tear him limb from limb for how he had hurt her. Especially since he had chosen to give her up to the man she loved without so much as a fight.

Through the blur of tears, Tessa finally pulled away and looked up at her old friend. Her first love.

"I thought you were never going to come and see me," she said brokenly.

Brian held her at arm's length, thinking how she looked just like a wilted rose, slumped there before him. "Nor did I."

"Thank you for making an exception."

"Ye *are* the exception. Always have been, lass. I saw that about ye long before Chandler Tate."

Tessa brushed away her tears with the back of her hand, trying not to wince too openly at the sound of his name. "I thought you hated me," she said miserably.

"Oh, lass, I only made ye believe it because I thought ye needed to follow yer dream," Brian said huskily. "I knew ye couldn't do that with an old commitment to me hangin' over your head."

His voice went suddenly lower as he gazed down at her sallow, tear-stained face. "Never once did I imagine when I sent ye away that somethin' like this would come of it."

Blanched cheeks and dull, vacant eyes replaced her spirited grin and the rosy complexion that had always made him smile. It broke his heart to see her like this.

"Put on your shoes."

"Why?"

"Does it matter, lass? Ye need to get out o' this place. See somethin' different from these four plain walls. Think different thoughts from those o' Tate."

Tessa sank back onto the bed and gazed absently out of

the little paned window, her weeping subsided now. "Did Mary tell you what happened?"

"Only that he is not a widower after all. That there is still another wife."

"It is true, you know. I saw her with my own eyes. She was beautiful. Tall and elegant. So full of the confidence that comes from being born into that wealth. All the things I could never be for Chand—" Tessa did not finish the name that had come in a long, exhaled breath.

Brian sat down on the edge of the bed beside her. It shifted beneath his weight as he took up her small, chilled hand. "Can ye be certain there isn't more to it than that, lass?" he asked her carefully. "Even I could see how he worshipped ye."

She let out another, more ragged breath. "He told me she had been unfaithful."

"There, ye see? If the woman shamed him that way, and they divorced over it . . . Well, all I'll be sayin' is that perhaps things are not so awful for ye as they seem. And with a right proper explanation—"

Tessa's eyes suddenly glittered like green fire. "I don't want to hear it, Brian!" she declared. "Don't you see? He didn't utter a single word to me, even then, about divorce."

"Did ye give him a chance? The way I heard it, there was a fair lot o' confusion all around."

That much was true enough. She hadn't given Chandler a chance to explain. The pain and the betrayal had been too great. Each word Cynthia spoke that night had been a venomous dart. They had pierced her heart in rapid succession until she felt nothing but the overwhelming urge to flee.

"It doesn't matter anyway, Brian," she said tiredly. "Chandler has been doling out his version of the truth to me in little bits ever since we met, apparently never trusting our love enough to tell me all of it."

She took a breath, feeling the anguish and the loss flair up inside of her again. "Thanks to him, I was forced to hear it in the worst way possible. From his other wife!"

She clenched her eyes against the sound of her own words.

"I trusted him," she said now, in a pained whisper. "I believed he had begun to trust me."

They were looking at one another, their faces and bodies close, both of their voices low and barely audible across the little room. Brian felt his loins tighten at her nearness. It brought back the memory of the kisses they once had shared. Promises made and broken. But what Tessa needed from him right now was only a friend.

"Well, one thing is certain. Ye cannot go on sittin' around here frettin' about the past. Mary is as busy as ever and helpin' her once again with the less fortunates, should take yer mind from all yer own troubles."

Tessa closed her eyes. "Will the work make the pain go away, do you think?"

"Aye, in time," Brian promised, pressing a chaste kiss on her cheek.

Tessa opened her eyes again. They glittered with tears as she looked earnestly up at him. "But tell me, Brian," she achingly pleaded, "what do I do until then?"

"What is it that's givin' off that scent then?" Mrs. O'Neil asked impatiently as Kathleen opened the window seat in Tessa's closed up, grey bedroom.

Light seeped into the room in a small pale stream from the crack between the heavy velvet draperies. Another slightly more golden flow of light poured more boldly through the partially open door across the room.

"Smells like thyme. But yet not quite."

"Herbs?" Kathleen asked.

"A good cook knows her stew," Mrs. O'Neil shot back proudly as she stood, hands on wide hips, behind the smaller, younger maid crouching before her.

After a moment, Kathleen pulled forth the small brown pouch cinched tightly at the top with black string. The powerful aroma of medicinal herbs from Mrs. Gallagher's private cache filled the room in an instant.

"Well, will ye look at that."

"No doubt they belonged to Mrs. Tate," Kathleen surmised sadly as she sank back on her heels. "She told me once that she helped a midwife back in New York. They must have used these in their work somehow."

"I miss her so," Mrs. O'Neil declared with a heavy-winded sigh. "'Tis not the same house without her in it."

"We're none of us the same. Especially not Mr. Tate."

"She had a way of wrappin' herself around your heart. Especially the master's heart. 'Twas plain enough to see."

"What'll we do with these?" Kathleen asked as she held up the fragrant pouch. "They're sure to remind him of his wife if he ever has the strength to come in here again."

"Put them back as they were."

Chandler's voice startled them both. But not for its harshness. His tone was surprisingly thin and hollow. It had come more as a plea than as a command.

They both looked up and saw him silhouetted slack-shouldered in the doorway.

Kathleen quickly put the pouch back inside the open window seat and closed the lid. As her face colored with embarrassment, she thought of apologizing for having trespassed in a place where he clearly did not wish them to be. But when she looked up again, he was gone.

The only sound came as his own bedroom door clicked softly closed. It was the refuge he had sought exclusively these past few days, but for this brief and clearly anguished interlude.

Chapter

43

THEY STEPPED FROM THE PLATFORM OF THE HORSE-DRAWN BUS AT the stop near Mulberry Street. Tessa looked out with a familiar sadness at the crush of tenements, as dense as rabbit warrens, bathed now in misty morning light. After the opulence she had encountered in Boston it was even more difficult to come here with Mary than it had been before. To see so glaringly how different life could be.

Tessa rubbed her hands together. They were cold and stiff, like the rest of her slim body. She had not wanted to come. Not even after the talk she had with Brian the day before. She had pleaded with Mary to let her stay in bed. But the feisty Irish woman refused to take no for an answer.

Tessa's ears strained now at the unexpected sound of children's laughter. Women calling out around them. Sopranos. Contraltos. All swarming about and speaking in foreign tongues, which together sounded like nothing more than gibberish.

It had been right for her to come with Mary Gallagher this morning, even though she could not bring herself to admit it. She needed to get away from the boardinghouse. Just as Brian said, she needed to think of other things besides Chandler. How desperately she missed him in spite of everything.

She cringed and felt a shiver that such a thing was possible after what he had done to her.

Mary and Tessa walked up a staircase in a dim stairwell littered with old bottles, crumpled paper, and two sleeping children, both covered with a single old, gray coat. Tessa's heart lurched and she felt suddenly ill as she paused over one, a sweet-faced boy near James's age. Emotionally, she felt like a pendulum. Belonging and not belonging here, with each beat of her heart.

The apartment they entered was small and dirty. No different from all of the others. Here, too, there was a woman, slim and gaunt, lying limply on a bare cot. The room was heated by just a single weak pink ray of morning sun through a dirty paned window above.

The baby girl, with a prominent mop of inky hair peeking out from a coarse green blanket, had been born the night before and lay sleeping on the woman's unmoving chest. Mary took up the woman's slim wrist and then froze.

"Take the child, Tessa."

"What? I—"

"Take the child from her, I say!"

"But she's sleeping."

"She's dead, lass! The woman has died in the night."

Tessa felt the blood drain from her own face. It was suddenly so cold. She began to shiver. She was overwhelmed with the sensation of darkness and the urge to run.

In the past, it had always been the babies who had been claimed. Never a mother. Never had she seen a tiny child, a defenseless child, left so cruelly orphaned. She tried to speak but her throat closed. It was not fair at all.

Tessa went down onto her knees and lunged forward toward the woman, taking up her other hand.

"There must be something you can do. She can't die! The poor child will be—"

The woman's hand was cold. It shocked her, and Tessa let go. It was true. She had died and left this precious child alone here in so cruel a world to fend for itself. As alone and vulnerable as she herself had ever been.

"But the baby," she whispered frantically. "What will become of this little baby?"

"Faith, I know not, lass."

"Where is the rest of her family? Her father? A brother or sister?"

"There isn't another livin' soul. The woman told me she had lost everyone on the boat comin' over."

Tessa's mouth trembled. "So have I."

Gently, she lifted the sleeping infant from the woman's cold chest and brought it against her own warm bosom. The little girl nestled against her instinctively and let out a tiny, almost inaudible sigh. The sensation was very slight and very sudden or she might not have noticed it at all. But the grief that had been strangling her heart since she had arrived back in New York suddenly let her go.

She took a breath and gazed down at the peacefully sleeping baby in her arms. Tessa wanted to sing and to cry at the same moment. This child was motherless. She had no family. They each needed someone and God in his mercy had brought them together.

Mary rose back up after she had covered the woman's face. Her expression was grave. "She'll need to be taken to the foundling home. Cryin' shame, it is, beautiful little girl like that. Never had a fair chance."

Tessa glanced down as the baby stirred. She then opened her coal-black eyes and looked directly up at Tessa. "She will have a chance with me."

The furrow in Mary's brow deepened. "Ach, don't be speakin' nonsense, lass . . ."

She did not finish the sentence when she saw how entirely serious Tessa was. "You've no way to care for a child, and besides she's a . . . well, she's not . . ."

"She's Italian, Mary. You can say it. She's dark and I'm not. It means nothing, really. Only that she'll need to know

405

about her heritage one day." Tessa stroked the top of the baby's head and smiled down at her.

"I can't imagine what good it would bring to your life. You've got too much to contend with already."

"I can't imagine the harm. Mary, after what I've seen here, after what you and I have endured, making a difference with one of these children matters to me. And I do believe I need this sweet little baby every bit as much as she needs me."

"Have ye any idea what's involved?"

Thinking of Alice and James, remembering the challenges and the joys she had found so briefly with them, she stubbornly affirmed, "I believe I do."

Then with a characteristically stubborn smile, which Mary had not seen since the day she left for Boston, Tessa declared, "You needn't waste anymore breath, Mary. It's decided. I mean to be a mother to this child."

"Are ye certain ye know what ye're in for?"

"I'm certain that woman will go more easily to her grave knowing there is someone left behind to love her sweet angel."

Tessa looked up, the former conviction now alive and glittering in her wide green eyes. It was unmistakable, thought Mary. The old spirit was back. Thank the dear Lord, Tessa had come through her trial and she had survived it.

"I want to do this, Mary. I need to do this."

Mary Gallagher glanced back at the rigid body of the dead woman behind them. Then she looked back at the baby lying so peacefully and happily in Tessa's arms.

"I'll not be much help to ye. Ye're aware o' that. I've my own work to contend with."

"I understand."

Softening, she laid her thumb and forefinger around her chin. "I believe there is an old cradle up in the attic ye could—"

"The white wicker."

"That's the one," Mary smiled, seeing the first hint of color blossom and warm Tessa's cheeks.

Mary pulled the blanket back from the baby's face and gazed in at the wide-open eyes and the tawny rosebud mouth beginning to search for milk.

"We'll have to be gettin' her home soon. She'll be hungry, and when that happens she's not at all likely to be put off."

Tessa glanced back one last time at the woman who had given birth to the child. "What was her name, Mary?"

"I believe it was Sophia. Yes, that was it."

"Claire Sophia," Tessa proclaimed. "Her mother's name and the name of my own. What do you think of that?"

"Pretty enough."

Tessa smiled. "Thank you, Mary."

"Oh, don't be thankin' me, lass. You're the one who's in for a time of it."

"And isn't it splendid," Tessa said as her smile broadened.

Chapter

44

THROUGH BLEARY EYES, CHANDLER WATCHED HIS SISTER DEscend the two steps into the dark parlor and approach him. "What the hell are you doing here?" he growled.

"Saving you, just as I always do. Open these, why don't you?" she said, jerking back the draperies to let in the daylight. "It's positively tomblike in here."

"Leave them."

"But Chandler, it really is so lovely—"

"Leave them, I said."

"Well, you simply cannot go on like this. That is all there is to it. It has been over a month. Cynthia is back in Paris and life should go on."

"So everything has turned out for the best," he said thickly.

"I won't lie to you about it, Chandler. I'm glad Tessa is gone. She wasn't right for you. She never would have been."

Chandler's twisted features were bathed in shadows in the moment before he leaned forward in his chair and ran a heavy hand across his unshaven face.

"Then your work is done, isn't it?"

"Not since you're still angry with me."

Chandler groaned. "What do you want from me, Daphne?"

"I want you to say you're not angry anymore."

Christ! Was he to forever face this particular agony as well? Tessa's loss and Daphne's selfish, shallow smile and her ever-present ingratiating tone of voice? What greater hell was there on earth than that?

Day after endless day he tortured himself by forcing himself to recall his wife's sweet, beautiful face full of shock and betrayal as she faced Cynthia. It was part of his penance to recall it, he resolved. The rest of his penance was to live forever without the only woman he had ever truly loved.

"I'm not angry anymore, Daphne," he rasped. "I'm nothing at all."

She sank onto the ottoman before him with an expression of what looked dangerously like true concern. "Oh, come now, Chandler. You have a whole splendid life ahead of you, a clean slate."

"The reason I am not angry with you, Daphne," he said, struggling to control his grief, "is because I did this to myself. I alone brought the first bit of happiness into my life and I alone chased it away."

"Oh, now," she scoffed, straightening her skirts. "It can't be as bad as all that."

"Yes, Daphne," he countered drunkenly. "It most definitely is as bad as all that. And now that you have what you wished for and worked for, I shall thank you to leave me in peace."

He turned away from her and took a swallow of Scotch. The conversation was over. Daphne stood up.

"Well, I certainly never expected you to react like this. I don't suppose I had any real idea how much the little . . . how much she meant to you." Daphne took two steps backward, studying her brother's unshaven face, his rumpled shirt and trousers. "I really didn't mean to hurt you in this."

"You never do, do you, my dear?"

The response had not come from Chandler, but from Lincoln Forrester. Daphne's husband stood in the doorway to the parlor with an expression of exasperation highlighting his slim face.

"How the devil did you know I was here?"

"Because I know your penchant for taunting your victims, my dear. Remember, I am married to you."

"Well, that's not at all what I am doing here," she argued, approaching her husband in three short, skirt-rustling strides.

"Isn't it?"

"Not at all. I was trying to bring my brother to his senses. Trying to get him to open up this house again. He won't let Jennings open a single curtain."

"Then why not honor at least that one of his wishes without contesting it? Give him at least that much after what you have seen done."

They both turned and glanced back at Chandler, who stared blankly ahead as if they were not there.

"It appears that your brother would like to be left alone."

"I cannot do that," she huffed. "He cannot go on like this."

"Perhaps you should have thought about that before you acted," Lincoln said in a deeper, more remonstrative tone.

"Oh, now that's not fair at all. Chandler told me himself that he doesn't blame me for how things came apart."

Lincoln's thin mustache twitched as he pursed his slim lips. "Gracious of him."

Chandler took another swallow of Scotch and continued staring straight ahead.

"Come, Daphne," Lincoln clutched her elbow. "I think you have done quite enough here for one day."

She glanced back at her brother, void of noticeable life. Completely unmoving. "I didn't mean for this to happen. Truly, I didn't."

"Just an observation, my dear, but next time you may be

well served to consider someone besides yourself before you act."

Lincoln Forrester did not wait for his wife to argue the point before he pulled her through the entry hall and into the sun-filled carriageway.

"Sir?" Jennings formal tone came tentatively. He walked into the parlor after Daphne and Lincoln's cobalt-blue brougham had pulled out of the carriageway and back down onto Mount Vernon Street.

"I never thought I would hear myself say this, but I actually find myself agreeing with your sister."

The sound of the words was enough to tear Chandler from his clouded thoughts. He turned and tried to focus on his butler.

"Sir, she's right, you know. You really cannot go on this way."

"Good God! Why won't the lot of you leave me be?"

Jennings's words were crisp. "Caring, my dear boy, makes that quite impossible."

"I appreciate the sentiment, Jennings. I do. But I don't want to change."

"Not even for Alice and James?"

Again Chandler tried to focus, this time by closing and opening his heavy-lidded eyes. "Are they all right? Nothing has happened to them, has it?"

"Respectfully, sir, with their father sitting alone all of the time, in what closely resembles a cave, refusing anything but the palliative of liquor, what would you think?"

"All right, Jennings," he sighed wearily. "I suppose twenty years in this house has earned you the right to voice your opinion. What would you have me do?"

"I would have you go after her."

"Not possible."

"Then go to China."

Chandler's spine stiffened. His eyes widened slightly. "What the devil are you talking about?"

"To Hangchow, sir, where you were at peace. If you will not go after Mrs. Tate, then at least go after some sort of peace for yourself."

"Even in Hangchow I am not likely to find that."

"Chandler, my dear boy, this house with all of its memories, with the imprint of Mrs. Tate so heavily upon it now, is slowly killing you. Can you not at least relieve yourself of this one burden until the wound begins to heal?"

Chandler raked a heavy hand through his unkempt hair. "I don't deserve even that."

"That is not true. No matter what happened between you and Tessa, you still deserve to move on with your life."

"I deserve nothing but her wrath, Jennings, and I've gotten that in spades."

David Jennings moved a few steps nearer, hovering over the man he had cared for and nurtured since boyhood. "Wrath is a terribly strong word to assign a young woman who adored you."

Chandler looked up, his eyes wide now but still dull and vague. "Yes, she did adore me. As I did her. Which makes my actions all that much more heinous."

"You tried to protect your children from harm. When all of the truths are known, I believe Mrs. Tate will see that."

"Lies are lies, Jennings old friend," Chandler said, repeating Daphne's words. "Even the white ones."

The stalwart, dignified butler went to the grand window in four short strides and, with a flourish, pulled back the heavy apricot draperies as Daphne had tried to do. As the room flooded suddenly with light, he turned firmly back around leveling his eyes on Chandler.

"You are a lion in the business world. You and I both know you are accustomed to making things happen. Make your bride see why you did what you did."

"If I thought there was even a ghost of a chance that she would listen . . ." His words trailed off as he looked toward the sun.

Jennings continued. "If I did not believe with my whole

heart that the poor girl is every bit as miserable without you as you are without her, I wouldn't have said a word."

Chandler leaned forward in his chair. "Do you honestly believe that?"

"I would stake my life on it. She took a chance on you once, Chandler. Instead of allowing herself to believe the worst, as you are doing now, she found the courage to confront you."

Cynthia's gun, he silently recalled. The scene, the violence he had unleashed upon her, made him grimace. "She spoke to you then?"

"Who else did she have here?"

Who indeed? Chandler wondered. He had been more taken with concealing the truth than seeing how desperately she needed to be trusted.

"All I am asking is, do you not now owe Tessa the same bit of courage? A confrontation at the very least?"

He sprang to his feet and stood on uncertain legs. "She left Boston, Jennings! She went home to New York."

"May I suggest a compromise that your honor could bear?"

"By all means."

"Why not arrange a trip back to China for yourself and the children? You could all do with a bit of time away from Boston, time as a family, after what you all have endured."

"That much is true."

"In the meantime, send a letter to New York. Take the time to tell her everything that is in your heart. Spare nothing. You will know soon enough after that whether to stay or to go."

There was a silent pause as Chandler looked around the room still so full of his vibrant young wife. He could almost hear her sweet laughter again. Dear God, if there was even the slightest chance . . .

"Tell me something, Jennings," he began, with slightly upturned lips as he moved a shaky step nearer. "How did you become so wise?"

"There are few benefits to growing old, my boy," the butler chuckled in reply. "One of the few, if one is fortunate, is a bit of wisdom. I have long believed that one concession was meant to make this whole wretched business of aging a bit more tolerable."

"Perhaps I would do well to defer to you then. It certainly stood me in good stead with Li Kao Chen."

Jennings's reserved smile broadened. "I have a good feeling about this, sir."

"If she would just agree to see me. To hear me out. Perhaps we could slowly begin to put the pieces back together, one at a time."

"Anything is possible, sir."

"For the first time in a month, old friend, you have actually made me believe that."

Tessa lay back against the iron bedstead, watching the tiny child sleep on the bed beside her. The wicker cradle beneath the window was empty for the third night in a row. Both of them slept better like this. The reassurance of nearness. Human warmth. Tessa needed it every bit as much as Claire.

The stone that had pulled so relentlessly at her heart had been lifted by this little child, and Tessa felt happy again. Or almost happy. At least there were no more tears left to cry. No more secret hope that Chandler might appear at her door. Tessa had taken the wounded, empty place inside herself left by him and filled it with this sweet, innocent little girl.

Certainly there were times like this, in the stillness of the night, when Tessa considered how her husband had made no move, in the month of their estrangement, to try to see her. It was tantamount to an admission of everything she had fought against believing.

But the pain was no longer so raw. As Brian had promised, day by day, it slowly was healing. The scar would always be there. But it was finally over, she sadly resolved. It was really over between them. Chandler Tate had gone on with his life. And now she was getting on with hers.

Chapter

45

NEW YORK'S NOVEMBER WAS ODDLY WARM. THE BREEZES BLEW heavy, sultry cloaks of air as Tessa and Mary Gallagher returned home from Hester Street. She had assisted in the birth of twin boys that morning. It had been a revitalizing experience to see the two healthy, squalling infants come into the world, in spite of the harshness they would soon face. It was still new life, the possibility the future held, Tessa thought. She smiled to herself for the first time in a month.

She raised her head. The music sung by birds in the branches of the trees above was another tonic. Clear and sweet, it matched the glorious fragrance from Mrs. Kerrigan's rose bushes planted near the front steps. Like the rose bushes outside the Tate house on Mount Vernon Street.

Tessa was surprised to realize, as they climbed their own front steps, that it was the first time in the six weeks since she had returned to New York, that she did not think of Chandler and her brief time as his wife with a searing jolt of pain.

"Ye did a fine job today, lass."

"It was quite a sight to see."

"That it was," Mary smiled wearily.

Tessa inhaled the rose-scented air as they paused on the landing before their own front door. "Thank you for urging me to come along these last few weeks, Mary. Claire is the light of my life, but I do believe your charity has been the thing to help me keep my sanity through all of this."

"'Twas no charity about it, Tessa. Ye are now, as ye were before, a fine help to me."

Someone was waiting inside when they entered the house. She was a stout woman in a blue-and-white dress and bonnet, sitting in the parlor with her hands crossed on her lap, speaking in a low tone with Brian Sullivan. They both rose as Tessa and Mary came into the room. As always this late in the afternoon, before the lamps were lit, the room was bathed in shadows and an evening breeze came in from the open windows.

"Mrs. Kerrigan," Mary smiled.

"Mrs. Gallagher," their next-door neighbor returned a cordial nod. "I've come about this."

She held up a letter addressed with a firm, masculine hand in bold black ink. Tessa felt her own face blanch. Looking down at the letter, she could see unmistakably that the handwriting belonged to Chandler Tate.

"I am terribly sorry it wasn't brought over sooner, but I have been in Philadelphia visiting my sister and I am afraid my maid didn't recognize Miss Murphy's married name on the envelope. She said it was delivered almost a week ago."

Mary looked over at Tessa with concern. "Are ye all right, lass?"

The question sounded very far away to her. Tessa's heart was pounding above it. She glanced down at the handwriting once again. His hands had touched this, she thought disjointedly as her heart beat like the wings of a small bird. They were the same powerful hands that once had touched her so tenderly. So lovingly. They had to be divorce papers.

She sank into one of the chairs near the fireplace as Brian

loomed nearby, his ruddy face taut with concern. Mary walked Mrs. Kerrigan to the door.

"I really am sorry. I only hope it was not all that important," Tessa heard the woman say from very far away. She unfolded the letter and with a painful sensation, like hot coals burning deeply inside her, she began to read.

My dearest Tessa,

Over these past weeks that you have been gone from our home, I have wanted to write you a thousand times. Most of those times come at night when this old house is still and the memory of you in it is the strongest. It calls to me when there are no other busying sounds of the day to chase it away.

You are everywhere, Tessa. In the parlor that you so lovingly revitalized. In the bed we shared too briefly, and in the eyes of my children, who learned to live again when you were here.

At first, I resolved to respect your wish to be apart from me. What I did to you, to us, was unforgivable. For the rest of my life there will be a price to pay for that. But, I humbly implore you, my sweet wife, let not that price be the end of what we had just begun to build.

Tessa stopped reading when she could no longer see the words for the tears in her eyes. Breathing was almost painful, her heart was beating so fast.

"Are ye all right, lass?" Brian softly asked, taking a step nearer.

"I need to be alone," she replied in a whisper and stood. Then she went out of the house and sank onto the front steps.

A cool evening breeze caught her hair and tossed the ends close around her face. The hem of her skirt rustled at her ankles. She felt as if she had been hit in the stomach. The ache was intense. It was coupled with the longing. Her slowly healing wound was open again. Raw. Bleeding.

She looked out across the street. There were children playing. A carriage passed before her. This letter was the last thing in the world she had expected. The thing for which she dared not hope.

> I am not a fool, nor am I a child. I know we have much to resolve between us before things could ever be as they were. All I ask, Tessa, is for a chance to speak with you. To explain what I had no time to explain. Then I shall ask for nothing more. The decision from there of what will become of us shall rest entirely with you.
>
> If I do not hear back from you within a few days, I shall sadly assume that you cannot find a way even to hear me out, and I will accept that. I have purchased a ticket to China, back to Hangchow, departing on the 10th of this month. But I will pray God that you will allow me to pay my debt to you every day and every night for the rest of our lives.
>
> I bid you, darling, to remember all that we have shared and all that we might share again in time. I love you now as I will love you always, truly, openly, and completely, whether we are reconciled or not.
>
> > I remain faithfully, your husband,
> > Chandler William Tate

Tessa nearly tripped over her hem dashing back into the house and into the parlor where Brian had remained. "What is the date today?" she asked frantically, her eyes clear with resolve.

"I believe it's the ninth. Why'd ye ask?"

"I've got to go to Boston!"

"You've found it in your heart to forgive him then."

"I don't know anything anymore, Brian, only that I must see him. Beyond that, I don't know what will happen."

"I shall take ye to the train station myself."

"Will you watch Claire for me, too?"

He looked down at her and spoke in a lower, huskier tone. "Need ye even ask?"

Tessa took Brian's hand and touched it softly to her lips. "How can you still be so gracious to me after—"

"After lovin' ye, lass," he smiled, "'tis as easy as breathin'."

One last time she kissed the infant who already was as much like her own as if she had given birth to her. Tessa pulled the delicate pink-and-yellow blanket up around her shoulders and then held Claire close to her breast.

"I will miss you, my little darling," she whispered, kissing the top of the baby's head. "But this is something I must do. I may have waited too long already."

It was difficult to lay her back into the cradle, since Tessa knew she would not be there to see her wake from her nap this time. A painful longing streaked through her. Tears swelled behind her eyes. She loved this sweet, beautiful child.

"I wonder if she'll realize I'm not here."

"Without a doubt. But I'm not a bad second to ye," Mary Gallagher said with a reassuring smile.

"I can't thank you and Brian enough for this."

"Thanks are not necessary, lass. Only your happiness is."

The two women embraced. "What would my life ever have been without the two of you?"

"'Tis a blessin', to be sure, that none of us shall ever know the answer to that."

"I've never been so nervous about anything," Tessa confessed, her stomach still tightly clenched.

"Give him a chance to explain, my girl. He loves ye, and I've no doubt he'll set things right between ye."

Anxiety loomed before Tessa like a heavy dark mist that she could not quite shake away. "I shall pray for that, Mary," she said softly.

TESSA EMERGED FROM THE CAB NEAR DUSK. THE HOUSE ON BEA-con Hill sat on a grassy knoll before her like a formidable opponent. One now vanquished. Crisp lines. Bold, black trim. Iron railings. But it was no longer the imposing structure it once had seemed.

She turned back around to pay the driver and across the horizon Tessa caught sight of a thick plume of black smoke rising up from somewhere across town.

"Dear Lord, is that a fire?" she asked the gap-tooth driver who held out his hand.

"That it is, Miss. Down in the business district, near as I can tell."

"Is it bad?"

"Wouldn't be if we had enough horses to pull the fire wagons. But those poor beasts are still dropping fast as flies."

"Well they'll certainly find a way to put it out before it spreads, don't you think?"

"You never know, do you? I hear Chicago burned almost

420

to the ground last year. I suppose it could happen here just as well."

Tessa paid the driver. She was anxious to go inside as the tension stretched through her. She did not want to think of anything just now but seeing Chandler and the children.

She removed her gloves as the horse clopped slowly back down the drive and onto Mount Vernon Street. She recalled that these were the gloves that Chandler had bought for her that afternoon at Lord & Taylor. She only hoped now that it was not too late for them to talk. To hear his explanation.

As she walked slowly up to the door, Tessa noticed things. They were things that had escaped her attention before. A perfectly planted terra-cotta pot with a blue-and-white-painted spinning top tossed inside. The rose bush beside it, still bearing four crimson blossoms. Home, she thought, missing Alice and James more than she had expected. Eager for them one day to meet Claire.

She did not need to use the knocker. The formidable black lacquer door opened with a squeal as she lifted her hand. Kathleen was on the other side.

"Saints preserve us!" At first her face was full of shock. Then she recovered herself. "Welcome home, ma'am."

"Thank you, Kathleen."

Tessa's knees were weak as she came into the foyer. There she had added potted palms and a new soft watercolor hung on a pale-blue velvet cord. Her decorations were there six weeks later. It surprised Tessa how much of herself lingered in this once-imposing house. Even without her. Just as Chandler had said.

She turned slowly around. "Is he here, Kathleen?"

"No, ma'am. I'm afraid Mr. Tate is away."

Tessa slumped against the door. Her throat closed. "He can't be. My luck cannot possibly be that dreadful."

"I know 'tis not my place to say so, ma'am, but in his absence I'd like to tell ye that the master did miss ye. He wasn't the same after ye left. But glory be ye're back. Everythin' will be all right now."

"How can it be all right, Kathleen, now that I am here and he is on the other side of the world?"

She pressed a hand against her forehead feeling the lifeblood drain out of her. Disappointment taking its place. If only she had not been so stubborn. If only she had listened that night.

"Mr. Tate has gone to Maine, ma'am. No further than that."

Tessa swallowed and opened her eyes. "Then he's not . . . bound for China?"

"No, ma'am. He's gone 'til this evenin' on business. But we expect him back for supper."

Tessa felt a great rushing sensation of relief, yet she also felt filled with an almost painful anticipation. In the cab, and on the slow walk up the entrance stairs, she had steeled herself for their meeting. The expression on his face. What he might say. What she would say in return.

The sound of small collective footsteps barreling down the staircase filled the silence. Alice and James nearly tripped over one another to get to her.

"It *is* Tessa!" James cried out smiling.

"You've come back!"

Both children rushed at her, nearly pushing her onto the carpet as she knelt with open arms to receive them.

"Why did you stay away so long?" Alice asked. "Papa wouldn't tell us."

"No one told us anything," said James.

"It's a very long story, my sweethearts, and I am just so very glad to see you both. Give me another hug, would you?"

She drew them nearer, both children only too happy to oblige her, as Kathleen stood over them, still not quite believing herself that what they all had hoped for had now actually happened.

Their reunion was cut short by the sudden presence of Daphne, in sweeping cherry red, who had silently descended the staircase behind them. Contriving civility, she said, "So you've returned, Tessa."

"I've come to see Chandler and the children."

"I am quite certain all will say that you have been missed."

Her face heated, uncertain of this new tactic. "I did not expect to see you here."

"I'm certain that is true. But with my brother away, the care of these children must fall on someone, mustn't it?"

"It is good of you."

"They are family, Tessa," Daphne said in a low voice, yet with a slight, incongruous smile. "I am certain you recall my loyalty to family."

"How could I ever forget?"

"How indeed," she conceded with a nod.

Suddenly, the front door slammed back against the wall with a thundering crash, shaking all of the paintings on their frames. Everyone turned. Jennings stood in the opening, his face stricken and white as chalk.

"Oh, dear God," Daphne mouthed, pressing her fingers to her lips.

"What is it, Jennings?" Tessa asked, not bothering to say hello. Her heart raced. By his expression it was clear that whatever news he carried it was not good. "Tell me, please, Jennings," Tessa mouthed, pushing down the panic. "Has something happened to Chandler?"

The butler slumped against the doorjamb, out of breath. His face was pale and his narrow gray eyes were wide now and panic-stricken.

"Jennings! Out with it!" Daphne charged, bolting toward him. "Is it my brother?"

"No, Miss Daphne. Nothing like that. There's a fire."

"What do you mean, a fire? Where?"

"They say it started down on Summer Street. It has spread from the Tebbitts Building to the one next to it already. Destroyed them both."

"I saw the smoke myself from the cab," Tessa confirmed.

"Summer Street?" Daphne gasped, sheer black fright sweeping across her face. "Our offices are there."

"Yes, ma'am."

"Well, we mustn't panic. Surely they'll have it contained before long."

"I was told that the horse epidemic is making containment difficult," Tessa somberly offered. "They've few animals left to pull the water tanks."

"Men are dragging them," said Jennings, "but it is slowing things considerably."

Daphne pressed a hand to her forehead as her heart jumped wildly in her chest. "The epizoöty! I'd forgotten about it. Dear Lord above! The silks! We've just gotten a shipment from England worth a fortune. Oh! And all of the contracts! The cash!"

"Should we do something, do you suppose?" Tessa asked, pivoting around to face her sister-in-law.

Daphne was breathing in quick, shallow gasps. She began nervously to wring her hands. "I don't know," she muttered. "I don't know what to do. My brother has always dealt with this sort of thing, ever since . . . Oh, my Lord! Where on earth is Chandler? What would he have me do now?"

Tessa paced back and forth wearing a path into the priceless Aubusson carpet that warmed the parlor floor. Jennings perched on a settee, his hands rigidly steepled. Alice and James were silent as they sat together near the fireplace with Kathleen.

"We should not have let her go," Tessa muttered, shaking her head. "It has been more than an hour and we haven't heard a single word."

The gold mantle clock ticked out three beats before Jennings replied. "There was nothing we could have done, ma'am. Miss Daphne was determined."

"Perhaps I should have gone with her, Jennings."

His gray eyes lifted to meet hers. "After the dreadful way she has treated you?"

"She loves Chandler, as I do. She is his sister. If anything should happen to her, what would he . . . what would the children think of me if I did not at least try to—"

Tessa moved to the grand bay window, not finishing her

sentence. She looked out across a horizon choked now with thick black plumes and the acrid odor of smoke.

Even from this distance, they could hear the ominous, far-off clang of the fire bells and there was no sign of the fire abating.

Anxiety knotted inside Tessa, coiling up her throat as she tried to push away the disturbing thoughts of what might happen. She had done her best to convince Daphne that Chandler would never have put either of their lives in jeopardy, no matter how rare the silk. Jennings had tried to echo those thoughts.

But Daphne had been determined not to make the same costly mistakes she had when her brother had first abandoned her for New York. "My foolishness not long ago cost my family's company an enormous sum," she had said in a voice full of conviction. She then began pulling on her gloves and hat, preparing to leave. "I have no intention of seeing that look of disappointment in Chandler's eyes ever again!"

"At least let me go with you," Tessa had pleaded, as her stomach had clenched tightly with dread.

But Daphne would have none of it. It was something she meant to do alone to recapture Chandler's affection, and the respect she knew only too well that she had lost.

Jennings and Tessa had watched helplessly as Daphne then strutted fearlessly out of the house, taking her carriage down to Summer Street with every intention of single-handedly saving B.W. Tate & Company from total ruin.

"How long has it been now?" Tessa asked anxiously, pivoting back from the window in a swirl of light blue skirts.

Jennings's reply was somber. "Five minutes since the last time you asked, ma'am."

"I don't like it a bit." She glanced out of the window at a darkening blanket of smoke that was steadily blotting out the sun. Carried by the autumn breeze, bright-red cinders had even begun to fall on the walkway and onto the two elm trees in front of their house.

Tessa tried to keep hold of herself, but the dread was

gnawing away at what self-control she had left. She spun around. She saw the faces of Alice and James, wide and full of fear for their aunt.

"I am going after her."

"All right. Then I am going with you."

"I thank you for the thought," Tessa said, trying her best to smile in a way that would push back her own fear and the fear so raw on the faces of the children. "But someone has to stay here with Alice and James."

"I'll not let you go alone, ma'am," Jennings countered loyally. "Besides, Kathleen and Mrs. O'Neil are both here to look after them. Respectfully, Mrs. Tate, we could be wasting precious time with a debate like this."

The ebony-colored carriage rolled steadily back into a dark and eerie ash-covered Boston.

"What the devil—" Nelson Winthrop murmured, gazing through the window as his eyes played over the horizon. Chandler pulled his head from the back of the seat and opened his eyes.

"What is it?"

"It's a fire," Nelson said in an incredulous whisper. "Dear God, it has actually happened . . ."

Chandler dashed into the house, with Nelson behind him. The grounds outside and down on Mount Vernon Street were already covered with a thin layer of gray ash.

"Jennings! Jennings, where are you?" he shouted frantically.

Kathleen came out of the parlor and met them in the foyer. Chandler gripped her shoulders, his face heated red, a blue vein of panic pulsing in his forehead.

"Are the children all right?"

"They are upstairs with Mrs. O'Neil, sir."

"Thank the lord for that," he breathed a sigh of relief. "There is no telling how fast or how far this fire will spread. It's heading over toward Broad Street as we speak!"

"Yes, sir."

"And, in the meantime, where is Jennings?"

Kathleen was not able to mask the look of concern shadowing her own freckled face. "Gone with Mrs. Tate, sir."

Chandler went deathly pale. The words and their meaning wrapped themselves around his heart and began viciously to squeeze the life from it. "There must be some mistake."

"No sir," she bobbed a nervous curtsy. "'Twas Mrs. Tate all right."

Nelson stepped forward as Chandler turned away. "You don't mean Tessa, now do you, Kathleen?"

"Tessa. Yes sir. They went after Miss Daphne when she didn't return, sir. I heard Mr. Tate's sister say that she was worried about some bolts of silk and some contracts. She said, sir, that she had no intention of disappointin' ye again, Mr. Tate."

"I don't understand. She didn't answer my letter. I believed she had chosen not to . . . This cannot possibly be."

Chandler tried to take a breath. His heart pounded. Was such a thing possible? He was to be granted this miracle only to have the joy of it dashed by such an unbelievable tragedy? Daphne, Jennings and . . . dear blessed God in his heaven, even Tessa?

"How long ago did they leave?"

"Only a few minutes ago, sir."

"How many?" Chandler rigidly pressed, doing his best to control the desperation in his voice.

"No more than ten, sir. Since there was no carriage left, they went on foot. If you hurry, I am quite certain you could beat them there!"

427

Chapter

47

"WE HAVE TO DO SOMETHING!" TESSA CRIED OUT IN PANIC. "WE cannot just let her die in there!"

The fire was quickly spreading in every direction. Orange flames hissed and crackled. Windows burst and shattered from buildings nearby already engulfed by flames. Walls fell and thundered into bright pools of fire, as whole buildings were crushed into ash. The cooling November wind whistled above the clanging bells, beckoning the bright waves of flame forward, calling the fire to consume everything in its path as it moved steadily toward the Tate warehouse, a tall granite building into which Chandler's sister had dashed.

"I've got to go after her!" Tessa shouted above the roar. "It's been too long. She could be hurt!"

"It's too dangerous. This building could go up like a matchstick, with you inside!"

"Didn't you see the faces of those two children? How could I ever look at them again, Jennings, if I simply let their aunt die?"

"Then we'll go together!" he declared loudly.

"I can't let you do that!"

"Respectfully, Mrs. Tate, try to stop me!"

There was no longer any time to wait for the firemen or the horse-drawn steam fire engines, already overburdened by the out-of-control blaze as the flames steadily neared the building. In the midst of billowing gray-and-black smoke, they could hear shouts of desperation and utter chaos. Casting aside their own fears, Tessa and Jennings covered their mouths with soaking wet cloths and raced inside through a river of heat.

It was difficult to see anything through the thick billows of smoke that rolled and seeped their way up the stairs and through the corridors, clouding the air like a heavy shroud.

"Where is the Tate office? The smoke's confusing my senses!" Jennings shouted through the wet cloth as they ran together up a second flight of stairs and down another long, dark corridor.

"We haven't much time," Tessa shouted back, willing herself not to panic, as she tried doorknob after doorknob. All were locked.

In the distance, they could still hear the clang of fire bells. Men shouting. A scream.

"What about in here?" Jennings asked as one of the doorknobs finally turned and clicked open.

Tessa raced to his side and was the first to push inside the Tate office. She took two long steps in the darkness and felt the thud of a body against her shoe. It was Daphne, limp at her feet. Tessa knelt and listened to her heart. The room was not yet filled with smoke but there was enough to make them both begin to choke, even with the cloths covering their mouths. The only explanation for Daphne's condition was that she had panicked in the growing darkness and fainted.

"Is she alive?" Jennings shouted.

"She's only fainted, I think, but we've no time to waste before the smoke entirely invades this building too! We've got to get out of here!"

As Tessa gasped for breath, fighting the searing, burning sensation beginning to fill her own lungs, they dragged

Daphne's limp body out into the corridor in the direction of what they both silently prayed was the stairwell.

Unable to revive her, Tessa had given up her own wet cloth to cover Daphne's face.

Am I to die this way? she wondered as they trudged slowly down the stairs. So close to Chandler, to his arms.

Tessa and Jennings were both disoriented by their own mounting panic. Tessa struggled to catch her breath. Carrying Daphne's limp body made it more difficult.

Rousing at last, Chandler's sister began to gasp and choke, but Tessa did not dare stop long enough to see if she was all right. Each moment was critical, and for the first time in her life, Tessa actually began to fear dying. But out of the fear came determination. Tessa pulled Daphne even more forcefully down the stairs.

This is not how it was meant to end. I will see Chandler again. I *will* hear him out. I *will* give him a chance to explain! Tessa silently vowed.

"I can't . . . go on," Daphne gasped and choked.

Nearing the bottom of a second flight of stairs, Tessa stubbornly declared between her own painful gasps for breath, "Oh, no! I will not give up! And neither . . . will you, Daphne Forrester. We're not finished . . . with one another, you and I. Not nearly finished!"

Chandler and Nelson Winthrop arrived on Summer Street in time to hear that a well-dressed man and woman had dashed into the building, now steadily being engulfed by smoke and flames.

As the flames and the smoke spread from the building next door and began to eat at the Tate building, Chandler knew it was Tessa and Jennings, selflessly, bravely going in after his sister.

In the beginning, he had been afraid to trust their love, to trust her. But in spite of everything, she had returned to him. There was a good deal to be mended. He understood and accepted that. But their hearts belonged to one another completely and always would. He simply could not lose her.

As he lunged toward the building, two well-meaning strangers held him back. Nelson gripped his shoulder. Chandler struggled wildly to break free.

"It's too late, Chandler," Nelson said.

"Let go of me! You don't understand! My wife's in there!" He shouted desperately above the din of screaming and sirens and the torrid crackle of flames.

"Only the good Lord can save them now," one of the strangers shouted back.

Chandler struggled like a madman, fighting and kicking with every once of strength he possessed. But the two were stronger, and Nelson Winthrop was trying to spare the life of a friend.

"It's over, Chandler," he told his old friend, tears filling his own burning eyes.

"Tessa! Tessa!! Oh, God, no!!"

Through tears and flames, suddenly they all saw two figures staggering out past the thick cloud of smoke, like a mirage. A crowd of pallid-faced, stricken Bostonians watched the rescue through the smoke and the spray of fiery cinders. They were covered with soot, staggering and gasping for breath. But Chandler knew it was Tessa, and that she had escaped with Daphne. Jennings, however, was not with them.

Tessa took two steps forward into the street and collapsed, just as the building erupted behind them like a volcano of flames and ash.

Chapter

48

AFTER THE PHYSICIAN HAD SEEN HER, CHANDLER REFUSED anyone's aid in tending to his wife. Alone with her in her bedroom, filled now with fresh flowers and lit with the amber glow of a single flickering lamp, he had removed her black button shoes, her soot-stained dress, and the ribbons that had bound her hair.

Then, with infinite tenderness, he had washed her delicate face and neck. Her hands and fingers. But her hair and skin still bore the acrid smell of smoke, a reminder of the lengths she had gone to for love of him.

As she lay now in her huge mahogany poster bed, surrendering to a restless, fitful sleep, Chandler held her hand and watched her, the pale, peach-tinted skin dusted with freckles, hair the color of brushed copper. She looked like an angel in a fresco, so perfect and so pale. *His angel*. And by a miracle she was here with him again. Safe in her own bed. Unharmed.

Beyond the windows, the north end of Boston was still burning out of control. The reports were grim. Entire buildings, factories, storefront shops, had already been reduced to rubble. People had lost their homes, their businesses, and their lives. And poor Jennings. He had been a part of Chandler's life for as long as he could recall. Such patience and kindness. He had defined those words, Chandler thought.

There would never be anyone else like Jennings.

Chandler looked upward, whispering a silent prayer of thanks, and pushing back the tears, that the same fire that had taken the life of his dear friend had spared his wife. His hand played along the smooth surface of her cheek, and he could not help thinking back to all that she had endured for him. Tonight, and since first coming here as his wife.

He ran a fresh cloth through the basin of cool water beside the bed and tenderly pressed it onto her forehead. "God, I am so sorry. I do love you, Tessa. And, if you will let me, I will speak those words until my dying breath."

Then he slumped exhausted beside her sleeping body in the stiff-backed oak chair, still holding her hand. Tomorrow they would have much to discuss, and he would have to tell her about Jennings. He would have to tell her everything. But now, none of that mattered. The past did not matter. Not even the future. Nothing was important at all but Tessa. And having her safe, here in this house again, beside him.

"How is she this morning, sir?" Kathleen asked anxiously as she waited outside the bedroom door. It was clear by the look of him that Chandler had not slept at all. His eyes were glazed and darkly rimmed. But at least they were together, Kathleen thought. At last perhaps things will be as they should be once again.

"Mrs. Tate is weak," Chandler replied wearily, "but she asked for tea and honey for her throat before she drifted off again."

"Saints be praised," Kathleen said softly, looking heavenward, then remembering. "Then she doesn't remember about Jennings, sir, does she?"

"No, Kathleen, it appears at the moment that my wife doesn't remember much about yesterday."

"It's bound to be hard on her, sir, them becomin' so close and all."

"Yes."

"But Mrs. Tate is a fighter," she said loyally, and whispered it, not wanting to wake her.

"That she is," Chandler quietly agreed.

"I must tell you, sir, I did everything I could to stop her from goin' down there. But she wouldn't hear of it. She was goin' on and on about loyalty to your children and helpin' your sister."

"Speaking of Daphne," Chandler said with a sigh. "How is she this morning? Have you any word?"

"Better than both of us, I can honestly say. She's already had her bath and taken breakfast, and is bein' cared for at this very moment downstairs by Mr. Forrester. I don't know that her husband has told her about Jennings either, sir."

"Daphne spent the night here?"

"I do hope that was all right, Mr. Tate," Kathleen said. "I sent for her husband once you had returned, and he came directly. He did not think she was up to the carriage ride home."

"That's fine," Chandler said, thinking, as he ran a hand across the day-old, coarse golden stubble on his chin, just how well Daphne had fared and what her impulsive behavior had cost David Jennings.

Kathleen hung her head. "Much of Boston was not so fortunate as you, if I may tell you, sir. They say 'tis like a battlefield down there," she said somberly. "It really is devastation, but I hear that by dawn they'd gotten most of it under control at last."

Chandler leaned against the doorjamb, exhausted.

"I don't imagine Boston shall recover from this for a very long time."

"Will you kindly stop your whispering over there," Tessa suddenly rasped, calling out across the room. "I can barely make out a word the two of you are saying."

Chandler pivoted around and dashed across the room. "I thought you were sleeping!"

"I should be drinking my tea," she countered, mocking frustration as she looked across at Kathleen.

"Oh yes, ma'am!" she smiled obligingly. "I shall see to it at once."

When they were alone again, Chandler came and sat with her on the edge of the bed, uncertain what to say. Uncertain of the barriers still between them. But most of all, he was uncertain how to tell her about Jennings.

Chandler smoothed the hair back from her forehead with heart-rending tenderness. Then he pressed a gentle, tentative kiss on her cool skin. As he pulled back, it was the first time they had looked into one another's eyes since that night when everything had first come apart.

"You needn't look so worried, you know."

"That was a foolish thing you did, going into a burning building like that," he said achingly. "You should know better than that. If I had lost you—"

Chandler caught himself and the deeper implication of his words. She was here but things were far from settled, and he must grant her the time to set the pace between them. But first he needed to tell her about Jennings. She had a right to know, no matter how painful. For better or worse, Chandler was finished keeping secrets.

"How do you feel?"

"Truthfully, as if I had swallowed hot coals. But other than that, I will be fine."

Chandler breathed an audible little sigh of relief. Then his voice went low, and he took her hand.

"There is so much I want to say. So much I need to tell you. But first, there is something more important you must know."

"All right."

"How much do you remember, Tessa, about yesterday?"

She looked at him with wide eyes, still bloodshot, still so very tired. He could almost see the images and the memories dash across her mind, like mice skittering across a bare floor, as she considered the question.

"There was so much smoke," she began tentatively, putting a voice to the images. ". . . and Daphne, oh, I was so angry at her because she would not even try to save herself. She wanted to give up, and so Jennings and I had to—"

Chandler watched the tears flood her eyes as she looked at him in that first excruciating moment of realization. "Oh, no," she said softly, achingly, shaking her head. "No, Chandler, not Jennings . . . Please, tell me no."

She steepled her hands and pressed them to her lips, trying to be strong, finding it impossible. He had been her first friend in Boston. So strong in the face of her weakness. So sage when she had behaved so foolishly. "Oh, God, it cannot be. Not Jennings. Not my dear friend . ."

Chandler gathered her into his arms and held her, trying to bear the weight of her grief for her, along with his own, and yet knowing that such a thing was impossible. They had both lost someone important in their lives. They both ached for what it meant, a future without him.

He cradled her gently as she sobbed into his shoulder, whispering "No, no" over and over again until he thought his heart would break from the anguished, keening sound.

"Oh! I tried to save them both! I tried, Chandler. He just stumbled and wood started falling and—"

"I know, darling," he whispered and touched her hair.

"There was just so much smoke, and then he seemed ill, like my father, and Daphne was crying and saying she couldn't go on . . ."

He tightened his arms around her. "But you survived, and I will thank God every day the rest of my life for that."

She was sobbing now, curled against him like a child. For the moment, everything between them, all of the anger and betrayal, was forgotten, covered over by need, and healing, and this horrendous tragedy. Yes, Tessa needed him. Chandler needed her. He always had. But from the tragedy of David Jennings's death came threads of hope, almost at once, as they sat together. It began the process of mending their two broken hearts.

"I loved him," she sobbed and trembled against him. "He was so very kind to me."

"And to me."

"He really believed that I could do this, that I could be your wife."

"David Jennings was a very wise man."

"I miss him already, you know."

"Yes," said Chandler tenderly. "God, so do I."

She slept in fits and starts most of the day. Chandler stayed by her side, holding her hand, cooling her brow with wet cloths, as Boston burned out of control.

Jennings had not been the only one to lose his life. Others had perished, and with them, businesses, homes, hopes, and dreams. They would rebuild, but the city would never be the same. Boston would never forget so massive a tragedy.

Chandler was sitting beside her holding her hand when Tessa finally woke to a room full of afternoon shadows. His face, so full of concern and marked by fatigue, was the first thing she saw.

"You needn't have stayed with me like this."

"I wouldn't have been anywhere else on this earth." Chandler smoothed the hair back from her face and gazed down at her with such an expression of tender concern that Tessa nearly cried.

"I couldn't believe it when Kathleen told me that you'd come back."

"Things were left unfinished between us. I had no idea what we would say to one another, I only knew that I couldn't leave things as they were."

Still uncertain where they stood now, and not wanting to push her, Chandler sat not moving, only looking at her and holding her hand.

"I shouldn't have run away like that, at least not without letting you explain. I owed us that much."

"Right now I want to say everything to you. There is so much to be explained. It is difficult to know where to begin."

Tessa squeezed his hand. "There will be plenty of time for that."

His eyebrows arched slightly. "Will there?"

Chandler fought the urge to pull her to him at that moment. To touch her in the ways that had once so briefly filled their nights, and made him believe that his soul might actually have been worth saving after all. But they were not nearly ready for that. Too much had happened, and there was still too much to be resolved between them.

"Right now," Tessa answered, her voice still raspy. "I would like to know how Daphne is."

Chandler straightened, eyes widening. "My sister, who has thwarted us at every turn? Who nearly cost you your life, and did cost Jennings his?"

"It's not fair to blame her, Chandler. Jennings was determined to go with me."

"And you, my darling, after everything, were you determined as well?"

"Yes."

He shook his head. "You are a remarkable woman, Tessa. I only wish that I could tell you——"

Tessa pressed two fingers gently to his lips. "Tell me about your sister for now."

Chandler collected his thoughts and tried to quell the rush of love filling his heart. "Kathleen tells me she is fine. She's downstairs at this very moment, having tea, and no doubt doling out orders to poor Lincoln already."

They both smiled knowingly and their eyes met again. There was passion there. Whatever became of them now, no amount of tragedy, misunderstanding, or even estrangement could extinguish that. Chandler brought her hand to his lips and kissed it tenderly.

"I cannot quite believe you ever found it in your heart to come back here and, at least, to let me explain."

"Time heals a great many things," Tessa said.

It would never be able to heal the loss of you, he thought. But he knew she wasn't ready to hear that.

Later, after she had dressed, Tessa asked Chandler to take her downstairs to see Daphne. She was sitting with Lincoln in the little walled, ivy-covered garden off the breakfast room and he was helping her sip her tea.

There was little joy among them, with the ground, even in this walled garden, covered with a thin layer of gray ash. The air was still choked with the scent of charred wood. Reminders of yesterday. And of Jennings.

Seeing her brother, Daphne sprang to her feet and began to weep. She wrapped her arms around his neck and fell against his chest. "Oh, I'm so sorry, Chandler. It's my fault. All of it. Jennings is dead and the business is in ruins! It's gone! Everything has been burned to the ground! All that you and father worked so hard for, and that poor, poor man losing his life, and I'm to blame when I only meant to help!"

Chandler felt a surprising rush of tenderness for her at that moment, in spite of their history, in spite of everything. They had all been through so much these past few hours, and never in his life had he heard such a repentant tone in his sister's voice. That, in itself, was a small miracle. And after all, he thought, if there was even the slightest chance that Tessa might forgive him, didn't he owe his own sister that same thing now?

"You tried to do what you could. It was very brave of you."

"I'm just so sorry," she sobbed. "I wanted to save at least something. I didn't expect . . . I didn't think anyone, least of all Jennings and Tessa, would follow me."

"I just thank God that you are all right," he charitably told her in a soft tone.

She pulled back and looked at him, her wide eyes flooded with tears. "I have caused so much suffering, it seems. I honestly never meant to do that. We will get through this, won't we? We will rebuild the company?"

There was such a vulnerable expression on her face, such remorse as she looked up at him, that Chandler felt he had little choice but to tell her what she needed to hear. "Of course we will," he answered her, trying desperately to believe it himself. "We're Tates, remember?"

Daphne ran a napkin across her eyes to dry them. Then she looked back at Tessa. There was a kinder, softer expression on her face than Tessa had ever seen.

"So," Daphne sniffled. "I understand that I had the intolerable lack of breeding to faint yesterday, and that it was you who saved my life."

"Jennings did his part," Tessa replied carefully as she and Chandler sat down on the green iron chairs facing the Forresters.

"And he lost his life because of me."

Tessa lowered her eyes slightly.

"So, this morning I find myself in one very awkward position," Daphne continued, her voice straining slightly. "Owing a debt of gratitude, and my life it seems, to someone of whom I have never approved. Someone I treated badly."

"You owe me nothing, Daphne."

"In a curious way, Tessa, I actually admire your courage," Daphne continued, and dabbed again at the corners of her eyes. "I cannot honestly say that I would have done the same for you, if the tables had been turned."

"Well, there really is no one else quite like my wife."

Everyone watched Daphne swallow back a hefty lump of pride and stiffen on the carved iron bench, twisting her small, bloodless hands, and the handkerchief, into a knot, as Chandler's declaration hung like a cloud between them.

"After what happened yesterday, I realize now that I was horribly hasty in my judgment of you, Tessa. You deserved better than that from me."

She drew in a breath and looked at Tessa squarely. "You are what my brother wants. And after what you did for me, after all that you have done for this family, I have actually begun to see why. My only regret is that I did not see it sooner."

Chandler's mouth came open as he looked at Daphne. "Tessa is always saying that people can change, but I would scarcely have believed it of you, had I not heard it for myself."

Lincoln cleared his throat. "Nor would I."

"The point is, Tessa, I am truly sorry for how I behaved toward you."

"If you do mean it, I thank you for that."

"And I shall not be acting as an impediment to the two of you any longer. If you have survived all that fate . . . and I have thrown across your path, at the very least, you do deserve a chance at making a real marriage of it, after all."

"You wouldn't mind committing that to paper this time, would you?" Chandler asked.

"You doubt me?"

"Well, you must admit, we have every reason in the world to do so."

"Very well then," she said, pleating her ivory-and-green checked skirt with rigid fingers as she shifted in her seat. "I shall prove to you just how sincere I really am. Once this whole dreadful mess is cleared up and Boston is on its feet again, I would be honored if you would allow me to host a belated wedding supper for the two of you."

"Supper at your house?"

"Well of course at our house."

Chandler coughed into his fist, unable to refuse himself at least one tiny bit of sarcasm to alleviate the tension between them all. "Without an official food taster, I don't know."

"Not to worry," Lincoln joined in with a wan smile. "I shall be there, eating the very food you do, and my wife would not dare poison me."

Chandler cast a glance at Tessa. "He's right you know. Who else would have her if not Lincoln? The man has the patience of Job."

"So then may I count on you both to accept?"

Tessa and Chandler exchanged a glance. "There is a great deal to be worked out between us yet, Daphne, and perhaps a wedding celebration will not be appropriate. But that decision will be up to Tessa."

Daphne gritted her teeth as a hint of her old, proud arrogance glittered in her eyes. Then, still so unexpectedly to those around her, she softened again. "I understand."

"Well, that is a beginning," Chandler said.

Daphne then looked to Tessa, her former rival. "Tessa? Since I am certain a great many things shall be up to you from now on, then I ask you, may I do at least that for you and my brother?"

Tessa's mind whirled like the child's top she had seen outside beside the door in the terra-cotta pot. It was so like her. The city had nearly burned to the ground, Jennings had died, and Daphne was organizing a supper. She was rushing things. Experience had made Tessa wary. So much had happened. But it really did seem as if she was trying to make amends.

Her reply was cautious. "Let's just get through today first, shall we Daphne?"

"Fair enough."

"And in the meantime, I am going to have a memorial for Jennings. Perhaps you would like to help me organize that."

It surprised everyone that Daphne's eyes filled once again with tears, and for a moment she seemed unable to speak.

"Oh, I would like that very much," she finally said.

Tessa had insisted on coming.

Late on Sunday afternoon, she and Chandler walked slowly, silently, through the charred, twisted rubble of what once had been Boston's business district. The devastation was sweeping.

They walked beneath a red-streaked sunset and Tessa's stomach churned at the sight of the beautiful curves of what she remembered as Franklin Square. It now lay in total ruin. Otis Street. Summer Street. Their once proud and gleaming buildings were nothing more now than a tangle of twisted black iron and ash.

As they stepped carefully, Tessa heard the echo of the rattling, snapping flames and the hiss of water against melting walls. She grimaced at the memory of the frightening sights through which she had pressed in order to save Daphne. But she kept silent, looking at the remnants of a fire that had laid waste to an entire city. Thirty-seven streets. Warehouses. Grocers. Carriages. People's livelihoods. People's lives. From Washington Street all the way down to the harbor, nothing more now than a lurid graveyard of skeletons remained.

A pall had descended upon the historic city as merchants searched through the smoldering ruins for account books or even traces of any of their merchandise that the greedy fire had not claimed.

As the wind whipped at Tessa's cloak and gown, finally she and Chandler stopped. They stood together gazing out across the ravaged heap of stone and ash that once had housed B.W. Tate & Company. Everything was lost. Tessa had no idea what she could possibly say. And yet she had wanted to be here, needed to be here for Chandler. She shuddered, feeling suddenly cold as she watched his face, pale now and stricken.

"I know what I told Daphne," he said painfully, crouching to run his hand through the still warm ashes, trying to comprehend the utter desolation, all of the loss. "But I really don't know what we're going to do."

Tessa felt her heart lurch at the tone in his voice, and how low it had gone, almost to a whisper. They had lost everything. A fortune in beautiful silks. Velvets. All of those new satins. Files. Ledgers. Contracts. A business into which his father had poured his life's blood. A business that Chandler had nurtured.

"Well, I don't see that there is much of a choice in the matter," she said firmly.

Chandler came back to his feet. He put an arm around her waist and clutched her tightly, in spite of their estrangement, needing the supportive feel of her near to him.

"The Tates *will* rebuild," Tessa declared. "There's an example to be set for the rest of Boston. They need you Chandler. They need to see your strength."

Chandler pulled back and looked at her. "Do you honestly believe that we can?"

And suddenly that indomitable Irish spirit of hers, that spark of something exceptional with which he had first fallen so in love, was there shining up at him against all of this destruction. "I never thought I would set foot in Boston again," she said. "And yet here I am. Yes, I suppose I do believe anything is possible if you want it badly enough."

By evening, the fire had been entirely extinguished but Boston still reeled from the devastation. Tessa and Chandler returned home together after helping those they could to salvage what few possessions were left. Both of them were exhausted as they climbed the long, lamplit staircase.

"May I come in?" he asked tentatively, almost awkwardly, outside her door. "I know that it's late, but we still must talk."

"It has been an awfully long day, Chandler. What we have to say to one another can wait, I think."

"Well I cannot wait. This void between us has torn a hole in my heart, Tessa, and if there is even the slightest chance of mending it, I would like to begin now. Please," he said brokenly, "let me come inside with you."

They sat beside one another on the daybed that was near the fireplace. The only sound between them at first was the crackle of the logs as they shot rich brassy flames in the hearth, and cast a ring of gold and shadows into the room.

"First, I have to tell you how sorry I am for all of the pain I caused you. You certainly didn't deserve that," Chandler said haltingly.

"You were in a difficult position. Your wife had made a fool of you, and risked your children in it. I began to see that once I was away from here for a while."

"But you don't know the entire story. I want you to hear it, all of it. What tore Cynthia and me apart was far more

444

than simple infidelity. The story won't be pretty, that I can promise you. But it will be the truth this time, Tessa. All of it."

Her voice was suddenly high and thin as they looked at one another. As they held hands. "For now, tell me only one thing."

"Anything."

"Would you ever have told me the truth about Cynthia if she hadn't shown up as she did?"

He lowered his head. "I don't honestly know. I wanted to. That much I can tell you from my heart. I was trying to find the words. In the meantime, I told you what I could. A little more each day. I know now that was not nearly enough."

Tessa looked away, then stood. The firelight touched her hair making it glow.

"I should have trusted you to know the time. If you sent her away, I'm certain now that it was for a very good reason. I should have believed in you, Chandler. But things will have to be different between us."

"Does that mean then," he asked cautiously, the emotion raw now on his face and in words that still came from him so haltingly, "that we have a future together . . . as husband and wife?"

Tessa cupped her chin in two fingers, trying to remain calm, as emerald tears shimmered in her eyes. "That depends."

"Upon what?"

"Upon whether I ever truly was your wife."

Chandler stood and pulled her close to him. He clasped Tessa tightly in his arms, searching her face. "Oh, God. All this time we were apart you've believed our marriage—"

"Well, in this country a man can have only one wife."

"And I do." He took her face in his hands. "Cynthia and I were divorced quietly before she went to France the first time. It was part of the arrangement."

The rest of the truth came in fragments as they sat together. Holding one another. Talking in low tones. Forgiving one another for the pain both of them had caused.

"It was just so dark and vile, what I had done. How I chose to protect Cynthia. No matter what my reasons, I played a part in a man's death."

"But you didn't kill anyone."

"No, but I covered it up. And there is as much guilt in complicity as there is in the deed itself."

She leaned against him, remembering. "And I informed you, so self-righteously, that I could never accept the lengths to which some people were driven. I was the one who kept you from wanting to tell me the truth."

"I couldn't bear to lose you, Tessa, not when it took an entire lifetime to find you."

She was trembling now, from surprise and from relief. It was so splendid to be this near to him again, to hear his deep, reassuring voice, and to know that when they had given themselves to one another, as they had done so many glorious times, they had done so as man and wife.

"I'm just so sorry," he murmured, kissing her tear-moistened cheeks, her nose, and finally her lips with the excruciatingly delicate touch of his lips. "I despise myself for putting you through all of this."

"Shh," she quietly implored him as she moved closer against him. "It's over now."

"But I want you to know everything. It's important to me that you hear it all."

"We have a lifetime for all of that."

Chandler took her up into his arms and lay her beneath him on the bed. His body strained above her. "We have hurt one another so badly," he muttered softly against her mouth. "What I want more than anything now is a chance to begin again with you."

And so the moment she had hoped would come was here. It was what she had worried and wondered about on the trip back from New York. What she would say. But now that she was here again it seemed so simple and so right. In spite of everything, she felt that rightness of them down to the very core of her soul.

"It is what I want, too, Chandler," she finally said.

His mouth covered hers at last, and yet the kiss between them was surprisingly gentle. "Oh, my sweet, sweet angel bride," he murmured against the smooth column of her neck.

Tessa could feel him trembling as he pressed himself against her. His heart was racing as she wrapped her arms around him, and they were bathed in each other's forgiveness. And their love. "You know I don't expect more . . ." he began. "It has just been so long, all I really want is to be close to you like this, if that is all right."

"Oh yes, it is more than all right."

"Only tell me that you'll never go away again. Swear it."

"I do swear it."

When he could begin to breathe again, Chandler rolled onto his side and took her palm, then gently kissed it.

"You are so beautiful."

"You're prejudiced," Tessa smiled, rolling to face him on her side.

"Hopelessly."

"I wonder if you'll feel the same way once you know about my surprise."

"I will always feel the same way, Tessa."

"Then how, I wonder, will you feel about more children?"

Chandler gulped back a groan of shock. "You're not . . . I mean, you can't possibly be—"

"So then you're not angry?" she asked a few moments later, when the whole story of Claire had been told. "You do understand that the child is Italian. She's far darker than any of us."

At the sound of the warning in her tone, Chandler took her hands and steepled them inside of his own. "Heart of my heart, I love whom you love."

"I love you."

"That is not so easy," he said as he looked away.

Tessa pressed a soft kiss against his unshaven cheek until he turned his eyes back to hers. "I have forgiven you. Can you not do the same for yourself?"

"I let Cynthia return to Paris. A second time, when I had the chance I did not right the wrong of a man's death."

"Who would it have served to turn her in after all this time?"

"My conscience, at least," he said with a grim smile.

"You have spared your children the rest of their lives. You knew from the first it was what was best for two sweet innocents in spite of the guilt you would forever bear from it. There is great honor in that."

"This from the woman who said that there is a right and there is a wrong? That life is as simple as that?"

"I was a fool ever to have said that."

Chandler considered her retraction for a moment. He had never expected to hear her say it. "I suppose, in some cases, people's experiences can change their beliefs."

"And hopefully, if one is lucky, one gains some maturity along with it. I cannot honestly say to you now that, had I been in your place, I would have acted any differently."

"That means a great deal, Tessa, coming from you."

"I told you once that I loved those children as if they were my own."

"And that is how I shall love Claire."

"We're being given a second chance here, aren't we?" Tessa asked as she lay her head against his chest.

Chandler lightly kissed the top of her head and then smiled to himself, feeling happy, complete, at last. "I think, my darling, we are giving it to ourselves."

Chapter
49

IN THE TATES' ENTRYWAY, TESSA HELD CLAIRE SO TIGHTLY IN her arms she felt certain she must be crushing her. But the baby cooed happily against her breast then closed her eyes with a little sigh as Tessa showered her with tender kisses.

"Oh! You cannot imagine how much I have missed you!" she said with a tender smile, kissing the top of the baby's head.

"I'd say the feelin' was quite mutual," Mary Gallagher said, standing back and surveying their reunion. "Poor wee thing hardly stopped her cryin' from the moment ye left New York, as if she knew."

"Well, that certainly won't be a problem ever again! Claire Sophia is a member of this family for better or worse."

Chandler took a step forward with Alice and James as they both stood on tiptoe to catch a glimpse of their sleepy new sister.

"She's beautiful!" Alice proclaimed with a satisfied smile.

"I must thank you, Mrs. Gallagher, for bringing her home to us. I'm sure it was not an easy trip to make with a baby."

"I would do anythin' for Tessa, Mr. Tate," she said devotedly to Chandler.

"As would I."

"I'm sorry to hear about your company. 'Twas a devastatin' fire. You lost so much."

Chandler put his arm around Tessa as she held the baby. "That much is true, but we also have a great deal to celebrate, tonight. My wife and our new daughter are safe and well. My sister, Daphne, too was spared, and may well have even learned her lesson at last. I think just now I would prefer to concentrate on that."

"It is a wise man who appreciates what he has instead of what he might have lost."

"I don't know how wise I am," Chandler smiled. "A truly wise man I once knew might have pointed out that I almost lost the greatest treasure in the world."

"True enough. But would he not also have said that ye have her back again?" Mary Gallagher asked.

"We have each other back," Tessa corrected her with a smile of pure joy lighting her eyes. "And believe me, there is nothing else in the world that matters so much as that!"

Acknowledgments

The Great Fire of Boston was the initial inspiration
for *Angel Bride*. Although it has been eclipsed in
history by the Chicago fire a year before, it was no less
significant and caused no less devastation. From that
as a starting point, Chandler and Tessa weaved themselves steadily into my mind and heart, as I thought
about the real story—the people whose lives a cata-
strophic fire like that would have changed. The rest of
their story unfolded from there.

I would like to thank the Boston Public Library for
all of their help in uncovering details of the fire; a
special thanks to Jann Walker, Director of Public
Relations, Lord & Taylor, for her help with details
about the original store; to Ted Huters, Professor of
Eastern Languages at The University of California,
Irvine; to the growing number of male readers who
have been so unexpected and so wonderfully encour-
aging of this ever-changing journey that began in
Renaissance France and has led now to 1870s Boston.

Among them are George Hanke, Neil Haeger, Terry Harnish, Clyde Kelly, Bill Judy, Philippe Tartavull, Lew Holton, Archie Morrison, Bob Alger, and Reg Pye.

Also, a very special thanks to Julie Garwood, a writer of unparalleled class, for her professionalism and her kindness. She continues to be an inspiration.

And last, but by no means least, thank you to the many kind readers who continue to write to me with wonderful comments. I do love hearing from you!

Diane Haeger

P.O. Box 9136
Newport Beach, CA 92658

THE ENTRANCING NEW NOVEL FROM THE
NEW YORK TIMES BESTSELLING
AUTHOR OF *PERFECT*

Until You

by

Judith McNaught

COMING SOON IN HARDCOVER FROM
POCKET BOOKS

POCKET
BOOKS

987-01

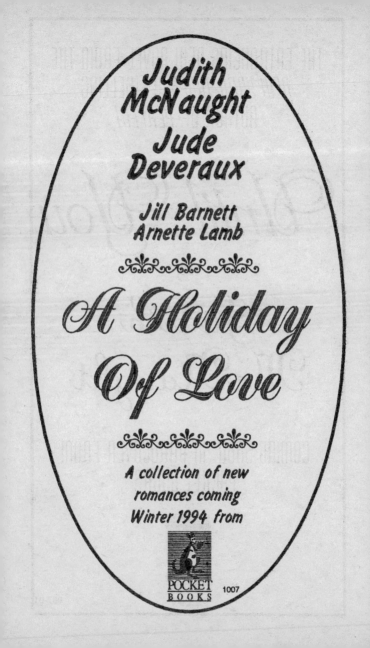

Judith
McNaught

Jude
Deveraux

Jill Barnett
Arnette Lamb

*A Holiday
Of Love*

A collection of new
romances coming
Winter 1994 from

POCKET
BOOKS

1007